LOTTIE AND THE LAND OF DOFSTRAM

THE BATTLE FOR DOFSTRAM

MA Haggerty

LOTTIE AND THE LAND OF DOFSTRAM

THE BATTLE FOR DOFSTRAM

MEREO
Cirencester

Published by Mereo

Mereo is an imprint of Memoirs Publishing

25 Market Place, Cirencester, Gloucestershire, GL7 2NX
info@memoirsbooks.co.uk www.memoirspublishing.com

Lottie and the Land of Dofstram - The Battle for Dofstram

M A Haggerty

ISBN: 978-1-86151-006-8

Contents

ACKNOWLEDGEMENTS

With huge thanks to my husband Jim for all his encouragement, and to the rest of my family for their kind support.

The story so far

Lottie Montmerencie enjoys a pleasant and peaceful life, thanks to her job in the local library. As more readers join, Ms Beckett, the manager, recruits two students from the local college, Peter Martindale and Penny Barker, to work on a part-time basis alongside her. Lottie soon takes Peter and Penny into her confidence and tells them of the scares and torments she has suffered recently. She explains that her parents, David and Jayne Montmerencie, were cave explorers, and on their last expedition some years ago they failed to return home. As she was only twelve years old, she was left in the care of her Aunt Jean, moving into her own home at the age of nineteen.

Lottie has discovered that her friend DaVendall comes from the magical land of Dofstram and has special powers. He is here to protect her. She learns that her parents' friends Sam and Lucy Walters are also there to watch over her. Having acquired two pets, Allsorts the dog and Scruffy the cat, from an animal rescue shelter, Lottie is surprised to discover that they too come from Dofstram. She is astonished to find that her pets are able to converse with her, but she very quickly accepts it and finds herself talking back to them. She learns that most of the animals in Dofstram can talk, the exception being those belonging to the evil tyrant Zanus.

Zanus has been made aware of Lottie's existence and knows that two of the prisoners in his dungeon are her parents. Eager to have Lottie in his power as well, Zanus sends a team to Lottie's land, led by Crocanthus, his right-hand man and chief torturer. Using the disguise of Jeremy Thackett, Crocanthus tries to deceive and befriend Lottie.

Having imprisoned a magical stone within a large boulder, the witch Imelda, ally and rival of Zanus, manages to extract some of its powers, but is prevented from gaining all of them. Unaware of the danger he is putting himself and Jayne in or the significance of the stone, David finds it and removes it from the boulder. On escaping from the cave he is surprised to discover that he can converse telepathically with the stone. Back in Lottie's land, in the form of a magical seahorse brooch called Beauty, the stone finds its way to an antique shop owned by Moff, a friend of DaVendall, and Lottie acquires it.

Furious that the stone is gone, Imelda is desperate to get her hands on it again to extract the remaining powers it holds. She gives Crocanthus potions to enable him to disguise his appearance in order to carry out her mission.

Lottie suffers many frightening moments both at work and at home as the Zanuthians try to capture her and find the brooch, with which, like her father, she can communicate by telepathy.

Lottie, Peter and Penny visit Dofstram by way of a portal within a grandfather clock in Moff's shop. The land is now under threat of being taken over by Zanus and his Zanuthians. With the aid of Zanus' ally Sizan and his monstrous Gorgonians, the Zanuthians set about killing the Outlander people and destroying their dwellings. These atrocities reach the ears of King Alfreston in Castle Urbone. The King is determined to stop Zanus and Sizan from taking over Dofstram. Having fought many battles against Zanus' father, he had not expected to have to battle against the new tyrant.

Lottie and her friends are shocked to discover how many prisoners are held within Zanus' stronghold, the Tower of Zorax, as well as her parents, and offer to help free them despite the dangers. Zanus and Imelda do not yet know that the stone has been adapted into a brooch, but they realise that it has somehow found its way to Lottie.

Having promised to return with the stone and Lottie, Crocanthus faces a dilemma: who would he give them to, Zanus or Imelda? If he gives them to Imelda he might be killed by Zanus for his treachery. Yet he fears what Imelda might do if he should hand them to Zanus.

In this third and final volume, the story concludes with the return of Lottie and her friends to Dofstram to free her parents and the other prisoners and to help rid the land of the tyrants as they had promised King Alfreston and his people.

Chapter One

Trouble Brewing

With the departure of DaVendall, Frances and Bertram remained in the hallway, each hoping their friends would have a safe journey to Dofstram. After a while, Bertram took his wife by the elbow and led her back to the kitchen.

Winston, however, was still getting over the excitement of his strange journey to Lottie's house under the protection of DaVendall's cloak. It left him secretly wishing it could have lasted longer. Disappointed at not going with the others to Dofstram, he left his parents in the hallway and made his way to the kitchen.

Standing in the doorway and looking round at the empty kitchen, he felt a feeling of emptiness inside which he could not understand. Then he remembered his mother's remedy for all problems, and set about making a pot of tea. As he placed the last cup and saucer on the table, he noticed his parents coming through the kitchen door. Absorbed as they were in their discussion about their friend's departure, it took a moment for Frances and Bertram to see what Winston had done. Frances beamed across at her son.

"Winston, you have been busy!" said Frances. "This is just what we need, a cup of tea and a bite to eat."

Winston looked to see if he could find the biscuit tin. After searching several cupboards he finally found the biscuits and placed the container on the table. As he did so, he noticed the kettle was billowing out steam. He took the kettle from the cooker and poured the boiling water into the teapot. Meanwhile he was listening intently to the conversation between his parents. He noticed the concern in their voices when they discussed the departure of their friends, and his interest became more acute.

At the mention of Dofstram, he paid closer attention and was surprised at some of the things he heard. He was keen to ask about the talking animals and the battles that had taken place, but decided this was not the time to ask questions, as he didn't want to stop the flow of conversation.

With the teapot full, Winston set about pouring the tea out, placed the cups in front of his parents and waited for a lull in their conversation. As they sipped their tea, Winston thought this might be the time to speak.

"Do you think they've got there yet?" he asked. He took a bite of his biscuit and glanced at his parents. Bertram was surprised at the tremor in his son's voice. He hesitated before answering.

"Try not to worry, Winston," he said. "DaVendall will take care of them. I should think they'd have arrived by now, it doesn't take long once they leave Moff's shop."

Winston was slightly reassured by this answer, but he was curious as to how a grandfather clock could take someone from one land to another. He decided to return to the question another time.

Now his parents were deep in discussion again, about some of their more pleasurable past memories of Dofstram. Winston, losing interest, decided he would go into the living room and watch television. He made his way into the hallway and hesitated for a moment before opening the living room door, not knowing why. As he pushed the door open he felt a definite lack of warmth. Winston hadn't considered how empty and lonely the house would feel without Scruffy and Allsorts.

He was about to switch the TV on when he heard a knock at the front door, but decided to ignore it. He searched through the channels and finally opted for a science fiction programme. He plonked himself down unceremoniously into an armchair before realising it was the chair he'd seen Scruffy occupy.

Bertram and Frances were equally surprised to hear the knock.

"I'm sure Winston said something about going into the living room," whispered Frances. "It might be best if you go to the door, dear. I don't want Winston answering it at this time of night."

"Who do you think that could be?" grunted Bertram.

"You don't think it could be, you-know-who?"

Bertram grimaced. "Just let it be him. I'd love to give him some of his own medicine," he said.

"Don't say that, Bertram, you know how evil he is," said Frances. Feeling a shiver of fear run though her body she added, "Don't forget, Winston is in the other room. I don't want any harm done to him."

"Now take it easy, Frances. I'll go and see who it is. No harm will come to Winston, or us," Bertram stated in a quiet voice, which belied his true feeling of concern.

As he was about to walk out of the kitchen, Winston was surprised to hear another knock at the door. He was now wondering why neither of his parents had answered. Reluctantly he got up to head for the door. As he was about to enter the hallway he noticed his father had come through the kitchen door.

"I was just going to answer it," said Winston. Bertram smiled. "It looks as if we both had the same idea then, son," he said. "You go and watch your programme. I'll see who's calling this time of night."

Winston wasn't too happy about going back into the empty living room. Although the programme he'd selected would normally have him glued to the television, on this occasion he was finding it difficult to concentrate. Not thinking it worthwhile to search the channels again, he decided he would join his parents in the kitchen.

With mixed feelings of concern and fear, Bertram halted for a moment before opening the door. Noticing Winston had gone to join Frances in the kitchen, he cautiously undid the latch.

Before either Frances or Winston could say another word, they heard Bertram's booming voice echoing down the hallway. "Come on in! How lovely to see you again. It's been such a long time since we last saw you."

The kitchen door opened to reveal Sam and Lucy. Delighted to see who it was, Frances wasted no time in getting up to welcome them. She stood up with open arms and a beaming smile, ready to give Lucy a welcoming hug.

"Frances, how lovely to see you," said Lucy. "It's been such a long time, hasn't it? I couldn't believe it when Moff told us things had gone from bad to worse. I guess this is what made them leave so soon." She sat down next to Sam.

"I can't believe how long it's been since we were together," said Frances. "I wish it hadn't come about because of the troubles in Dofstram. I never thought this could happen again." She suddenly remembered her manners, "I bet you'd like a cup of tea or something?"

"I bet you'd like something a little stronger than tea, eh Sam?" Bertram butted in.

"You remembered, Bertram!" Sam replied, grinning. "We brought a couple of bottles with us, as we weren't sure what Lottie would have in." As he placed the bottles on the table he suddenly noticed Winston sitting at the table. "I guess this must be your son. Now, let me see if I remember rightly, your name is, er let me think, Winston? Am I right?"

"You remembered then, Sam," Bertram replied. Turning to his son he murmured, "Come on over here and meet Sam and Lucy Walters."

Somewhat amused at watching his parents with these visitors, Winston guessed they must be more of their friends from the past. He wondered if they were friends from that other place.

Noticing the raised eyebrow his father was giving him, he stood up and made his way round to greet Sam. He wondered if they were able to work some kind of magic, and if so, if they would tell him.

"How nice to meet you too, Winston, please call us Sam and Lucy," said Sam, smiling. Winston made his excuses to leave the kitchen, but as he was about to pass Sam's chair he suddenly heard Sam whisper, "Not magic, Winston, just our ability."

"Can you hear thoughts then, like DaVendall and the others?" Winston asked in a quiet voice.

"Lucy and I have the ability to sense when someone is troubled. On occasions we are able to hear other thoughts. But like our other friends, we use it with discretion."

"Thank you for telling me." Noticing his parents smiling, Winston wondered if they had known this.

"I think I'll go back to the living room and finish watching my programme, if that's all right?" Winston declared, ready to leave the kitchen. He slipped out and quietly closed the kitchen door. Back in the sitting room, he turned the sound back up and sat back. But he found it difficult to follow the programme. His thoughts were elsewhere. The one thought which kept churning over in his mind was wondering what abilities Sam and Lucy might have. Deep within his own thoughts it took a while before he heard his mother calling. "Winston, not too loud with the sound please."

"OK Ma," Winston replied, bringing his attention back to the television.

Back in the kitchen Bertram was keen to get on to the subject of Dofstram. Opening one of the bottles, Bertram asked, "How much do you know about this business concerning Lottie, Sam? Is this all to do with what's taking place in Dofstram?"

"I think before we get into deep discussions we should at least have a drink to help us," Sam replied, watching Frances as she removed several glasses from the cupboard. Placing them on the table, she went to see if Lottie had left any little tasty bits for nibbling. After looking in a couple of cupboards, she noticed the list Lottie had left explaining where everything was. She smiled to herself. Collecting an assortment of extras from the nearby cupboard, she put them out.

"Dear Lottie, she's even put some cans of drink in the fridge for Winston," she said. As if on cue, Winston called out, "Is there anything for me?"

"Come and get it lad, your Mum's not running after you with it," called out Bertram. Winston made his way to the kitchen, collected what he wanted and went back to his programme. Meanwhile, settled with their drinks and knowing Winston was content with his refreshments, Frances asked, "Please, can you tell us what's happening?" Sam noticed how tense Bertram and Frances were.

"I'm not sure how much you know, but if I start from the beginning you can tell me when to stop," he stated. "As you probably know, we've had a lot of trouble from Zanus and Sizan. Once again Zanus is threatening to dominate Dofstram, as his father did before him. He's ensured assistance from Sizan and his beastly Gorgonians. Before you ask, he is still deeply involved with that dreaded Old Crone Imelda. I've no doubt she's managed to create other monstrous beasts. I don't need to tell you what horrors she can conjure up. Going by the destruction and brutality on their last encounter with the Outlanders, Zanus isn't going to stop until he's taken Dofstram. He's adamant he won't surrender as his father did."

Taking a quick sip of his drink, he continued, "It wasn't long after the battle which you were involved in, when King Alfreston and Queen Matilda ensured Dofstram was restored. Although Zanus continued to send out troopers to try and take the Outlanders' properties, he failed to achieve anything from it. We can only guess that's why he's been set on invading all the villages. Zanus is determined to get rid of King Alfreston and rule Dofstram. He regards Dofstram as his by right and has never forgiven his father for being so weak. Zanus despised his father for surrendering to King Alfreston."

Remembering the last battle they had fought brought to mind the many friends they'd lost. In a quieter tone of voice Sam went on to say, "I fear this will be an even bloodier battle than any of the previous ones."

"Just how long have these battles been going on, Sam?" asked Bertram.

"I'm afraid they've been going on for some time. Zanus and Sizan have strategically attacked the Outlander communities and they've managed to seize some of the Outlanders' land. Unfortunately some Outlanders have been killed and others have been taken prisoner. Zanus was crafty enough to start on the villages at the farthest parts of the land, which enabled him and Sizan to pick off the villages one at a time. It was some time before the King knew what was happening, but as soon as he heard how some Outlanders had been taken prisoner King Alfreston sent troops to help prevent any more being taken."

Sam took a drink from his glass, then continued. "Alas, by the time the troops arrived many villages had been burned, and the villagers were left dead and dying. They could only guess that the survivors were now being held in Zanus' dungeon."

Shocked at what they'd been told, Frances and Bertram took a moment to digest what he'd said. Bertram asked Sam to continue.

"We think Zanus must have suspected troops were being sent from the castle. Owing to the troops returning from each mission and reporting the same thing. No surviving Outlanders or enemy were found in the villages."

As Sam finished talking, Frances' thoughts turned to the survivors. Fearing the worst, but wanting to know, she asked quietly, "What happened to the survivors, Sam?"

"That, Frances, is something we aren't sure of. Many of the surviving wounded from other villages said any surviving Outlanders had been rounded up and taken prisoner, but they thought some villagers had managed to escape. Where they went or who they were remains a mystery, but as none of the survivors came out to show themselves to the troopers it's hoped they are still alive. We don't know for sure, so it's all guesses."

"It's been a long time since the people of Dofstram have enjoyed freedom and peace," added Lucy.

"I dread to think how many casualties there were as a result of these attacks. I can still remember the number of lost friends from when we were there," Frances remarked in a sad voice.

"A great number of our friends have been lost or taken prisoner," said Lucy in a sombre voice. "What we don't know is how many. We fear some will have been taken to Imelda." Lowering her voice to just above a whisper, Lucy continued, "I dread to think what tortures those poor people will have been subjected to."

Shocked but not surprised to hear of the lives lost, Frances shivered at the thought of prisoners being tortured.

"Does anyone know? Is it possible we might know if David and Jayne are there?"

Lucy took hold of Frances' hand and whispered, "Unfortunately not. There have been several attempts to find out, but without success."

A sudden silence fell over the four people. Each one was recalling sad memories of the devastation and destruction they'd witnessed.

Sam cleared his throat. Waiting until he had gained their attention, he said, "I think perhaps this might be a good time to let Bertram and Frances know as much as we know, Lucy." Sam noticed the look of concern flash across Bertram's face.

"One of the biggest shocks we all had, including their majesties, came after one of the bloodier battles," he went on.

"What was that, Sam?"

"Discovering Zanus had learned of Lottie's existence." Giving Bertram and Frances a moment to absorb what he'd said, Sam continued in a softer voice. "When their majesties heard this, they raised many questions. King Alfreston was keen to know how Zanus knew about Lottie. Who told him and for what purpose? These were questions the King was eager to have answered. But then comes the big question - how long had Zanus known? And why would Lottie concern him?"

Noticing the look of surprise on his friend's faces, Sam halted for a moment before continuing. "It wasn't until some time later we discovered Zanus had sent troopers to capture Lottie. The question we were all keen to know was - why did Zanus want her?"

Listening to the gasps coming from Frances, Sam felt he knew the question Frances was about to ask. "I wonder who really wants her, Zanus or Imelda?"

"I'm reluctant to say it, but what if he is holding her parents and intends to use Lottie to make them tell Imelda where the coloured stone is?" said Bertram. "If I remember rightly, David upset the Old Crone when he removed the stone from the big boulder."

Frances let out a loud gasp. Lucy added, "That's right, Bertram. Thankfully they are not aware how the stone looks now. I hope they don't capture Lottie, or they will have the both she and the stone."

Thinking for a moment or two, Lucy added, "One thing we all know, and that is what the Old Crone would use them for. As for Zanus and that cruel Crocanthus, perhaps they just want some kind of power over Imelda."

Frances was stunned by all she'd heard and was trying to

understand how and why this should have come about. "Does anyone think this could this mean Jayne and David might still be alive?" she asked. "I'm going to suppose they are, and that's why Zanus is so eager to get her."

"Has anyone any idea who, or how many, of Zanus' brutes have been sent across, Sam?" asked Bertram.

"That, my friend, is another mystery. We have managed to discover one or two. That dreadful duo Evoc and Harbin we all remember well. As to who the others are or where they might be, we have never been able to find out. Last but not least, we know Crocanthus is also here. What concerns us we know he must be using some kind of disguise. What, we aren't sure. Where these terrors are is another question. They seem to have secured themselves somewhere where we can't find them."

"With regard to Jayne and David, no one knows what happened after they were taken," said Lucy. Fearing she was about to mention Beauty by name, Sam interrupted. "Our mutual friend has tried on many occasions to get through to the telepathic prisoners, but has always been blocked by a kind of grey mist," he said. "This mist has been overshadowing the tower for many years."

Realising why Sam had interrupted her, Lucy thanked him. Giving Lucy a warm smile, he continued, "With the latest attacks on the Outlanders, we have learnt from the warning birds that there are increased numbers of Zanuthians and Gorgonians gathering beyond the Outlander villages. Having become aware of this, King Alfreston organised a large troop force to head out there. As soon as DaVendall returns, the King will be heading out there with more troops."

Sensing the shock from Frances and Bertram, Sam took a drink before adding wistfully, "Zanus has to be stopped at all costs. He mustn't be allowed to defeat the Outlanders. Dofstram has been free of those dark and gloomy days for many a year now, it mustn't return to the dark and cruel times when his father ruled."

"I suppose with the help of that brute Sizan, and the Old Crone, it might be possible for him to achieve this?" asked Frances.

"We can only hope not. That could be another reason they want the stone. They are aware of the power it holds, which they fear more than they fear their majesties. The King will need more than just the troops he has at the castle. He will need to seek the help from all the Outlanders, or at least the ones who are able to fight." He glanced towards Bertram and Frances, wondering if they'd understood his meaning.

Frances added wistfully, "Let's hope the King succeeds, and doesn't let Zanus triumph."

"You mean us, Sam? You mean the King might need our help once more?" Bertram burst out. Frances stared at her husband with her mouth slightly open. "He would only have to ask and we would be there in no time," she whispered.

Gripping tightly onto her glass, Frances realised Lucy had placed a hand on top of hers. Frances could see by the look on her face that there was more she wanted to say.

"I just knew you would agree," said Lucy. "But I think this battle will be a lot bloodier and a good deal harder to fend off Zanus from gaining control. He's a much crueller and meaner brute than his father was." Having noticed how much quieter Lucy's voice was when she mentioned Zanus, they waited for her to finish what she was saying before speaking themselves.

"I do hope King Alfreston will let us help. I sure would like to help with freeing Dofstram of those brutes, Zanus and Sizan!" Bertram bellowed, surprising everyone with the anger in his voice. Sam wondered if Bertram or Frances were aware that Lottie had been betrayed by a person from this land.

Anxious to try and discover who the informer could be, and feeling the anger Bertram had expressed a moment ago, Sam said, "We have another nasty problem to deal with. A little matter of discovering who the informer is who revealed to Zanus the existence of Lottie." Looking across at Bertram and Francis Sam he went on, "Have you any idea who this despicable person could be?"

"Sorry, Sam. I can't begin to think who would do such a thing," said Bertram.

Disappointed, Sam continued, "Let's see now, what do we know so far? We know the informer is from this land. What we found difficult was - why and how did this person know of Zanus and Dofstram? Whatever the reason, that's a person I'd like to get my hands on." As Sam finished speaking they could hear the anger in his voice.

Aware how hard Sam had tried to find the person and knowing the frustration he had felt in not doing so, Lucy leaned over and quietly said, "We will find this person, Sam. And soon. Something will give the informer away." Sam smiled at Lucy and reassured her he was all right.

"If I knew who it was, his or her life wouldn't be worth living," said Bertram. "But be reassured, Sam, you aren't alone on this subject. There are many of us who would like to get our hands on that person. I can't think who would be so wicked and cruel as to inform Zanus of her existence." Then, as if talking to himself, and remembering Sam's comments earlier, he said, "How did you discover it was someone from here, Sam? How did someone from this land know of your land? How would disclosing Lottie to Zanus be of use to the informer?"

Bertram took a drink and twisted the glass round in his hand. "It certainly makes you wonder what this informer gained by letting Zanus know who Lottie is," he said.

"Hasn't anyone got any idea who it could be?" asked Frances.

"Unfortunately not," said Sam. "It's been made harder for us to detect this person because, as I said earlier, everyone was surprised to discover it was someone from this land."

"How did you discover it was someone from this land?" asked Bertram. "Is that why Zanus sent his brutes to capture Lottie?"

"That's a very good question, Bertram. I doubt if we'd have known anything about an informer, or of Lottie's danger, if King Alfreston hadn't sent some of the Jaspers to quietly fly round the enemy and observe what was happening. This was on his last encounter with Zanus' brutes. What the King hadn't expected was what they came back and told him."

"What? What did they tell him?"

"Fortunately for the Jaspers, the unicorns had given them a veil of invisibility. Some of the Jaspers took a chance and flew closer to the enemy. They were about to return to the King when they heard several of the enemy moaning about Zanus sending troopers to the humans' land. On hearing this they waited to see if more would be revealed. It must have come as quite a shock when they heard the reason for their being sent. However, when they heard Lottie's name mentioned, knowing David and Jayne had a child by this name, they ventured closer to hear more. I'm not sure what happened next, but the Jaspers did manage to hear that it was a person from the humans' land who had informed Zanus of her existence. I guess this must have annoyed him, and as a result he must have felt it was essential she was found and brought to Zorax." He watched as Bertram poured him another glass of malt.

"This is awful!" Frances muttered, as if talking to herself.

"Surprisingly, the Jaspers heard the troopers boasting and laughing about some other human," Sam went on. "They were shocked to hear they were laughing about the informer from the human's land. They were doubly shocked to hear another trooper say Zanus was to spare the informer's life if Lottie was brought to his tower. They flew back to King Alfreston and reported what they'd heard."

"Is that what decided their majesties to send their own protectors across?" asked Bertram.

"Yes," replied Lucy. "We were the first to arrive. We were given strict instructions to report any happenings direct to the King. Soon after that more friends came to join us."

"Wow!" Frances exclaimed. "So now we know how Lottie's life was put in danger?"

"I think the hardest thing to comprehend is being aware the informer originates from this land," said Sam. "It made us think about every customer who came into our shop. I'm still curious as to how this person got to our land."

"I keep thinking that myself," said Bertram. "But possibly more important, how did the informer know of Zanus? And how did the informer know where to find him?" Brushing his hand over his nose and mouth he cautiously added, "There's many unanswered questions surrounding this informer. How come he wasn't killed on sight? We all know Zanus is a brutal killer. How did the informer know he would be interested in Lottie? Which leads me on to question three - is it possible this informer knows David and Jayne and is using Lottie as a way of getting revenge for something?"

"Wow Bertram, that's not something I'd even considered. Why, if it was a friend of theirs, would Lottie be offered up like a sacrifice?" said Frances.

"The people of Dofstram have asked the same questions. But as Sam said before, when we first came to this land we suspected anyone and everyone who came into the shop," Lucy said, in a voice only just above whisper. With concerns and other thoughts going through their minds it was a while before Sam broke the silence. "I do hope our friends have arrived safely."

Hearing a sound from outside the kitchen door, Frances called out, "Are you all right, Winston?"

"What is it, son?" asked Bertram.

"Just getting a bit tired, Dad. I think I might pop off to bed. I've put the television off and it's all tidy in there." He turned to make his way out of the kitchen.

"Just before you go, is there anything you want before you settle down?" asked Frances, concerned at how quiet her son had gone.

"No thanks, Mum. I know which room to go to, Penny showed me before she left," he replied in a tired voice. Frances felt her son wasn't his usual self, but not wanting to quiz him any further she called out, "Goodnight then son, we'll see you in the morning."

"Goodnight son, sleep well," called out Bertram.

"Goodnight, Winston, nice to have met you," called out Sam.

After acknowledging them with his own goodnight, Winston made his way through the hall and up the stairs, still unable to shake off the despondent feeling. As he dragged himself up the stairs he knew he was feeling down due to the absence of Scruffy and Allsorts, but knowing this did little to comfort him. As he changed into his pyjamas he sat on the side of the bed for a while then quietly said, "Take care Scruffy and Allsorts, I hope you've arrived safely in your land." Then he burrowed under the duvet.

Meanwhile, Frances was struggling to shake off the feeling that something was troubling Winston. Gaining Bertram's attention, she told him, "I'm a little worried about Winston, Bert. He doesn't seem to be his usual self this evening. I hope he's not going down with something."

"It's probably all the excitement over the last couple of days. He'll be all right after a good night's sleep," Bertram replied, hoping his explanation would prove correct. Pouring out another drink, Bertram asked Sam to continue with what they were talking about.

"Well. Let me see. Oh yes. Queen Matilda suggested it would be a good idea to send her pets across. I won't say their names, you never know who might be listening. Queen Matilda and DaVendall discussed a variety of ways of getting Lottie to give them a home. Thankfully it happened just as they'd planned. They knew from talking with us that Lottie enjoyed long walks in the park. After discussing this with Matilda, DaVendall came up with an idea on how he could approach Lottie without scaring her. His idea was to discard his cloak and hat and dress himself as men here dress. Knowing Lottie's habit of walking in the park, he planned to make her acquaintance during one of her walks. He'd quietly observed Lottie over a few days and began to sense her loneliness. It was only after she was at ease in his presence that he planted the suggestion of having a couple of pets to keep her company. When Lottie agreed to the idea, he told her of an animal shelter close by."

Carried away with his explanations, Sam appeared to have forgotten where he was as he suddenly blurted out, "That's where Pointer and Marmaduke had been placed."

Realising he'd used their true names, Sam clamped his hands over his mouth, and murmured an apology. "Oh! Good grief, what have I done? I'm so sorry! I meant to say, Allsorts and Scruffy." He was half expecting something extraordinary to happen, but the only thing he heard was the calm voice of Frances say, "I don't think anyone other than us heard you, Sam."

Waiting for Sam to take in what Frances had said, Bertram commented, "So that's how DaVendall got the relevant parties together, I was beginning to wonder how they had."

Lucy continued with the story. "After letting the animals know Lottie would be visiting the rescue home, DaVendall left it to them to do the rest. Almost at once Lottie was drawn to her pets. I'm sure a little bit of magic played its part. That aside, as it turned out they were soon going to witness the torment Lottie was going through. Of course that didn't answer the problem of how to bring our friend and Lottie together. That took a bit longer than DaVendall hoped, but he eventually succeeded."

Stopping for a moment to gain her breath and to take a sip of her drink, Lucy continued, "Going back to where we first began, when we first arrived here we weren't sure what danger Lottie was in or from whom. It soon became apparent when we saw Evoc and Harbin. At that moment we knew for certain her life would be under threat. What we didn't know until later was there had been many other scary moments at Lottie's house. It was through Allsorts and Scruffy we learned something of what she was going through. Lottie had put these happenings down to a variety of reasons like strong winds, noisy neighbours, speeding cars, you know the sort of thing. But we knew as soon as we heard what was happening it could only be those two morons. What we weren't sure of was – was this being done to scare her out of the house, or was it their attempt to capture her? One thing that did puzzle us for some time was how they knew where she lived. We could only guess it must have been another of the things the informer disclosed."

Taking a moment to catch her breath, Lucy noticed her friends were staring at her and waiting to hear what else she had to say. After another quick drink Lucy continued, "I got a little ahead of myself. Let me go back a little. Sam and I had become more than a little suspicious of her neighbours and listened carefully for any slip of the tongue whenever any of them came into our shop. When we let King Alfreston know what we'd found out he became increasingly alarmed for Lottie's safety. I'm sure that's what made him agree with DaVendall that he should remain here as long as was needed."

Realising that Lucy had stopped speaking, Sam waited to see if Frances or Bertram had any questions. Looking at their expectant faces, he decided to continue. "We knew Moff had brought the stone across and was safely settled in his shop, but what we didn't know was how he would manage to attract Lottie's attention and get her into the shop. Thankfully that was taken care of by DaVendall. On arriving here, it wasn't long before he came to see if we had any more news about other Zanuthians. Up until then we hadn't seen or recognised any others, but DaVendall assured us he hoped to be able to discover who had come across and where they were."

Lucy, feeling the remorse from Sam, took up the conversation. "We understand from Moff that our friend sensed Lottie right away. But we all know them to be compatible, Lottie had to take hold of it herself. Moff told us it happened almost as soon as Lottie entered the shop. He'd been careful to strategically place it in the window. When our friend sensed the person looking in the window was the one she should be with she sent out her gentle glow. It was the glow coming from the stone that attracted Lottie to look at it more closely. As soon as Moff placed the tray on the counter Lottie lifted our friend, and as she observed the stone Lottie was captured by the delightful orange glow it emitted."

Lucy caught the whispered voice of Frances as she asked, "What did Lottie do or say when the glow appeared?" Giving a gentle laugh Lucy explained, "Moff was quick to comment that it must be the winter sun shining on the stone."

"What about Crocanthus, when did he come on the scene?" asked Frances. Lucy creased her brow in thought and then replied, "I'm afraid that is only something we can guess. It's our belief the kidnappers were taking too long to do the deed. I guess that must have made Crocanthus want to come and complete the task himself."

"You know what I find most peculiar?" said Sam. "Not being able to discover the whereabouts of other Zanuthians that came across, especially as their smell is so atrocious. I wonder if it was only ever Harbin and Evoc."

"Why Sam?" asked Bertram. "Apart from their disgusting aroma, what made you think it could only be those two bullying morons?"

"Well, with everything that had been happening at the house

and the events in the library, it's only those two goons who have ever been spotted. I wonder if that was another reason why Crocanthus came here. And that brings me to another of my concerns – disguises. We all know Crocanthus has certain powers of his own in his own land, but do they extend to here? If they don't I wonder what, or who, Crocanthus became?"

"I never thought of him in disguise," said Lucy. "Do you think he could have been to our shop?" With only a touch of Sam's hand on hers Lucy added, "I know one thing. Lottie and that young lass of yours have had a great deal of torment from those morons."

Remembering the times they'd been called to help Lottie, she quietly added, "I'd like just one minute with those bullies. I'd soon give them what for!"

Chapter Two

Unwelcome visitors

As everyone considered this latest discussion, Bertram took the plate of biscuits and offered them to his friends. As he was about to place the plate back on the table a loud crash came from outside the back door. Not wanting to jump to any wild conclusions, especially as the wind had increased since they'd be chatting, they hoped it was just a dustbin blowing over.

Bertram made his way to the back door to make sure, but before he had reached it a coarse voice yelled out, "We knows yer in there, an' we're gonna get yer!"

A loud thump echoed off the back door. Halting in his tracks, Bertram placed a finger to his lips to request quiet. Making his way back to where he'd been sitting, he indicated they should get closer together before speaking. I guess it can only be those two morons," he whispered. "They obviously don't know Lottie and Penny aren't here. How about we give them a fright?"

"What do you have in mind, Bertram?" whispered Sam. But before he could say anything further a crashing noise came from outside the kitchen window.

"This is getting too much!" said Sam in an angry voice. Rising from his seat, he noticed Winston enter slowly through the kitchen door. Not wanting to scare Winston any more than he was, Sam sat back down as Winston asked nervously, "Dad, what's going on? I heard crashes and bangs. It's not that horrible man come here is it?"

"Your Dad is just going to sort it out. We're not sure if it's the wind blowing over a dustbin, or if it was something else causing the noise," Frances told him, hoping this would reassure her son. Sam noticed Bertram had left his chair and was making his way to the back door again.

"Hold on, Bertram, I'm coming with you," he whispered. Bertram slowly opened the back door and peered out into the darkness. "I can't see anything," he said. "I'll just take a walk round the garden and make sure everything's all right." Making sure the back door was securely closed, Sam and Bertram set off into the garden.

As they moved away from the house, Sam whispered, "I noticed you didn't mention it could be a certain person making that noise, Bertram."

"Thought it best not to," whispered Bertram. "Winston probably hadn't heard the threats, only the banging and crashing."

They continued to look around as they made their way to the bottom of the garden. Both men pondered over what other forms of torment Lottie and Penny might have gone through. Then Sam grabbed Bertram's arm and pulled him to a stop.

"I'm sure I heard some movement coming from the side of the house," he said. "Let's see if it's who we think it is." They hastily made their way up the garden. On reaching the corner of the house they slowed their pace and stealthy crept round the side of the house. They were surprised and somewhat frustrated at not seeing any sign of the people they'd hoped to find.

As they made their way down the side of the house, Bertram caught the disgusting aroma of the Zanuthians. "Just as we suspected," he whispered. "It must be those two morons Evoc and Harbin. The only question now is, is Crocanthus with them?"

Then a loud bang came from the front of the house. Alarmed, they wasted no time in setting off in the direction of the noise. Reaching the corner, they hesitated for a moment before edging their way round, not knowing what they might see. They slowly turned the corner to see Evoc attacking the front door with some kind of weapon. Meanwhile Harbin was busy shouting threats to the people inside.

"We's are gonna get yer, jus' yer wait an' see!" he shouted.

Forgetting their concerns over Crocanthus, Sam and Bertram set off in pursuit of the two men. Aware how frightened the people indoors might be, they felt a sense of urgency at getting hold of them.

Unaware of the attention they had attracted, Evoc and Harbin failed to realise how close Sam and Bertram were. Continuing with his abuse, Harbin rattled the letterbox as if to enhance his abuse. "We're gonna get yer, jus' yer wait."

Evoc was about to bang on the front door window when he caught something out the corner of his eye. Not seeing anything obvious, he passed it off as some sort of night creature. Turning his attention away from the front door, Evoc left Harbin to continue his banging and threatening and moved across to the window facing the front of the house. Violently knocking, and not caring if he broke the glass, he only wished he could see the fear on the faces of the two women inside. Then he realised Harbin had stopped. He looked round to see what had caused him to halt and was shocked to see Sam and Bertram heading in their direction. Without thinking he darted across from the window to grab Harbin by the arm. Catching his breath, he managed to squeeze out, "Let's get out of 'ere!"

Not having seen Bertram or Sam, Harbin tried to shake Evoc off his arm. Evoc dropped his grip on Harbin and set off down the front path as fast as he could. Having ignored Evoc's warning, Harbin decided to continue tormenting the people inside. But as he raised his weapon to crash it onto the door, he suddenly became aware of Sam and Bertram closing in on him. He had little time to think. With instinct taking over, he found himself racing down the front path behind Evoc.

Sam and Bertram set off after him. Age not being on his side Sam breathlessly muttered, "I wish I could run faster." They hear the sudden voice of Harbin screaming at Evoc to get the car.

"Bleedin' 'ell, why does she need such a long path?" he muttered breathlessly to himself. Gasping for breath, he took a hasty look behind to see how near the men were. He knew that if he was caught they would show him no more mercy than he would them.

Bertram thought he would catch at least one of the men. Closing in on Harbin, he reached out to grab hold of him when Harbin suddenly dodged out of the way. Bertram was surprised to see his quarry leap over the gate and take off up the road. Angry with himself for not being able to get hold of either man, Bertram stood panting by the gate. Without noticing that Sam had caught him up, he started to make his way up the road.

"We'll have to leave them, Bertram. Now they're in their car we don't stand a chance of getting them," Sam said, trying to get his breath. Annoyed at letting Harbin get away, Bertram wasn't keen on giving up, but on hearing what Sam had said, he turned and grunted, "I have to agree with you, old fellow, but I was so near to catching that brute."

"Never mind, Bertram at least the ladies weren't here to suffer this torment," Sam said, still panting for breath.

"Luck was not on our side tonight, Sam," Bertram said. Hearing a car start up, Bertram was determined to make sure it was the two men. He stepped off the pavement and didn't have to wait long before the car appeared racing down the road. It did indeed contain Evoc and Harbin. All Bertram could do was shake his fist at them, to be rewarded with sneering grins from both men as the car went zooming past.

"Blast it! I thought we would at least have caught one of them. What I wouldn't do to have them in my grasp!" said Bertram. "Come on Sam, let's go and make sure the others are all right. I wonder what made them decide not to get into the house."

"I guess they're afraid of Scruffy and Allsorts, which only confirms what we were discussing earlier," said Sam. "I wonder if those men gave a thought to the animals not responding to their threats. I do know one thing - if this is what those men have been doing here, it's no wonder Lottie and Penny have been frightened."

"I did wonder if they had considered why Allsorts hadn't barked. But it reassures me they were lucky to have had Allsorts and Scruffy here," Bertram replied.

As they continued on up to the house they suddenly heard a loud squawk and stopped in their tracks to see what it was. Bertram tapped Sam's arm and whispered, "What on earth was that terrible noise?" Aware of having heard the sound before, Sam knew exactly what had caused it. He was about to explain to Bertram what it was when the squawking noise came again, only louder.

"What on earth..." exclaimed Bertram, but before he could finish Sam whispered loudly, "You know what creature makes that sound, Bertram?"

"It can't be."

"It can. And it is. That's the sound of Zanus' spy birds, and we all know it means they're about to attack. I think we should let Lucy and Frances know what we've seen."

With a nod in agreement, Bertram hastily followed Sam as he turned the corner along the side of the house. Keeping a constant lookout for any further intruders, they reached the back door in no time.

Entering the kitchen, they could see by the looks on the three faces that they did not need to relay everything that had taken place.

"I guess this must be something of what Lottie and Penny have had to put up with," said Lucy.

"That, Lucy, is exactly what we were saying outside. It's a good thing they had Lottie's pets to protect them," replied Sam.

"Don't forget our friend. She would be able to help her friends," added Frances.

"Quite right Frances," Bertram said, sitting on the chair next to hers. "I just wish I could have got my hands on at least one of them. One day I'll get them. One day!" He started to pour himself a drink. "How long have those dreadful birds been here, Sam?" he asked.

"Birds, Dad, what birds?" asked Winston.

"Sorry, I forgot you might not have heard their terrible squawking. We heard them when we were walking up the pathway. It made me think how little I knew of the danger Lottie and Penny had been in," Bertram told his son.

Before any more questions could be asked, Sam took this moment to respond to Bertram's earlier question.

"I've been thinking about the first time we heard those birds," he began. "That was an occasion when we came to the aid of Lottie. It did take us a while to discover where they were. You can imagine the shock when we found they were perched in that big tree outside Lottie's gate. As soon as we knew that, we took great care not to let the birds know we were aware of them."

Then a fearful thought entered his head and he added in a cautious voice, "You don't think they were sent in place of Zanuthians do you?"

Turning to face Bertram, Winston replied, "Dad, who did you say you were you chasing outside? I thought it was the wind making all that noise. Now you tell us about some weird birds in the tree outside Lottie's gate!"

Hearing the quiver in Winston's voice, Lucy turned to Winston ready to answer his questions. "You heard the same bangs and crashes as we did, Winston. What you might not have heard was the threatening voices warning us they were going to get us. We knew at once it was Evoc and Harbin. I have to say they are two of the nastiest people I know. Regretfully they come from our land. They are from a race of people called the Zanuthians. They got away this evening, but we'll get them another day. With regard to the birds, those are Zanus' spy birds. They can speak, but all his other animals have had that ability taken away. These birds are cruel and vicious, just like their master."

As if on cue, a mass squawking sound came through the cold and windy night air. Sam got up to make sure the back door was locked. Then, to make certain, he slid the bolts across, top and bottom. Walking back to his seat, he noticed the strained expression on the faces of Lucy and Frances and saw Winston shrinking low into his chair.

"Thank you for telling me this, but are those birds about to attack us in here?" whispered Winston in a scared voice.

"Well they won't get in here now. The doors and window are locked," Sam told them. Hoping that was correct, Winston pulled himself back up into his chair and looked round at the people present. As he did so, Lucy surprised them by asking, "Did I hear right, Sam, do you really think these birds were sent in place of Zanuthians? If so, that's probably why none of us have picked up that awful Zanuthian aroma, except for Evoc and Harbin." Noticing the shock on their faces, Sam waited for a moment before replying.

"I fear so, Lucy. They could only have come across with help from the Old Crone." Noticing Winston was about to speak, Sam sensed what was coming next, and brought the subject back to what had taken place outside.

"We did give those morons a fright didn't we, Bertram? It was sheer pleasure seeing their scared faces when they saw us getting close to them. However, I'm not sure they will stay away for good. Remember they won't know the ladies aren't here, or that we're just visiting."

Winston had no desire to be on his own at this moment. When he saw fresh drinks being poured out, he whispered, "I could do with one of those."

"Not this time of night son," said Bertram. "A hot chocolate if you like, but nothing stronger."

"Can I stay here and have it then? I don't really want to go back upstairs just yet," Winston pleaded.

Please to have something to ease her mind from the last discussion, Frances turned to Winston and said, "Sit where you are, Winston, it won't take long to make you a drink." Sensing Francis' concern, Lucy leaned towards Winston and whispered, "Bit scary, eh Winston? But at least Sam and Bertram sent them off with a flea in their ear. With regard to those birds, have no fear they will not enter the house." Moving his chair nearer to Lucy, Winston was surprised to feel the same comforting warmth from her as he felt from his mother.

"How dangerous are these spy birds, Lucy?" he asked. Remembering the dreadful things she'd seen and the carnage they had left behind, Lucy considered the best way to explain about the birds. She didn't want to make Winston any more afraid that he already was.

"They are very dangerous, Winston. They're known by the folk of Dofstram as demon or devil birds. They obey Zanus' every command," she explained gently.

"This man Zanus sounds really awful. Would he order these birds to kill us?" Winston asked nervously. He took a drink of his hot chocolate. Placing her glass on the table, Lucy took a moment before saying, "I guess there's quite a bit you should know, Winston. So the simple answer is, yes. If he thought it was necessary to eliminate you and thought any of us were a threat he wouldn't hesitate.

"Let me explain a little about Zanus and his dealings with Imelda, the Old Crone. At some time, and no one knows when, Zanus and Imelda joined forces in wanting to gain power over the land of Dofstram. It isn't known for certain if she was constructive in giving Zanus the power to kill his father. One thing we do know for certain is that she gave him a potion to take away the ability of all his animals to talk, but not his birds. Fortunately she failed to stop all the animals in the land from speaking. There again, we can only guess he used the potion to make sure his animals couldn't refuse to do his bidding."

Taking in the rapt attention on Winston's face, Lucy continued, "That's not the only potion she's created, she made a potion which enhanced the birds size and killing power. I'm glad it didn't work on all the animals, eh Sam? It must really annoy Imelda and Zanus that the other animals still have the freedom to talk."

"That's right, young Winston," said Sam. "We found it very strange to discover your animals don't have the ability to talk. But we were glad to find out it wasn't through some evil potion." Now beginning to feel a little tired, Sam finished his drink and declared it was time he and Lucy went home. Thinking it would be nice for Bertram and Frances to come to their home, Sam added, "Don't forget our shop is only at the bottom of the road. Please come and see us sometime. But we must remember to be ready for any message from DaVendall requesting our presence."

"Cor, I hope he does, and soon," Winston called out. Walking their friends to the front door, they bid each other goodnight. Closing the door behind their visitors, Frances felt an overwhelming moment of tiredness come over her. Stating as much to Bertram, and realising Winston was still with them, she said, "I think we should think about retiring for the night." Murmurs of agreement came from Bertram and Winston.

Bertram checked to make sure the downstairs was securely locked up for the night. As he left each room he took a quick glance round, then switched off the lights. Joining Frances and Winston at the foot of the stairs, he quickly assured them everywhere was secure. "Right everyone, let's take ourselves off to bed," he said.

As they were about to go to their rooms, Winston asked, "They won't get in here will they? Those birds I mean." Bertram moved closer to his son and stated solemnly, "No Winston, they'd sooner attack in the open. They wouldn't come inside." Then he added, "I think after this little episode tonight we'd better take care when referring to Lottie's pets. We mustn't give them away by calling them anything other than the names Lottie gave them."

"I agree," Frances and Winston replied, almost as one. Without further discussion, they turned in.

Chapter Three

A Visit from Crocanthus

Seething with rage at failing to complete their task, Evoc and Harbin began to argue as to who was wrong. With neither taking responsibility, they agreed it was the fault of those interfering humans. With both men ranting on about their failure neither was listening to the other until Harbin shouted, "Shut up yer moron! 'Ow was we to know they'd be at 'er 'ouse?" With his own thoughts on what had taken place at the house, Evoc opted to remain silent. But as they turned the corner Evoc said, "Didn't we 'ave the pleasure of seeing 'em standin' like idiots? They was real shocked when we went by."

Harbin was still annoyed that his partner had run off and left him to face the two men. He now attacked him verbally and physically, punching Evoc with every word he spoke.

"Why didn't yer see 'em earlier? Yer ran off an' left me. I was nearly 'ad by one of 'em."

"What abart me, I was nearer to 'em, an' anyways, yer didn't run when I tried to pull yer along wid me. So there, now yer know why I went off!" whined Evoc. Furious with the answer and annoyed at him for answering back, Harbin landed a fist on the top of Evoc's arm, causing him to make the car swerve across the road.

"Now look what yer gone an' made me do!" shouted Evoc, trying to gain control of the car. Ignoring the situation Harbin, with his usual contempt for his partner stated, "'Ow was we to know some interfering 'umans was there?"

Failing to realise Harbin had become annoyed at his

continual repeating of the question, Evoc was not prepared for the torrent of abuse Harbin hurled at him, warning him not to keep repeating what he said.

Evoc was terrified of upsetting his partner, so he refrained from saying anything, until a sudden thought crossed his mind,

"I didn't' see none of 'em women, nor did I 'ear that dog bark. Did yer see 'em?" Evoc asked in a quieter tone of voice.

"I always said she 'ad some weird magic abart 'er, but I 'spects they was 'iding somewhere inside," Harbin remarked, "Odd we never 'eard no dog," he added to himself.

Turning the next corner, and attempting to ignore the grunting and groaning coming from his partner, Evoc drove on in silence. Having covered a fair distance, Harbin was relieved to see that they were approaching the street where they were staying. He was looking forward to a proper drink, and his thoughts suddenly turned to Crocanthus.

"I was jus' finking, 'ow do we tell Crocanthus we failed, 'specially when we know e's gonna ask...?" Before he could finish his sentence, Evoc interrupted. "Don't let 'im 'ear yer say 'is name, yer know 'ow mean 'e gets if 'e 'ears yer." Wondering if perhaps Harbin had seen something of Crocanthus, Evoc started looking round, but could see nothing to cause concern.

"Don't be stupid, 'ow's 'e gonna 'ear me?" asked Harbin scathingly.

"Cos 'e's crafty, that's 'ow," Evoc replied, just as scathingly. Fearful of discussing the subject of Crocanthus, Evoc brought the car to a halt outside the gate. Harbin, eager to get inside, turned to his partner and glared, "Let's get in an' get a proper drink, I needs a big mug of ale." Snorting in response, Evoc flung his door open and exited the car. He slammed the door shut and glanced across to see Harbin standing by the closed door.

"What yer gonna do abart telling Crocanthus?" smirked Evoc. Angered at Evoc's smile, Harbin made his way round the back of the car and grabbed his partner's arm. Flinching from the impact Evoc shouted, "Ow! What yer do that fer?" Ignoring Evoc, Harbin dragged his partner round the car and up the pathway.

About halfway, Harbin sensed something was wrong and stopped. Looking nervously around, he knew this had to be

Crocanthus. Swinging his body round, he searched to see where their tormentor could be. He pulled Evoc closer and whispered, "Do yer feel it?"

Evoc attempted to shake off Harbin's hand. "Feel what?" he moaned, "I don't feel nuffin. Leave go my arm."

Dropping Evoc's arm unceremoniously, Harbin took another look round before continuing up the path. Noticing Evoc had kept pace with him, Harbin was sure Crocanthus would be waiting for them. He approached the door, convinced that what his gut was telling him was right. Urging Evoc to hurry and open the door, he turned to face him and stated, "I still feel summat's abart." Observing the dim expression on Evoc's face, Harbin stated, "Me gut tells me it's Cro….."

Not wanting his tormentor's name mentioned, Evoc interrupted Harbin and said, "Don't say it. 'E's not 'ere. I don't see 'im." Even though Evoc couldn't feel Crocanthus' presence, he was nevertheless relieved he hadn't seen any sign of him being around.

"I don't see 'im. An' I don't fink 'e's 'ere," Evoc whispered. The pain in his arm caused by Harbin pulling him up the pathway was only just beginning to fade. Angered by that, and with the fear of Crocanthus being around, Evoc turned to Harbin.

"'Ow come I can't feel 'im? I can't see nuffing nor no one. Yer mus' be goin' mad."

Giving Evoc a glaring look, Harbin replied nastily, "I don't know. I jus' know 'e's gotta be somewhere close by."

By this time, Harbin wasn't sure if he wanted to enter the house or not. For a moment he considered getting in the car and driving far away. Failing to notice how unsettled Evoc had become caused some surprise to Harbin, when Evoc uttered, "I still can't see nuffing, nor 'ear any bird noises." Not wanting to mention Crocanthus by name, he whispered coarsely, "Let's get indoors, jus' in case…."

Taking another look round, Harbin was still hesitant on entering the house, but found himself agreeing with Evoc. Grabbing the key from Evoc's hand, Harbin halted for a moment before unlocking the door. Ignoring Evoc's whining voice, "Get a move on, it's freezin' out 'ere," Harbin swung round and hissed, "Shut yer mouf an' listen."

Making sure Evoc was still close to him, Harbin unlocked the door and cautiously entered the house. As he eased the door open, the creaking made him shudder. He was convinced the door was giving him a warning. Disturbed by this thought, he moaned inwardly as he ventured further inside the door.

They slowly entered the hallway. Scared of Crocanthus and angered at the rough way Harbin had grabbed him, Evoc stammered, "'E's not 'ere is 'e?"

"I can't see 'im, but I knows 'e's around," whispered Harbin.

Removing Harbin's hand from his jacket, Evoc stood and watched his partner's odd behaviour. Evoc could not resist gloating. "See, no one's 'ere," he scoffed. Harbin lifted his hand ready to bring it down on Evoc's face, but his hand suddenly changed direction. He thought he had seen something moving. Harbin grabbed Evoc's arm and pointed to where he'd seen the weird movement. "Did yer see that?" whispered Harbin.

Creasing his forehead and wondering what Harbin was talking about, Evoc suddenly caught a flicker of something pass by the bottom stair. It was the warning glare that came back from Harbin which prevented Evoc from uttering a sound.

Moving cautiously, they made their way further into the hall and nearer to the stairs. Keeping their eyes focused, they avoided walking too close to the bottom of the stairs, neither man feeling able to speak.

Harbin suddenly nudged Evoc's arm and pointed to a shimmering figure emerging in front of them. They stared. The figure was drawing them closer. A sudden movement of the figure startled them, preventing them from being drawn any closer.

Then they saw the figure slither its way towards them. Jumping back in alarm, Evoc grabbed his partner's arm. Evoc was somewhat taken aback that Harbin hadn't flung it off. It appeared Harbin was hypnotised by the moving figure. Giving Harbin a shake, Evoc was surprised when there was no response. He was shocked to see how white Harbin had gone. He was surprised to see his own fear reflected on Harbin's face.

"Let's get away from 'ere!" hissed Harbin. Evoc sidled up behind him. "Don't yer know what it did to yer?" Evoc whispered. Closing the front door and wondering what Evoc was talking about, Harbin whispered, "It didn't do nuffing to me."

"It did, yer was sort of 'ypnotised," Evoc told him, warily. Expecting some kind of punishment for telling Harbin he was affected by the figure, he followed quietly into a nearby room. Nervously they edged their way into the room, and only then realised that the shimmering figure had entered with them. Standing in the middle of the room they were startled to see how close the figure had come.

"What is it?" whispered Evoc, nervously. Certain he knew the answer; Harbin wasn't prepared to give it. The more he watched it, the more he felt he was losing control of his thoughts and body. Evoc, experiencing a similar feeling, knew instantly what was taking place. Not wanting this figure to take control of his mind, he began shaking his head and summoned enough strength to look away.

Harbin, not wanting to give any sign he was able to resist being hypnotised, suddenly felt Evoc's trembling hand touch his arm. He gave a slight movement to show he wasn't hypnotised. Noticing the figure move a little away from where it had stood, Harbin turned to face Evoc.

"Did yer go funny, like yer wasn't yerself?" Harbin asked abruptly.

"Me 'ead went funny, but I jus' give it a shake an' then I was all right," Evoc replied. Catching a glimpse of what was emerging from the shimmering figure, Evoc let out a loud scream.

"What the 'ell yer do that fer?" Harbin asked in a trembling voice. Mouth wide open and pointing to the emerged figure, Evoc shook his hand for Harbin to look at what made him scream. No sooner had Harbin turned his attention to where Evoc was pointing, than a long thin arm appeared before them. Before either man could say or do anything they found themselves in the grasp of two sets of bony fingers. Harbin wondered if this thing had been sent to kill them.

As he attempted to remove the bony fingers from his arm, Harbin felt a burning sensation run through his body. He was bent over with pain and finding it impossible to move. But then he heard the voice he feared more than anything else.

"Oh no you don't!" the figure hissed, followed by a guttural laugh. Evoc, unaware of Harbin's struggle to get free, found himself staring at the person he feared the most: Crocanthus. With the grip on his arm increasing, Evoc feared what horrible torture lay in store.

"Oh no you don't! You won't get away that easily," Crocanthus taunted, tightening his grip on their arms. Trembling, but knowing there was no escape, Evoc and Harbin knew they would have to wait until Crocanthus decided to release them. What was it he wanted? Unknown to both men, Crocanthus had been reading their thoughts, so he knew the fear they were feeling. That only served to increase his power over them.

"Yer got us now. Yer can let us go," said Harbin. But Crocanthus was laughing at their discomfort, and it seemed as if his grip had got firmer. Evoc, thinking he would try walking away, panicked when he failed to lift his foot off the floor. He tried several times to walk away and each time was met with firm resistance. He made one more try and was relieved when at last he was able to lift his foot from the floor. Taking a step forward and thinking this would be the moment to get away, he felt a firm tug on his arm, followed by a taunting Crocanthus saying, "Not yet, you moron, there's things to discuss."

In his eagerness to get away and hearing the taunt from Crocanthus, Evoc suddenly realized he hadn't seen any movement from Harbin. Unconcerned, he tried to walk over his partner's legs when he tripped on his partner's foot. Receiving a punch from Harbin's fist, Evoc yelled. "What yer do that fer?"

With his attention on Evoc, and wondering what Crocanthus was waiting for, Harbin checked to make sure Crocanthus had actually released his arm. Shaking life back into the numb arm, Harbin peered sideways, trying to see where Crocanthus was moving. Not taking care of what he was doing, Harbin found himself losing balance and falling flat on the floor. He stood up slowly and began waving a fist at his partner, threatening to get his own back.

Ignoring Harbin and his shaking fist, Evoc soon became aware that Crocanthus no longer had hold of him. Unlike Harbin, Evoc had watched Crocanthus move away. Amazed at how Crocanthus was able to move across the floor without apparently walking, Evoc whispered, "'Ow the 'eck does 'e do that?" He was surprised to hear Crocanthus reply, "You don't need to know."

As he stared at one of the cruellest men he knew, Evoc wasn't prepared to enter into discussions about magic and people's powers. Reading Evoc's thoughts, Crocanthus contented himself with a smirk aimed at Evoc. With more important things to do Crocanthus wasn't prepared to waste valuable time with these morons.

Harbin was decidedly disgruntled at the appearance of Crocanthus and failed to see the cruel expression clouding over in Crocanthus' eyes. If he had done, he might have thought twice before exclaiming rudely, "What yer 'ere fer? We ain't found no glowin' stone."

Taken aback at hearing Harbin daring to speak to Crocanthus in that tone of voice, Evoc stepped back and waited to see what would happen. Seeing Crocanthus advancing towards Harbin, Evoc felt as if he was watching something beastly moving in slow motion. But what was even more discerning was the malevolent look Crocanthus was giving Harbin. Unable to take his eyes off what was happening, Evoc became even more terrified of what Crocanthus would do.

Crocanthus drew back his hand and without warning brought it down hard on Harbin's face. Harbin staggered back from the blow as blood began running freely from his nose and mouth. Shocked, Evoc feared he was going to get the same treatment. Slowly walking backwards away from Crocanthus and Harbin, Evoc heard the cold voice of Crocanthus demanding, "Where do you think you are going?"

"What the 'ell….?" But before Harbin could finish his muffled question, Crocanthus had turned his attention to Evoc.

"What you staring at, scarface?" Crocanthus sneered menacingly. Still shocked at how quickly Crocanthus had punched Harbin, Evoc halted where he was. Still fearful of being punched, he stared unblinking as Crocanthus made his way closer to where he stood. He suddenly heard his own voice saying, "We didn't fink yer was comin' 'ere no more." Waiting to see if Crocanthus would punish him for answering back, Evoc noticed Harbin was still busy trying to stem the flow of blood.

With his usual feeling of contempt for these two men, and enraged at having to leave Dofstram, Crocanthus vented his anger on them. "Sit down, shut up, and listen to ME!" he warned them. Impatient that the men weren't moving quickly enough, Crocanthus began lashing out at them with his fists, drawing moans and groans as each blow landed. Content that he had put sufficient fear in both men, Crocanthus stood over them in a threatening manner and stated, "That stone needs to be found, and it needs to be found now!" Pacing back and forth, he ignored the wailing sounds coming from the men. He was obsessed with claiming the stone. He now concentrated on what the next move should be.

Trying to fathom what might be going through Crocanthus' mind, the two men stared nervously at him as he continued to pace back and forth. Suddenly they noticed his expression change from a creased brow to an angry one, which soon turned to a smirk. As Evoc and Harbin passed a glaring look at each other they were shocked when Crocanthus spun round and was staring them straight in the face. Through his cold dark eyes and his thin narrowed lips, Crocanthus demanded their full attention.

"There have been some very disturbing developments in Dofstram," he said. "These disturbances have been brought to the attention of Zanus."

Watching the men to see what their reaction would be, he wondered why neither of them had asked, 'what developments?' Waiting impatiently for one of them to speak, he entered their thoughts to discover what they were thinking.

Squirming on their seats, not sure how to respond, Evoc and Harbin were unaware of this. Angered by what their thoughts had revealed, Crocanthus began to taunt them. "So! You thought I was going to let you return to Dofstram, eh? Well you won't be going back if you fail to get that stone," he said. Walking round them and enjoying their discomfort, he continued, "You were sent here to complete a certain task, in which you have failed. Through your stupidity the stone hasn't been found. So guess what? You have one more chance to complete that task -

or else!" He put his face inches away from the men and clenched his teeth. "Find that stone!" he hissed.

Alarmed at the nearness of Crocanthus, and guessing he must have read their thoughts, Evoc wailed, "But we's told yer, we's can't find no dratted stone." Seeing Crocanthus lift his arm, Evoc managed to step back just in time to avoid the impact of his fist.

Angry at Evoc managing to avoid his punch, Crocanthus glared at him and uttered in a cold voice, "Listen, you moron. It's vital that stone is found. You might like to know we are aware of DaVendall and friends being in Dofstram. And yes, that includes those women. Lottie, the woman you were supposed to capture, her interfering mate Penny and that other kid, Peter." Leaning into the faces of Evoc and Harbin, he uttered, "Guess what, they were seen arriving at the castle along with others of our enemy."

Taking a threatening step closer to the two quivering men, he continued, "Zanus is ready to punish all who fail him. He is angered that the woman had escaped being captured." Halting for a moment to let the message sink in, he waited to hear if either man would make a comment. With nothing forthcoming, he continued in a taunting voice.

"Zanus wasn't in a good mood when he discovered who had arrived at the castle, and without the stone." Staring at Crocanthus with wide eyes, and showing clearly the fear he was feeling, Evoc waited anxiously to hear what else Crocanthus had to say.

Just for a moment they appeared to have forgotten Crocanthus was waiting to say something else. Neither man had seen the cruel, pinched expression on his face. Not the most patient of men, Crocanthus decided he wasn't going to waste much longer with these two, and quickly brought their attention back to him.

"So scarface, what should we do now?" he taunted. Casting his eyes towards Harbin, he noticed he had shrunk further back into the seat. "I suppose you can't guess either?" he taunted him. "Well, I suppose I'll tell you what we've got to do now." Noticing Harbin was about to speak, Crocanthus slapped him across the mouth and told him, "Keep it shut, I haven't finished yet!" Evoc gasped when he saw the blood start to flow again from Harbin's nose and mouth.

Crocanthus turned to Evoc. "Well, do you idiots have any ideas where the stone could be?" he asked.

Watching Crocanthus standing so imperiously with arms folded, Evoc suddenly thought of a question. "Why can't yer find it? Yous 'ave magical powers, we don't."

"How dare you speak to me like that!" Crocanthus roared, landing a fist on Evoc's face. Reeling back from the attack, Evoc wailed, "Look what yer've done. I'm bleedin' all over the place."

"Shut your wailing, or I'll give you another one," Crocanthus hissed. Wishing he would leave, Harbin stated, "We don't know 'ow to find a stone which glows. 'Ow will we know when it will glow?" Feeling drawn to where Crocanthus had previously been standing, they were shocked to see he'd moved and was now standing behind them. Trying to ignore his presence as he hovered over them, the two men feared he would read their thoughts again. This left them struggling to remain alert and to think of other things, not Crocanthus.

Now Crocanthus had moved from behind them to a position in front of them. They were unable to take their eyes from him as he transformed himself into a ghost-like image of himself. Gawping at the image, Evoc stammered, "'Ow'd yer do that?"

Sneering at the men as they cowered away, Crocanthus maintained his new form and began to slither and dive around them. Disconcerted by what was taking place, Evoc drew Harbin's attention to where Crocanthus was moving. Mesmerised by the gliding movements of Crocanthus' new image, Evoc failed to see a long bony finger aimed straight at his chest. Screaming at the impact, which left a burning sensation, Harbin jumped back for fear of having the same done to him.

Just when he thought he was safe, Harbin felt a sharp pain in his side and shouted out in agony. He looked down to see blood oozing through his clothing. Meanwhile Evoc, terrified of what other terrors Crocanthus had in mind, was trying to work out where he had gone. Laughing at the discomfort of the two men, Crocanthus floated back beside them. Then, to their amazement, he rose up off the floor and grew in height, almost reaching the ceiling.

"Get on with finding that stone or you'll never return to Dofstram!" he spat, stabbing them each with a sharp fingernail as he spoke each word. He laughed cruelly as he watched them trying to move away from him. Before either could respond, they realised Crocanthus was once more beginning to change shape. Terrified of what he would now become, Evoc was making his way to the door, while Harbin stood transfixed.

Before Evoc could reach the door he was shocked to see that his way was being barred by a creature he had seen before, an enormous cobra-like snake. It opened its mouth wide to display unusually long fangs. With a guttural laugh, the creature slowly dropped to the floor and began slithering over to Harbin. Waiting for the inevitable, Evoc remained where he'd fallen.

Rearing up and displaying its large fangs, the snake hissed in the voice of Crocanthus "Find that stone, or else!" Terrified he was going to be attacked; Harbin fell back on the seat he'd vacated, leaving Evoc where he was. Looking across at his partner, Harbin grunted, "Don't move, 'e needs us to get that dratted stone."

"Yer 'opes 'e won't kill us yet," replied Evoc. Crocanthus let out a loud hiss and vanished. Looking round to see where the creature had gone, Evoc nervously stated, "I fought yer said 'e wouldn't kill us? Why 'as 'e gone wivout telling us what 'e 'spects us to do?" Just as stunned as Evoc on seeing the creature, Harbin was in no mood to be spoken to in that manner. "Jus watch yer mouf, 'e ain't done wiv us yet," he scowled.

By this time, Evoc had scrambled up off the floor and was peering round the room. Not seeing any sign of Crocanthus or the creature, he was about to relay that information to Harbin when he noticed that his partner was about to rise off his seat. What neither man was prepared for was the sudden arrival of Crocanthus, standing and staring them in the face.

"So, thought I'd gone did you? Well I ain't. Just take a warning, I want that stone found. If you fail I'm not going to say what will happen to you, but I promise you won't like it."

Crocanthus, seeing the fear on Harbin's face, let out a

raucous laugh and turned his attention to Evoc. "Well, what about you, ugly mug, nothing to say?" Without waiting for a response, but seeing the fear on Evoc's face. Crocanthus stepped towards him, making Evoc jump back.

Crocanthus strolled casually over to the door. He had not quite finished with them. He spun round to face them.

"Find the stone or die!" he hissed.

"We don't know fer sure she 'ad it," whined Evoc. "If she did 'ave it, where's she 'idden it? 'Member, we bin to 'er 'ouse to look an' nearly got 'ad by that there shopkeeper. Not fergettin' 'er mate's ol' man."

Hearing how quiet his mate's voice had gone, Harbin looked to see how Crocanthus was going to react. Then, to the surprise of both Crocanthus and Harbin, Evoc shouted, "I know one man. Not 'im, the shopkeeper, the one 'oo was wiv 'im. 'E was one of them 'umans 'oo came to fight us afore."

"What yer yakking on about?" shouted Harbin.

"Yous 'member, the 'umans 'oo came an' 'elped to fight with those 'umans what was there. Yer know, the ones what's being 'eld in 'is dungeons."

Evoc was stumbling excitedly over his words. Realising who Evoc was talking about, and ignoring the shopkeepers, Crocanthus sneered, "Think you're clever, eh? I know all about those interfering shopkeepers. They'll be taken care of later."

Evoc, wondering why Crocanthus hadn't commented on the other man he saw, sneered, "Yer missed out 'er mate's old man. 'E was at that 'ouse."

Realising he must have missed part of Evoc's statement, Crocanthus shouted, "What? What other interfering humans?" He moved back into the room and made his way over to where the men were still cowering. His anger increasing by the moment, he recalled the moment he'd been at Penny's house with every intention of getting rid of them. Remembering how he'd been thwarted by the presence of DaVendall and his interfering companions did little to calm the anger gathered inside him.

"What are they doing at her house?" roared Crocanthus. He began to storm round the room, so busy considering his own question that he failed to notice Evoc and Harbin had moved away from their seats. The pair had hastily moved across to the door, intent on making a quick exit should Crocanthus change into something else. Surprising the two men, Crocanthus added in a distant tone, "I wonder what brought them there?" Then he noticed where Evoc and Harbin were standing.

"Just where do you two morons think you're going?" he bellowed. The two men made their way sheepishly back into the room. Observing the cruel expression on Crocanthus' face, they resisted the compulsion to sit down.

"Why ain't yer said somefing about the other 'umans? The shopkeeper ones, yer never told us yer'd seen 'em," Evoc asked, in a hushed voice. Keeping a wary eye on Crocanthus, Harbin waited to see if Evoc would be punished for challenging him. But the minutes past with no response from Crocanthus, either verbally or physically, and Harbin wondered if Crocanthus had heard what Evoc had said.

"I 'ope 'e goes soon," grumbled Harbin. Just then Crocanthus unexpectedly announced, "I'm going to pay a visit to her house myself. I need to discover what is going on. It might be Lottie has returned."

"So what we s'ppose' to do?" whined Evoc.

"Shut your whining. Let me think, moron!" retorted Crocanthus impatiently. Pacing back and forth, he finally continued, "This is what you will do. You are to go and see that library boss woman and find out if she's found the stone. If she has, I want it. I wouldn't want her to get any ideas of keeping it from me!" Turning and glaring at the men, he warned, "Do whatever it takes to make her talk. Don't return until you have found the stone!"

Neither man was looking forward to returning to the library, but neither could they summon the courage to tell Crocanthus this. Deep in his own thoughts, and thinking about his forthcoming visit to Lottie's, it now appeared to Evoc and Harbin that Crocanthus had forgotten them. Evoc turned to Harbin and gave a shrug of his shoulders. Returning the gesture, Harbin noticed Crocanthus was about to exit the room. He opened his mouth to speak, but Crocanthus glared at him with cold black eyes, making Harbin close his mouth in an instant.

"Get going, you idiots! You've been told what to do. Remember, that stone is the most important thing, if you wish to return to Dofstram. If it means tearing that library apart, then do it. Just remember, no stone, no going back," he warned in a cold threatening tone. He gave a last warning glare and left the house.

Not sure what to make of Crocanthus' sudden exit, Evoc and Harbin stared at the doorway wondering if he would return with another warning. After waiting for a while and with no reappearance of their boss, Evoc crept stealthily towards the door to check he wasn't waiting for them in the hallway. Turning to Harbin, Evoc stated, "Good, 'e's really gone."

With the strain of what had taken place over the past few moments, Harbin felt a need to vent his anger on someone, and the only person available was Evoc. However, before he could carry out his desire, Evoc remarked angrily, "I ain't goin' to no libr'y. I 'ates goin' to that libr'y, that old woman'll make us leave as soon as she sees us." Unaware of Harbin's vengeful intentions, Evoc walked towards the door ready to exit. Seeing he was about to leave the room and annoyed at not being quick enough to give his partner the thumping he felt he deserved, Harbin called out rudely, "Where yer goin', idiot? What yer mean you 'ates goin' there? Yous know we gotta go back there fer that darn stone. Yer knows what 'e'll do we don't get it."

"I know we won't get out of this 'orrible land if we don't find it," Evoc called back. Deciding he'd had enough for one day he started to climb the stairs.

"I'm gonna go ter bed," he called back. "See 'ow I feels in the mornin'."

Shocked at Evoc's response, Harbin stomped out the room and took himself up the stairs, moaning and groaning at what they had to do come morning.

Chapter Four

The Impostor

Crocanthus was still going over what his menials had told him and wondered why these other humans would be at her house if Lottie was still in Dofstram. His mind filled with his forthcoming visit to Lottie's house, he considered the various disguises he could use. Aware he couldn't go as himself, or indeed Jeremy Thackett, he suddenly thought of the answer.

Perfect! That would do it. He couldn't help congratulating himself on such a clever idea.

When he reached his house, he took a moment to look round to make sure it was clear to change his disguise. Not seeing anything to concern him, he side-stepped behind a shrub and concentrated on changing his appearance to that of Mr Jeremy Thackett, well-dressed gentleman about town. Transformation completed, he strode confidently out from the shrub and made his way to the front door. He did not care who saw him now.

He opened the front door and took a moment to check the hall. Satisfied it was safe for him to proceed, he closed the door quietly. Remaining alert to any unsuspecting tenant he made his way across the hallway to his apartment.

With his concentration taken up by what he'd planned, he was eager to see which of his potions remained. Thinking about the potions brought Imelda to mind. He was annoyed at having to give her the stone and the woman as a reward, but he rejected those thoughts and turned his attention to making certain the disguise would be good enough to fool those interfering people. He berated himself for not getting rid of them before this could happen.

Checking through the potions, his curiosity turned once more to why those people would be in Lottie's house.

"I'll soon find out why," he muttered to himself. "I might even get a chance to do away with them." Not thinking of anything other than his desire to get to Lottie's house, he was suddenly interrupted in his thoughts when he heard a sound from outside his door. He decided to take a look before removing the potions from their hiding place.

He walked quietly across the carpeted floor, continuing to listen. At the door of his apartment, not hearing anything, he slowly opened the door just enough for him to see out. He could see nothing, and closed the door as quietly as he'd opened it.

Now he had only the potions on his mind. He made his way to the far corner of the room and lifted up the corner of the carpet, but then he hesitated for a moment before pulling it away from the floorboards. Satisfied whoever or whatever cause the noise had gone he lifted the relevant floorboard to reveal the hiding place for his potions. He was relieved to see the box was still as he'd placed it earlier.

Absorbed with what he was doing, he suddenly heard voices outside his door. "I don't think he's in," said a distinctive voice. Clutching the box in his arms, Crocanthus wondered who and what the speaker could be referring to. He had never had any time for his fellow tenants, and wasn't prepared to speak to them now. As he placed the box back under the floorboard, he became agitated and wondered how he could get rid of them.

He knew his powers were limited, but his immediate desire was to make these people go away. Pushing all other thoughts from his mind he concentrated on what he would do to make them leave the hall.

"These idiots don't know who they're dealing with," he sneered to himself. "They might know me as Jeremy Thackett, but they've no idea who I really am." With that in mind, he wasted no time in turning to a scare tactic he'd used on Evoc and Harbin. He concentrated his energy on changing his appearance, and it was with some satisfaction that he looked down at himself to see the transformation was complete. His new ghostly image enabled him to noiselessly exit the room through the keyhole. A group of people were standing across from his door, and Crocanthus floated across the floor until he was close to them.

It didn't take long for him to lose interest in the conversation. He began to blow out icy cold air, and had to restrain himself from gloating when he saw them shudder. Watching them vigorously rubbing their arms, he waited for someone to comment on the cold. No one did, so he decided he needed to give them something that would really scare them. Building up his energy, he gradually showed them an outline of his ghostly image. Getting the reaction he wanted, he frightened the group further by weaving round them and blowing cold air on each one as he flew past.

Now the intruders were so paralysed with shock that they stayed rooted to the spot instead of leaving the hallway. Crocanthus was furious. Ignoring their wide-eyed stares and the open mouths ready to scream, he murmured to the person nearest him, "Let's see if this will make you move." Startled by hearing a voice from nowhere, the man called John let out a low scream.

Satisfied he'd scared at least one of the group Crocanthus started prodding and scratching the others with his long skeletal fingers. Enjoying their shrieks, he considered a different attack. Then one of the men whispered, "Did that thing attack you? Look, I've got blood coming through my sleeve!"

"I'm bleeding too," whispered his friend.

"What was it, Freddy?" asked Mary, one of the women. "I thought it looked like a ..."

"Don't say ghost! You're frightening me," called Anna. "Look, we're all bleeding. Do your scratches burn? Mine does. Can anyone see where it went?"

The group peered round, fearful that their attacker was beside them. Shivering from the cold and fright, Freddy pointed in the direction of the front door. They were shocked to see it open all by itself.

Crocanthus had opened the front door with such force that

it slammed against the back wall and rocked backwards and forwards. Their reaction didn't disappoint him. The women were hanging on to the men's arms, pleading with them to make whatever it was go away. What he found more amusing was when one of the men tried to sound brave and called out, "How did that happen? I didn't think it was that windy."

"I was about to say the same thing, Ivan," whispered Michael, staring at the gap where the door should be. Shocked to see blood on his friend's clothing, he checked to see if he was bleeding too and found blood oozing through his sleeve. A stinging sensation was going through his arm.

"Is there somewhere we can wash this blood off?" he asked. "My arm is stinging like crazy."

"We could use the washroom over there, but it's pretty basic," Mary told them. She little knew Crocanthus hadn't finished with them just yet.

Not sure how long he could keep this disguise, and desperate to discover what was going on at Lottie's house, Crocanthus decided one last vicious attack should make these wretched people leave. Recalling someone mentioning the wind, Crocanthus murmured to himself, "So it's not windy enough. Eh? Let's see if this will make you go!" He let out a blood-curdling laugh which echoed round the hallway, then watched with cruel amusement as the group huddled together.

"I don't like what's happening here," said Mary, in a nervous voice.

"You think that's bad? Just you wait and see what's next," Crocanthus said to himself. He turned his concentration to the pictures hanging on the walls. With one huge blast of air he blew many of them off their hooks, sending splinters of glass everywhere. The few remaining pictures that remained on the wall were swinging from side to side.

"What the blazes? Look what's happened to the pictures," called out Freddy. "I don't think much of your accommodation, Michael. Does this go on all the time?"

"So many of those lovely pictures, smashed on the floor!" exclaimed Anna. "I've never seen that happen before and I've lived here for some time." Noticing Mary was making her way to where the glass had fallen, Anna called out, "Be careful. I'll fetch a dustpan and brush, we don't want any cut fingers."

Anna hurried into her room, trying to shrug off her fears, and dashed back with the brush and pan. Forgetting about using the washroom, the remainder of the group waited for her to return.

"Is someone there?" Michael called out. "Whoever you are, what you're doing isn't funny."

"I agree, it's not in the least funny. I dare you to show yourself," called out Freddy.

Arriving back with brush and pan in hand, Anna set about clearing up the glass, while Michael and John stood the pictures against the wall. Anna asked, "Who's playing tricks, John? I don't know about you, but I've never seen anything like this before. Can you make out what happened with the door and the pictures?"

"Never, Anna. I don't understand it," said John. Just then the front door swung violently shut.

"What the blazes is happening here?" shouted John. Hearing no response, he looked at Michael and asked, "Have you ever known this door to open and shut on its own?"

"Not as long as I've lived here, and that's coming up to two years now," replied Michael.

Freddy could feel himself becoming annoyed. Before he could stop himself, he called out, "Who's there? Come on, show yourself."

Then one of the women started to whimper. "Who's there? Look everyone; something is making my jacket move," she shrieked.

"I think this place is haunted," whispered Milly.

"Have you noticed how cold it's gone?" said Michael. Rubbing their sore and stinging arms, their attention was drawn back to the door.

"I don't think the cold air can be coming from the front door, because it's shut," said John

"Well what could it be?" asked Milly. "I've lived here for some time, and I have never experienced anything like this. It's making me too scared to stay here."

Moving as near as he could to the person called John,

Crocanthus landed a cruel punch in his stomach. John buckled over.

"Ouch, what's going on here?" John gasped as he recovered.

Before any of the others could make a comment, Crocanthus landed a vicious blow on the arm of Freddy. Then, noticing the women had turned deathly pale, he couldn't resist taunting them further. Floating over to where they were standing, he laughed menacingly as he floated past their faces. But even Crocanthus was suddenly deafened by a loud scream from Milly. Thinking he'd really give her something to scream at, he began to trail his bony fingers up and down her arms, leaving scratch marks.

"What's that? What's happening?" screamed Milly. Michael took hold of her hand and led her towards the door. The rest of the group followed.

Stepping eagerly onto the footpath, Mary said, "Oh god, this place is haunted. I'm never coming here again!"

Listening to the words from the departing group, Crocanthus let out a loud raucous laugh which left the group with no other thought than to get as far away from the house as possible. It wasn't until they were a good way along the road that they took a quick look back to make sure that whatever it was hadn't followed them.

Still a bit breathless, Anna drew a breath and asked, "What do you think was going on? I've never seen anything like it before, have any of you?"

"I've been wondering that myself," said John. "Do you think the house has a ghost?"

"I don't know and I don't care. I know I've never seen anything like that before. And I'll be looking for other accommodation. I can't go back there!" whimpered Milly.

"Nor me," John stated in agreement.

"May I suggest you and Michael come over to my place for the night?" suggested Freddy.

"Milly and Anna could stay with me," suggested Mary.

"Thank you," said Milly. She took hold of Anna's and Mary's arms and they set off down the road.

Crocanthus gave no further thought to the people he'd frightened. He made his way back to his room and waited for the disguise to fade away. Then he stomped over to the far end of the room and threw back the carpet. Snatching up the floorboards, he lifted the precious box from its secret place and tucked it under his arm. Making his way to a nearby chair, he opened the box to reveal what potions remained. Just then he suddenly heard a voice outside his door. "Where is everyone?" Not another interruption!

Crocanthus was about to go and see who it was when he heard a door shut. Turning his attention back to the box with the potions, he opened it once more and pondered over which one to use. As he cast his eye over the phials, he suddenly became convinced some were missing. Surely no one would dare to enter his room?

"Someone's been in here and stolen my potions!" he fumed, pacing round the room. "If I find out who he is their life won't be spared."

He lifted the phials from the box, studying each one carefully, hoping to recognise which one had gone. Moving aside one of the phials, he realised that some of the smaller ones had been hidden from view by a larger one. Although he was relieved, his anger was not so quick to subside.

"If I ever discover anyone coming in here, I will carry out my threat." He muttered. He took out the phial he sought and sat twirling it round in his hand. Then he suddenly remembered he would need the phial that would reverse the disguise. He selected the correct one and placed the remaining phials in the box. As he did so, he had a sudden thought. Would the selected potion be enough to sustain his disguise for the length of time required?

He decided to wait until he had reached Lottie's house before taking the potion, and he wondered if he could take all the phials with him. But he soon realised this was not possible. He arranged the rest of the phials in such a way that he would know if anyone had touched them. Closing the lid, he stomped across the floor and replaced the box under the floorboard, throwing the carpet back to its original place. Then he checked his pockets to make sure the required phials were secure. Now he made his way to the door. He opened it just far enough to see into the hall, where he could see that there were no other tenants around. Casually walking over to the cupboard at the end of the hallway, he removed his bicycle and wheeled it out.

Crocanthus rode on down the road, churning over different scenarios he could use. After discounting a few of the ideas, his thoughts suddenly turned to Zanus' spy birds. Not wanting them to become aware of his presence, he also knew he would have to careful not to be seen by the shopkeepers.

As he approached the corner of the road, he checked to make sure no one was observing his movements. As nightfall approached he remained alert for any spy bird that might be flying round. The darkness would give him extra cover, and it was a while before he continued on his way.

As he turned the corner, he could see the lights were out in the shop. He made his way as near as he dare to Lottie's house, taking care not to stop under any of the street lights. He left his bicycle against one of Lottie's neighbour's high hedges.

As he approached the gate he could hear the muffled squawking of the birds, which made him take extra care on opening and closing the gate. He walked slowly up the pathway, cursing the birds for making such a loud noise.

Staring at the darkened house, he gave no thought that the occupants might have retired for the night. Instead, his thoughts turned to different ways in which he would enjoy teaching Lottie a lesson. Remembering what his menials had told him about the people who had been in the house on their last visit, he groaned. "Damn it. How am I supposed to know who she's got in there?"

Having made the decision to see who was inside, he wasn't going to let a darkened house stop him. He took shelter behind a nearby shrub, certain the potion would now last long enough for him to complete his mission. Then he took the phial from his pocket and drank it.

Once it had taken effect, he gathered himself together and stepped confidently onto the doorstep. With the potion transforming him to the desired disguise, he looked down at himself and was pleased to see how clearly he resembled the person he was meant to be. He knocked loudly on the door, smirking at his cunning plan.

"Are you ready?" he called. But he was horrified to hear it was his own voice, and not that of his disguise, he asked again. "Are you ready?" he asked again. Relieved to hear the voice sound as the true person would talk, he uttered, "Aah! That's better."

He could see no signs of life or movement from within the house, so he gave a loud knock on the door. Impatient at being kept on the doorstep, he quickly repeated it. It was then he started to wonder why Lottie's mangy dog wasn't barking. Just then the door opened, wide bringing him face to face not with Lottie but with Bertram.

"Why hello, Sam, is something the matter? Come on in!" Bertram said, moving aside to let the disguised Crocanthus in. Taking a step through the door, Crocanthus couldn't resist quietly gloating at how easily he'd fooled this man. Bertram, surprised to see Sam returning so soon, wondered what could be wrong.

"What's the matter, Sam?" asked Bertram. "Something bad must have happened for you to return on such an awful night. Is Lucy all right? You weren't attacked by those birds, were you?"

Realising he'd better say something before Bertram became suspicious; Sam replied, "We're all right. We weren't attacked by anything."

Just then Frances called out, "Who's there, Bert? Is everything all right?"

"It's Sam, Frances. I'm not sure what's happened, but if there's any trouble I'm sure we can sort it out," called back Bertram.

Crocanthus quickly realised that the real Sam must have visited them earlier. Trying to think of a suitable response and not able to think how best to answer, he decided to change the subject.

"I wondered if perhaps Lottie and her friends might have returned," he asked, trying to look round. Bertram considered asking why he should ask such a strange question, but decided to wait.

"I forgot to ask earlier, have you seen Lottie wearing any special items?" asked Crocanthus. Shocked to hear Sam ask this, Bertram frowned and looked directly at him.

"That's a funny question to ask at this time of night. I wouldn't know what Lottie wore," Bertram replied. He was beginning to feel something wasn't quite right, and that there was something different about his friend.

"Would you like to come in Sam? It's not very nice out there," Bertram asked. "Did something happen to you and Lucy on the way home? You seem different."

Crocanthus turned to face Bertram. Had he said or done something to make him suspicious? With a forced a smile on his face, replied, "What made you say that? I don't feel any different. As I say, everything's fine with both of us."

Unable to explain what was causing this uneasy feeling, Bertram decided he would ask Frances to come downstairs and join them. He knew she would soon detect what was wrong. Without giving Sam a chance to say anything further, Bertram called Frances and asked if she would join them in the kitchen. Not waiting for a response, he invited Sam into the kitchen, assuring him that his wife would not be long in joining them.

Surprised that Frances hadn't responded, Bertram put his head through the kitchen door and called, "Frances, would you mind coming down? Sam and I would like a drink. We're in the kitchen."

Frances wondered why Bert wasn't making a drink himself. Then it dawned on her that Bert must want her there for a reason.

"I wonder what Sam is doing back here?" she asked herself in a hushed voice. "Be right there!" she called down, reaching for her dressing gown.

Meanwhile, downstairs in the kitchen, Bertram was having great difficulty in shaking off the uncomfortable feeling he was getting. Sam, oddly, was saying nothing. Bertram went over to fill the kettle. Waiting for the kettle to fill, he had a horrible thought - 'What if ...' but just then he heard Winston calling, "Dad, what's going on?"

"You go back to sleep son, it's only Mum and me," called Bertram. "We're going to have a quick drink. Just a bit unsettled tonight." Curious as to his father's response, Winston settled down in an attempt to sleep, but at that moment he noticed his mother standing on the landing. He couldn't help thinking there was something strange going on.

"Can I come and get a drink too?" he asked. Frances looked at his eager expression and replied, "Come along then, Winston. Seeing as you've been disturbed, you might as well come and join us. Perhaps a hot drink will help us all to settle."

Waiting for Winston to put his dressing gown on, Frances whispered in a cautious voice, "Did you hear someone knocking on the door a little earlier? Is that what disturbed you?"

"So it was our door," replied Winston. "I thought I was having a dream." Down in the kitchen, Frances greeted their unexpected visitor.

"Hello, Sam, is Lucy all right? It's such a horrible night for you to be out, is something wrong?" she asked, taking the tea tin off the shelf. Making a show of putting fresh tea leaves in the teapot, she checked to see if the kettle was near to boiling.

"Why didn't you bring Lucy?" asked Winston in a tired voice. Trying to ignore Winston, Crocanthus turned his attention to Frances. He felt if anyone would know if Lottie had anyone in particular she cared for, she would have mentioned it to this woman. But he knew that if he didn't respond to Winston his parents would get suspicious.

"I just felt a little concerned about Lottie and came to see if she had returned," he said. Seeing Winston was about to say something, Bertram placed a hand over his son's and gave a small squeeze indicating he should remain silent. Winston nodded and remained silent. He too was beginning to feel something wasn't quite right, and hoped his Dad would find out what.

"Why would you think Lottie had returned, Sam? Have you heard something to make you think that?"

"I was a little unsettled, and said as much to, er, Lucy," replied Crocanthus, cursing himself for having to struggle to remember the woman's name. "It was her suggestion that I should come and see if Lottie had returned safely." He glanced at the three faces round the table, hoping he'd been successful with his explanation.

"Why didn't Lucy come with you? Is she all right?" asked Frances, looking enquiringly at Sam. She wondered what it was about Sam that didn't feel right.

"Have any of you ever seen Lottie with anything special?" asked Crocanthus. "Like something of her mother's, for instance?"

"Whatever made you ask such a question, Sam? You know as well as us that Lottie doesn't have money to spend on luxuries, she needs all her earnings to keep the bills paid." She was now convinced that something wasn't right.

"Come on Sam, what's with the question?" asked Bertram. Noticing Bertram and Winston were giving each other querying looks, Frances asked, "Why would Lottie come back so soon? You know where she is and who she's with." Without taking her eyes off Sam, she waited for an answer. Then she turned to Winston and asked casually, "Winston, be a good lad and fetch a plate for the biscuits."

Winston knew his Mum never put biscuits on a plate at this time of night; they always helped themselves from the tin. And why was Dad giving him such strange looks? Passing his mother to get to the crockery cupboard, he felt a kind of tension coming from her he'd never experienced before. Whatever was causing it made him feel nervous.

"Are you all right, Mum?" he whispered. He watched her spread the biscuits on the plate.

"I'm fine," said Frances, not wanting to scare him. "Just keep your ears and eyes open and watch Sam."

"Ah, that's a good cup of tea, just needs a little sugar I think," boomed Bertram. He offered the sugar bowl to their visitor.

"No thanks," Sam curtly replied. Now Bertram knew for certain that this was not his friend. Sam had a real sweet tooth and always had three sugars in his tea. He only had to take a glance at Frances to know she must have had the same thought.

"If you've finished your tea, Winston, I think you should take yourself off to bed," said Frances, anxious for her son's safety. Winston gave his mother a wary look and placed his empty mug in the sink.

"Leave that, Winston, I'll see to that later," Frances told him, giving him a warm smile.

"OK. Thanks, Mum," Winston replied, in a tired voice. Giving a big yawn, he bid his parents goodnight and made his way out the kitchen door. They were surprised to hear him call out, "Night Dad, night Sam, night Mum, see you all in the morning."

As Winston made his way up the stairs he had a sudden thought. Why hadn't Sam called goodnight - and why hadn't he had sugar in his tea?

Relieved that Winston had gone to bed, Bertram wanted

answers to certain questions he had not wanted to ask in his son's presence. Turning to Sam he asked abruptly, "Now, what's wrong with you, Sam? You're different from only a couple of hours ago. Are you sure there's nothing wrong?"

Annoyed he'd given them cause to doubt who he was, Crocanthus was struggling to keep his frustration under control.

"There's nothing wrong with me. Surely I can ask if Lottie's all right? After all, she might have come to some harm in Dofstram."

"What makes you say that, Sam? Lottie would never come to harm when she's with her friends!" Frances said sharply.

"I think it might be a good idea if you give Lucy a ring to let her know you're all right," suggested Bertram.

"I don't need to do that, she knows where I am and she knows I won't stay long," said Crocanthus.

"That's not like you, Sam, you care deeply that Lucy worries about you," Frances remarked, placing her empty mug next to where Winston had left his. Crocanthus was now struggling to remain civil while fighting off the urge to do these interfering people some harm. He rose from his seat and said rudely, "I think I will leave now." Shocked at Sam's rudeness, Bertram and Frances were surprised at how quickly their visitor left the kitchen. They followed him into the hall to find him already at the front door. Briskly moving forward, Bertram opened the door ready for Sam to leave. But Sam hadn't got all he'd come for. Taking a chance he asked again, "Are you sure Lottie hasn't acquired any new items?"

"Frances has already told you Lottie has bills to pay," Bertram said sternly. "Anyway, it's none of our business if she decides to treat herself now and again."

Glancing at the pair as they stood close together, Crocanthus struggled to control how he felt. "I agree," he grunted. "Now I really must go. Goodnight."

"Give our best to Lucy," said Bertram.

What Sam did next alarmed Bertram and Frances. He simply halted where he was, half in and half out the doorway. Staring up the stairs, he was trying to reach into Winston's thoughts. Bertram, seeing the cold, dark, half-closed eyes, was becoming alarmed for Winston's safety. He wasn't sure what was taking place, but he knew he had to get this person out of the house.

Crocanthus, concentrating on the occupant upstairs, continued peering into Winston's mind, frustrated at not being able to break through. He was convinced he could make the boy tell him what he wanted to know.

Bertram and Frances stood observing him, newly afraid for their son. Aware of how many a mind has been infiltrated, Bertram wondered if that was what was taking place now. He knew he had to get this person away from here as quickly as he could. He thought he could guess who the 'Sam' person really was and knew this would have to de done with great care, or both Winston and Frances would be made to suffer.

"Good night, Sam," he said brusquely. Annoyed at having his concentration broken and frustrated at the rubbish that was going through the boy's thoughts, Crocanthus stepped noisily out onto the doorstep. He glared at Frances, who responded by saying, "Go home Sam. Lucy will be wondering where you've got to."

Bertram closed the door with a slightly louder bang than he would normally have done. Hearing the door bang brought Frances out of her worried thoughts.

"You know as well as I do who that was," she said to her husband. "Did you see that horrible look on his face when he stared up the stairs? I'm so glad Winston wasn't in sight. You don't think he'd harm him, do you?"

"I don't think so," replied Bertram. "But I'm sure he would have harmed us if he could." Noticing how pale Frances had gone, Bertram didn't want to worry his wife any more that she was. Placing a gentle hand on her arm he asked, "How soon did you realise?"

"I don't exactly know, but I knew for certain when he refused sugar in his tea. I'm so glad you didn't say his name. I knew there was something wrong when you called and asked me to make a drink. That was a good idea. It alerted me that something wasn't quite right."

"Well done Frances, I hoped you would think it was strange. But I didn't know how else to ask you to join us." He took her by the arm. "Who would have thought he'd dare to come here, disguised as our Sam? That really was terrible. I don't know about you, but I could do with something stronger than tea. I feel as if we have had a lucky escape."

Having had similar thoughts herself, Frances suddenly felt tears run down her face. "Come along Fran, time for a glass of something special," Bertram whispered. He gently led his wife into the kitchen and sat her down on a chair. Reaching across the table for the malt, Bertram poured out a drink for them both.

"Thank you, Bert," said Frances. "I really need this. I've never been so frightened as I was tonight. You don't think he would have harmed us do you?"

"Well I'm not too sure. I was somewhat worried for a moment about our Winston. I was relieved he went off to bed without asking any awkward questions."

"Me too, but he's a good lad, and he was very tired."

They sat in silence for a moment, sipping their whisky.

"I know it's late, but I think I might just give Sam a ring and let him know what's taken place," said Bertram.

"Are you sure you should disturb them?"

"I do. What if he goes disguised as one of us?" asked Bertram.

"He wouldn't, would he?" asked Frances anxiously.

"I wouldn't put anything past that evil, conniving swine."

"Go on then, Bert. I'll pour us another small drink while you ring Sam," Frances said, still very nervous at having had that dreadful man so near to her family.

Bertram took out a slip of paper from his pocket on which he'd written Sam's telephone number. He dialled it, hoping they weren't too deep in sleep. Just as he was thinking this, a sprightly Sam answered: "Sam and Lucy's shop, can I help..."

"Did you get back all right, Sam?" Bertram interrupted.

"What do you mean, Bertram? We arrived home safely some time ago, thank you."

"I don't mean you and Lucy, I meant you. You only left here a couple of minutes ago."

"I still don't know what you're on about, neither of us has left the shop since we got back from visiting you," Sam told him, wondering if Bertram had perhaps been dreaming.

"Sam, please listen very carefully. We've just had a visit from your good self. Only it wasn't the real you."

He heard Sam call out to Lucy, "Come over here my dear. It's Bertram on the phone and guess what? They've just had a visit from me, only it wasn't me..."

Lucy put her hand on his arm to stop Sam from saying the name.

"Bertram, are you still there?" asked Sam.

"Yes, I'm still here."

"Did you let on you knew it wasn't really me?"

"No, and neither did Frances. We were only sure it was an impostor when he refused sugar in his tea." He heard a gentle laugh coming from Lucy, which seemed to lighten the dark moment Bertram was going through.

"Well done for your sweet tooth, Sam," laughed Lucy. "I'll never tell you not to put so much sugar in your tea again."

Just at that moment Frances came through to join in the conversation. Tapping Bertram's arm she mouthed, "What does Sam say about all this?"

"They're as shocked as we are," said Bertram. "At least if he goes to their shop pretending to be me or you, they'll know it's the impostor. I mustn't say the name, but we all know who it is." With a moment's silence, Bertram then added, "There was one small thing; he asked if we knew if Lottie had acquired any new items."

Hearing the gasp coming from the people at the other end of the telephone, Bertram continued, "I might tell you he got no joy from us. In fact we told him it was none of our business if she had."

"I think we should get together in the morning and discuss this again, what do you say, Bertram?"

"I agree, but for now, I think we'd better let you settle for the night, and we'll come and see you in the morning."

"That sounds good to us," said Sam.

"Goodnight, my friends. See you in the morning," called out Frances. With each one bidding their goodnights, Bertram replaced the telephone and returned to the kitchen with Frances. Pleased to see his drink ready on the table, he picked it up and toasted the air.

"Let's see what tomorrow brings," he said.

"Cheers," responded Frances. Feeling more settled after talking to their friends and finishing off the evening with a small drink, Frances and Bertram took themselves off to bed.

"What do you make of him asking about Lottie acquiring new

things?" Frances asked Bertram as he climbed into bed. "Do you think he knows…?" With the room in darkness, Bertram said, "That's something we can discuss in the morning. Now try and get some sleep Frances, who knows what tomorrow will bring."

* * * *

Wheeling his bicycle down the road, Crocanthus was pleased not have given himself away, but disgruntled at not being able to confirm if Lottie had the stone. With his mind on the stone, and the punishment he would receive if he returned to Dofstram without it, he was even more desperate to know who had possession of it, and where it was. Noticing his Sam disguise had finally worn off, and disturbed by the numerous thoughts going through his mind, he set off for home.

Arriving at his accommodation, he opened the door and checked to make sure he was alone. Securing his bicycle in the relevant cupboard, he strode across the vast hallway to his room. He heard someone call out, "Good evening," but ignored the greeting and entered his room.

"How rude!" muttered the tenant, little knowing how lucky he was.

Chapter Five

Encounter in the Library

With a new day beginning, and having had a surprisingly undisturbed sleep, Jeremy Thackett drew back the curtain. Staring out of the window, oblivious to the misty damp fog still hanging over from the night before, his mind turned to the plan which he would put into action today. After dressing he scoffed down a slice of bread, then went to retrieve his bicycle. As he left the house, he thought it would be too early for others to be around. In fact the street was full of people going in all directions, some calling out greetings and well wishes for Christmas.

Ignoring everyone, he made his way into town. As he approached the outskirts, he noticed a car approaching behind him. Thinking it was too close, he glanced behind with every intention of hurling abuse. He was shocked to see a car he recognised, for he was in no mood for those two morons Evoc and Harbin now. Seeing a convenient passage he rode down it, stopping just inside to confirm what he'd seen. Then he waited until they were well past before continuing on his way, making sure there were a few cars between them and him. What Crocanthus didn't know was the argument Evoc and Harbin were having about being made to go to the library.

Evoc annoyed Harbin by pointing out that they were nearly at the car park. With great reluctance Harbin drove in and parked the car, leaving Evoc to fetch a parking ticket. Sauntering back to the car, Evoc whined, "I'm not goin' in 'til I'm ready. What if she's not in?" Turning to Evoc, Harbin uttered through clenched teeth, "Stick yer ticket in the window, that ol' man over there 'as spotted us parking." Evoc secured the ticket without argument. Acknowledging a cursory nod from the car park attendant, Evoc made an exaggerated point of closing the car door.

While Evoc had been busy with the ticket, Harbin had had his mind on how they might achieve what Crocanthus wanted. Casually observing Evoc waiting round the other side, Harbin closed and locked the car. After considering several ideas, he decided the best plan was to drag the boss lady into a room and beat it out of her. Then he remembered she had early morning readers, so he dropped the idea.

Watching Evoc make his way round to his side of the car, Harbin wondered why Crocanthus would think the library woman would have the stone, or hide it from him. He did not want to consider what they would do if she didn't have it.

"Come on, we gotta lot work to do," Harbin said gruffly, making his way to exit the car park. Ignoring Harbin and still reluctant to carry out Crocanthus' orders, Evoc asked, "'Ow we gonna get 'er to talk? What do we do if she don't 'ave it?" Expecting Harbin to give him a thump him, Evoc stepped a little further away from his partner.

"I bin finking that meself, what if it's not in there? We know it's not in 'er 'ouse, so it must be wiv the boss lady in the library," replied Harbin. Stepping outside the car park, they barged through other pedestrians, ignoring the calls of 'how rude, watch what you're doing, mind out'. They continued to plough their way towards the kerb, ready to cross the road to the library.

As they waited impatiently to cross the road, they began swearing and cursing at the traffic for not letting them cross. Stepping out into the road, Evoc glared and raised his fists at the drivers as they blasted their horns. One driver called out, "Watch out, look where you're going!" and other drivers joined in. Suddenly there was chaos as verbal arguments began to take place between, pedestrians and drivers. Harbin left Evoc to the angry drivers and strode casually across the road. Reaching the other side, he called Evoc to follow.

"Idiot, that was a stupid fing to do. We don't need to let 'er know we're 'ere," shouted Harbin. He was about to give his partner a thump, but Evoc swung round to face Harbin and sneered, "We got 'ere didn't we?"

Realising how near to the library they were and not wanting to draw any more attention to themselves, the pair made their way slowly and somewhat reluctantly to the library door.

Inside the library, Ms Beckett was becoming curious about the noise outside, but she was more concerned that none of her staff had so far turned up, so she ignored it and concentrated on preparing the library for the early morning customers. Just at that moment the door bell rang, indicating someone had entered. Disappointed it wasn't a member of her staff, she found herself looking across each time the bell rang, hoping it would be one of her staff arriving.

As she greeted her regular readers, Ms Beckett was becoming quite perturbed at not hearing from any of her staff.

"I wonder where they've got to? It's not like any of them to be this late," she muttered to herself. Noticing the time, she could see several customers waiting at the front desk. Apologising to them for keeping them waiting, she attended to their needs and was somewhat relieved when she'd said goodbye to the last person in the queue. Looking round without seeing anyone needing her attention, she glanced at her watch and muttered, "It's not like Lottie to be late."

Hearing the doorbell ring again, she hoped it would be Lottie. It was now nine thirty. But it wasn't Lottie, nor either of the students, Peter and Penny. Instead she was facing those dreadful men she had banned from the library.

Seeing the way the two men sauntered down the steps, Ms Beckett felt sure they were up to no good, as usual. She realised to her dismay that they were staring directly back at her. She remained behind the counter, ready to evict them if they started any trouble.

Ignoring the people in the library, Evoc and Harbin walked threateningly over to where Ms Beckett was standing.

"If you're here to cause trouble, I will not hesitate to get the police to turn you out," Ms Beckett warned them.

"We're not 'ere to cause bovver. We've come to look at books," grinned Evoc.

"We'll be over at that table," said Harbin. Seeing how near the table was to her desk, Ms Beckett couldn't help feeling apprehensive. She watched as they made their way to the table, failing to notice that another person had now entered the library.

Evoc began to feel uneasy and knew instinctively why. Turning to Harbin he asked warily, "Is 'e 'ere?"

"'Oo?" responded Harbin.

Looking around and convinced there was someone close by, Evoc whispered nervously, "'Im, our boss man, is 'e 'ere?"

Scanning round as far as he could, and not seeing anyone or anything out of place Harbin snorted, "You idiot, 'course 'e's not 'ere. 'E sent us to see to 'er." But even as he spoke, he could feel himself becoming nervous. Wondering why Evoc could feel Crocanthus' presence and he couldn't, Harbin looked around once more.

"I can feel 'im, 'e must 'ave sneaked in usin' 'is powers," Evoc said gruffly. Unnerved by what Evoc had said, Harbin rose from his seat and started making his way towards the nearby stairs to look at the floor above. He left Evoc sitting at the table. Wondering why his partner was climbing the stairs, Evoc secretly hoped their boss would show himself to Harbin.

"You think you'll find the stone by sitting here, do you?" hissed Crocanthus into Evoc's ear. Jumping off his seat, Evoc peered round about, but couldn't see where Crocanthus was. Rubbing the ear Crocanthus had spoken into Evoc whispered, "Where is yer 'iding?"

He heard a low menacing laugh from close by and thought he could see the faint outline of a person. Shaking his head and blinking rapidly he wasn't sure he wanted to see that person revealed. It looked like Crocanthus, but whoever it was, he was only just visible.

Evoc stood open-mouthed, wondering if anyone else could see what he was seeing. Reading Evoc's thoughts, Crocanthus surprised Evoc by saying, "No one can see me or hear me. Only another Zanuthian can do that. Shut your mouth before the old woman sees you and thinks you've gone more stupid than ever." Giving Evoc a moment to gather what wits he possessed, Crocanthus asked, "Where's the other moron?"

Evoc was wondering that himself. Before he could tell Crocanthus where Harbin had gone, he heard him mutter, "So, he thinks the stone could be up there, does he?" Having adjusted his eyes to where the ghost-like image of Crocanthus had stood, Evoc noticed it was no longer there. Thinking he might have gone fully invisible, he looked round nervously, not sure what to expect.

This was soon answered when he saw Harbin hastily running down the stairs.

"'E's 'ere. 'Es up them stairs!" said Harbin. Stretching his neck to scan the stairs and the immediate area, Harbin grabbed Evoc's arm and tried to pull him towards the door.

"What yer doin'? We can't move from 'ere. I know 'e's 'ere, 'e was 'ere afore 'e found yer up them stairs. Only 'e's Crocanthus, not 'is pretend self. An' 'e's changed into a 'orrible shimmering fing, all ghostly-lookin'."

"If we go now, 'e could deal wiv 'er ladyship," replied Evoc.

As eager as his partner to get away, Evoc was more nervous of what Crocanthus would do if they disappeared. They waited nervously to see what Crocanthus had planned. It wouldn't be long before they would find out.

Ms Beckett, having been observing the two men, wondered why one of them had gone up to the next floor, but equally wondered what had made him come down again so quickly. The other man, the idiot one as she thought of him, was standing open-mouthed staring at something – what it was she couldn't imagine. Whatever it might be, it had made him stay transfixed in the one position.

With her own nerves feeling stretched, she wondered what their next move would be. She wasn't aware of Crocanthus' entry into the library, or how near he'd moved to her. Neither of the men could see him, so they were equally surprised when Ms Beckett jumped to one side.

"Hello there, it's me, Jeremy," Crocanthus whispered menacingly. "Guess what, I've come to collect my property."

Unable to see where he was but recognising the threat in his voice, Ms Beckett slowly looked around to where she thought he was. Still not seeing him but feeling his threatening presence, she stammered an attempt to explain. "I – I haven't been able to find it. I haven't found any stone of any colour here in the library. But where are you? Why can't I see you?"

Giving a low menacing laugh, Crocanthus replied, "Because it suits me not to let you see me." Pausing for a moment, he considered a thought that had just come to him.

"I might just take a look round the library myself. It has to be here," Crocanthus muttered directly into her ear. Remembering her customers and fearing for their safety, Ms Beckett pleaded, "Please don't. I've looked everywhere, but it's not here, really." Ignoring her, he slithered across the floor and started shifting the books from place to place, deliberately dropping several as he discarded them. Shocked by what he was doing, Ms Beckett went across to try and cover his movements. Picking up the fallen books, she began pretending she was reorganising them. Noticing the peculiar looks some of her customers were giving her, she tried not to show her surprise when one of them asked, "Are you all right, Ms Beckett? You seem a little edgy today."

"I'm all right, thank you, Mr Plumb. My staff haven't arrived yet so I'm trying to cover as many jobs as possible," she replied, hoping to reassure him.

"I was going to ask where Lottie was. Perhaps she's caught this flu bug that's going around?" Mr Plumb responded, turning his attention back to his paper. Thankful that no one else sought to question her she continued straightening the books. Then she made her way back downstairs, hoping that at least one member of staff would put in an appearance.

Feeling free of Jeremy's presence, Ms Beckett settled herself sorting invoices, hoping he had left the library for good. She would soon be made aware that this was not so. Hearing the clatter of falling books coming from a different part of the floor above, she glanced across to see if those other two awful men were still where she'd last seen them. She was surprised to see them staring in the direction she'd heard the books fall.

Conscious of not wanting to alarm her customers, she calmed herself down and with a purposeful step she hastened to the area from where the noise had come from. Nervously she approached each aisle. Satisfied there was no one there and all the books were still on the shelves, she was shocked to see the state some of the books were in. Gasping at the wanton destruction they had suffered, she gently lifted the damaged books and turned her attention to discovering where Jeremy Thackett could be.

There was no sign of him. She replaced the undamaged books back on the shelf and held onto the damaged ones. Certain there was no sign of her tormentor, she then made her way to the end of the aisle, still clutching the damaged books.

Crocanthus was frustrated at not finding the stone. He waited impatiently for Ms Beckett to reach the end of the aisle. Thinking she was taking too long, he was about to go and speed her along when he realised she was almost upon him. Deep in thought about how she could repair the books, she was surprised to see someone she thought was a customer standing at the end of the aisle. As she was about to ask him if he needed help, a hand shot out and grabbed her by the arm.

She stifled a scream. "What do you want? You don't need to grip my arm so hard!" she shouted. She suddenly felt herself being shaken. Terrified at what was happening, but wanting to confirm who it really was, in a low voice she asked, "Is that you, Jeremy? Is this some sort of disguise?"

Without answering any of her questions, Crocanthus pulled her back up the aisle, where he thought he wouldn't be heard. "It doesn't matter who I am. I've come for the stone." He was amused at watching her peer at him, but determined not to reveal his identity, just yet. That would keep for later.

If you don't give me the stone, I have certain ways to deal with you. They aren't pleasant for you but I find I quite enjoy them."

Terrified by what he'd said and still not certain who this person was, Ms Beckett asked, "Are you someone who knows Jeremy?"

Throwing back his head, Crocanthus laughed raucously.

"Do I look like a friend of this, er, Jeremy's?" he asked, in a contemptuous voice.

"I wouldn't know. I don't know Jeremy that well," Ms

Beckett answered, trying to wrench herself free from his ever-tightening grasp.

"I'm not interested in anything other than the stone. I know you must have found it, so hand it over," he warned through clenched teeth. Terrified of what he would do, Ms Beckett started to panic. How could she convince him the stone wasn't there?

"I don't have it. I never found it," she stammered. Staring into his dark cold eyes, she felt immediate fear, which Crocanthus immediately picked up on.

"You need to feel fear. But we will deal with that later," he goaded her.

"What do you mean?" she asked nervously. Noticing the two men from downstairs were now standing level with her, she began to wonder what was going to happen. If only her staff had turned up. She wondered who she could turn to for assistance. Taking a chance, she called out, "Help! Would someone help me?"

Before she knew it a large hand had been placed over her mouth and there was a hissing sound in her ear warning her to shut up. As this happened, two customers appeared at the other end of the aisle.

"Are you all right, Ms Beckett?" one of them asked. Breathing hard, Ms Beckett tried to calm her voice down.

"Thank you for coming so quickly. These people were getting annoyed with me for not having a book they wanted." Looking the men over, and obviously not liking what they saw, one of the women commented, "This is a respectable library where people behave properly. We don't want any unpleasantness."

By this time some of the other customers had come to see what the chaos was about. Annoyed at what was taking place, Crocanthus spun round and rudely told them, "This is none of your business. Go back to where you came from."

Taking the opportunity to escape from his grasp, Ms Beckett wasted no time in walking to the other end of the aisle to join the customers.

"How rude!" said one. "Who does he think he is, ordering

us about?" asked another. Not wanting it to go any further Ms Beckett assured them she was all right and thanked them for their help.

"I'll be at my desk if anyone requires assistance," she said. Hastening back to her desk, Ms Beckett wasn't too sure where the two men had gone, or the man who'd threatened her.

Shaken by what had taken place, and surprised that Lottie still hadn't rung in, Ms Beckett glanced at her watch and noticed it was nearly time for lunch. Although she was in need of a break, she was hesitant about closing the library.

She settled for getting a drink and bringing it back to her desk. With drink in hand, she made her way back to her desk to notice that many of the customers were leaving. Fearful of being left and still not aware of where the men had gone, she looked round to see how many people remained. She was relieved to see that several other customers had come in. She settled herself down at her desk, worried about what she could do about finding that stone.

As she thought about the places she'd searched, her attention was drawn to the sound of the door being opened. At first she couldn't see who had come in, but as she was about to go on with her work, she noticed the two men skulking out of the door. Relieved they'd gone, her main thought now was where Jeremy had gone. Then she heard his voice.

"Not to worry, I haven't left yet," he said. "We've still got work to do. Haven't we, boss lady?" Shocked to hear the familiar voice, Ms Beckett tried to remain calm as she quietly replied, "I fear the stone isn't in the library. I've looked everywhere."

Jeremy's voice seemed to be coming from the man she'd spoken to in the aisle.

"Who are you?" she asked him. "Your voice is exactly like someone I know." Without responding, Crocanthus stood in front of her, staring with his cold dark eyes. Then, before her eyes, he began to change his appearance. Mesmerized by what was taking place, she tried to speak, but the only sound she could make was a dull squeak.

Crocanthus was enjoying her discomfort. He glanced round to see if any of the interfering people were around. He was desperate to have the stone, and still convinced she had it.

Keen to change the subject, and seeing the Jeremy she knew, Ms Beckett asked again, "Were you that strange man? If it was you, how did you change from that man to Jeremy?"

He peered straight into her eyes, and she could almost feel the coldness from them. Terrified of what he would do, she became even more alarmed.

"If I need to do something to harm these people, I will," he said.

"There's no need to involve them. They don't know anything about a stone," she whispered nervously.

"Irrelevant. If they get in my way I will make certain they don't do it again," he added, in the same warning tone. "I'll be gone for a short while. Use the time to decide whether to live and hand it over, or die when I take it from you. Let's hope you see sense and hand it over."

Remaining still and telling herself to stay calm, she waited for him to leave. Only now did she fully realise what a despicable man he was. She took in his apparel, noticing his long black coat and knee-length black studded boots. She wondered why she hadn't heard him going up the stairs. He slammed the door as he left the library, and Ms Beckett could only give a huge sigh of relief.

"Thank goodness he's gone," she thought, clinging onto the edge of the desk for support. For one moment she thought she was going to faint, but she managed to stave off the feeling. In the back of her mind was the threat he'd made. What would he really do, knowing she couldn't give him something she hadn't got?

* * * *

When Crocanthus had ordered them to leave, Evoc and Harbin thought he had meant he wanted them to leave the library. It wasn't until a moment later that they realised he meant they had to leave this land and return to Dofstram. Delighted, but reluctant to actually believe it, Harbin asked nervously, "Do yer mean we can really go back 'ome, to our 'ome in Dofstram?"

"Return to Zanus," snapped Crocanthus. "Tell him I will be back shortly. Don't you dare tell him anything else. Understand? Go, you idiots! Zanus will need all his troops. I have some unfinished business to complete."

Without waiting to see if Crocanthus was going to change his mind, the two men hastened towards the door. "What made 'im tell us to go now?" asked Evoc.

"Idiot! Cos we're needed by Zanus," Harbin sneered. "Ain't 'e fightin' wiv them Outlanders?"

"I wonder what 'e's gotta do 'ere?" asked Evoc. Checking Crocanthus wasn't nearby, he added, "What did 'e mean we wasn't to tell Zanus anyfing?"

Harbin glowered at Evoc. "'Ow would I know?" he glowered. "P'r'aps 'e's 'idden the stone fer 'imself. 'Oo knows?"

"Why would 'e keep the stone? 'E know Zanus will kill 'im if 'e's done that." Annoyed Evoc was continuing to question Crocanthus' remarks, Harbin punched his partner on the arm.

"Keep yer mouf shut when we get back. I don't want no 'arsh treatment from 'im." One look at the expression on Harbin's face prevented Evoc from doing so.

Maintaining silence, but each with their own thoughts, they set off for the portal that led back to Dofstram.

* * * *

With. no sign now of Jeremy, Ms Beckett wondered how he could alter his appearance in front of her. Her thoughts turned to Lottie.

"I wonder if she knows Jeremy is able to change his appearance?" she said to herself. Concerned at how far she'd got involved with him, Ms Beckett decided to ring Lottie's home and find out if she was all right. While dialling her telephone number Ms Beckett's thoughts were on how she would bring the subject of Jeremy into the conversation.

The phone rang out unanswered. Unaware of what had taken place the night before, she was at a loss as to why she was getting no response. Placing the telephone back on the holder, she wondered what to do. Meanwhile there were customers to deal with and queries to answer. Making her way back to the counter, she settled on closing the library early and possibly paying Lottie a visit. She realised this wasn't an evening for Penny and Peter to come, so she wrote a hasty note explaining an early closure and placed it on the library door. Receiving one or two comments from people about the notice, she answered the questions by explaining she was short of staff.

As the newly-stated closing time approached, Ms Beckett began to have some concerns about Jeremy, and wondered why he hadn't reappeared at the library. With some reluctance she made her way to the door, indicating to the customers it was time for her to close. They expressed their concern that Ms Beckett would be all right, and in return she wished them a safe journey home. As the last of the customers left the library she closed and locked the door. Unsettled by her strange day, she remained where she was for another moment before going off to collect her coat and bag.

As she approaching the door to leave the library she felt apprehensive about something, without knowing what. A feeling of reluctance to leave the library came over her. Taking a deep breath, she told herself not to be silly, but she gave up the idea of going to Lottie's, instead concentrated on getting home as quickly as possible. As she locked the library door and tested it to make sure it was secure, Ms Beckett had that apprehensive feeling again. She didn't know that Crocanthus hadn't finished with her yet.

Crocanthus was considering what he should do next. Should he make her stay open, or should he observe her and see where she went? Opting for the second choice, he had another thought. This one gave him more satisfaction. Moving away from the library window he sheltered in the doorway of a conveniently boarded-up shop, situated close by.

Ms Beckett felt sure she was now safe from those awful men. She knew it wasn't Evoc and Harbin themselves that caused this feeling, but Jeremy. At that moment she stopped still and slapped a hand on her forehead. She cursed herself for being so stupid. "They're all in it together," she said out loud, surprising the pedestrians who passed by. "Why didn't I see that before?"

Setting off at a fast pace, it wasn't long before her street came into view. She slowed down to a more sedate walk, then looked behind and across the road.

She was convinced someone was watching her. Unnerved, she stopped and took a longer look round hoping to see it was possibly one of her neighbours. Alas, she saw no one. As she set off again, many things were going though her mind. Should she stop off at a neighbour's? Should she walk past her house? But then she thought, what good would that do? She'd have to go home some time.

She knew the only one who could be giving her this uncomfortable feeling was Jeremy. She was loath to mention his name, even to herself. As she stepped through the gate and removed her house key from her coat pocket, the feeling of dread seemed to be even stronger than before. Placing the key in the lock she drew a deep breath and unlocked the door. What if he was in her house now, waiting? As she pushed the door open, she half expected to see him standing in her hall, as he'd done once before.

She was about to enter the house when she heard Jeremy's voice in her ear. "I think we should go inside, don't you?" he whispered.

She turned to see that the man beside her was not Jeremy but the brutish man from the library. He pushed the door wide open, making her drop the key on the floor. As she bent to retrieve it she felt a terrific blow on the back of her head and fell flat on the floor. Clutching her head and wishing the spinning sensation would go, she waited to see if he was going to hit her again. It seemed an age before he spoke.

"Get up! I need that stone, now! You have it hidden here. Now get up and fetch it."

Ms Beckett scrabbled to get off the floor, her head throbbing. She was terrified.

"I don't know where the stone is!" she wailed. "I don't even know what it looks like." Steadying herself by holding onto the banister rail, she only just managed to avoid the fist that was aimed at her body.

"You were told to get that Lottie to tell you if she had an

orange stone. Weren't you?" Crocanthus demanded. Seeing the cold black eyes staring straight at her, Ms Beckett wondered why his voice had changed. No longer was it the voice of Jeremy. She could only guess that this was the true voice of the brutish man from the library.

"I did ask her if she had any special thing, possibly with an orange stone," she explained tearfully. "She said she didn't have anything orange, only jewellery which belonged to her mother." Half expecting him to attack her again, Ms Beckett stumbled towards the room nearby, fearing for her life. She wondered how she could convince this man that she didn't have what he was looking for.

She was startled to see the brutish man sitting in the chair opposite her, and wondered how he'd got there without her noticing. Just then her thoughts turned to the annoying dragonfly which had pestered her in the house before. Why on earth was she thinking about that?

Then she noticed that the man had moved off the chair. Looking to see where he had gone, she wondered how she could get him to leave her house, knowing deep down that he would only leave if she was to miraculously produce this stone he wanted.

For want of something to say, and not wanting to avoid annoying him further, she began to ask, "Would you like some... ?" But before she could finish offering refreshments, she was struck in the face by a large fist. She put her hands up as a kind of protection. Slowly removing her hands, she was shocked to see how much blood there was. Concerned at the blood on her clothing, she thought she ought to go and clean it off. But as she lifted herself off the chair he pushed her back down.

"I just want to wipe my face over," Ms Beckett sniffed. But now there was something different about her attacker - something about his face.

"Take a good look, Ms Beckett," he taunted. "Do you prefer me to look like Jeremy?" Shocked, Ms Beckett sat wide eyed, not knowing what to say. Gathering herself together and wiping the blood on the only tissue she had available, she stammered, "How do you do that? How can you change yourself so easily?"

She felt as if she was faced with half Jeremy and half the other man. His clothes were those of the other man, but his face was that of Jeremy.

"What do you think of the disguise I used to get to Lottie? I might add, you were so obligingly helpful in helping me to keep track of her," Crocanthus stated. "Just one thing wrong. You failed to find the stone. That and Lottie are the things I need to find. The woman was easy, but not the stone."

Learning she had played a part in Lottie's discovery made Ms Beckett rue the day she'd ever made a friend of Jeremy.

"So, is this the real you, or is it the monster who appeared out of the blue in my library?" Ms Beckett asked. As he stared straight back at her, she felt an instant chill run through her body. His cold, black eyes made her feel he was reaching deep into her soul. With a sudden raucous laugh, he responded, "Well done. So now you know who I am. Perhaps you would like to know my true name as well? Crocanthus is my name. It wouldn't fit in with your land, so I had to pick a name that would. What do you think?"

Not sure what to say, Ms Beckett sat staring at the cruel look on his face. Then without warning he took out a long, sharp knife. With one swift movement he leaned over and plunged the blade straight into her stomach.

"This is what happens to people who fail me," he hissed.

Screaming, Ms Beckett fell to the floor. As she lay cradling her stomach, she saw him moving towards her and thought he was going to stab her again. But to her surprise he stood by her armchair and wiped the bloodied knife down the arm.

Ms Beckett decided to try and stand up. She felt a searing pain going through her stomach and saw that her hand and jacket sleeve were covered in blood. She fell back onto the floor, trying to stop herself from losing consciousness. She clutched her stomach as the sound of his voice started to drift away.

"You are no longer needed. You gave me all the information I wanted. Shame about the stone, but I will enjoy searching your house before I leave," he taunted her.

Ms Beckett lay on the floor wondering if she would survive, but knowing that wasn't going to be possible. She was beginning to feel cold. Trying to stem the flow of tears and the warm blood that ran freely from her wounds, the only sound she could hear was the dreadful man rifling through her property. Somehow, this gave her an element of satisfaction. She knew he would never find the stone here. It was her last conscious thought as her life slowly ebbed away.

As Crocanthus searched Ms Beckett's house he was inflicting as much damage as he could. When he had opened every drawer and cupboard and failed to find the stone, he began ranting and raving. Finally he stomped down the stairs and made his way to the room where Ms Beckett lay. Sneering at the figure lying on the floor, he coldly stated, "That's that then. A fair reward for failure to complete a simple task."

He made his way out of the house, still enraged at not finding the stone. Then he had a sudden thought.

"What if the stone is with Lottie in Dofstram? Isn't that something one of those idiots said?" It now looked as if Dofstram would have to be his next destination. One way or another he had to capture Lottie and the stone.

Chapter Six

Council of War

In Dofstram, Lottie and her friends had safely arrived at Castle Urbone. Discovering the true identity of Jeremy had been a bit of shock to them all, especially Lottie, who was still trying to come to terms with his deception. She wondered how she could have been so easily duped.

Thinking of her conversations with Jeremy, Lottie was hoping she had not said anything to give her friends away. She felt fairly sure she hadn't. She recalled her first meeting with DaVendall and the others. As she was going over these thoughts, she heard the gentle voice of Beauty whisper, "Don't worry Lottie. Neither you nor your friends have given us away."

"Thank you, Beauty," whispered Lottie. "It's good to hear that." Then, remembering Crocanthus' sneering comment about Ms Beckett, Lottie wondered what he meant: "Be warned, Lottie. Ms Beckett might not be who you think she is." Thinking about Ms Beckett, Lottie remembered accusing her of being friends with those two awful men. At the time this had left her with a feeling of guilt. But that made her wonder how, and when, Ms Beckett had become involved with their enemies.

Realising how near she had come to revealing her friends on that cold and damp Sunday after visiting him from their walk in the park, she could feel tears starting to well up and struggled to stop them falling.

"Hold on Lottie, we will have a little talk later," she felt Beauty say. "I think you are being a bit hard on yourself." Lottie replied telepathically. "Thank you, Beauty, but I think I'm all right now." Giving her a warm smile Beauty added, "You don't need to worry about Crocanthus or what he said about Ms Beckett. I'll try and find out how she became involved." Knowing Beauty would be true to her word brought an element of comfort to Lottie.

Placing her brooch on the corner of the table, she smiled in acknowledgment of Beauty's wink. She hoped her thoughts hadn't been picked up by any of her other friends. She turned her attention back to the opened maps, which had been placed in an orderly fashion on the table. Taking a momentary glance round the people at the table and noticing how absorbed they were in looking at the maps, Lottie felt it was unlikely they'd heard the conversation between her and Beauty. However, unlike Penny and Peter, Lottie hadn't noticed what was holding the maps in place.

She felt a gentle tap on her arm and looked to where Penny was pointing. At first she couldn't see it, but then she spotted a movement from one of the corners, and was amazed to see a delightfully coloured tortoise sitting there. There was a tortoise at each corner. Giving Penny a nod to confirm that she could see the tortoises, Lottie took a closer look at them. They were very different from the tortoises back in her land, but she wasn't sure if it was polite to mention it, so she remained quiet.

"Good day, young tortoises. I hope all is well with you?" Beauty greeted the creatures.

"Hello, Beauty, it's super to have you back," replied one of the tortoises. With the other tortoises echoing his words she gave them each a warm smile in acknowledgement. To the delight of Peter, Penny and Lottie, one of the tortoises asked, "I take it these young people are friends of yours, Beauty?" "Indeed they are, and loyal friends they are too," she replied.

Although Lottie, Penny and Peter had met a variety of animals and spoken with many of them, Peter was still enthralled whenever an animal spoke. He couldn't take his eyes off them, with their delightfully different colourings.

Without thinking, he found himself saying, "I thought these tortoises were ornaments."

Quick as a flash, one of the tortoises shouted, "Ornaments?"

Another echoed indignantly, "Ornaments indeed! Who could possibly take us for ornaments?"

Before the tortoise could add anything further, another stated grandly, "We're very important map holders." At this, four tortoise heads rose up in the air. "That we are," said one of them.

"Now, now, my friends, don't forget these youngsters aren't used to you yet," Beauty said gently. Still feeling indignant at being called an ornament, a quiet but firm voice replied, "Sorry Beauty, but we had to make it clear we are not ornaments."

Having heard enough, and aware of what was happening to the Outlanders, King Alfreston shouted, "Right, let's get down to what we are all assembled for. Tortoises, hold the map still and please move your heads. I need to see the whole of the map." The tortoises quickly drew their heads back into their shells, and Lottie tried desperately to concentrate on the conversation being discussed. Unfortunately, her thoughts had wandered back to her first encounter with DaVendall.

Recalling his arrival in her car on that dreadful evening as she had been making her way home after a long day at work, she wondered what it was about him that had made her accept him so readily. Taking a glance across at him, and thinking she saw a glimmer of a smile, Lottie wondered if he'd picked up on her thoughts.

"Is everything all right, Lottie?" DaVendall asked in a low gentle voice.

"I think so," Lottie whispered, hoping she hadn't disturbed the intense conversation that was developing. She noticed DaVendall had turned his attention back to the King. What did surprise her was how serious the King's voice had become.

"Firstly," the King stated, "there is the matter of the prisoners." Glancing across at Beauty, he knew he didn't have to say it, but for the benefit of the others he added, "Beauty, I think this is probably best left to you." Acknowledging the nod of agreement, he continued. "We all know there will be many difficult and dangerous times ahead, for all concerned. Now with regard to getting more Outlanders to join us..." Before he could ask the question, DaVendall stated, "My operation, I believe."

Noticing the expression of surprise on Peter's face,

DaVendall added, "We need to defeat Zanus and his crony Sizan. This will be a dangerous mission so we need as many helpers as we can get." Then, in a quieter voice he added, "We must complete our task this time and prevent them from ever attacking the Outlanders again."

Taking a look round and seeing the intent expression on all the listeners' faces, Lottie found herself looking at her sea-horse brooch. Studying the beautifully-designed brooch, she found herself wondering yet again how she had come to purchase such a beautiful thing. She was surprised to hear Beauty say, "Why don't you ask, Moff?"

"Sorry, Beauty, I didn't think I was talking out loud," Lottie whispered, looking round and wondered if anyone else had heard what she'd said. Casting her eyes in the direction of Moff she caught him looking at her with a gleam in his eyes. Feeling a little awkward, but curious about many aspects of her being accepted by Beauty, she asked, "How...?" But before she could continue, Moff interrupted her by gently saying, "I understand there are some things you feel haven't been explained. Am I right, Lottie?"

Lottie was unsure if this was the appropriate moment to ask the questions that had crossed her mind on many occasions. Then, as if Moff knew what she was thinking, she heard him say in a low voice, "All the signs were right for you to be the one. But I think it's about the price. Did I not charge you enough for the brooch, Lottie?" Noticing the wry smile on Moff's face, Lottie wondered if Beauty had told Moff about her thoughts.

"Er. I don't think you did Moff. I mean, I don't think you asked the correct price. I was convinced the brooch would be more than I could afford, but when I saw that gentle orange glow reflected through the window something told me I was meant to have it. Does that make sense to you?"

"Indeed it does, Lottie. If it had been any other person who'd come to buy the brooch, I would have asked a great deal more. But when Beauty gave me the signal indicating you were the one, I made certain the price was one you could afford. Remember, some of this has been already been explained. Beauty is the only one who would know if the right person claimed her."

"So I was right. Is Beauty made from a real orange stone and real diamonds?" Lottie asked, unaware that her voice had gone a little louder than a whisper. Concerned that everyone seemed to be looking at her, she was relieved to hear Queen Matilda say, "You are quite right, Lottie. Beauty is indeed a true gem. She has been called by that name right from the time your mother remarked on how beautifully she glowed."

"What would Beauty have been called if she had not been called Beauty?"

"I think it's best if Beauty answers that question," replied Queen Matilda kindly.

"I'm not sure Penny. I was known in the lagoon as the carnelian stone," Beauty whispered. Pondering over the name, Peter was convinced he'd never heard the name before. Without realising it he was voicing his thoughts.

"That's an unusual name. I don't think I've ever heard of a carnelian stone."

"The carnelian is known as the energy stone, Peter," King Alfreston replied, before Beauty could answer.

"Is that how you have powers others haven't, Beauty?" asked Penny. Aware that she had always had her powers, Beauty smiled at Penny and replied, "Possibly." Before any more questions could be asked, Queen Matilda added, "Lottie is right about the other stones, they are indeed real diamonds."

"Wow, Moff. Just think what you could have got for it!" stated Peter, looking at Beauty in an admiring way.

"Yes, but if Moff had asked a higher price, I definitely couldn't have bought it," Lottie said wistfully. Penny, absorbed in the conversation, quietly and slowly joined in, "You know what, Moff, I'm glad Lottie was the right one. And I'm glad I got to be her friend or I'd never have come to your land and met all these lovely people." Smiling across at Penny, and warming to her as she did her parents, Bertram and Frances, Queen Matilda said, "I have to agree with you, Penny. We too have been lucky in meeting more friends. Especially friends who offered to help us."

Taking up the conversation, Letswick added, "We were all surprised to discover how Beauty's powers could be enhanced, but I think the biggest surprise to us in this land was discovering her powers could be enhanced by someone from your land. The first time this came to light was when your father rescued Beauty from the boulder. Whereas with you Lottie, Beauty felt the bond as soon as you looked in the window, and knew for certain when you lifted her from the tray."

For just a moment everyone remained still and quiet, absorbing what they'd been told. Remembering something Beauty had said on a previous occasion, Penny broke the silence by saying, "That's just what Beauty told me ages ago."

"What else did Beauty say?" asked Queen Matilda, keen to hear all.

"Let me see… oh now I remember, Beauty told us what you just said, about her powers I mean. I admit I was disappointed when she explained her powers could not be enhanced with me. But I have a very important role to play in keeping Lottie safe." Embarrassed at seeing everyone looking her way, Penny decided she'd said enough. However, she wasn't going to let them think she had forgotten what Beauty had said.

"And a very good job you've been doing too," Pointer called out from the opposite side of the table.

"Hear, hear. I agree with Pointer," added Marmaduke. Anxious to get back to what they had been discussing, the King cleared his throat, bringing a halt to any further discussions. He looked round to ensure he had their complete attention. Although Lottie was listening to what the King was about to say, the mystery of what had happened to her parents still hung heavy in her mind.

"We'll soon discover that, Lottie," Beauty whispered. Accepting what Beauty had said, Lottie was brought back to the moment, just as the King was saying, "Do I have everyone's attention?" Feeling a nudge on her arm, Lottie looked to see who'd done it and saw Penny was smiling at her.

"Are you with us, Lottie?" she whispered. Seeing a nod and a smile from Lottie, Penny indicated to Lottie to look at the maps. Lottie looked at them and was surprised to see that they were beginning to reveal the features held within.

"Wow, look at that!" exclaimed Peter. "It's as if the maps are in 3D!" Watching the hills rise to varying heights, and the trees spreading out their leaf-filled branches, Lottie and friends were completely mesmerised by it all.

Just then Penny shouted, "Look. Look at those beautiful waterfalls! They're sending ripples of water along the streams. Aren't they just magical? Look at the way they flow round hills and through the dales, isn't that a delight?" With the maps presenting more and more features, Penny looked to see if her friends were as excited as she was.

"I do have to agree with you, Penny," said Queen Matilda softly. "Each time I see the maps they seem to reveal more of the country. But this time I think they have really excelled themselves." Leaning over to take a closer look, Peter noticed something developing in front of his eyes. At first he was unable to make it out, but then, to his great surprise, he realised it was a tower rising from the map. It didn't look like any tower he'd ever seen. It seemed as if there was something threatening about it. He felt a shudder run through him and wondered why he felt so threatened. Staring down at it, he suddenly noticed the tower was placed beyond a dark, densely-wooded area.

Peter gasped. Letswick had said something about this area. Transfixed with what was happening on the map, and with a strange sense of fear coming over him, Peter suddenly remembered what Letswick had called this dark area - The Forbidden Wood.

He wondered if he might see that dreaded woman emerge from the map. Almost as soon as that thought appeared, he felt something strange begin to happen. Not knowing how or why, he felt himself going into a hypnotic state. Now he was struggling to stop himself being drawn away from the table. Letswick, hearing Peter's gasp and sensing his somewhat turbulent thoughts, whispered, "Is something troubling you, young Peter?"

Hearing Letswick's voice Peter wasn't sure if it was real or if he imagined it. Still drawn to the map and sensing the same fear, Peter heard the voice again: "Come along Peter. Close your eyes and stand away from the map." Peter closed his eyes and tried to step away from the map. When he discovered he couldn't move his legs, he felt fear and panic. But at that moment the calm voice of DaVendall entered his thoughts.

"Move away, Peter. The Tower of Zorax is trying to invade your mind. Close your mind to everything but my voice."

The others' attention was still on watching the map evolve, showing various images. Slowly emerging from his hypnotic state, Peter was relieved to feel the fear start to leave. He looked at Letswick and DaVendall, wondering what to say. To his surprise, Letswick said, "Don't try to understand it just now, Peter. All will become clear soon."

"What is that tower thing over there?" asked Penny. "Isn't that the evil wood where that old woman lives?"

Quickly realising what she was referring to, Letswick felt concerned that the Old Crone had not only picked up on Peter's presence, but had also sensed Penny. He soon realised he wasn't the only one who'd thought that. He heard Beauty and DaVendall telepathically say, "You don't think Peter was hypnotised by the Old Crone do you?"

"Watch out for Penny," said Beauty. "We don't want the same happening to her."

By this time they had all been drawn to the area Penny had pointed to. Standing between Peter and Penny, Letswick telepathically replied, "I think it's possible. The Old Crone was trying to weave her way into their young and vulnerable minds, but I don't think Peter was held long enough to cause any harm. As for Penny, I don't think her mind was affected. I do think we will need to keep a wary eye on them in case anything like this should happen again."

Giving Peter a reassuring smile, Letswick settled himself on the box to view the maps on the table. The tower, which he knew to be Zorax, had fully emerged. Letswick couldn't help saying, "This is the first time I have seen one of the maps reveal Zanus' tower in such detail."

"If that's true, I wonder why they are revealing so much today?" asked Peter.

Before Peter could ask another question, Lottie interrupted by asking, "Does that mean my parents could be in there?" Feeling Penny's hand slip into hers, Lottie waited anxiously for someone to answer her question.

"It is quite possible, Lottie," Queen Matilda replied softly. With a tear beginning to roll down her cheeks, Lottie gave a sniffle and said quietly, "Can we go and get them out?"

"All in good time, my dear. We have many things to sort out first," King Alfreston replied, hoping his voice wasn't too harsh. "Now let's get on with it. The more time we spend here, more of our Outlander friends are dying."

"Strategies, that's what we need. Strategies!" said Letswick. King Alfreston placed the tortoises on the far corners of the map again and began rubbing his chin, considering the best way to manoeuvre his troops. All eyes were upon him.

"Right, we will send more troops to the Outlanders," he began. "We need to be careful when it comes to the tower. We need to have a clear view of freeing the prisoners. I'm not sure if troops are the answer, but I will leave that to Beauty. We could spare a few, but remember we'll have to leave some here to defend the castle and the people in it. You never know with Zanus, or Sizan, where or when they will attack."

"I think the first thing we need to do is give assistance to the Outlanders who are deep in battle on the other side of the Forbidden Wood," stated DaVendall. Not waiting to see if anyone had anything to add, he continued, "My mission will be to round up as many of the other Outlanders from the furthest corners of the land."

Looking round, he added, "As the King will arrange groups for the other missions, I will only take a few people with me. I would like to take along Themis, as she's part Zipher and part Jasper. I might, if I may, take a few additional troops? I will also need Cedar. Being one of the older unicorns his powers will work well with mine." Taking a moment to look down at Gamlon, his trusty cane, DaVendall knew without speaking that Gamlon agreed with his choice.

Agreeing with what DaVendall had said, King Alfreston asked, "May I suggest you take along a few extra Ziphers and Jaspers?"

"Thank you, Alfreston, that would be a good idea," replied DaVendall warmly. As the King and DaVendall were speaking, Lottie and friends were surprised to see the King's marker had left a trail going round the Forbidden Wood. Penny indicated where other parts of the land had been pointed to.

Fascinated by what he'd seen, Peter couldn't stop himself from saying "Wow, that's some marker you have. Look, it's leaving a visible trail."

Somewhat amused by Peter's remark, the King told him, "That, my young man, is a very special marker. It will show us where the enemy are hidden. At the moment it is marking out the best route for DaVendall. Before we go any further I think we'd better bring in Kestron, Rouand, Drewan and Eram. I think it might be an idea to let them lead the troopers. Krast, would you please run and bring them here? We need to get our troops on the road."

"Kestron - isn't that the driver we met on the way here?" asked Peter.

"It is indeed, but he's a valuable scout," Queen Matilda replied. "Being part Zipher and part Jasper, not only does he have extra sensitive hearing, he has the ability to fly."

"That's odd," said Penny, "I'm sure we were told he was a Zipher when we first came here."

Giving a gentle chortle, Queen Matilda replied, "That's because he sees himself more as a Zipher than a Jasper. Kestron very seldom talks. He prefers to sign or use telepathy."

Before anyone else could speak, the throne room door opened to reveal Krast and the requested people. Pleased to see the men had responded so rapidly, King Alfreston urged, "Come on in and join us, we have many things to sort out. As you will be leading the troopers you need to know what is being planned." With everyone keen to do whatever was requested, they remained silent while the King informed them of his plans.

"My task will be to go and assist the Outlanders, who are currently defending the barriers. I'll take Rouand, Moff, Kestron and Drewan along with as many troops as can be spared. Plus, I think Pointer should come with us. We'll go the long way round so we can avoid entering the wood just as the marker has indicated on the map."

Taking only a moment to catch his breath, King Alfreston turned to face Moff and asked, "It might be advisable to get a message to Sam to ask him to come along with Bertram. It's quite possible we will need their help." Taking a moment to consider his next request, and knowing the dangers they faced, King Alfreston turned to Peter and asked, "Would you come with us? It won't be an easy task, but the more helpers we have the better."

"Wow! I most certainly will, Your Majesty," Peter replied excitedly.

"This is a very dangerous mission, Peter. It won't be a joy ride. Think carefully before you decide to come along. As the King stated earlier, there will be many dangers," warned Pointer.

"Knowing you'll be there Pointer, I just know I will be all right," said Peter firmly.

Remembering what the King had asked, Moff queried, "Would you like me to go now, Your Majesty?"

"I think that would be a good idea. It might be wise to stress we need them to come immediately," replied the King. "Matilda, my dear, I think it might be a good idea to have Lucy and Frances remain here with you. Krast will remain as well. Marmaduke, if we need extra help, I'll get a message to you. I'm certain there will be many wounded who will be returning in need of attention."

Turning his attention to the lions, he asked, "Would you remove yourselves from the table and be ready should trouble arise?"

Pleased at last to be asked to contribute something, the lions replied as one, "We will. If you need us to go with you, we are not afraid." As if by magic, as soon as they finished replying, they stood free of the table top.

"Thank you lions, we will call on you if we need you, but we must protect the people remaining here," King Alfreston assured them. Content with that, the lions sat on the pedestal of the table holding the maps. Queen Matilda turned to her husband and replied, "I agree, Alfreston. If any of us are needed to leave here I will make sure enough helpers remain to treat any wounded."

"Now with regard to the tower. That is going to be a very dangerous mission," King Alfreston stated solemnly. He looked across at Beauty. "That's my task, I believe," said Beauty.

Noticing the hesitation before Alfreston nodded his head in acknowledgment, Beauty looked at Lottie and Penny. "Would you be prepared to come with me on such a dangerous mission?" she asked. Giving no thought to what dangers might lie ahead, Lottie and Penny said almost in unison, "You can count on us." To which Lottie added, "We agreed to help, and help we will." Then, lowering her voice to just above a whisper, she added, "After all, my parents might be prisoners."

Aware of Lottie's feelings, Beauty declined to make a comment. Instead she went on to request the assistance of others to ride with them.

"Eram, would you consider coming along?" she said. "I'd appreciate it if Yemil, Binro, and Letswick could come as well."

"I think you have made a wise choice, Beauty," said the King. Then to everyone's surprise, he started looking round the room. Alfreston suddenly boomed out, "Where is that daughter of ours, Matilda? She's always missing. She knows this is a bad time for her to be out on her own." Aware of Alfreston's fear whenever Rubie left the castle, Matilda softly replied, "Rubie will be here soon, she took Ferdi out for some exercise."

"May I just say something before I forget?" asked Letswick. Lost in thought about Rubie, and having only caught the last few words from Letswick, King Alfreston asked, "What is it Letswick? Have I forgotten something?"

"I was wondering, is Petra here? It might be a good idea to take her along with us, Beauty. She would be able to help with seeking out all the prisoners."

"That would be an excellent idea," Beauty added. "Does anyone have any idea where Petra could be?"

Just at that moment, Krast re-entered the room with Nain by his side. "Excuse me, Your Majesties, but Nain has a request," Krast stated.

"Come along in, Nain. What is your request?" asked the King, trying to control his eagerness to get going. Making his way slowly into the room, Nain asked, "Could Rista and I help the people who are going to the tower? Our friend Petra might be in there." Shocked to hear this, Alfreston replied, "We were just asking if anyone knew where Petra was. Am I to understand she was taken prisoner?"

"Yes, Your Majesty," replied Nain in a timid voice. Remembering Nain was one of the Jaspers who had helped to free David and Jayne, Pointer said, "I think it would be a good idea if Nain went along with Beauty. He will be able to guide her group to the places where Zanus holds his valuable prisoners."

Stroking his chin and pondering over what had been said, King Alfreston suddenly said, "I agree." Then, remembering Nain had requested if one other could go he turned to Nain and asked, "Rista, your friend, is she willing to go? Does she know how dangerous it could be?"

"Oh yes, Your Majesty, she's busy in the stable at the moment. I could let her know if she has permission to join us," Nain hastily replied. Smiling discreetly at the speed with which Nain had responded, King Alfreston quietly stated, "If you'd like to go and let Igorin know, you'd best collect Rista and sort out your ride."

Not waiting for the King to change his mind, Nain hurried from the throne room and headed straight for the stables.

King Alfreston gave a slight cough to gain their attention. Then he continued where he'd left off.

"DaVendall, would you like to round up your troops along with Themis and all the other people? You will need to ride hard and fast to bring further help. I'm not sure how long we'll be able to keep Zanus at bay. I fear this is going to be a very hard and bloody battle. And by the way, if any of you should come across Rubie, please remind her she has parents who are worried about her."

"We will do that, but before we leave I think it might be a good idea if Beauty made up several phials of her invisibility liquid," DaVendall suggested. "While we're together I can give them the necessary cover, but if we get parted this will enable our friends to have protective covering should they need it."

Considering what DaVendall had said, Gamlon added, "We know this won't be a permanent measure, but it will offer some protection."

"Gamlon, you've been very quiet up until now," replied Beauty. "But DaVendall's suggestion is a good one." She turned to Queen Matilda. "Would you please come and help me with this?" Turning to leave the room, Queen Matilda said, "We know you want to get going DaVendall, so we'll be as quick as we can."

"See you when the phials are ready," said Beauty. Lifting Beauty off the table, Queen Matilda sensed a moment of panic from Lottie, just as Beauty had. To reassure her Beauty gently told her, "Don't worry Lottie, we'll soon be back."

Not realising her feelings had been sensed by Queen Matilda and Beauty, Lottie concentrated on using her telepathy to reply. "Sorry, Beauty, I've been so used to you being attached to me I forgot you really belong to this land."

Penny and Peter were still absorbed in watching the differing movements taking place on the map. Giving Penny a nudge, he pointed to a certain area. Turning her attention to where Peter was pointing, Penny wondered what she was meant to be looking at. Not seeing anything different, she whispered, "What is it Peter?"

"I'm not sure - perhaps we should ask someone," Peter replied anxiously. Taking another look, he became even more shocked when he saw a dark mass looming over the area close to the tower.

"Your Majesty, look at this!" he shouted. "Something strange is moving near the tower." Everyone moved back to the table where the maps were placed.

"Now young Peter, what's caught your eye?" asked Letswick, gaining his breath. Not taking his eye off the map, Peter pointed to the area.

"Look - there by the tower. It's as if the tower itself is moving."

DaVendall, having also noticed what Peter was pointing to, realised what was happening. "What you are looking at, Peter, is Zorax, Zanus' tower. This will be him sending reinforcements to the battlefield. He'll want reports on what is taking place. To do this he sends his demon birds ahead of him. Some will return and report whatever is happening on the battlefield, while the others will remain and wait for Zanus to appear. I wouldn't be surprised if Sizan is at the tower ready to ride with Zanus."

He glanced over at Peter. "This will be a dangerous mission and will need every bit of courage you can muster," he warned him. Taking in what DaVendall had said and having had a similar thought himself, Peter replied, "Don't worry, DaVendall, I won't let the King down. I will do my best to help defeat these brutes."

"Well done, young Peter. I knew from the beginning you would help us." Marmaduke said. "Be very aware of everything around you. Things might not be what they seem. Take great care, young Peter."

Wondering what Marmaduke was referring to, Peter concluded that it must be the way Lottie had been deceived by Crocanthus. About to ask the question, he noticed the immediate company were absorbed watching the mass move over the map. Gathering his courage, he asked, "Can we get going? It looks like the Outlanders could do with some reinforcements of their own."

Just then, Moff entered the room with Sam, Lucy, Bertram and Frances, with Winston following close behind. Trying to take in the wonders inside the castle, Winston had found himself lagging behind his parents. When he saw the doors open to reveal a large and wondrously decorated room he wasted no time in catching up. Feeling a little overawed by the situation, he sought his father's hand. He wondered what adventures had taken place in this room.

Not sure what to expect, Moff and friends were surprised to see everyone bent over a table deep in conversation. It was some moments before King Alfreston realised that the door had been opened and someone had entered. As soon as he saw who it was, he called out, "Welcome, welcome my friends. Please come on in!" With such a greeting, and with such a broad smile on his face, they couldn't help but smile back.

"We are pleased to be here, Your Majesty. Any time we can help we'll be right there," said Bertram in his usual straightforward manner. Delighted that his friends had once again answered his call for help, King Alfreston went across and warmly greeted them by offering his hand. After shaking hands, the King turned to Winston and asked, "And who do we have here?"

"It's so good to see you again, Your Majesty. This is our son, Winston," said Bertram, pride in his voice.

"Welcome, young Winston. Unfortunately we don't have time to stand and talk properly, but we will do so at a later time." Turning to Sam and Bertram, he stated sombrely, "I need to go and help the Outlanders. They have been defending their lands against the Zanuthians and those dreadful Gorgonians. I wonder if you will ride with us? You know how bloody the last battle was, but I fear this one could be even bloodier. Zanus is set on taking Dofstram and ruling over it. But as we all know, he can only achieve that by capturing our friend and giving him more power than the Old Crone."

The friends saw by the expression on his face that it wasn't going to be easy. As if to confirm what they thought, King Alfreston added, "I can only stress how dangerous it will be."

Remembering the fierce battle they'd undergone before, it didn't cross any of their minds to refuse. Sam stated as much to the King, and Bertram added, "After all, isn't that what friends are for? I might just add how honoured we are at being requested to come and help."

With a bemused but warm smile, the King stated, "I'll take this moment to thank you for once again for your help. Beauty and Matilda are in the process of preparing a few phials of invisibility liquid. DaVendall is taking some along for his group. It's likely we might need some in an emergency."

Winston had stopped listening to the conversation. He was still trying to come to grips with how they'd come to this place. One minute he was eating his breakfast, the next Sam had telephoned to ask if they would all come to his shop immediately. Winston recalled his parents telling him to get a move on as they were needed urgently at Sam and Lucy's shop. No sooner had they arrived there than they were mysteriously transported to Moff's Antique Shop. Before he had chance to speak to his parents, the most amazing thing happened. He was being asked to enter a grandfather clock.

Winston had had to ask himself how they had all got inside. His recollection of the journey in the grandfather clock was just as vivid as the journey. Travelling through a wonderful maze of colour, he tried to think if anyone had told him what to expect, but knew none had. Passing this thought off, he saw before him the kaleidoscope of colours and shapes he'd seen on his journey.

What he hadn't expected was what would happen at the end of their journey. Surprised at seeing so many dwarf-sized people, he'd tried very hard not to stare. This he found even more difficult after noticing some of the people had wings and others had two pairs of ears. Moff explained the different races, and Winston recalled the fierce looks on the guards' faces as they tried to enter the land. Having met Moff at his house, then Sam and Lucy at Lottie's house, Winston wondered how he was going to remember who everyone was. That was when he realised he was in for more surprises.

Following close behind his parents, Winston couldn't be sure who had asked if they were ready to be taken to the castle. Still staying close to the adults, he was ushered into a waiting carriage. Relief followed when he was joined by the others. He became absorbed in watching people fly past with beautiful coloured birds, waving back when others waved and called out a welcome. He was lost in what was happening outside the carriage, so he jumped when he heard a voice say, "Are you ready to leave?"

Looking to see who'd asked the question, he was stunned to see one of the unicorns smiling at him. "Are you ready, young man?" asked the unicorn, kindly. Winston stared in amazement before stammering an answer. He reasoned that Lottie's pets talked, but felt he must have missed the part of the conversation about other animals in Dofstram having the same ability.

Winston realised the surprises weren't over when he saw that the coach was flying alongside many of the people and birds he'd been watching. He happened to look down, and was shocked to see how far from the ground they were.

Deep in his own thoughts he heard his name being called and realised his Dad was trying to get his attention. "Well my lad, what do you think of Dofstram? Winston. Winston my lad, are you listening to me?" asked Bertram.

"Sorry Dad, I was just trying to get my head round our incredible journey here. Dofstram is an amazing place. I wonder if I missed anything," stammered Winston. Giving a gentle laugh,

Bertram told him, "You'll have time to learn of many different things in Dofstram." He faced his son and added quietly, "I will be riding with the King and his people, so I would like you to assist with whatever you're asked. No one is sure how events will turn out, but I trust you will take care." As he finished speaking, he noticed Queen Matilda had entered the room with phials in her hand and Beauty pinned to her dress.

Thinking they would be leaving shortly, Bertram placed a hand warmly on Winston's shoulder, just as King Alfreston made a further request for Rubie to be found. After being assured by Queen Matilda it would be done, King Alfreston turned his attention back to Beauty and said warmly, "Take care Beauty, I hope all goes well at the tower."

Placing the phials in a secure place, he turned to his wife and quietly said, "Take care Matilda. Let's hope this battle will not last long." Not waiting for any response, and keen to get going, he called for his group to make their farewells short and follow him. In a matter of moments King Alfreston and his group were making their way round to the stables, where Igorin was waiting with the unicorns and horses.

Following behind the King, there was considerable muttering between the people, mainly about their forthcoming battle. Acknowledging the greetings and calls of 'take care,' they continued on their way to the stables.

On seeing the King approach with his group of people, Igorin ordered the stable hands to bring out the animals. Without hesitation they brought forward the unicorns, horses and ponies. They led the horses and ponies to the mounting blocks, where the animals waited patiently while the Ziphers and Jaspers placed themselves, two to an animal, on their backs.

Checking to make sure their riders were secure they waited whilst others made their way over to the unicorns. With Kestron settled on his unicorn, Kerez and the King settled on the other unicorn, Gazer. King Alfreston turned to Igorin.

"Sam and Bertram will need rides, Igorin," he said. Giving a bow, Igorin replied, "Yes, Your Majesty, right away." Running into the stables, he gathered another two horses while telling them, "We need you to take Sam and Bertram. They are going with the King. He's heading out to the battle against Zanus." With the horses saddled and harnessed, one of the horses remarked, "Troubles again, eh Igorin?" Giving the horse a gentle slap on the rear, Igorin replied, "I'm afraid so. Now take care of yourselves. There will be a warm stable waiting on your return."

"I remember the last battle we were involved in," said the other horse solemnly. "Many of our friends failed to return." Not wanting to get into further discussions about what could happen, Igorin whispered to each horse, "Please take care, and come back soon." He led them across to Sam and Bertram and handed over the reins to the men while telling King Alfreston, "I'll set about arranging the animals for DaVendall's group." Taking the reins, Sam and Bertram settled themselves in the saddles. They thanked Igorin and watched as he set off towards the stable.

Having joined the troopers, Sam and Bertram noticed King Alfreston had raised his arm, indicating he was ready to leave. After a brief moment he brought down his arm and urged Gazer to walk on. Watching the King lead his people, Igorin, along with many others, shouted, "Take care, come back safe." Many others looked on fearing what these people faced.

As soon as they were free of the castle, the animals were urged to gallop on, and did so. Everyone seemed relieved that the rain appeared to be holding back. Knowing this was going to be a long hard ride, there was one thing that crossed each rider's minds - how they would avoid going through the Forbidden Wood. As if sensing their thoughts, King Alfreston suddenly called out, "The marker has shown the way for us to avoid entering the Forbidden Wood."

On hearing this Bertram stated, "That's funny, I just thought about the wood. How did King Alfreston know what I was thinking?" Hearing gentle amused laughter behind him, Sam laughingly replied, "Don't forget this is Dofstram. Many weird and wonderful things happen here, including the King knowing such thoughts." Joining in a moment of gentle laughter, Sam and Bertram remained in line with the troopers.

Chapter Seven

Departure from the Castle

Watching King Alfreston leave the throne room, DaVendall turned to Themis and said, "I think we should be on our way too." With a gentle nod of the head, she made her way across to stand by his side. Before leaving the throne room, DaVendall asked Queen Matilda if she had the phials he requested. Placing the phials in his hand, Beauty gently reminded him, "Advise your people to use them sparingly, DaVendall. Remember the cover will only last a short while. Take care until we meet again."

DaVendall thanked Beauty and Queen Matilda for the phials and turned once more to Themis. "Are you ready?" he asked. Acknowledging DaVendall's request, they set about bidding their farewells to Queen Matilda and Beauty.

Entering the hallway, Krast was in his usual position at the main doors, ready for them to exit. He wished them well, then added, "I hope many volunteers will come." With only a smile from DaVendall and a quick hug from Themis, Krast slowly closed the door behind them as they started to descend down the castle steps.

Concerned with their forthcoming journey, they were about to step away from the castle steps when a voice halted them. "Take care, DaVendall, and you, Themis." Seeing the concerned looks on the lions' faces, DaVendall quietly replied, "Thank you, lions. We will indeed take care." Wasting no further time, DaVendall set off to gather the other volunteers. Considering the trials that lay ahead, he requested Dylan and Rowena to ride with him. Pleased to be asked but nervous at the same time, they soon rounded up their horses. Settled and ready to follow when DaVendall gave the word, they waited and watched as DaVendall made his way to the stables.

On the way to the stables Gamlon sensed DaVendall was trying to plan for the inevitable. Wondering if he should say anything, he waited for a moment before whispering, "I guess you want Dylan and Rowena to come along because of their friendships with many of the Outlanders."

"How perceptive of you, Gamlon," DaVendall whispered with wry humour in his voice. Gamlon then asked, "I wonder if we'll encounter any of the spy birds."

"It's not a question of if they appear, Gamlon, it's a question of how soon. King Alfreston suggested the warning birds should fly further afield than they usually do. They will be able to let us know if the spy birds are about, and where they are. We need to ride hard and fast if we are to reach the outer villages. It's essential we gather as many volunteers as possible. I can't count on everyone riding with us," DaVendall finished in a low voice.

Making a quick check to make sure his group was ready, he thanked Igorin for his help and gave the signal for his group to walk on. As they set out for the castle they were greeted by the sound of many voices calling out, "Take care. See you soon." DaVendall and friends acknowledged their calls, giving a warm smile as they passed.

Anxious to get as far into the journey as possible, DaVendall requested that everyone should stay close together. Sending a signal for the men at the gates to open them, they waited patiently as the heavy gates were slowly opened. DaVendall thanked the men and signalled his group to follow. With the last of the riders safely on their way, the gatekeepers proceeded to close them. As they were doing this, one of the men stated, "This isn't going to be an easy task. I just hope they keep an eye open for the Old Crone." Shocked to hear the dreaded name spoken, one of the listeners stated, "You shouldn't mention that name here. We all know things happen when it's spoken out loud."

Realising his mistake, the man quietly agreed with what was said, before adding, "Let's hope nothing happens." The men proceeded to make sure the gate was securely closed.

Setting off at a fast pace, DaVendall took a moment to transmit his thoughts to Beauty. When she responded, he telepathically said, "We are on our way now, Beauty. I only hope we can gather enough people together and get to Alfreston soon. You have a difficult and dangerous task ahead of you, so please take care. Perhaps with Lottie's help you might be able to break through that weird grey mist surrounding the tower."

"That is what I am hoping, DaVendall. You take care also, and we'll all be together soon," replied Beauty. Listening to their conversation, Gamlon added his own best wishes. "Good luck, Beauty, see you soon." As the conversation finished, Lottie, thinking she'd heard voices in her head asked Beauty, "Is DaVendall all right? I thought I heard his voice."

Beauty whispered, "You did indeed hear DaVendall, Lottie. He was wishing us well and telling us to take care." Lottie was convinced she'd heard more, but she accepted without question what Beauty told her. Meanwhile DaVendall, keen to get further along, refrained from speaking and concentrated on getting to his destination.

Somewhat confused by what had taken place, Winston edged his way towards his mother, who was standing talking to Lucy and Queen Matilda. Giving her arm a gentle tap, he quietly asked, "Mum, what's happening?" Trying to keep her own fears under control and not wanting to make Winston any more alarmed than he already was, Frances smiled at her son and said quietly, "I will explain everything later, Winston. We'll see everyone safely off, then we can talk."

Meanwhile Beauty was checking that her group was prepared to leave. Lottie, having noticed the amused faces when they saw her attach Beauty to her jacket, told them, "Force of habit". Fearful of what Beauty and friends were heading into, Queen Matilda remarked, "Good idea, Lottie. We're sure our enemies haven't discovered what it is exactly they are looking for. It's possible they think our friend is still a misshapen stone. I think that when you leave here, it might be advisable to refer to your brooch as 'our friend'. We don't want to let our enemies know of her transformation."

"That's a good idea Matilda, thank you. Now, before we

leave, Eram, would you please ask Yemil and Binro to come? I think they should hear what I plan to do." Beauty asked. Turning to Letswick, she asked, "Letswick, would you just check with Igorin that our rides are ready?" Without feeling a need to comment, Eram and Letswick made their way to complete their respective tasks.

"Cor, are you going with them, sis?" asked Winston, with a hint of envy in his voice.

"I am, and please don't call me sis," replied Penny.

"Now you two, that's enough," whispered Frances. She was scared and anxious about their forthcoming rescue mission and her voice was harsher than she had intended.

"Try not to worry, Frances, we know this isn't going to be easy but we'll take care of each other," Beauty responded, hoping this would allay some of Frances' fears.

"Will you be able to see into the tower, Beauty? If I remember correctly, you said something about a kind of mist surrounding it which you thought had been created by a certain person?"

"Indeed, Frances," replied Beauty. "That's something that has been causing me some concern, but I think it will need to be sorted when we get closer to the tower. If you take a look at the map over there you'll see there's a grey mist still hovering over it. For part of the journey you will be able to track where we are."

Just at that moment Letswick entered the room to confirm the animals were ready and waiting at the stables. As he finished speaking Eram entered the room with Yemil and Binro. Waiting for them to settle, Beauty asked, "Could you all come a little closer please?"

Watching them make their way to where she sat proudly on Lottie's jacket, Beauty began to lay out her plans. "Before I go under cover of Lottie's jacket, I suggest we ride as far as we can. Eram will lead and warn us of any dangers. Now let's see who can ride together. Letswick, I know you will be with your unicorn Doran. I think it would be better if Penny rode along with you. Is this all right? Lottie and I will ride with Yemil on Dandy."

Seeing Penny grin and acknowledging that she would be delighted to ride with Letswick, Beauty continued, "I think, Binro, you should ride up front with Eram. That will leave Nain and Rista, who will have sorted out their ride by the time we get to the stables. Knowing Igorin has prepared our rides, I suggest we make our way to the stables."

"What have you worked out for going through the Forbidden Wood?" asked Letswick. Aware that she had left that out, Beauty smiled at him and replied, "I think we will need to think about that on the way." Penny turned to Letswick and asked, "You don't mind me riding with you, do you?" Being just a little shorter than Penny, he looked up at her and assured her that he would be delighted to have her with him.

Frances was desperately trying to hide the fear she was feeling for her daughter, and tapped Penny on the arm. Penny wasn't surprised when she turned and saw her mother looking at her with tearful eyes.

"Take care my girl, I'll be waiting here for your safe return," Frances murmured. Penny flung her arms round her mother's neck.

Having heard the fear in Frances' voice, Queen Matilda quietly said, "Take great care everyone and look after each other. I think it would be better if we stayed here while you take yourselves off to the stables." Turning to address Beauty, she asked, "Please keep us informed as you progress, Beauty." Noticing the concern in Matilda's voice, Beauty softly replied, "I will, Matilda, I'll keep you well informed."

While they had been conversing, Marmaduke had been observing the lost look on Winston's face. Jumping off the chair, he made his way across the floor to Winston. Placing a paw on Winston's hand, he asked, "Would you like to come and have a look at our maps, Winston?"

Startled at the touch from Marmaduke, Winston whispered, "Hello Scruff... sorry Marmaduke, I nearly forgot to call you by your true name. This is all so odd I'm not sure if I understand it all." Seeing the amused look on Marmaduke's face, Winston explained how he knew his real name. "Moff told me your real name is Marmaduke," Winston whispered.

"No harm done, Winston," Marmaduke assured him. Taking in how regal Marmaduke looked, Winston commented, "You sure do look different here, Marmaduke. Not at all like the Scruffy I've come to know."

"Just a slight disguise, Winston, I wanted to fit in with the neighbouring cats," Marmaduke explained. Admiring Scruffy's new look, Winston stated, "You certainly used a good disguise."

As they made their way to the table, where the maps were still in place, Winston said, "I was just thinking how beautiful this land is. I can't believe that some awful people want to dominate it." Stooping down to face Marmaduke he whispered, "Will you ever come back to Lottie's? It wasn't the same after you left. It was really awful."

"Who knows, young Winston, who knows? At the moment everyone is hoping to keep Zanus and Sizan from taking over our land." Then in a low voice, he added solemnly, "Which is what they will do, if they defeat King Alfreston and the Outlanders."

"Why do you call them Outlanders?" asked Winston.

"Because that's where they live, on the outlying parts of the land. There are many different races of Outlanders. They live in small villages on the farthest parts of Dofstram." Taking a breath and letting out a deep sigh, Marmaduke went on, "Some will offer help willingly, but DaVendall will need to do a bit of bargaining for others to help. That's why King Alfreston agreed to let DaVendall go on this mission. The King is hoping that when DaVendall asks for help they will respond favourably. Only with everyone helping will we be able to fend off the Zanuthians and Gorgonians."

Thinking over what he'd told Winston, Marmaduke added, as if speaking to himself, "It wouldn't surprise me if DaVendall hasn't taken Rowena and Dylan."

Hearing that last comment, Winston asked, "Why would he ask those particular people to go?"

"Because, Winston, they are good friends with many of the Outlanders. If DaVendall can't persuade them it's possible Rowena or Dylan can."

Totally absorbed in what Marmaduke was telling him, Winston suddenly heard his name being called.

"Winston, come along! Beauty and her people are going to make their way," Frances called out in a nervous voice. Just as she finished speaking, Beauty asked, "Is everyone ready? I think we should make way, we want to try and get as far as we can before it gets too dark. We will have to rest overnight and set off for the tower at sunrise."

"Oh gosh, I hope not. I don't like camping much," Penny whispered to her Mum.

"This won't be like any camp you know, Penny," Frances whispered back. Making their way down the castle steps they too were greeted by the lions. With solemn voices the animals asked the group to take care.

"Thank you, lions, we will indeed take care," replied Beauty, and Letswick added quietly, "We'll see you all soon." Watching the group move away, one of the lions sombrely stated, "We all wish that to be very soon."

As they approached the stables, it came as no surprise to any of them to see Igorin and the stable lads standing with the prepared animals. What none of them heard, except Beauty, was Igorin wishing the animals to remain safe. Then repeating what he'd said to include all the animals, he then added, "Take care, warm bedding will be ready for your return."

Seeing his unicorn Doran waiting patiently, Letswick walked across to greet him. "Hello my friend. Not a pleasant mission this time."

"That's what I was told. But we need to get those poor prisoners out of the grasp of Zanus as soon as possible," Doran replied, giving a gentle nuzzle on Letswick's arm. Kneeling down, he waited until Letswick was safely on his back before adding, "I see some of our friends are ready to go."

"Right, let's go and join them," replied Letswick, settling himself on Doran's back. Amused to see the unicorns and the horses kneel down to let their riders climb up Penny asked Doran, "Will you do that for me please?"

"Certainly Penny, hold tight, Letswick I'm just going to kneel down," Doran responded softly. Trying not to stand too hard on Doran's leg, Penny took the offered hand of Letswick.

"Right Penny, are you settled?" Hearing a positive response,

Letswick continued, "I suggest we move on Doran and join the others." Having left Letswick to settle Penny, Beauty called out, "We'll follow you, Eram. Keep a steady trot. We don't want to wait until dark before we seek shelter. Binro, would you please listen out for you-know-who flying around." Agreeing with Beauty's request, Binro telepathically asked, "How will I communicate any information to the ones who aren't telepathic?"

"Don't worry about that, Binro, I'll make sure everyone is kept informed of what you relay to the telepaths. However, I would advise a little caution when reporting any information; Lottie has come a long way in using telepathy." Moving to the front position of the group Eram asked Binro, "Are we all ready to go?" He nodded his head. It wasn't long before they heard Eram call out, "Prepare to go. Remember, stay close."

Seeing the number of people gathered in the forecourt, Penny and Lottie were surprised to hear so many onlookers calling out their support. "Take care. See you all soon. Stay safe!" they were saying. With acknowledgments in response, Eram gave the signal for the men to open the gates.

"What a lovely thing to do, giving us such a warm farewell," commented Penny. Noticing how near the castle they were, she settled down for the long ride ahead.

"The people remaining at the castle will have concerns all the time we're away, but sadly they know their attention will need to be on keeping the castle safe and helping with any injured," Letswick explained. "Remembering other battles, there are often many casualties." Waiting for the last of the group to pass through the gates, the men were about to close them when they heard a voice calling, "Hold it. Just give us a moment." Recognising who it was, Letswick turned round in the saddle and called out, "Come along Nain, we need to be going." Observing Rista settled behind Nain, Letswick was satisfied they were set to exit the forecourt.

"Well young man, I thought I was the last one to get ready. We really should get going," Letswick gently chided. Blushing at Letswick's comment, Nain was quite relieved to hear Beauty say, "Right, Eram, lead on." Rista leaned closer to Nain and whispered, "Thanks for getting Beauty to agree." Smiling, Nain replied, "That's all right, Rista. Just remember this is going to be a very dangerous task, so please take care."

"Will do, and you too," Rista whispered. As they started out on their journey Beauty was busy considering the safest way to journey through the Forbidden Wood. Churning over several options, she was soon satisfied with what she thought would be the safest. Content to keep this thought to herself, or until as such time as she thought the moment was right to pass it on, Beauty moved closer to edge of the lapel, where she could look round for signs of possible enemy activity.

With a clear but darkening sky, Beauty concentrated her thoughts on gaining Letswick's attention. "Have you seen or heard anything that we should be aware of?" she said. Caught off guard by Beauty's voice, it took a moment for him to respond telepathically.

"Hi Beauty, you startled me there for a minute. I can't say I have seen or heard anything, but I have noticed how dark it's become." Taking another look at the sky, Beauty replied telepathically. "Me too, but I can't see why. It's almost as if that dreadful mist encircling the tower has started to make its way across the sky. I suggest we keep a watchful eye on it and see what happens."

With acknowledgement from Letswick, Beauty turned her attention to Eram. Changing from telepathy to verbal communication, Beauty called "Eram, would you please halt for a moment. I would like everyone to make their way closer to me." Giving a flick of the wrist, he steered his horse to the back of the group.

Wondering if something had happened, they hastened their animals to move closer to Dandy. Beauty put their minds at rest, and assured them she wanted to explain what she considered was the best way to journey through the wood.

"We're all aware of the care we need to take on approaching the Forbidden Wood, but when we journey through we'll be faced with many dangers," she began. "As the animals will also be in danger, I will ask Doran and Dandy to ensure they keep the animals protected. I will protect the people, that way we won't exhaust our powers." Taking a short pause, she continued, "As yet I haven't picked up on any dangers, but we will as we get closer to the wood. Some of us have experienced many of the horrors within, but there's no knowing what other horrors await us. With assistance from Lottie I'm hoping to discover what is beyond the mist. Remember, we face double the danger as we get closer to the tower. That's why I must try and break through the mist, but this protective cover was placed there by Imelda, so she will know as soon as it is attacked."

As Beauty finished speaking, Letswick added, "I guess Zanus will have taken most of the troopers to the battlefield, but we must be ready for any left behind."

Thinking of the differing abilities the Ziphers and Jaspers had, Eram said, "Could the Ziphers please listen out for any odd sounds and let us know? Jaspers, it may be we could use your flying ability later. It might be helpful to know if the sky is free of enemy birds."

"That's an excellent idea," commented Beauty. "Binro, I too think a little flying might be needed. But only after we have made sure it is safe for you to do so. Our main aim is to get all the prisoners out of the tower. Nain, Rista, that's where you will come in. With the knowledge you have of where Zanus keeps his 'special prisoners' we will be guided by you. I can't think of anything else, but does anyone have any questions?"

They heard Rista quietly say, "Nain and I will find the prisoners. We know there are a few areas where he keeps his prized prisoners. The other prisoners will soon be discovered."

With an earlier suggestion running through her mind, Lottie asked, "Before we set off, could I remind everyone what Queen Matilda suggested?" Pointing to her brooch, Lottie continued, "From now on this will be known as, 'our friend'. We must protect 'our friend' from the enemy."

"That's right," added Penny, "I think it's an extremely good idea." Seeing warm smiles coming back at her, Penny felt herself blushing.

"Quite right Penny. Now, I think we should be moving on, it will soon be dark," said Letswick. An eerie silence fell.

"May I suggest we ride a little faster?" said Eram. "I don't like the way it's become dark so quickly. We need to seek shelter before it gets much darker." Not wanting to add to their concerns, especially with Eram noticing how dark it had become, Beauty and Letswick refrained from commenting on what they were both thinking. Suddenly a different thought crossed Letswick's mind. Seeking Beauty's attention, he asked, "Have you heard any news of where the warning birds are? I can't see any around."

"I haven't heard anything yet, Letswick," Beauty replied. "I know some of them went with DaVendall and some with the King. Once they have made certain the skies are clear of trouble they'll return to the castle."

Surprised to hear that the warning birds were with DaVendall and the King, Lottie asked, "Why haven't any come with us, Beauty?" Beauty, who wanted to encourage Lottie to practise using her newly acquired telepathy skill, replied telepathically, "With your help, and with the help of other telepaths, we should be able to pick up the presence of unwanted enemies."

Elated by what Beauty had said, Lottie concentrated on her thoughts and replied telepathically, "I understand. I just hope it will work when we need it most. Somehow the more I converse with you this way the easier it seems to become."

"That's what I had hoped to hear you say, Lottie. Be reassured, when the time comes to put your telepathic gift into use you will not fail," Beauty told her telepathically. Realising the non-telepaths wouldn't have heard their conversation, and with Eram urging them on, Beauty refrained from passing on what had been said.

Eram was busy concentrating on the task ahead and had increased the pace from a canter to a gallop. Lottie was surprised at how easily she'd taken to riding, but guessed it could be Dandy who was ensuring her safety. Glancing over at Penny, Lottie was amused to see such concentration on her friend's face. Just for a moment Lottie wondered if Penny had ridden before.

Taking a moment to contact Queen Matilda, Beauty channelled her thoughts directly to her. It wasn't long before she heard the Queen say, "I'm here Beauty, is everything all right?"

Having reassured Queen Matilda that so far everything had gone to plan, Beauty went on to tell her how they were going to proceed into the wood, and told her to watch their journey through the wood. Queen Matilda feared this part of the journey the most. "I wondered what you had planned," she replied. "We've been watching the maps to see how far all the groups have gone. DaVendall's group has faded off the map. That happened soon after he left. I guess he found a different and possibly safer way to go. Alfreston is just coming up to the hills, the ones that shelter the wood. When he reaches them the maps will no longer be able to follow. That I fear is what will happen when you go into the wood - our marker won't be able to follow you."

Taking in what Matilda had told her, Beauty was pleased to hear that the other groups had remained safe for now, but she was wise enough to know this could all change in a moment. Without bringing Matilda's attention to this, Beauty asked, "Have the warning birds returned?"

"Not yet," replied the Queen. "Before Alfreston's group disappeared off the map Moff managed to send a quick message letting us know they had not seen any spy birds, but they knew they were around."

With their minds beginning to fade they bade each other goodbye, as Beauty left a last message, "I'll contact you when I can." Deep within her own thoughts and taking a moment to see if everyone was still close by, she settled back onto Lottie's jacket and waited for Eram to let them know when the time had come for them to stop. Beauty then turned her mind to Ms Beckett.

To her horror, she was shocked to see a dreadful vision. Crocanthus was standing over Ms Beckett with a bloodied knife. Shuddering, Beauty realised he had killed her. Sensing Ms Beckett's life leave her, Beauty withdrew her mind, fearing Crocanthus or Imelda might sense her presence.

"Are you all right, Beauty? You suddenly gasped," said Lottie. Not sure how to pass this information on to her, Beauty quietly gained Lottie's attention and began explaining what had happened. At first, Lottie struggled to take in what had been said. It was quite a while later when she asked, "Why, Beauty? Why did he kill her? Ms Beckett wasn't all bad."

Having realised it was Ms Beckett who had enabled Crocanthus to get information about Lottie, Beauty tried explaining how Ms Beckett had been tricked into revealing everything she had known about her. Giving Lottie a moment to think about what she'd said, Beauty then continued, "He needed to know as much as he could about you if he was to become Jeremy, your friend. Ms Beckett became too involved with him and was obviously too scared not to do whatever he told her."

Shocked at what she was being told, Lottie felt a tear trickle down her face. Wiping it away, she sobbingly asked, "Would he have killed her if I'd told her we were becoming suspicious of some of the things she was asking?"

"I don't think it would have made any difference, Lottie. By the time you suspected her of being against you, she was too involved to escape his grasp. I do admit I didn't think he would stoop to killing her. He is such an evil, cruel man."

Thinking about Ms Beckett, Lottie wondered what Beauty had discovered about Mr Thomas, the bank manager. Remembering the last time she had seen him battered and bruised, she asked warily, "What about Mr Thomas? Was he also in this with Ms Beckett?"

Unaware of the request Lottie had made to Beauty earlier, Yemil was surprised to hear what Beauty was telling Lottie. She waited to hear the answer.

"Oh no Lottie, he was telling the truth about falling over. What he didn't tell you, because he was too embarrassed, is that he wasn't totally sober when this happened," Beauty told her with a gentle laugh. Relieved to hear that at least one of her doubts had been a more pleasant discovery, she joined Beauty and Yemil in a quiet laugh, although Yemil had no idea what was so funny.

Galloping along and secretly hoping they would soon stop, Penny was surprised to see that they were moving closer to

Lottie and Yemil. Hearing their quiet laughter, Penny asked, "What's the joke, Lottie?"

Lottie told her what Beauty had discovered regarding Ms Beckett and Mr Thomas. "Why would he kill her?" asked Penny. Beauty offered up the same explanation as she'd given Lottie.

With regard to Mr Thomas, Penny and Letswick saw the funny side of it. Letswick commented, "No wonder he didn't want you taking his arm, Lottie. He probably thought you would smell the drink on him."

"Nevertheless I feel guilty at suspecting him of being the informer," Lottie told them.

"You and me both, Lottie, I was convinced it had to be him, especially with that battered and bruised face," Penny echoed.

"I'm sorry what happened to your boss lady, but she never gave a thought about what happened to you two," Letswick pointed out. "Remember Lottie, if you hadn't had your pets it would have been a lot worse."

"I know, but to kill her, that's so awful!" Lottie replied in a sad voice.

"This sounds terrible," Yemil whispered. "Crocanthus killing people in your land is awful." Turning to Letswick, she asked, "How is it possible for him to do that?"

"Because he has sufficient power to carry this out, wherever he goes. But I feel certain that to make sure the deed was complete, he would have got a little help from another evil individual. He was possibly given a poison that would be added to the blade. That would make it impossible for anyone from Lottie's land to revive her, even if the stabbing alone hadn't worked."

Riding on in silence, but pensive about what Letswick had said, Penny asked, "What about that nosy neighbour, Lottie? That woman in the park? Didn't you say something about not seeing her husband?" Not having given the Shepherd's a further thought, Lottie asked, "Beauty, do you know anything about Mr Shepherd? Could he be the informer?"

"I'm not sure, Lottie. I wasn't over keen on Mrs Shepherd but from what I heard I can't say if he is or he isn't," Beauty replied. "What about you Letswick, have you any thoughts on this?"

"Can't say I have Beauty, I've not met either of the Shepherd's. It might mean Lottie will have to be alert as she's the only one who knows him," Letswick replied. Having been joined by other members of the group they continued on in silence, each with their own thoughts. Galloping on it didn't take long to see how close they'd come to the dreaded wood.

* * * *

Back at the castle, Queen Matilda had been relieved to hear from Beauty, but she was becoming anxious at the lack of news from her husband. Her attention was brought back by Winston calling out, "Look, isn't that Dad's group fading off the map?" Fearing the worst, they all turned their attention to the map. Frances whispered, "Winston, you gave us all a bit of a scare just now. But we knew this would happen when they got closer to that area." Lucy was taking in what the map was revealing. "Looking at where the marker is going, it looks as if they will go round those hills," she said, pointing. "This will mean they could avoid going through the wood."

Queen Matilda felt a growing concern as her husband and his group began to fade from the map. No one took their eyes off what was happening as they watched the marker bring their attention to where King Alfreston was going. Suddenly the marker stopped. "King Alfreston and his group have gone beyond where I can follow," the marker told them. Everyone gasped.

"Thank you, marker," Queen Matilda quietly replied. Failing to notice the look of surprise on Winston's face she added, "I do hope they take care." She turned to Winston, and gently asked, "Are you all right, Winston? I was going to ask if you can still see those spy birds."

"Did I hear that marker speak?" asked Winston, ignoring the question in amazement. He was surprised to hear soft laughter. Wiping his whiskers, Marmaduke assured him it was indeed the marker. Trying to keep a straight face Marmaduke suggested, "I think you'd better let the Queen know the answer to her question."

Winston put aside his question, telling himself he would ask Marmaduke about it later. "Does Queen Matilda mean that black mass over there?" he whispered. Looking to see where Winston was pointing, Marmaduke replied, "That's right, Winston. You'll need to let Queen Matilda know they are still in sight."

Thanking Marmaduke for his help, Winston turned to Queen Matilda. "Yes, the spy birds are still in sight" he said. "But there's so many I can't count."

"Thank you, Winston," said the Queen. "That's a bit worrying. I only hope the warning birds have let Alfreston know how close the birds are."

Taking another glance at Winston, and aware there were many things he didn't know about Dofstram, she gently asked, "How are you feeling, Winston? I see the surprise on your face has gone. There are many things you will learn once you have been here a while."

"I'm all right thank you, Queen Matilda," Winston replied. Although he still wanted an answer to his original question, he thought this wasn't something he should ask the Queen. Turning her attention to Marmaduke, Queen Matilda asked, "Has anyone reported the warning birds' return?"

"Not yet, Your Majesty," he replied. "They will stay with the King until it is safe for them to return." Edging his way closer to Winston, he continued, "The warning birds will let King Alfreston know there are many more spy birds heading in their direction." Letting out a low whistle, Winston concentrated on watching the black mass of spy birds until they too faded off the map.

"Where did those birds go? They're not there any more," said Winston, as if talking to himself. He jumped back in surprise when he heard Krast's voice say "They have flown too far for the marker to continue following them."

"Does that mean we will no longer be able to follow the group, as well as the spy birds, Krast?" Winston asked.

"I'm afraid it does, Winston," Krast replied. Following his response they became aware of a heavy silence which seemed to engulf everyone in the room. It was some time before the silence was broken, and then it was only a whisper, as Marmaduke said, "I do hope they stay safe." It wasn't long before other voices echoed the same thought.

"Marmaduke," Winston whispered, "How does a marker speak?" With an amused expression on his face, Marmaduke whispered, "That marker, Winston, is very special. Beauty gave the marker the power of speech many years ago. This has enabled it not only to show the way, but to explain any difficulties that might arise. You might have seen earlier when it stopped at the point where the King and the spy birds faded."

With his attention now on the marker, Winston thought he saw it move. He was about to mention it to Marmaduke when to his surprise, the marker spoke to him.

"Young lad, do you not have talking markers in your land?" it said. Winston gaped open-mouthed.

"I - I don't know of any," he stammered. He didn't know what else to say. He placed an arm round Marmaduke and whispered, "You're so lucky to have such wonderful things. I think I'd like to stay here."

"We'll see, young Winston. For now we have other things to consider," Marmaduke replied gravely. Stroking Marmaduke's back, Winston felt comforted by his purring.

Chapter Eight

Council of War

As they waited for any sign to come from DaVendall, Queen Matilda, Frances and Lucy tried to cover their anxiousness by catching up on the events that had taken place since they were last together. At last, unable to restrain herself any longer, Queen Matilda exclaimed, "I do hope we hear from Alfreston and DaVendall soon. I'm not sure which is worse, waiting here or going on a mission. One thing I do know, we'd best be prepared for the worst. Earlier battles with Zanus and Sizan have proved that their respect for human life is nil."

Marmaduke was only half listening to what was being discussed. What he really wanted to know was if the things he'd heard about the monsters were true. Waiting for a lull in the conversation, he cautiously asked Queen Matilda, "Is it true Imelda has created some obnoxious creatures for the Gorgonians to ride?"

Krast was astonished to hear Marmaduke ask this question. Before the Queen could respond, he exclaimed, "Wow Marmaduke! How did you know that? We were only told a short while ago that Zanus had ordered such creatures to be created."

Seeing the look of shock on some of the others' faces, Krast gave them a little time to absorb what he'd said. Then he slowly added, "We have managed to discover very little about these beasts. We know they are like nothing the troops have encountered before. Apparently they are of immense size and extremely vicious with it. According to some who have had the misfortune to come across them, they can also cover the ground at high speed."

"How did you know that, Marmaduke? About these monster creatures, I mean?" Winston asked. Noticing that all attention was on him, Marmaduke explained, "Beauty informed us we would be facing more of Imelda's unearthly creations. They had been discovered when the Ziphers and warning birds were taking a fly round, the usual routine to make sure none of Zanus' spy birds were around. It was one of the Ziphers who noticed a peculiar-shaped creature, and she alerted her companions. When they flew closer to the beasts they realised this wasn't anything they'd ever seen before. They were terrified of being seen, so the warning birds and Ziphers wasted no time in reporting it back to the King."

"How did Beauty know?" asked Winston.

"I'm afraid I told her," said the Queen. "It was when we were discussing how to get Lottie and her friends safely to the castle. I warned her to be careful of such beasts."

"That's really something," Winston remarked. "But how can Beauty converse with people in Dofstram when she's in our land?"

Krast wasted no time in responding. "Beauty has great powers, Winston. Many some we don't know about. Somehow Beauty and DaVendall are able to share this ability. This proved to be invaluable in keeping the people of your land safe."

Absorbed in the conversation and thinking of earlier times, Frances asked in a solemn voice, "I thought that after the long battle with Zanus the Elder, King Alfreston had managed to get him to surrender."

"Soon after Zanus had been captured, Alfreston made him agree to leave our land and never return," explained the Queen. "Very reluctantly he agreed, to save his own skin. Many of the Zanuthians were against this, especially his son, Zanus. Where they went no one knew, but for many years after that, Dofstram returned to its pleasant state. It came as a complete shock to hear Zanus had been plotting to overthrow his father. With help from his cruel ally Sizan, he achieved his goal. We have never been certain whether it was Zanus or Sizan that dealt the final blow which killed Zanus' father. It wasn't long after the killing of his father; Zanus started waging war against the Outlanders.

He vowed to take over the land and rule Dofstram as his father once had."

Stunned to hear how this battle had come about, Lucy took a moment to gather her thoughts. Then she surprised everyone by asking, "Is that why he began his reign of terror on the Outlanders?" Acknowledging Lucy's question, Queen Matilda stated, "It was some time before we were made aware of what was happening to the far distant Outlanders. By then it was too late to save many of the people and their homes." Her voice saddened by the memory, she continued in a firm but positive voice. "We have to make sure we remove Zanus and Sizan for good. If we fail, I fear Zanus will rule Dofstram for ever."

There was no reply, and the Queen wondered if her friends had heard all that she'd said. She could see the look of concern etched on their faces. She left them with their thoughts.

Queen Matilda turned to face Lucy and Frances and surprised them by saying, "I see Marmaduke and Winston are absorbed with the map. Perhaps we should go and see what's happening."

After encouraging Winston to look at different areas on the map, Marmaduke pointed out one specific hill and quietly drew Winston's attention. "See that hill there? That's where King Alfreston and his group are aiming for. If you look a little closer you'll see they just miss going through the wood."

Fascinated by the map and trying to take in the variety of areas, Winston surprised Marmaduke by asking, "This Imelda, what's she like, Marmaduke? Is she truly that ugly? How old is she? What does she look like?"

Hearing Winston mention the hated name, Marmaduke felt a shiver of fear run through his body.

"Imelda – well, let me see," he replied. "How can I best explain what's she's like? Firstly she's really evil and cruel, and yes she's ugly, very ugly. Her hands are a fright to behold; they're not properly developed like yours. Her fingers are long and bony. Her fingernails, ugh! They are long and disgusting. They curl over at the tips, just like an eagle's talon. But worse still, when she wants to secure her prey, they unwind and become long, like tendrils from a tree. Take care she never gets close enough to prod you with one of those nails, I fear it would be enough to kill you."

Marmaduke, trying to keep his voice steady, hesitated before adding, "Many of her torture victims are failures."

Seeing the expression of horror on Winston's face, Marmaduke asked if he should continue. With a nod from Winston he continued, "She has uses for these poor devils as well. She hangs them on the passage walls inside Zanus' tower. We have never been sure why she does this, but we think they are put there to put fear into Zanus' prisoners."

Recalling the many horrors he'd seen and heard, and seeing fear on Winston's face, Marmaduke told him in a more light-hearted voice, "She's really ugly. The ugliest thing you can think of." As the tension slowly eased Winston laughed and said, "Is she really that awful? And, with fingernails that could kill? Wow!"

"Take my word for it Winston. There is nothing in the world uglier than her, and no one I know has more lethal fingernails." They burst out laughing, failing to notice that the lions had moved from the pedestal holding the map table. Seating himself at the feet of the Queen, one of the lions said, "I don't think that young man has noticed us yet." The Queen gave each lion a stroke on the head and whispered, "Give it time boys, Winston is trying to take everything in. Don't forget, he's never been to a place like Dofstram before."

Reaching the table on which the maps lay open, Frances asked, "What's made you both laugh?" Winston tried to explain what Marmaduke had told him about how ugly Imelda was, and her funny fingernails.

Queen Matilda gave a sudden gasp. The laughter came to a halt. They were surprised to see that she had joined them at the table.

"What's wrong?" asked Frances. Without saying a word, Queen Matilda began pointing at an area on the map. At first they couldn't see what she was pointing at, but then Marmaduke surprised them by saying, "There, over by the hill I told you about. Winston, look what's happening, Zanus' spy birds are flying in the same direction Alfreston went."

"Can you follow them?" asked the Queen.

At this request, the marker slid across the map until it reached the hill. It stopped, then turned to Queen Matilda and said, "I can't see round the hill, Your Majesty. The warning birds will let King Alfreston know they are close." As the marker was speaking, they all watched the dark mass of birds fly over the hill.

Wondering what they could do to alert the King, Lucy thought of an idea, "Can't we try and reach the telepaths? We could let them know what we've seen."

"Good idea Lucy, but there are so few of them here," Queen Matilda replied.

"If we use all our strength we might just manage to get through," suggested Marmaduke.

"You're right Marmaduke, we have to try something. Let's join our thoughts and concentrate on the minds of the telepaths," Queen Matilda said. Looking round to see who she knew was telepathic, she asked, "Are you ready?" Nodding, the telepaths proceeded to close their minds to everything else and concentrate on trying to contact their fellow telepaths riding with the King. Sadly, after several valiant attempts, it proved to be impossible. Each time they thought they'd succeeded they were halted.

"It isn't working. There's a sort of grey mist preventing our minds from getting through," Lucy observed. "I saw that too," replied Marmaduke.

Exhausted at trying to get to the telepaths, Queen Matilda decided it was time to stop. Unaware of the difficulty they were having, Winston moved across to his mother and whispered, "Is there anything we can do?"

"We can't do anything at the moment, Winston," replied Frances. "We'll have to wait and see if they are successful."

Releasing their minds, Lucy turned to Frances and in a sombre voice said, "We've had no luck. A thick grey mist is preventing our thoughts from getting through. We can only hope the warning birds have been able to alert Alfreston. It might be his group is beyond the hill." Then in a lowered tone, she added, "But I'm not sure."

"I agree with Lucy, it could be the mist preventing us from getting through, but then it could be something simple like being out of range," commented Marmaduke.

"I think you might be right, Marmaduke. But didn't Beauty tell us about a thick grey mist hovering over the tower which prevented her from reaching the telepaths in there?"

"That's right," Lucy replied, "but we mustn't give up."

Seeing the despair on her friend's faces, Queen Matilda tried to think of something to say, but nothing came to mind.

Quietly entering the room, Krast caught the end of the conversation and realised they must have failed in reaching the telepaths. He thought there might be another way to reach King Alfreston, before he could voice his thoughts Frances asked, "What now? Is there anything else we can try?"

There was silence. But suddenly Lucy surprised them by suggesting, "I was just wondering something. I was wondering if I could get through to Sam. There have been times when one of us has been in trouble we've managed to sense help is needed."

"Try it Lucy. Please try it!" said Krast. Surprised at the pleading tone in his voice, Lucy gave him a smile and closed her eyes. Removing everything from her thoughts, she concentrated on trying to contact Sam. Coming across the same barrier of mist they'd come up against last time, Lucy tried to ignore the mist and concentrate on reaching Sam's thoughts. She drew a picture of Sam to the front of her mind, and was surprised to see a small space appear in the mist. Lucy called his name then waited to hear if he would respond. Not hearing anything, she took a chance and relayed what they'd seen on the map. After repeating the same thing three more times she waited again for a response.

Then, just as Lucy had convinced herself she'd failed and was about to withdraw her thoughts, she thought she heard something. She concentrated as hard as she could. A faint voice seemed to say, "Birds over..."

Silence followed, and Lucy hoped he'd heard everything she'd said.

The others were becoming worried at the time Lucy spent trying to contact Sam and were delighted to see her coming back to them. Lucy was feeling faint. Frances, seeing Lucy start to sway back and forth slipped an arm round her friend's back. Frances was quietly urging Lucy to take her time.

Finding more strength than she'd ever used before, Lucy hadn't realised how weak she'd become, but hearing the soothing voice of her friend she slowly and quietly said, "Thanks Frances." Without removing her arm, Frances asked, "Lucy, are you all right?"

"I'm all right. Just took a little more out of me than usual," Lucy replied weakly. Aware her friends were eager to know if she'd been successful, Lucy thanked Frances for her help and settled herself back into the chair. Sitting for a moment, Lucy took a deep breath and relayed what had happened.

"I had to try lots of times, but I'm sure I managed to reach Sam's mind," she said. "I was in the process of explaining what we'd seen on the map when a veil of mist came between us." Noticing the disappointment on her friend's faces, Lucy added slowly, "I hope he heard all I said. I think he must have heard some of it because he repeated, 'birds over,' then it went silent. With that horrible grey mist separating our thoughts, I wasn't able to contact him again."

Pleased Lucy had at least made contact with Sam, but slightly disappointed that he might not have heard everything, Frances said warmly, "At least you reached Sam. That might mean Beauty could be lucky enough to break through the mist too. Let's see if the map can show us what's happening."

"I agree. Well done, Lucy," said Queen Matilda. "If Sam was able to repeat the word 'birds,' let's hope he received the entire messages. Which as you say, gives us hope for Beauty."

"Look Mum, those big black birds are flying towards the wood," Winston stated warily. He wondered if there was any way the birds could escape from the map and get into the room. Marmaduke, picking up Winston's thoughts, gave him a gentle tap on the hand and whispered, "Don't worry Winston, they can't escape from the map." Relieved, but surprised at Marmaduke's comment, Winston looked at Marmaduke, only to see a large smile on the cat's face. With everyone's attention on the map, they were surprised when Krast asked, "If everything has been sorted, I wonder if a little light refreshment might be required, Your Majesty?"

"Oh Krast, what a good Idea," Queen Matilda replied. "A

pot of tea for us please, and cream for Marmaduke, and whatever Winston would like."

Thinking of the decanters in the Queen's cabinet, Lucy quietly asked, "Perhaps Winston would like one of your special drinks, Your Majesty." Acknowledging the wink Lucy gave, Queen Matilda said, "Leave Winston's request to me, Krast. Lucy's idea is a better one." She turned to Winston. "Would you like to come and choose your drink?" Thinking he would be offered the same drinks as those he was used to back home, Winston made his way slowly to join her. Lucy and Frances watched in amusement as he made his way to the cabinet. Knowing what was behind the closed doors, they waited to see his reaction when they were opened.

Waiting patiently for Winston to join her, Queen Matilda placed her hand on the ornate door handles. Then she slowly, almost teasingly, opened the cabinet doors.

Unprepared for what was about to be revealed, Winston was immediately struck by the melodic music that came from within. As the inside was revealed he stood wide eyed, not sure what he was really seeing. Blinking rapidly, as if trying to clear his eyes, he tried to take in everything he could for fear of it disappearing. There were many beautiful sea-horses floating round. Stunned at their variety and colour, he was lost for words. He stood mesmerised as the gentle creatures floated round the back of the cabinet. Absorbed with watching the smaller sea-horses darting here and there, he was taken in by how beautiful they were. He couldn't believe anything as marvellous as this lagoon could really exist.

He was suddenly surprised by one of the larger sea-horses saying, "I think we are a big surprise to your visitor, Matilda." Winston, noticing that the sea-horse had not called her Queen Matilda stepped back in surprise when the other sea-horses floated towards her.

Amused at the impact the sea-horses were having on Winston, Queen Matilda whispered, "What do you think?"

For just a moment, Winston was again lost for words. "Sorry Your Majesty, what did you say?" asked Winston, not taking his eyes of the lagoon.

"I asked what you thought of our sea-horses," Queen Matilda repeated warmly.

"They are the most beautiful and unusual sea-horses I have ever seen. They're not like the ones back in the zoo aquarium. These are truly splendid." As he finished, he was surprised to see one of the creatures give him a wink as it swam past.

"Thank you for telling us we are beautiful. You must know our friend, Beauty?" it said. Winston, lost for words, wondered if he'd ever speak again as he stared at the sea-horse smiling at him. Feeling a gentle tap on his leg, Winston looked down to see Marmaduke, with a big grin on his.

"Aren't you going to answer the sea-horse, Winston?" Marmaduke asked.

"Why er, er yes I think so," Winston stammered. He was about to respond when he noticed that several other sea-horses had come closer.

"Sorry, I forgot my manners. You really are the most wonderful sea-horses ever. And yes, I do know Beauty; she's out on a mission," he said. Realising what he'd done, he clasped a hand over his mouth and wondered if he was in for a warning. Instead he heard Queen Matilda say, "Don't worry Winston, our sea-horses are aware of all that's taking place. Now young man, what would you like to drink? Pick your colour and I'll pour it out."

Reluctantly taking his eyes from the floating sea-horses, Winston cast his eye over the variety of decanters. Stuck for choice, he asked, "Can I have some of that one, the one with mixed colours in, and later some of that blue please?"

"You can have both now if you like."

"Oh yes please," Winston replied excitedly. With the drinks poured out, Queen Matilda bid the sea-horses goodbye and closed the cabinet doors, much to Winston's dismay. Seeing the disappointment on Winston's face, Marmaduke explained, "The sea-horses prefer shade to light, so the doors are only opened for a short time."

"I understand." Hoping the sea-horses could still hear him, Winston called out, "Goodbye sea-horses." Content with his drinks, he made his way back to table.

While this was taking place at the cabinet, Krast had placed a tray of tea on the centre table. He made his excuses to leave, remarking on various works to he had complete.

"Time for tea, or in your case, Marmaduke, cream," Lucy called out.

"What did you think of the cabinet, my son?" asked Frances, smiling as she spoke.

"Fantastic. Mum, those sea-horses are just great. The ones back at the aquariums back home don't have the same colours as these," Winston replied, taking a drink from first one glass then the other. Amused at the way Winston was savouring his drinks, Lucy explained, "The sea-horses are from the royal lagoon, Winston. There are many more young ones in the other lagoon. Perhaps you will get to see them one day."

"I hope so," Winston replied wistfully, helping himself to another drink. Noticing Marmaduke had gone to where his saucer of cream was waiting, he thought there was something different, but didn't know what. Looking round, he suddenly realised that it was the lions. They had been by the map table, but now they were by the Queen's chair. How on earth had they got there?

At that moment he heard a voice say, "Hello there Marmaduke, enjoying the cream?"

Wondering who had spoken, Winston looked to see who had entered the room. To his surprise, he heard Marmaduke say, "Mm. I certainly am enjoying the cream, thank you."

"How are you? It's a while since we last spoke together," Marmaduke said. Curious as to who he was talking to, Winston asked, "Who are you talking to, Marmaduke? I don't see anyone else in the room."

"Why, my friends the lions," Marmaduke told him, licking the cream off his whiskers. Thinking he'd misheard, Winston gave a laugh and asked, "Did you say lions?"

"That's right, lions. Look, sitting close to the Queen's chair."

Staring at the lions, Winston tried to see if one of them actually spoke. Just as he was doing that, he suddenly jumped back when one of the lions said, "It's all right, we won't bite."

"Good day, young sir," another lion said. Staring back,

Winston wasn't sure if he should reply or run. Then he was surprised to see the lion wink at him. Not sure what to say or do, Winston stammered, "G - good day, Mr Lion."

"Come close, Winston, we won't bite. Correction, we bite if you are the enemy," said one of the other lions, in a teasing voice. Looking all round, Winston checked to make sure none of them had bared their teeth.

"Do you have names?" asked Winston, in a low cautious voice.

"Oh no, we are just called lions," replied the lion who'd spoken first.

"Would you like names?" Winston asked, still with caution in his voice.

"We've never thought about it. Would you like us to have names?"

Unable to take his eyes off the lions, Winston wondered if he'd made an error in asking if they would like names. Glancing across at Marmaduke, then turning to face the Queen, he wondered if he dare ask if they should have names.

Sensing his confusion, Queen Matilda said, "If you can think of suitable names, I'm sure the lions would like to have them."

Winston hesitated for a moment, then asked, "How did you get over here? I thought I saw you sitting over by the table?"

"Just a precaution young man, just a precaution," the lion repeated. Not sure if that needed a response, Winston went back to the subject of names, and asked, "Perhaps there are names you would like to be called by?"

"Never thought about a name," one of the lions said, with another of the lions adding, "It might be nice to have a name, like Marmaduke has."

"May I suggest Winston decides what you should be called?" Marmaduke replied, giving the lions a knowing wink.

"Well young Winston, have you decided what to call them?" Marmaduke asked.

"I'll have to think," Winston replied, as he placed the glass of blue drink on the table.

Absorbed in what was taking place; Queen Matilda suddenly said, "I wonder if everyone has arrived safely at their destinations?"

"Perhaps someone will let us know soon," Frances replied.

A moment of silence fell over the room. Winston was busy concentrating on suitable names for the lions, with Marmaduke sitting close beside him. Suddenly the sound of a door opening made them both jump. Marmaduke, noticing it was the side door, knew who would be coming into the room.

"Hello everyone," called out Princess Rubie. Surprised but pleased to see her daughter enter the room, Queen Matilda asked sternly, "Where have you been, Rubie? Your father was quite cross that you weren't here when he left to ride out to the Outlanders. He was very worried about you."

Embarrassed at her mother's stern words, Rubie explained in a low voice, "I was never in any danger of being caught, Mamma. I was with Ferdi and our friends." Suddenly noticing Marmaduke, she ran over and gave him a hug. "It's wonderful to see you again. I hope you're all right, and no one has been treating you badly?"

"I'm quite all right, thank you Rubie. Now please release my neck or you'll strangle me," Marmaduke said in a friendly voice. Releasing the cat, she noticed Winston sitting close by.

"Hello there, my name's Rubie, what's yours?" she said. Startled by what was happening, Winston could only reply, "Winston."

"Rubie," Queen Matilda called out, "would you come and meet Frances?" Not wanting to upset her mother further, Rubie made her way to where Frances was sitting. Passing Lucy on the way Rubie greeted her, "Hello Lucy. You and Sam have been gone for such a long time. Are you home for good now?"

Lucy smiled warmly at Rubie and replied, "That I don't know, Rubie. It will depend on the outcome of the battles." Queen Matilda stepped towards Rubie and introduced her to Frances.

"Rubie, this is Frances. You have heard your father and me discuss the invaluable help Frances and her husband Bertram gave us in the past." Moving closer to Frances, Rubie held out her hand and politely said, "Pleased to meet you. May I call you Frances?"

"Why yes, Princess Rubie. It's lovely to see you," Frances replied, as she shook hands with Rubie.

"Please call me Rubie. It's much shorter and friendlier than Princess Rubie," said the Princess, releasing Frances' hand. Casually observing Winston and Marmaduke, Rubie could see they were busy conversing with the lions. Rubie whispered to her mother, "Who is that person with Marmaduke?"

"That's Winston, son of Frances and Bertram," Queen Matilda replied. Wanting to return to Marmaduke, Rubie made her way over to join him. She took a seat beside the cat and was cordially greeted by the lions.

"Winston is thinking of names for us," said one of the lions.

"What a good idea. Perhaps we can think together?" Rubie suggested.

Before Winston could answer, the throne room door opened to reveal an anxious-looking Krast. With one thought in mind, to let the Queen know the warning birds had returned, Krast failed to see expressions of concern on the people's faces.

Queen Matilda stopped what she was doing and asked Krast to tell her what was troubling him. She feared bad news, so it was a relief to all when Krast told them, "The warning birds have returned. King Alfreston and his group are safe. So are Beauty and her group. Apparently the two groups are resting for the night."

"Oh thank goodness for that. Is there any word on how DaVendall's group is getting on?"

Not recalling the birds mentioning DaVendall, Krast slowly replied, "No word at the moment. I think his group might be out of reach, or in a dangerous position for the warning birds."

"I guess that could be the answer," murmured Queen Matilda. Realising Krast hadn't left the room, Queen Matilda turned to him and asked, "Please make sure the birds are well tended, Krast." With a quiet response, "Yes, Your Majesty," Krast made his way out of the throne room. Relieved to know the warning birds were back and that at least two of the groups were safe, Queen Matilda asked Lucy and Frances to come and help prepare the rooms that had been set aside for the injured.

Leaving Rubie, Winston and Marmaduke in discussion with the lions, Frances commented, "I suppose the lions will have names by the time we come back?" Murmuring their agreement, Queen Matilda, Lucy and Frances left the throne room.

Chapter Nine

In the Dungeons

With events taking place at the castle, and the three groups well on their way, the prisoners in the dungeon were expressing their despair of ever being freed. Many of the prisoners had been held in captivity for so long they'd given up hope of ever seeing daylight again. Now, sitting hunched over on damp and grimy floor, they began to sense a heavy, evil atmosphere around the tower.

Just then the stomping feet of guards were heard approaching the cells. Holding their breath, the prisoners waited for the inevitable slamming of a door, indicating they had selected a cell and were about to remove a prisoner. They heard clunking keys being rattled against the cell bars. It was a relief to the occupants of each cell when the guards moved onto the next. The sound of thundering boots and the noise of keys dragged along the cell bars set everyone's nerves on edge. Desperately trying to discover who they had come for, the prisoners waited anxiously, not uttering a word.

It wasn't long before a coarse voice called out, "'Urry up, we gotta find the right one fer Zanus." Muttering and cursing at having to do a menial's job, the guards continued in their search for the wanted prisoner. As they moved further along the passage and passed a number of cells, the noises stopped. Now everyone was aware that the guards had found the cell the unfortunate prisoner was in.

They heard the door crash against the wall as one of the guards shouted, "'E's in 'ere all right. This is where we left 'im to rot." Entering the cell, the guards raised the lanterns to eye level as they began searching for the wanted man. Peering at each prisoner in turn, their cold dark eyes sent shivers of fear through the prisoners' bodies. Disregarding the screams as they trod carelessly on the prisoners, the guards grunted and moaned, still not seeing who they wanted.

Just as one of the guards was about to kick away what he thought was a lump of filthy straw, he realised the lump was the prisoner they were looking for. Seeing the lantern being placed near to his face, the prisoner kept his head down and tried to move closer to the back wall. Then he felt a rough hand on his chin. Before David could move any further, he was staring into two pairs of cold dark eyes.

"'Ere 'e is, lets get 'im to Zanus afore 'e gives us a whippin'," shouted a guard. Giving David a harsh kick, they ordered him to get up and follow them. Enraged that he hadn't submitted to their threats, they pushed aside the nearby prisoners and dragged David over the cell floor. Ignoring the cries from his fellow prisoners to leave him alone, they continued on their way to the door.

Jayne sat in horror as she saw the guards dragging her husband along the floor. Begging them to leave him alone, she tried to reach him, but was harshly pushed aside by the guards. She wasn't prepared to give up as easily as that, despite the pain she was in. But when she tried to push herself up off the floor she discovered she had very little strength left. She found it impossible to stand, and fell back onto the floor. Then she began to plead for David's life.

Disturbed by Jayne's screams and pleadings, David continued to struggle in the hope of freeing himself from the guards. Unfortunately, the more he struggled the more the guards laughed. With the captured prisoner adding to their troubles the guards quickly became irritated with David and began viciously kicking and punching him.

Scared, but furious at what the guards were doing to their friend, several of the prisoners tried to grab the guards' legs. The reward for this action was more vicious kicks, followed by cruel laughter. Fearing his fellow prisoners would be severely punished, David called out in a pained voice, "Please don't, my friends, you will be punished if you continue."

David continued to struggle against the guards, even though he knew it was useless. One thing he was sure of was that he wasn't going to make it easy for them. Noticing they were close to the cell door, David tried one last attempt to get free. What he hadn't expected to see was Bacjo leading other prisoners in attacking the guards. But the guards laughed cruelly as they kicked the prisoners away.

The guards began taunting David about the beating he was about to receive, telling him it was for defying Zanus. Not taking in what the guards had said, and being weak from lack of food and the continual beatings, David wondered if he would survive whatever lay in store.

On reaching the torture room, the guards threw David through the door and onto the floor. David knew of the various instruments within this terrible room and felt sure they would be using their favourite, the whip. As he lay on the floor helpless to prevent what they were about to do, he found himself thinking of the many friends that had died in this room from the torture they had endured. One thing he vowed to himself - he would not die without a fight.

Laughing raucously, the guards made their way over to where he lay and hauled him up off the floor. As they tied him to the iron rungs, David couldn't help noticing how bloodied the wall was. Feeling them tear the blood-matted shirt from his back, he tried to prepare himself for what he knew would be coming. As he hung limply from the rungs he could hear the whip being thrashed through the air. Tensing himself ready for impact, he screamed as the whip made contact with his bare back. Before he knew it he felt the muscle-tearing jerk on his arms as his legs gave way. Burning pain shot through his arms as they took the full impact of his swinging body. Going in and out of consciousness, he lost track of how many times the whip lashed across his body. Convinced it was near the end for him he almost relished the release, as numbness began to overwhelm his body.

Gathering his thoughts for one moment, he strained to hear

if any other prisoners were there. Tears running down his face, he suddenly thought of Lottie. With a fragmented vision of his daughter waving farewell as he and Jayne set off to the cave, he doubted he would ever see her again.

Left hanging on the wall, he suddenly became aware that the guards were returning.

"He ain't gone, 'as 'e? 'E ain't movin'," said one guard. Tentatively moving closer to David, the other guard uttered, "I ain't gonna tell Zanus if 'e is. I don't want no whippin'."

"'E's gotta be dead, 'e ain't movin'," said the other.

Taking advantage of the light thrown out by the flame, through half-closed eyes David thought he saw other prisoners. He strained his eyes to take another look, but he could not be sure. Turning to telepathy, he could only manage to say a few words. "Is there anyone in here with me? My name is David." He was about to try once more when he suddenly heard a weak voice enter his thoughts.

"Hello David. It's me, Kira," came back a voice. Kira was one of the Ziphers who had been held in the same cell as himself.

"Why have you been tortured?" asked David. "Don't they know Ziphers can't speak?"

"Zanus is going to torture all the prisoners in turn," said Kira. "He thinks you told us where the stone is." Exhausted by the effort of using telepathy, she told him, "Tired, can't say any more, hope to see you soon." Closing her mind to any further telepathic communication, she failed to hear the sadness in David's voice when he apologised for getting them all involved.

As he lay prone against the wall and alone with his thoughts, he soon sensed someone approaching. He pretended to be unconscious, and it took all his strength not to respond to the rough hands which suddenly grasped his arms. Stifling a cry of pain, he felt one of the guards undoing the iron cuffs from his wrists.

"Get up 'uman!" grunted the guard. "Yer might fink yer dead, but yer ain't, not yet." Laughing at what he'd said he gave another David another kick and grabbed hold of his arm.

Noticing his partner hadn't taken hold of David's other arm

the guard shouted in a coarse voice, "Get 'is arm, yer idiot, we ain't 'ere to jus' guard 'em, we're 'ere ter fight." Having suffered being tortured and now being dragged from the torture room, David hoped he was going to be taken back to the cell. That hope was soon dashed when he felt himself stumbling up the now familiar slimy steps. Wondering how much more his pain-racked body could take, he tried to shut out the jeering guards. But then he heard his daughter's name mentioned. Waiting to hear if anything more was going to be said, he became aware that the taunts concerned Crocanthus. He tried to wait patiently to hear what else they would let slip. Fearing Lottie had been captured, he was terrified of what they would do to his daughter. At that moment, he suddenly caught more of their conversation.

"I 'ope that Crocanthus gets that stone fer Zanus. If 'e fails it's a whippin' 'e'll get," said one guard.

What concerned David now was how Crocanthus had got to Lottie. The guards suddenly laughed in his face and told him what Zanus had planned for his precious brat. Receiving another harsh kick from a guard, David closed his eyes and breathed in deeply, trying to absorb the pain inwardly. Slowly releasing his breath, he half opened his eyes. He realised they were only a short distance from Zanus' room.

Without any warning he was given a vicious kick that landed squarely on his ribs. Despite the pain and with the thought of Lottie in the hands of Zanus, David felt a sudden surge of energy soar through his painful body. Surprising the guards, he crawled towards the door and warned them, "If any harm has comes to my daughter, or any of my friends, I will kill you." Exhausted by his sudden burst of energy he lay limply on the floor.

Laughing raucously, one of the guards taunted, "An' 'ow yer gonna do that 'uman? Yer'll be dead afore yer can kill us." Wishing he had the energy to carry out his threat, David couldn't even find the strength to reply. Then a studded boot landed on his thigh.

"Get up," one of the guards ordered. David grimaced, but he was determined not to give the guards the satisfaction of knowing how much pain he was in.

"Yer best tell Zanus 'oo 'as the stone, an' where it is," said a guard coarsely. Wondering why Zanus was so desperate to possess the orange stone, David also wondered what made his newly-acquired friend so important to this monstrous man.

As they arrived outside Zanus' room he felt a tremor of fear coming from the guards on hearing Zanus' voice cursing and swearing at his cowardly troopers. Using this to his advantage, David looked up at the guards with swollen bruised eyes and taunted, "Scared of him, aren't you?"

"Shut yer mouf," warned one of the guards, at the same time as another guard landed a punch on David's back. Annoyed that this prisoner had noticed their reluctance to open the door, one of the guards uttered, "Yer'll get more whippin's if yer don't tell."

Finally opening the door, they pushed David through the door and watched in cruel amusement as he stumbled and fell. They failed to notice the angry glare Zanus was giving them. With the increased pain from this latest attack and his mind still on Lottie, David attempted to stand up. Before he could complete the move one of the surly guards placed a heavy boot on David's back, pushing him back down. There was a pungent smell of sweat, sour ale and raw meat, which made David feel sick. Striving to stay alert, he recalled how he'd rescued the gem from the boulder, but he shook that thought from his mind in fear of Zanus reading his thoughts.

Lying prone on the steps, David's mind began to wander. Was he going to end up like one those other poor creatures hanging off the walls round the tower? Zanus rose from his seat slowly and deliberately and swaggered forward. He halted a short distance away from him, then slowly and deliberately drew a large dagger from his belt. Stroking the blade back and forth on the palm of his hand, Zanus placed it on David's left cheek and drew it slowly across the skin. David felt warm blood run down his face. He wiped his cheek with a piece of the tattered shirt sleeve. Trying not to show the fear he was feeling inside, he wondered if this was going to be a long-drawn-out death.

"Where is the stone?" roared Zanus. "'Oo 'as it? Tell me, or yer'll get worser cuts." David's immediate response was to wonder how he could get away from this uncouth beast. Failing to answer Zanus brought on another warning, "Where is it? I demand yer to tell me."

With the blood from his face mingling with the dried blood on his body, David knew it was fatal not to answer. Before he could utter a word Zanus was leaning over him, almost touching his face.

"Where's the stone? 'Oo 'as it?" he demanded, through clenched teeth. He placed the dagger blade on David's right cheek. He let it stay there for a while, then slowly and deliberately cut deeply into the cheek. There came a stream of blood, and David could feel himself becoming faint. Not wanting to satisfy Zanus' lust for power, he drew in as much breath as he could. He closed his eyes, then started to regain his balance and wiped some of the blood off his face. He stared into Zanus' cold black eyes and replied in a firm and determined voice, "I don't know where the stone is and if I did I wouldn't tell you."

Angered that this human would openly defy him, Zanus swiped his heavy crooked stick across David's body. He laughed cruelly as David sank back to the floor.

"Bring the other 'uman, an' 'urry up!" he roared.

Dazed and weary as he was, David's fear overcame all that on hearing what Zanus had just shouted. Convinced he was going to see Lottie, he blinked rapidly, desperate to clear the blood and sweat from his eyes. As he did this he struggled to remain calm and concentrate on not losing consciousness. He could feel his heart racing.

Ignoring the jeers and taunts coming from Zanus, David suddenly heard the door slam against the back wall. He wriggled into a better position, hoping to see who would be coming into the room. Just as the person stepped through the door, his view was blocked by the guards. It seemed an eternity to David before he finally caught sight of who the newcomer was.

It was not Lottie but Norman Mansfield, the man who had betrayed them. Although he was relieved and thankful that it wasn't Lottie, David felt a sudden desire to kill Mansfield for his treachery. He wondered how this man whom he had once called his friend could have done such a wicked thing.

Incensed with rage, David attempted to grab hold of the

informer. "Don't try it, 'uman, 'e's mine to deal with," warned Zanus. The guards yanked David away from the steps and sent him sprawling on the floor. Amused by what had taken place, Zanus stared at Norman and jeered, "'E wants to kill yer. That's nice, innit?"

Not concerned with David, Norman was more nervous about what Zanus intended to do with him. Fearing it would be something harsher than the whipping he'd received earlier, he tried to edge away from Zanus.

David made no effort to hide his feelings, but he knew he would get his moment. Staring directly at Norman he wished he could convey this telepathically, but soon realised how dangerous it would be to others if Norman possessed the same gift. Watching Norman calmly stroll round the room, David guessed he was trying to give the impression he was a friend of Zanus', however, David couldn't help noticing that he maintained a safe distance away from him.

His pain pushed to one side, David shouted, "You despicable demon, how could you do this to your friends? Through you, Crocanthus has been sent to bring Lottie to that vile creature sitting up there. How could you do such a dreadful thing?" As he vented his anger David was deaf to the jeering and raucous laughter coming from Zanus, and others in the room. Instead, he concentrated all his attention on Norman. Through clenched teeth he warned, "Be certain of one thing. If any harm comes to Lottie, no matter what happens I will find you and kill you." Taking in a quick breath, and with all the contempt he could muster David added, "I will never forgive you, Mansfield."

Although Norman felt somewhat uncomfortable in David's presence, he couldn't help noticing the state of David's battered and bleeding body. Seeing this reminded him of the severe beating he'd received from Crocanthus after he was discovered entering Dofstram, which had resulted in him betraying Lottie, Norman felt little remorse. He had convinced himself long ago it was the only offering he could make to save his life.

Standing some distance away and staring back at David, Norman smirked, "Aah, your daughter Lottie, I know her well. Let's put it this way Mr David Montmerencie, it was her life or mine. Look at the state of you. Face bleeding all over the floor, bruised and beaten within an inch of your life. Tell me, what would you have done if you had been in my place?"

Looking straight at this informer and aware of how they'd met, David replied in as strong a voice as he could.

"I wouldn't have become a coward and a traitor like you. I hope you haven't involved her Aunt Jean. But then I wouldn't put anything past you."

Conscious of David's affection for Jean, Norman sneered, "Well now David Montmerencie, that's something you might never know." Then he leaned towards David as far as he dared and added, "And where's that know-all wife of yours? Beaten and bruised like you?"

"Shut yer moanin! Yer can 'ave yer fight later," shouted Zanus. Waiting for the moment to get to Norman, David missed seeing the guards' raised fists until they pounded down on his tortured body. But as he gasped for air he knew he wasn't going to let Norman think he was getting away with this. Drawing in as much breath as he could, he looked straight at him and warned, "One day, Norman Mansfield, you will pay for what you have done." He saw no remorse from Norman only a sneer.

Tired of hearing the two men ranting at each other, Zanus roared, "Shut up! Now, where's Crocanthus? I need 'im 'ere." He leapt from his seat, giving his crooked stick a couple of hard bangs on the floor. Stomping round the room, he suddenly remembered Crocanthus was still in the other land. He span round to face Norman and bellowed, "You. Informer. Go back to yer land an' send 'im 'ere." Then in a more menacing voice he hissed, "Remember this, 'uman, if yer don't return, I 'ave ways of finding yer."

Stumbling away from Zanus, Norman thought of the torture room and all the horrors it held. He assured Zanus he would return, and Zanus sat back on his seat. David turned his attention to Norman again and demanded, "Why? How could you do this to us?"

"Look at you, David the wonderful cave explorer. Well you don't look so wonderful now. Just think my life was spared by offering up your daughter," Norman sneered in reply.

"I wouldn't have offered up my friend's daughter on a plate like you have," David uttered in a low warning voice.

Zanus ordered the guards to take David to the cell, then told Norman to be on his way. Only half listening to what Zanus had said, David's one thought was still to try and get at Norman. But the more he struggled to free himself of the guards, the more he was met with further punches until he collapsed on the floor.

Anxious to be free of Zanus' wrath, the guards dragged David through the door. Slamming the door behind them, they continued to drag him unceremoniously down the grimy stone steps and back to his cell. As the guards approached the cells, they could hear the prisoners scuttling about on the straw floor like rats. Laughing raucously at knowing how they were feared, the guards wasted no time in opening the cell door. They dragged David inside and dropped him disdainfully on the floor.

The prisoners waited in silence until they were sure it was safe to move. They heard the loud clunk of the key as it locked the cell door. Jayne started crawling her way to where David lay. Finally sitting herself beside him, she was shocked to see the vicious cuts to his face. Gently tapping him on the arm she placed her mouth close to his ear and whispered, "David, can you hear me? What made them cut your face?" then as if to herself she added, "Weren't the whippings bad enough?" She began gently wiping away the blood that was still flowing down his face.

Lying still and trying not to grimace, David left Jayne to tend to his wounds. It was some time before he was able to breathe properly, owing to the pains shooting through his body. Thinking they might ease off if he moved, he gingerly turned onto his side. Gently grasping Jayne's wrist, he eased it away.

"I'm OK, love. I just need a minute to get my breath." Breathing more easily, he continued, "I wasn't harmed, well not much, only a few cuts and bruises from the guards. These cuts were a donation from Zanus."

Jayne whispered, "Why did he do that? These will take a while to heal. He's cut them quite deep. David, please tell us what happened, and don't leave anything out. It's important we know. We all know how cruel these Zanuthians are. Remember what's happened since we were first brought to that bully."

David had been wondering how much he could reveal without upsetting his wife any more, but after hearing her request he decided to tell all. Taking a breath, he noticed many of their cell mates had edged closer.

"Give me a moment," he said. Looking up at his wife he whispered, "I will tell you everything." She gave David a warm smile.

They suddenly heard something rustling through the straw and heard a voice, which they instantly recognised as Petra's. On hearing what had happened to David, she nervously asked, "Did Zanus say he wanted other prisoners brought to his room?" Taking in the nervousness in Petra's voice, and aware she was waiting for him to respond, David cleared his throat and started to relay what happened.

"I didn't hear Zanus ordering further prisoners to be taken to him," he said. "He's desperate to find a certain stone. After I was taken from here my first trip was the infamous torture room. At first I couldn't see anything as it was pitch black, but I suppose you heard the screams just as I did. At first I thought I was the only one there, but when the guards came to see if I was still alive I could see other prisoners. I thought some were no longer with us, but I couldn't be sure. The screams made me aware that there were others being given a taste of the guard's favourite weapons."

Halting for a moment to catch his breath, he could hear the gasps of horror coming from his friends. About to continue, he listened as Jayne whispered, "We heard the screaming. It was horrible. Could you see who the prisoners were?"

"I'm afraid not. As soon as I was strapped to those dreadful iron rungs the whipping started," David explained. Taking another look at the cuts on his back, Jayne slowly stated, "I can see that, David. You've hardly any material left to cover your back. I've treated your cuts as best as I can."

"Thank you, Jayne. I think you should know what happened when I was taken to Zanus' room. I don't need to tell you how rough the guards were, you've all been on the receiving end of their violence. Almost immediately, Zanus was demanding I tell him where the stone was and who had it. He was outraged when I couldn't tell him. That was when he took his dagger to my face. He probably thought I would reveal all. He was wrong, I wouldn't tell him even if I knew. Deciding I needed further encouragement to tell him, he shouted someone else to be brought in.

"When Zanus said that I froze. Thinking it must be you Jayne, or possibly Lottie he was shouting for, I came out in a cold sweat and wondered what I could do to protect you. I can't tell you what a relief it was when neither of you came through the door. But it was a shock to see who it was."

Suddenly David's mind was flooded with telepaths entering his mind asking who the newcomer had been.

"It was our dearly beloved friend, Norman Mansfield." He felt his anger returning and took a moment to calm himself down. He then continued, "I was desperate to get my hands on him. I thought at one time I might get the chance to strangle him, but no luck. Zanus and his brutes stopped me."

There were loud gasps, but no one seemed to want to say anything. David wiped away a drop of blood from his face and continued in a more sombre voice.

"This will be of interest to us all. Zanus has ordered Norman to go back to our land and send Crocanthus back here. Norman must have been thinking he would be allowed to stay there, because in the next breath Zanus ordered the informer to come back, or else. You should have seen Norman's face."

Bacjo asked, "Why would Zanus want the stone?"

"That's something I wondered too. I can only think he might want it for its powers." He sat with his head in his hands, partly in despair and partly owing to the burning sensation of his injuries.

"Can I do anything to help?" Jayne whispered.

"Not really. It just stings a little, nothing worse. I wish I could find a way of getting us all out of here." He turned to Jayne and said, "I just hope Lottie is safe." As he said it he jerked back as a sudden thought that came to mind.

"I had a momentary thought when Zanus was demanding the stone. Is it possible it has found its way to Lottie?"

"David," Jayne whispered, "I agree we shouldn't mention

any names, but how would they know the stone had been given a name?"

"I've thought about that, Jayne. Do you remember when the stone was cleaned and you referred to how it shone? I know that wasn't exactly what you said, but they might just be clever enough to put two and two together. Even though they'll still be looking for an orange stone, we don't want to give them any help in finding it."

"If they are together do you think Lottie will be able to join us?" said Jayne. Petra whispered, "Hush Jayne, we don't know who's listening. But if they are together perhaps the stone will be able to contact us telepaths."

"Wow Petra, I hadn't thought that far," David whispered. "I know I've tried many times to reach our friends, but I have never been successful." Immediately he had finished speaking, many of the prisoners called out verbally and telepathically, "Me too."

As the murmurings continued, Jayne turned to David and asked, "Do you think they could be together? Do you really think it's possible?" David waited a moment before responding, as his thoughts had turned to the danger they could all be in.

"It could be possible," he said. "I wonder if that's why Crocanthus and others were sent to capture Lottie. Jayne, you remember how vicious Zanus turned when he discovered we'd released the orange stone from that rock. Added to the demands he made just now, it could be possible." Remembering his conversation with Kira, he added, "While I was in the cell I called out to see who was there. Kira, one of the Zipher people, had been badly beaten. She told me Zanus is convinced we have told the prisoners where the stone is. As a result, he is going to have all the prisoners punished until they reveal where it is."

Suddenly through the silence came a quiet voice into his thoughts: "I fear this must be them preparing to do battle." Not recognising the voice immediately, he telepathically asked, "Who said that?" It wasn't long before the quiet voice of Kira replied, "David it's me, Kira."

"Kira where are you? It's so dark in here I can barely see." Listening to the rustle of straw, he suddenly felt a hand on his arm. He knew instantly it was Kira. They smiled at each other.

"When did they let you go? Are you all right?" he asked her.

With her eyes on David, she telepathically told him, "They brought me back to the cell after they took you to Zanus. They weren't happy when they realised I couldn't speak. Being idiots none of them could sign, so they gave me another taste of the whip then returned me to the cell." Giving David a smile, she continued, "I wouldn't have told them about the stone no matter what they did."

Aware Jayne wouldn't know of his telepathic conversation, David reverted to speech, which everyone could hear.

"I'm so sorry they involved you, Kira, but it's a relief to see you here with us," he said. "They are absolute beasts with that whip. I hope they didn't use it too much?"

Jayne leaned across and said, "Me too, Kira. Would you like me to take a look at your back? I know what state David's back is in. I might be able to ease some of the soreness." Lowering her voice to a whisper, she added, "I agree with David we must not disclose any information about the stone." Then in a more tentative voice, she added, "Who knows what lies in store for us?" Having listened to the conversation, Bacjo whispered, "I don't know how any friend could betray another."

"That's something I haven't been able to work out. Why would this man do such a terrible thing?" David commented. Without showing any surprise that David had heard him whispering, Bacjo became aware of Petra edging her way towards him.

"Bacjo, I thought the battle was over. I guess this is another of Zanus' plots to take over our land," she uttered nervously. Taking hold of her hand, Bacjo replied, "I'm afraid so, Petra. You know we've had to face so many battles, but I fear this will be the biggest." Then, voicing his own thoughts, he said, "If only we could get out of this place. We'd be able to help rid these bullies from our land."

David noticed how eerily quiet the people were. Guessing they were listening to the conversation he added, "I've had an awful thought. Suppose the Old Crone got Zanus to send his bullies to retrieve the stone. This might be what led Zanus to believe it could be with Lottie."

Recalling when she first saw the stone and remembering the

state it was in, Jayne quietly added, "They won't know the stone has changed shape. They'll still be looking for a dull, misshapen orange stone. I hope that's made it harder for them. Let's hope they never find out how the stone has changed. If it is with Lottie it should remain safe." Then as an afterthought she said, "Do you think they know it sometimes glows?"

"That's a good point, Jayne. That why it's even more important that it must always be referred to just as the stone," David whispered, "We mustn't give anything away, or their lives would really be in danger. But then, if it's only the stone they want why would Zanus want Lottie as well?"

Suddenly, a timid voice from the corner of the cell replied, "I've had a thought. It could be he wants to get Lottie here as extra punishment to you and Jayne. Or it could be they will use her to get you to tell Zanus where the stone is."

Taking hold of David's arm, Jayne whispered, "I pray they don't succeed in getting Lottie. I'm terrified of that hateful man getting his hands on her."

"Me too, Jayne. The thought of him or Crocanthus with Lottie is not something I want to think about, at least not until we get free of this place. Then we'll see what happens." Staring into the blackness of the cell, David's thoughts were wandering off to what he'd like to do to those two men.

Feeling his arm being shaken, he looked to see who it was. Having gained David's attention, Mittoy signed, "I can feel the anger and frustration you are going through. Perhaps this might be the best time to concentrate on how we can get away from here."

Placing a tender hand on Mittoy's, David stated, "You're right, Mittoy. I should be using my thinking energy on how to get us out of here."

"I saw what you signed Mittoy, and I feel the same, but we've tried so many ways to get away and every time we've failed," said Norda in a wistful voice. Immersed in their conversation, they failed to see Bacjo edging closer to them, they jumped in surprise when he whispered, "I've been thinking. I wonder why Zanus ordered that horrible informer to go and bring back Crocanthus? Could it be that Crocanthus has captured your daughter and possibly the stone?"

Shocked at what Bacjo had said, Jayne wished at that moment that she had the telepathic ability David had. Then an idea came to her mind. In a firm but quiet voice, she said, "This would a good time for all the telepaths to join minds. We need to try and reach someone outside the tower. I wish I had the ability, but I haven't, so come on all you telepaths, get your minds together."

Turning to Mittoy she asked, "Would you please make sure everyone is aware of what I've asked?" Without wasting any time, Mittoy concentrated on reaching the minds of the telepaths, telling them to join their minds together and he would relay Jayne's idea. With minds gathered, Mittoy explained, "Jayne has asked all telepaths to join minds. When David gives the word we will try and get through to any telepath outside Zorax. Jayne hopes that by us all joining minds we might be successful in breaking through that swirling mist."

Before assuring Jayne he had done what she asked, Mittoy made one further request: "Please remember to inform the non-telepaths what we will be attempting." Satisfied that everyone would be informed of what had been proposed Mittoy, brought his thoughts back to wait for David's signal. Acknowledging the presence of Mittoy, David felt a sudden surge of minds as the telepaths declared they were ready.

"Well done, everyone," David replied telepathically. "Now, we will need to use all our strength of mind and concentrate on trying to contact any telepath beyond the tower. It seems we've all tried on our own, but have failed. I'm not sure if that grey mist is the only reason we failed, but we have to try and break through it."

"I hope we can. I know when I tried, I failed too," signed Mittoy.

"Same here," called out another.

"And me," said another.

Waiting for the other telepaths to finish speaking, David then asked, "If you are ready to concentrate as one, I'll relay a message and then we'll repeat it." Agreeing with David, they waited anxiously, ready to repeat the message. Feeling the telepaths were ready, David concentrated his mind and began.

"If there are any telepaths picking up our thoughts please try to respond," he said. "If you are unable to do this, please pass a message to King Alfreston. Tell him there are many prisoners in Zanus' dungeon." Thinking that was a long enough message, David urged the telepaths to try and repeat the message as one. As before, he felt the power of all telepaths becoming one. Giving a signal for everyone to speak at the same time, they set about relaying the message. The impact of so many telepaths repeating the same message seemed to give them hope. But, after a while, having failed to get any response, Mittoy telepathically asked, "Can we try one more time? You never know, we might be lucky this time."

"Are you strong enough to try one more time?" asked David. His mind was filled with replies of 'yes'. Concentrating their minds once more, they set about sending out their telepathic message.

Exhausted after so many attempts, Sanso weakly stated telepathically, "It's no good David. We don't seem to be able to get beyond the mist."

"I think we should let our other friends know we haven't been successful on this attempt, but tell them we will try again." responded David. "A big thank you for trying my friends, perhaps next time we will be able to break through the misty barrier. We should free our minds and get some rest." Withdrawing his mind from the telepaths, he noticed several sad faces looking in his direction and knew they must have heard of the failed attempts. Disappointed at not achieving what they set out to do, David's thoughts turned to wondering how they could escape.

Just then he felt something digging into his leg. Thinking it was a lump of stale straw, he moved to one side and attempted to brush it away. Then he suddenly realised it wasn't straw and that it must be something attached to his tattered trousers. Easing his hand down to the torn pocket he suddenly let out a quiet yell when he felt his fingers touch something solid. Drawing his hand carefully from the torn pocket, he realised it was Letswick's compass. He had forgotten all about the compass and was surprised that it had managed to stay in his pocket. Raising it to eye level, he studied it, wondering if it held the answer to their predicament.

As he opened and closed the compass case, a narrow beam of light shot out from it. Fearful the guards might have seen, it he closed the lid instantly. Not hearing any sound, he began turning the compass round, trying to discover if it held the key to their freedom. Remembering the light which had shone when he opened the lid, he wondered if the answer lay within the compass itself.

While thinking this he opened the lid again, and once again a beam of light came from it. Staring at the dial and wondering if there was some way of discovering its hidden secret, he was disappointed at not seeing what he had hoped for. He snapped shut the compass lid and sat staring into the darkened cell.

He sat for some time with his own thoughts, making a conscious effort not to let the situation beat him. He turned the compass over in his hand and slowly opened the lid just enough to let a small beam of light shine through. Apart from the light it still looked to him like other compasses he'd used. However, aware that this was Letswick's compass, he reasoned it might hold the key to their escape.

He began to study every part of the compass, hoping he'd missed a hidden clue. Sensing he was being observed, he whispered, "I was hoping this compass would show us a way out." Turning the compass needle to varying compass points, he soon discarded the idea. Reluctantly he closed the lid and placed the compass back in the pocket he'd recovered it from. Then he murmured, "I'm sorry, but it seems the compass isn't the answer to our escape. What with that and not being able to break through that weird mist, I fear we will be here for a while longer."

Hearing the despondent tone in her husband's voice, Jayne sidled closer to him and took hold of his hand. "It was worth a try, David. You never know, perhaps some of your thoughts got through," she whispered. From the murmurings echoing round the cells David knew he wasn't the only one feeling disappointed. He decided to ask if the telepaths would try again. With a firm assurance that they would, it wasn't long before all the telepaths merged in David's mind.

As before, they waited for David to give the signal, then as one voice they sent the message, "Please answer if you can hear us." They all waited. Then, thinking he had heard something, David asked, "Did any of you hear that?" But receiving a negative response, he reluctantly put it down to wishful thinking.

As he sat pondering over what could be causing the mist, he took the compass from his pocket and began unconsciously opening and closing the lid again. As he vacantly stared at the compass, his thoughts turned to Norman Mansfield. "I wonder what made me think of him," David uttered not taking his eyes off the compass. "Why did Norman turn against us? I thought he was a friend of Jean's." He turned to face Jayne. Surprised, Jayne turned towards him and asked, "What made you think of him at this time?"

"I don't really know. What I do know is that it's through him we're worried about the safety of Lottie," David answered in a sad voice.

Unable to avoid overhearing the conversation between husband and wife, Bacjo couldn't stop himself from saying, "Why would anyone do such a terrible thing to a friend?" To which another prisoner commented, "I wondered that myself. Perhaps he was offered something in return."

"I've just remembered something Norman said when I asked him that question," said David. His reply was, 'It was her life or his.' What he meant by that I don't know." The despair he felt was echoed in his voice when he uttered, "There's so much I don't understand."

Jayne refrained from speaking but placed an arm around his shoulders. Studying the now closed compass, David turned to her and whispered, "Do you think this will help us this time?"

"I don't know David. Before we had the help of Letswick," Jayne whispered back.

Opening the compass, David tried once more to discover if it had the answer to their escape. Twisting and turning it round he took another look from front to back, but still saw nothing different. Flicking the closed cover open, he turned the dial this way and that, wishing he could see some indication of a way out. Deciding this wasn't going to be of any help, he closed it and placed it back in his pocket.

"I wouldn't mind betting that Old Crone has something to do with the mist. I bet she's put one of her evil spells in it," David said to himself.

"We all think that too," whispered some of the prisoners. Surprised to hear so many voices making the same remark, David slowly stretched out his painful legs and said, "I guess as we're all thinking the same thing. That must be the answer."

David began shuffling back and forth to try and revive his numb feet. With the pins and needles gone, he shuffled along the straw-covered floor, trying to shake off the depression that was beginning to engulf him. Taking a slow walk round the cell and being careful not to tread on anyone he moved closer to the rear of the cell. Then he felt something or someone touch his leg. Stopping instantly he looked down to see what it was.

"Try not to worry David, someone will come and help us," Petra whispered. Surprised to hear her, he replied, "I hope so Petra. I just wish there was some way of contacting the outside."

"Someone will come," Petra whispered, trying to stop the tears which were ready to fall. Observing the tremor in Petra's voice, David took hold of her hand and sat silently beside her. Little did either of them know they were both thinking the same thought. Would they ever be rescued?

Chapter Ten

The strange light

Aware of the danger of the mission that faced them, Eram was eager to ride as far as possible before darkness fell. He reminded Binro to hold on tight and urged everyone to ride hard and fast. Following closely behind him, each person was concerned with what dangers they would have to deal with. They covered a vast amount of land and it wasn't long before the hills which sheltered the Forbidden Wood came into view.

By this time darkness was beginning to fall rapidly, a concern to them all. Wanting to find secure shelter, Binro tapped Eram's shoulder and waited for him to face him. Bringing the horse to a walking pace, Eram turned to Binro and watched as he signed, "Have you noticed how dark it has become?"

"I have," replied Eram. "Do you know a place which would be secure for us all to shelter?". Thinking of a place he'd seen on a previous occasion, but not sure if it would be large enough for everyone, Binro signed, "I think I know of somewhere. I'll have to check and see if it is big enough to hide everyone. I'll take a quick flight round and if it's not suitable I'll look for somewhere else."

"Take care, Binro," said Eram. "We aren't too far from that dreaded wood. While you are busy doing that, I will gather everyone together so we're ready to go when you return." With a quick flap of his wings Binro flew off, leaving Eram to complete his task.

While Eram and Binro had been discussing their plan, Lottie's thoughts had been on their forthcoming task. Her one big wish was to know if her parents were alive. Sensing Lottie's thoughts, Beauty waved her tail to gain Lottie's attention. It took a little while, but finally Lottie responded to the movement from her brooch.

"Are you all right, you aren't going to fall off are you? It's been a bit of a bumpy ride?" she said. Beauty responded, "I'm all right thank you Lottie. I was just thinking how quickly the darkness came."

"Is that why Eram is asking us to gather around him? I thought we were going to ride until we reached the wood," Lottie asked.

"We don't want to enter the wood at night, Lottie, it'll be dangerous enough in the daylight. Although the wood prevents much light getting through it should be enough for us to see what terrors lie waiting. If you look up, you'll see Binro has gone in search of a suitable place for everyone to be sheltered," Beauty explained in a low gentle voice. As she finished speaking, Beauty noticed Binro was flying back to Eram. Settling himself on the horse, he signed to say that there was a shelter large enough for all, just a little way away.

Relieved to see what Binro signed, Eram and Letswick agreed it would be wise to make for the shelter immediately. They urged the group to follow closely. "We only have a little further to travel, so we need to ride hard," Eram told them. Riding beside Letswick, she commented, "I've been looking for spy birds, but fortunately I haven't seen any. However, I think we will need to post guards through the night. You never know with him or Imelda what evil they will do."

"I agree with you. It could turn out to be a very long night," Letswick replied. Concentrating on where they were going, the group remained content to ride close to each other.

Just then, having had Lottie move her from under the cover of her jacket and into a position where she could see more clearly, Beauty suddenly caught sight of a flash of light in the far distance. She watched as it soared across the sky. At first she thought it was a rainbow, then she wondered if it was a streak of lightning, warning of a storm approaching. Before she had time to express her thoughts another stronger streak of light soared across the sky. Curious as to what it could be, Beauty reconsidered her previous thought. She knew this was no ordinary light.

From where she'd seen the light, Beauty's mind was on something completely different. Fully convinced she was correct, she took great care not to give away any of her thoughts. She was confident Lottie had not picked up on her thoughts. Not wanting to cause alarm, she calmly said, "I think we ought to ask Eram how much further the shelter is. I feel we could be in for a storm. I saw a flash of light which could be lightning."

Lottie wondered how Beauty could have seen a flash of light, as she couldn't recall seeing anything, but she knew that if Beauty had reported it - it must be real.

"Where did you see the light? I haven't seen anything," she said. "But I do think I could have heard a rumble of thunder." Lottie wondered what the noise had been, if not thunder.

"I only caught a sudden flash in the distance," Beauty told her. Then, recalling Lottie mentioning thunder, she added, "It sounded like thunder, but I wonder..." Beauty wasn't sure herself what it was; she had her suspicions, but wanted to be certain before saying anything.

Turning her attention to Dandy, Beauty asked, "Did you see a light, my friend?"

Breathing hard, the unicorn replied, "No, sorry, I haven't seen anything."

Concentrating her thoughts on telepathy, Beauty sought out the minds of Binro and Letswick and asked them the same question. Glancing at each other, they shrugged their shoulders.

Knowing her powers were greater than theirs and aware of the danger he would be in if their enemy knew she was there, Binro had a worrying thought. Gathering the telepathic minds, Binro reminded them that when referring to a certain item, it was to be called 'their friend'.

Assuring Lottie everything was all right, Beauty picked up on Binro entering her mind.

"What do you think, my friend? Will this make it a little safer for you?" he asked.

"Thank you, Binro, I hadn't thought of that, but yes it's

probably a good idea not to refer to me as the stone, or use any name," Beauty replied.

Riding on a little further, Binro thought about the beam of light his friend had mentioned. Surprising Eram, Binro manoeuvred Doran closer to Dandy and drew Beauty's attention. Telepathically he asked, "Have you seen something like this before? The beam of light, I mean."

He didn't have to wait long before he heard her reply, "I'm not sure what it was. I thought at first it was a flash of lightning, but I'm not sure." She was aware of that other telepaths might be listening.

Changing from telepathic conversation to verbal, Beauty whispered, "There were two streaks of light with not much time between them. At first I thought we were in for a storm but I'm certain it wasn't lightning." Beauty suddenly surprised them all when she added, "What I really wanted to say was, do you think it might just be possible one of the prisoners has the compass that belongs to Letswick?"

"Wow! My friend, whatever made you think of that?" gasped Letswick.

"Can't you explain what our friend was referring to, Letswick?" said Penny.

"It's just a possibility that it could be from the compass," said Beauty. "The one Letswick left behind on a previous attempted escape."

Then Letswick asked what many had been thinking. "If that is the case, would you be able to break through the mist and contact whoever has the compass?" he asked. Uncertain if they should attempt it there, Beauty turned to Eram and asked, "Are we near to where Binro found shelter?"

"Very near. May I suggest we move on? It's getting darker now and we don't want to be caught off guard," said Eram. Realising she hadn't answered Letswick's question, Beauty assured everyone she would think about it. Turning his horse in the direction of the shelter, Eram added, "I must say you certainly gave us all a surprise when you spoke of Letswick's compass."

Then Eram lifted everyone's spirits by saying, "Right

everyone, go over behind those shrubs. There's a makeshift cave we can use. Rest well and we'll make a move at early light."

Wanting to know more about Beauty's comment with regard to the light coming from a compass, Lottie decided this might be a good time to test her telepathy. Closing her mind to the sounds round about her, just as Beauty had taught her, Lottie channelled her thoughts to Beauty's.

"Do you really think the light might have come from Letswick's compass?" she asked. Taken by surprise at Lottie using telepathy, Beauty gently replied in the same manner, "Your telepathy is really coming along. The answer to your question is, I'm not sure. I don't want to get anyone's hopes up, but it is a possibility."

Having heard some of the telepathic conversation between Lottie and Beauty, Letswick drew Beauty's attention and suggested she should hear what Penny had to say. Wondering what Penny could have said that had caused Letswick to sound so concerned, Beauty called across, "What is it Penny? Are you all right?" Aware of the sudden silence after Beauty called her name, Penny noticed Doran had moved closer to Beauty. Being a little self-conscious she slowly and quietly told what she'd seen.

"I wasn't sure at first, but after hearing what you said I remembered seeing a flash of light soar across the sky. Like you, I thought it was lightning, but then another flash appeared. This one was different from any lightning I've ever seen."

Now Beauty knew her senses were correct; the light had indeed come from the compass. Drawing Penny's attention Beauty asked, "Penny, did you hear a rumbling sound soon after, like thunder?"

"I forgot about that," said Penny. "I did hear rumbling, but then I thought it didn't sound like any thunder I've heard before." Listening to their conversation, Lottie suddenly remembered hearing a rumbling noise earlier which she had passed off as thunder.

"That's funny Penny, I heard rumbling earlier. Thinking about it now, you're right, it didn't sound like any thunderstorm we've had back home." Having reached the shelter area and heard what Beauty and Penny had said, everyone was concerned with settling down the animals. While some dealt with the animals, others lit a fire to warm themselves and to give some light. In the meantime Nain and Rista had gone to prepare a makeshift meal. Thoughtfully watching the proceedings taking place and having spoken to the animals, Beauty realised they were too busy caring for their riders to notice any strange light. With regard to the compass, Beauty was aware an explanation was required, but that she mustn't raise their hopes about breaking through the mist.

Turning her thoughts to David, Beauty wondered again if he and Jayne were still alive. Then she began to wonder if it was David who had the compass. Hoping this might be possible, she hoped he would open the compass again.

She wished she could get through the mist to tell the compass holder to keep it open long enough for her to track its position. Observing how occupied everyone was, Beauty decided to give it a try. Closing her eyes, she concentrated hard on trying to break through. Having tried several times with no luck, she feared her thoughts might be picked up by Imelda. She remained in deep concentration. Closing her eyes, she brought forward a picture of David into her mind and tried mentally willing him to open the compass. Then, exhausted after her attempts, she could only wait to see if her thoughts would come to fruition.

Meanwhile, with the group now settled and enjoying the meal prepared by Nain and Rista, Beauty decided she would use this opportunity to explain about the compass.

"I know you must have heard some of the conversation between Penny and me," she began. "I think I ought to explain why I'm convinced the light came from the compass. Before I start, may I ask if the animals are settled?"

Eager to hear what Beauty was about to say, Letswick glanced over to where the animals were sheltered and reported that they were all safe and fed. "Let's hear what our friend has to say," whispered Letswick.

With a sea of expectant faces looking in her direction, Lottie placed Beauty on a nearby tree stump and said, "Right, my friend, we are all keen to hear what's going on." Beauty took a deep breath and began her explanation.

"First," she started, "The light which Penny and I saw was definitely not lightning. This left me with one other source, and that was the compass. On a previous rescue mission, Letswick left the compass to help light the darkened passages. My senses led me to believe someone had opened the compass. Whoever did so must have moved the part which throws out the bright light. When the compass was left by Letswick he didn't have time to explain how to create this signal. Having said that, we now have to hope it was a friend, and not one of Zanus' goons. Or worse still Zanus himself."

Ignoring the gasps, Beauty repeated, "I hope it hasn't fallen into the enemy's hands."

Ever curious, Penny asked, "Does this compass have any magical powers?"

With a gentle laugh, Beauty explained, "The compass doesn't have any particular magical powers, but what it does have is light. As you saw, it is a very powerful light. Whoever did this may not have been aware that they'd moved the dial to the beam selection. When it's moved to this particular position the light can penetrate anything. Not even Imelda can block it."

Silence followed the dreaded name. Then Dandy asked, "What about the dial? Would the light be powerful enough to reach us from the dungeons? Would it affect us animals?"

"I wondered that too, Dandy" said Lottie.

"The light can harm no friend," Beauty went on. "What it can do is search far into the sky, as Penny and I saw. However, whoever has the compass might not be aware of what the dial can do. If the person concerned thinks it will show them a way to escape I'm afraid it won't. If they leave it on long enough, my senses will discover where the compass is. After seeing the light I tried to contact any telepath in the tower, with no luck."

Beauty turned to Lottie and asked, "Would you be willing to take a risk and join your mind to mine? What I want to attempt could put us in danger." As surprised as her friends at such a request, Lottie only hesitated for a moment before agreeing.

"Before we do this I would ask all telepaths to join minds if I give a signal we're in trouble," Beauty asked. Looking round at the group facing her and noticing how attentive the animals were, it came as no surprise when Dandy asked, "Can we help?"

"Not on this occasion thank you Dandy, your help will be needed when we enter that wood," Beauty replied in a gentle tone. About to say something to Lottie, she was interrupted by Eram asking, "This sign. How will the telepaths know when you need help?"

"Sorry, I forgot to tell you. I will flick my tail to let you know we need assistance. Then I will need you to join your minds to ours quickly, to help us break free from danger," Beauty told them. Penny leaned across and whispered, "Aren't you scared, Lottie? It must be dangerous if our friend thinks she might need help."

"I am a bit, but also a little excited. I'm dying to know what's planned," Lottie whispered. Then Beauty asked Lottie to clear her mind. "Remember how we did this in your land. I want you to release any thoughts and concentrate on my mind."

Lottie did as Beauty requested. No sooner had she closed her mind to all other thoughts than she could see Beauty in her thoughts. "Concentrate on the wood and try not to be frightened of what you see or hear," Beauty was saying.

Lottie soon became aware of the image of a dark and foreboding wood forming in her mind. She heard the calm voice of Beauty say, "Take it easy, Lottie, we've only just entered the wood." With her mind Lottie could see how dark and dense the wood was. But then she caught sight of things creeping along the ground and noticed that the branches had increased their swaying. Wondering what had caused this, she heard Beauty say, "OK, Lottie. This is what we need to do. I want you to continue slowly through the wood. When you see the tower, cautiously move as close as you can. You will see it is shrouded in a thick grey mist. It will not harm you as you are protected by me, but that's what I'm hoping to break through. Remember, when it comes into view I want you just to concentrate on the mist. Don't try going through."

Following Beauty's request, Lottie's mind continued slowly

making its way deeper into the wood. Anxious she wouldn't let Beauty down, she concentrated on looking for a tower. No sooner had she thought about the tower than she saw it – the dreaded Tower of Zorax. As she looked at the huge tower, a sense of evil foreboding came over her. With gentle persuasion from Beauty, Lottie moved a little closer to it. Soon she found herself staring into a thick mist. She jumped back from it, sensing a threat being emitted by the eerie mist.

Concentrating hard, Lottie telepathically told Beauty she had reached the tower and could see the mist surrounding it. Having been with Lottie every step of the way, Beauty was delighted with what she had achieved.

"Now Lottie, please stay fixed on that mist," she said. "I know you feel threatened by it, but remember it can't harm you. I need to penetrate the mist in order to contact a telepath inside."

Holding the mist in her mind, Lottie felt Beauty searching for somewhere to break through it. Remaining still and as calm as possible, Lottie wondered if they would succeed in getting through. Then she heard an odd sound in her mind. Trying to understand what it was, but not wanting to break her concentration on the mist, she was unprepared for the voice which spoke.

"What's this? Is someone trying to break through me mist?" There came an eerie cackle, which unnerved Lottie. Not knowing where the voice had come from or whose it was, she was glad to hear Beauty say, "Stay calm Lottie. That was Imelda. She'll be trying to discover where we are. She won't know yet, so don't let her invade your mind any further. I'll put a cover round our thoughts, one she won't be able to get through. She will continue to work on your mind as it's not yet fully developed."

With a shiver of fear Lottie telepathically replied, "I'll do my best, but she really scares me."

"Well done. Just a few more moments while I try again," Beauty told her. Pleased to know Beauty was going to give some kind of cover, Lottie was nevertheless petrified of hearing that dreadful voice. For a while it seemed as if the voice had gone away, then a startling scream entered Lottie's mind, followed by the voice again.

"Yer won't do it, stone! Come to me an' yer friends in the tower can go," Imelda taunted. Terrified, Lottie tried not to let the voice upset her. Then she heard Imelda say, "Do yer know, we 'ave some very special prisoners. It won't be long afore 'e tells us where yer are."

Listening to that, Lottie felt certain Imelda was talking about her parents, but before she could ask, she heard Beauty threaten Imelda. "If you or any of Zanus' thugs harm my friends, I will hunt you down. You stole some of my powers, but by no means all. So be warned Imelda, I haven't finished with you yet." Wishing she could shout with joy, Lottie stayed true to Beauty and kept her mind on the mist.

"I can't break back through the mist, Lottie," said Beauty. "Now Imelda knows I'm close she's made it deeper. I've sent out a message and I hope some of my thoughts got through. I think we should join our friends and let them know what's happened."

They tried to withdraw their minds, but Imelda cackled, "No yer don't, yer'll be linked to me in a little bit." Lottie could feel Beauty trying to release their minds. Struggling to get free, Beauty quickly swished her tail, giving the signal for help. Within a moment Lottie felt a number of minds all coming in at once. Quickly explaining the problem, Beauty said, "I need everyone to concentrate and be ready to overpower Imelda. She is desperately trying to link our minds to hers. If she succeeds we will be in her power. I suggest we release our minds all together." Without a word of response, Lottie felt a sudden jolt as the minds merged as one. On hearing Beauty say, "Now!" their minds released together.

Drained of energy, Beauty sagged against Lottie and waited for her strength to return. Eagerly waiting to hear what had happened, Eram asked, "Lottie, is our friend all right?"

"It was a bit scary for a while," said Lottie. "This is what drained a lot of her energy. She'll be all right in a moment." As concerned as Eram, Rista took a glance at Beauty and was pleased to see her moving.

"That was something, wasn't it Lottie?" Beauty quietly said, then went on to tell the others what happened. "Unfortunately I wasn't able to get completely through the mist, even with Lottie keeping hold of it. It was a bit of a struggle breaking free from it, especially as the Old Crone had added depth to it. I tried to send a message, but don't know if it got through. But thank you all for coming so quickly. I'm aware she managed to draw off some of my power so I need to be careful when using telepathy, but with the assistance of Lottie, my powers are not reduced as Imelda thinks. The fear I have is of Imelda invading Lottie's mind, which would help her to discover where I am. My new shape will give me protection."

"Thank goodness we came in time, I don't know if we'd have had the energy to go up against Imelda," Binro signed.

"For the benefit of those who don't sign, I will translate what Binro said," Nain stated. Thanking Nain, Eram asked Beauty, "You said you left a message. How will we know if anyone heard it?"

"We won't, Eram. Hopefully it's in the hands of a friend. I did ask for the compass to be opened two or three times and kept open for a while," Beauty explained. Stunned by what had been revealed, Nain asked, "What if the enemy are the ones with the compass?"

"If that's the case young man, we will need to be more vigilant and make sure we don't fall into any traps," replied Letswick.

"I know if I had it, I would wish it held a secret power. I bet whoever has it has probably wished the same thing," Penny said in a matter-of-fact voice.

"The prisoners would need a guiding light to show them the way through the passages," said Beauty. "I guess that as before they would use the compass to do this. That's why I think and hope it's a friend who has the compass."

"Do you think it could be my dad?" said Lottie.

"I hope so, Lottie. As I said just now, whoever is opening the compass could be hoping to find a way to freedom. Unfortunately the compass isn't able to do that, but if the lid is opened and the dial turned my senses will be able to pick it up."

"Are you saying Lottie's parents are alive and in that terrible place?" burst out Penny.

"Our friend thinks it's possible, but none of us can say for certain who is in the dungeon," replied Letswick. "It could be one of the other prisoners who has the compass. We must try not to build our hopes too high." Noticing the saddened face of Lottie, Penny leaned over and said, "Try not to worry, Lottie. For all we know it was your Dad who opened the compass. Let's see what tomorrow brings." Lottie took hold of her friend's hand and whispered, "Thanks Penny. You're right, let's see what tomorrow brings."

With everyone agreeing it would be a good idea to take some rest, Yemil and Binro were appointed to first guard duty. Urging the others to settle and get some rest, Eram explained, "We have a hard and dangerous time ahead of us. I'll take over guard in three hours with Nain."

Assured they would be warned of any possible danger, the rest of the group set about settling down for the night. Everyone, that is, except Beauty and Letswick. Not wanting to be overheard, Letswick sought out Beauty's thoughts and asked telepathically, "What's the possibility of it being David who has the compass?"

"I'm not sure, I can only hope. It could be the telepaths are trying to break through the mist, just as I have on other occasions," Beauty replied.

"We'd better be well prepared for entering that dreaded wood."

"I'll make sure we have some protection, but how long it takes us to get to the tower will depend on what horrors Imelda has in store."

"I think I'm going to turn in now, Beauty. Try and get some rest yourself, you're going to need a lot of energy tomorrow trying to protect us," Letswick yawned. Somewhere in his distant thoughts he heard Beauty bid him goodnight.

* * * *

It was a disgruntled Norman Mansfield who set out to return to the land of humans. The prospect of the task Zanus had given him did little to curb the bitterness and fear he felt. Bitterness because he had to track down the person he hated, Crocanthus, and fear, knowing what would happen to him if he failed. He didn't know Zanus was going to order him back to Dofstram. The thought of his forthcoming meeting with Crocanthus reminded him of the cruel treatment he'd received on another occasion.

Pushing his horse to go faster, he wondered why Zanus had sent him to fetch Crocanthus back. He could have made one of his spy birds do this task. He wondered if it was a conspiracy between Zanus and Crocanthus to kill him.

Travelling over the muddy ground, he turned his thoughts on how his life had been changed since entering that cave. Thinking he had outsmarted David, and the triumphant feeling he had on entering another land, if he'd known what lay in store, he asked himself if he would have continued. He wished he'd never been so envious of David and Jayne being explorers.

He didn't like being called an informer and felt he had only helped Zanus because he had no other choice. Troubled by such thoughts, he urged the horse to a gallop, despite the constant battering of rain. Clinging to the galloping horse and trying to bar the rain from lashing into his face, he thought he saw movement ahead. He slowed the horse down to a trot and stared ahead, wondering if he should stop and see what it was. He slowed the horse to a walk and tried to make out what he was looking at. As he stared at an unfamiliar shape within the mist he sensed, more than knew, that this was no ordinary mist; there was something sinister about it.

He brought the horse to a halt and waited anxiously to see what would happen. It wasn't long before he saw a green mist rise up out of the ground. Staring at the mist as it swirled round in a circular motion, his thoughts turned to that of a whirlwind. It was then he felt himself being drawn towards the mist, almost in a hypnotic state. Shaking his head to break free of the mist's hold, he suddenly heard his horse neighing repeatedly and loud.

He tried to focus on how to get away and stared round, hoping to see some form of exit. Beginning to feel a little drowsy, he knew instinctively it was the effect of the mist. He rubbed the rain from his eyes and managed to wash away the drowsiness which was threatening to overcome him.

Taking up the reins and preparing to move, he had a sudden feeling of impending danger. As if to confirm his fears his horse reared up in fright, leaving Norman struggling to remain seated. In the place where he'd seen the green mist rising was a large snake-like creature. Norman sat terrified, not knowing what to do. Convinced this was one of Imelda's creatures, he knew his life was in great danger. He could only hope that as he was on a mission for Zanus, she might spare his life.

Thinking he might try going across the field, he turned and tugged on the reins to let the horse know which direction to go. He noticed the creature was reacting to all his movements. He could now feel the overwhelming presence of Imelda. Thinking he might try and get his horse to walk slowly round the creature, he ordered the horse to walk. He hadn't gone far when he was met with resistance. His horse began neighing wildly and kicking up its hind legs.

Then Norman felt a shiver run through the horse's body. Aware of his own fears, he gave his horse a kick to make him walk on. Shocked at getting no response, Norman wondered what he had to do to get his horse to move on. It was then he saw that the creature had turned into the frightening face of Imelda. He nearly fell out the saddle when he heard her screech, "So, informer! Scared of me little creatures is yer?"

Norman could say nothing. He was trying to keep from looking into the green eyes.

"What's the matter, thought yer might get away on yer own?" she cackled. "I'll be close no matter where yer go. So no double crossing!"

After witnessing the outcome of meetings between her and Zanus, Norman's fear of Imelda was like no other he had ever known. Recalling some of the failures that hung on the tower walls, he wasn't prepared to become one of them. Sensing his fear, and aware of the task Zanus had set him, Imelda warned, "Don't ferget informer, I'll know if yer fergets what yer to do." Now the green mist was beginning to engulf Imelda. Hoping this would see the going of her, Norman suddenly heard her crackling voice say, "I'll always be round to see yer gets Zanus' orders done. But remember, yer won't see me."

Watching the last speck of mist disappear, he remembered he still hadn't found this remote village. Anxious in case Imelda returned, he gave the order for his horse to gallop on. He made sure he was some distance from where the mist had first appeared before slowing the horse down, but it was some time before he managed to take complete control of the reins. Taking a final glance back, he could just see a pool of green gunge.

"Come on, boy," Norman whispered nervously, "Let's get away from here as fast as we can." He felt the horse shudder as it answered the order to move on.

Then he heard Imelda's voice again. "Take care yer do what yer bin told! Remember, yer can't hide from me."

Chapter Eleven

Encounter with Imelda

With the thundering sound of the horse's hooves and the eerie cackle of Imelda, it wasn't long before the Ziphers and Jaspers in their underground dwellings became aware of things happening above ground. Heads began appearing from the underground dwellings. Pleased to see the rain had stopped, Renka, one of the many Jaspers, began checking to make sure it was clear. Waving back in acknowledgment of being seen, she decided this would be the best time to take the sentries their food. She wondered who would accompany her on such a mission. Knowing the sentries at the entrance to Dofstram would be looking forward to their food, Renka was also anxious to return to the safety of her home before anything else happened.

Turning to her friend Arabel she explained, "It's my turn to take the sentries their meal, but I would like a bit of company." Noticing the wry smile on Arabel's face, Renka added wistfully, "I'm open to offers." Without giving it any thought Arabel asked, "Do you want me to come with you?" Renka smiled at her friend warmly, and replied. "Yes please. I think it might be wiser to fly."

"I think that would be a good idea. Also, if there are two of us we can look out for each other," Arabel said, giving Renka a gentle hug.

"Thanks for offering, Arabel. I think this could be a little more dangerous, especially after hearing those thundering hooves. But with no one seeing who it was, I admit to being more that a little anxious at having to go on my own," Renka told her friend.

Having arranged what they were going to do, Arabel wasted no time in taking two baskets from a nearby shelf. Handing one to Renka, Arabel said, "Come on then, let's make our way to the bakery and collect the food then we can get going." They took the offered basket and set off for the bakery. Keeping a constant lookout for any signs of possible enemy, it wasn't long before they reached their destination.

Paxal, the baker, had been keeping his eye out for Renka, but seeing Arabel with her he gave them a warm greeting as they entered his bakery.

"I see you've got company Renka. Would you like to see what I've prepared for the sentries today?"

"Yes, you always make something special for them, Paxal. We know they always look forward to whatever you send," Renka replied. "It's my turn today, but Arabel kindly offered to come with me. I didn't want to go on my own after the scare we had earlier."

"So, you heard the galloping horse too. That's very wise, to have a bit of company," Paxal said, busy filling two baskets with an assortment of goods.

"Cor, those meat pies look super. And those must be the biggest biscuits ever!" exclaimed Arabel. Taking a look round at all the other goodies on the shelves, she added, "What about these then Renka? Lovely apple pies with a touch of Paxal ingredient, I bet."

Paxal winked and placed a couple of extra pastries in the baskets, "In case you get a little peckish on the journey." But he couldn't help feeling concerned for their safety. Walking them to the door, he advised, "Now, take care and watch as you go. Those devil birds have a habit of appearing from nowhere."

"Did you see the Old Crone earlier?" asked Renka.

"I didn't. But I did hear her cackle in the distance. I pity the poor soul she was after," said Paxal.

Wanting to catch the attention of the Jaspers on lookout duty, Renka called out, "Is it still safe to go?" Giving Renka a wave, one of the Jasper guards called out, "All clear. Take care while you're on your way to the sentries. We haven't seen anyone since you've been with Paxal."

Another of the Jaspers called out, "I couldn't see who was riding that horse, but you can bet it wasn't a friend." Acknowledging the Jasper's comments, Renka said, "Come on Arabel, I think we'd better make a move. Make sure your basket is secure." Having moved alongside Renka, they prepared to complete their mission.

They took another glance round and nervously flew towards the portal linking the humans' world to Dofstram. They hadn't been flying long when they noticed other Jaspers had come to join them.

"Just thought we'd keep you company," called out a smiling Jasper. Returning the smile, Arabel thanked them for coming along but warned them to stay alert. Certain it was still all clear, they continued on their way, when Renka suddenly became aware of the sound of a galloping horse. Looking round, but not seeing where the sound was coming from, her first thought was seeking shelter. Before she could mention it to Arabel, Arabel whispered nervously, "Can you hear a horse, Renka?"

"I can, I was just about to ask if we should seek shelter, but I can't make out where the horse is. I wonder if it's coming in our direction," Renka whispered. With her own thoughts on finding shelter, Arabel voiced Renka's suggestion to the other companions. It didn't take long for the companions to agree that shelter was a good idea.

As she flew a little closer to the ground, Renka spotted what she thought would be the ideal place and flew down to take a closer look. Satisfied it would offer them sufficient protection, she indicated to the others to follow her. Reaching Renka, they began to check and make sure the burrow was free of any other residents. They secured themselves where they felt most comfortable and sat in silence, listening for any approaching enemy.

Arabel took hold of Renka's hand and nervously whispered, "We'll make a move once we know which direction that horse has gone. Don't you think it's funny the guards failed to recognise the rider?"

Renka whispered, "I know. It does seem kind of weird. If I didn't know Crocanthus was in that other land, I'd have said it was him. Whoever it was, they were in a hurry to get somewhere."

"I agree. But knowing it couldn't have been him, I wonder who else would have ridden so hard?"

Shalto, one of their companions, whispered, "I was thinking that myself. You don't think he came back unnoticed do you?" Renka whispered, "He wouldn't get past the sentries at the main entrance and certainly not the lookouts."

"Saying that, I wonder if he returned using a disguise created by that Old Crone?" suggested Renka. Hearing this sent a shiver of fear through each of the listeners.

Eager to deliver the food to the sentries, Arabel suggested they wait while she went and checked to see if it was all clear. She eased her way to the entrance of the burrow and looked to see if anyone was around. Her first concern was to make sure the horse hadn't come near to where they'd hidden. Not seeing anyone and not hearing any horses, she told the others she was going to take a look round the other side of the hill.

Her companions, keeping their eyes on Arabel as she ascended into the air, began churning over their recent conversation. As the murmuring voices calmed down, Renka replied in a distant voice, "I think we'd better be ready for when Arabel gives us the all clear to move."

Observing the group as they left the shelter, Jinta, one of the Jasper lookouts said, "I wonder who was riding that horse so hard. I wish I could have seen who it was, but when I heard that dreadful cackle I wasn't going to wait around." Feeling a hand on his arm, he turned to see his fellow companion Kula, sign, "I thought Crocanthus was in the other land?"

"I thought that too, but who's to say he didn't sneak back without any of us spotting him?" replied Jinta. Just as he said that they noticed a flag signal being sent from one of the other lookout posts. They were alarmed to see that it was a warning about possible danger. Taking a cloth from his pocket Jinta responded likewise and signalled, "What's the danger?" Almost immediately they received a message, "Be aware, we've heard a hard-ridden horse heading this way."

Signalling back and thanking their friends for the message,

Kula, the Zipher lookout, strained to hear for himself. Having picked up on the galloping horse, Kula signed to his companion that he could not tell which direction it was coming from. They were aware that their friends at the bottom of the hill would be waiting for the all clear. However, if Kula knew what Jinta was thinking he would have been more than a little alarmed.

Before acting on his thought, Jinta made sure their friends below knew it was safe to continue. As soon as he saw them take off he turned to Kula and told him of his plan. Shocked at what Jinta had planned, Kula signed, "I'm not sure that's a good idea. I know it would be nice to know who the rider could be, but is it worth the risk?"

"Stay here," said Jinta. "I will only take a short flight round. That way if anything unforeseen happens you could let me know." He placed an arm round Kula's shoulders. "I would really like to know who was riding that horse so hard." Assuring Kula he would take care, Jinta set off in the direction he thought the sound had come from.

Jinta, constantly vigilant, scanned the area close to where he and Kula were on guard duty. As he flew past the other lookouts, he gave them a wave, followed by the all-clear signal.

As Jinta flew out, he was determined not to retreat this time. He would just take extra care not to be seen. Taking a deep breath, he flew towards the copse, scanning carefully. As he passed over a barren part of the copse, something caught his eye. As he flew back round he was shocked to see ahead of him a horse and rider. So this must be what they'd all heard. But who was the rider?

Searching for a suitable place to hide, Jinta suddenly became aware of how far he'd ventured into the copse. He flew to one of the thicker branches high up in one of the taller trees. He landed with a sound of rustling leaves and cautiously moved between the branches, hoping he hadn't alerted the rider to his presence.

Jinta watched the rider, who appeared to be searching for something, or someone. But why would he want to come to such a dreary place? It crossed his mind there was a distinct lack of birds. It was like a smaller version of the Forbidden Wood.

Even so, he made up his mind that he wouldn't be leaving until he knew where the rider was going.

He soon got his answer. Ahead of him, hidden in a vale, he could see a crumbling village. The ground had been made muddy by the pouring rain and he saw how forlorn the villagers looked. Some didn't even have shoes on their feet, and what clothes they wore would do little to keep them dry. Jinta watched as the villagers struggled to go about their chores.

The horse and rider were heading for the centre of the village. Quietly and slowly Jinta made his way through the trees, settling on a branch as near to the village as he dared. Seeing the rider dismount, Jinta concentrated on trying to see who it was, but he could not. Frustrated, he wondered if it was wise to stay any longer, but as he thought this he was surprised to see the rider disappear from view again. He waited patiently for a few moments before reluctantly giving up his quest and preparing to fly back to his post.

As he searched for the path to the village, Norman Mansfield was unaware that he was being observed. Hampered by the drizzle, he wiped his eyes with a wet sleeve. In frustration he rode first one way and then another until at last he saw smoke coming through a clump of trees. At first he thought this might be another of the Old Crone's tricks, but he decided to take a chance and check it out.

Norman screwed his nose up as he smelled a strange odour. He thought he recognized it as the terrible odour that came from the Zanuthians, and wondered if Zanus had sent troopers to follow him. He wasn't too sure he wanted to continue, but knew he had no alternative. Seeing the open fire that was sending out billows of smoke, he cautiously approached the village. He took in the unkempt people and the rundown state of their dwellings, and soon recognised again the odour he had smelt earlier. He watched as the villagers dragged their dishevelled bodies towards the open fire, and felt sick when he saw what was being shovelled onto it, carcasses.

Turning his horse away, Norman made his way over to where he saw several women drawing water from a well. He was about to ask a question when he noticed an old man and woman scurrying across the muddied ground in his direction.

"This be Zanus' 'orse?" The old man said, trying to take the reins of Norman's mount.

"It is," Norman responded suspiciously, not sure he wanted to leave the horse there. He flinched from the old man's scrawny hand.

"I be Mr Tinks an' I runs 'is stables. This 'ere be Mrs Tinks, me old woman," said the man. He turned and called for assistance. "Get 'ere lad an' tek this 'ere 'orse to stable. Food an' water mind!" With some reluctance, Norman dismounted and handed the reins to Mr Tinks. Mrs Tinks remarked, "Yer ain't like none of them usual bullies."

Not wanting to stay any longer, and not interested in who she was referring to, Norman bid them farewell and set off for the portal. With his own concerns about what lay within it, he ignored the mutterings and moans as he made his way out of the village. Glancing over to the well, he was somewhat surprised to see the women were no longer there. He continued making his way back through the copse to the portal.

After being reassured by the lookouts that it was safe to leave the burrow, Renka wasted little time in gathering her friends and flying onto their destination. Having flown for quite a while, some of the younger Jaspers called out that they needed a rest. Hearing this, Renka flew to the back of the group and said warmly, "Thank you for your company, but as it's safe for us to continue may I suggest you return to your homes?"

Not sure if this was a good idea, some of the older Jaspers felt they should remain, and said as much to Renka. Thinking it over and aware there could be danger for the younger Jaspers if they were left on their own, Renka asked a few of the older Jaspers to return with them.

Meena, one of the older Jaspers, replied, "I agree. I think this is a good time for us to accompany the youngsters and return home. If you need help on your return please let one of guards know, and we'll come back." Agreeing to this, Renka and Arabel waved their friends farewell. With their friends safely on their way home, Renka had turned to say something to Arabel when she heard a voice behind her calling out, "I'm coming with you. After all you never know who else might come riding by." Recognising the voice, Renka turned to see Shalto and his usual beaming smile.

"Are you sure, Shalto? We might not be completely out of danger," Renka asked.

"All the more reason for me to come," replied Shalto, giving his friends a cheeky smile.

"OK then. Let's all three fly together. But we must stay alert," said Renka. Without any further comment the three friends set off to meet up with the sentries. They flew in silence until they were close to them.

"Should we make this a short visit?" said Shalto. "Once we've explained why we're late with their food the sentries will understand." Landing close to the stables, which were just a little away from the entrance to Dofstram, Arabel and Renka agreed it was a good idea. Leaving Shalto at the stable, Arabel and Renka made their way to the waiting sentries.

Shalto made his way to where most of the people and animals were.

After the usual greetings, he started to relay what had happened on the way. He didn't have to wait long before one of the horses said, "I'm sure you must be right about Crocanthus. We'd heard he'd gone to the humans' land."

"We would have known if he'd returned, disguised or not," said a unicorn. Hearing the agreement coming from the other animals, Shalto pondered for a while, then asked, "I wonder why Zanus is so keen to kidnap, you-know-who?"

Thinking this over, Flair, one of the many female stable-hands, replied, "That's something we've often discussed here. But we haven't been able to come up with an answer."

"I wonder if her parents are being held in the tower?" said Gina, one of the royal ponies. Continuing to brush down the pony, and not thinking about what the pony had said, Flair was taken aback when one of the unicorns called out, "Don't say that out loud, Gina. You never know who might be listening." Wishing she'd thought before saying such a thing Gina heard the shuffling of straw and noticed it was one of the unicorns moving in her direction. She raised her head a fraction, and saw that it was one of the unicorns that pulled the royal carriage.

"Don't worry, little one," said the unicorn quietly. "None of us really know who Zanus has in his tower." Flair stopped brushing and stroked Gina. "That's right, Gina, none of us know who's being held prisoner," he said. Shalto noticed a collection of stable hands and animals were deep in discussion.

Having much to tell about their journey, and feeling they would enjoy a little time with their friends, Renka and friends settled down to enjoy a moment's pleasant company. Relaying what had taken place on their journey, Venta looked at his companions with a thoughtful expression.

"Whoever it was hasn't come near here, or we'd have heard them," he said. His companion Gerda signed, "I agree. And we've been here since early this morning."

Some time later, thinking it was time to return to sentry duty, Venta signed, "This won't do. We need to get back on guard duty." Not wanting to keep them from their duties, Renka called across to let Shalto know they were about to leave.

Hearing Renka call, Shalto bid farewell to the animals and stable hands and made his way across to where Renka and Arabel were waiting. From the stables they heard were one or two voices calling out, "Take care." Confirming everyone at the stable was fine, Shalto went on to tell them no one at the stable had heard if Crocanthus had returned. Then he added, "The unicorns reckon that if he had returned they would have known it."

Uncertain as to how safe the journey home would be, Renka turned to Gerda and asked, "Could you get a message to Maisey and ask if they could meet us where we left them?" Assuring Renka she would do that, Gerda concentrated her mind on reaching the thoughts of the Zipher lookouts. Contacting the thoughts of Maisey, one of the Zipher elders, Gerda told her of Renka's request.

"I will gather my friends to meet up with Renka and Arabel at the place where we left them," promised Maisey. They bid each other farewell and withdrew their minds from each other. Turning to Renka, Gerda signed to let Renka know she'd been successful and to let her know that Maisey and others would be there. Thanking her, Renka, Arabel and Shalto bid farewell and set off back to their homes.

As he made his way through the dense copse, Norman tried to discard his thoughts about the rundown village he'd just left. His thoughts turned to Zanus. Keen to get this task over as quickly as possible, he continued making his way to the portal. But where was the cave that concealed it? Then, stepping round a group of thick shrubs, he noticed a clump of untidy undergrowth ahead, and stopped to take a closer look. Was this the shrubbery Zanus had told him to look out for? He had a sudden fear of Imelda mysteriously appearing.

Reassuring himself she was not around, he tried to recall the instructions. A mixture of thoughts raced through his mind, making him hesitate.

Aware of how he'd entered Dofstram by following Jayne and David, Norman cursed himself for not making a note of the location. He was in two minds whether to continue. But he had no choice.

It took him several minutes of hard work to penetrate the undergrowth and find that it was shielding a large boulder. He couldn't help but stare at it. Could it be the same boulder David had removed the stone from? But then he cast the thought from his mind. The more practical question was how he was going to move it. Knowing the portal had been created to allow Zanus' men to enter, and leave, Dofstram he felt a shudder of fear run through his body.

He started to push against the boulder, then suddenly remembered that you had to speak certain words to reveal the opening. For one fearful moment he couldn't remember what they were. He forced himself to be calm and finally remembered the words he had to say.

"Inkle abble dabble!" he said. No movement. Perhaps he had said the words too quickly or in the wrong order. As he was about to repeat the words, he noticed the boulder begin to shudder. Slowly it scraped its way across the ground, revealing the darkness beyond. Norman stared into the portal and instantly felt as if he was staring into a large black abyss.

Stepping nervously inside the portal, he strained his eyes to take in as much as possible. He was struck by how quiet it was. What could be lurking inside? And where was the light?

Suddenly a loud voice from within the darkness called out, "Shut the portal!" Norman froze in fear. "Shut the portal!" came the voice again. Swallowing, he uttered the words that made the boulder roll back. Realising it would bring about complete darkness, he fumbled in his pocket and retrieved a packet of matches. He struck a light just as the boulder sealed the entrance.

With the match burning down to his fingers, he cursed and struck another. His shaking hand lifted the flame in the air, wondering if the owner of the voice would appear. He slowly edged his way forward, hoping to find something which would give a more substantial light.

As he reached the end of the passage, he noticed a glimmer of light shining on the far wall, and cautiously made his way towards it. It seemed to be a reflection from somewhere down another passage. He eased himself around the corner and he saw what looked like a flaming torch. As he looked closer he was horrified to see it was being held by a severed human hand.

Reluctant to touch it, he failed to notice the last match was slowly reaching his fingers. At the shock of his fingers being burned he dropped the match. Now he knew he had no choice. It was either take hold of the hand, or grope blindly in the dark.

Terrified of what else the portal would produce, he edged slowly forward to take hold of the torch. He slid his hand along the slime-covered wall, unable to stop himself from flinching. He finally reached the torch, trying to conquer his horror at the thought that this had once been someone's hand. But he had no choice. He quickly snatched the flaming torch, recoiling at its touch.

Standing still and trying to calm his fears, he forced himself to continue through the portal. He could hear dripping water from somewhere up ahead. Then suddenly he heard the voice again.

"Look out the 'and don't get yer!" it taunted. He could see no one, but he knew who the voice belonged to. Sweating with fear, he tried breathing deeply to gain back some courage. Leaning against the slimy wall, he was alarmed to hear her next words.

"That 'and was on the end of a Rancouin's arm. 'E 'ad no use fer it after…" Not wanting to hear the finish he closed his ears just as her eerie cackle echoed round the portal.

Unnerved by what he'd heard, Norman called out nervously, "Where are you? I know who you are." Hearing no reply, but remaining alert he decided to move further along the passage. His one wish now was to get through this portal as soon as possible. His hopes were about to be shattered.

Continuing on, Norman made sure he kept his back as close to the wall as possible, taking care not to touch it any more than he had to. With his nerves so taut he couldn't say if it was a noise he heard or if it was his imagination. Standing still and listening all he could hear was his shallow breathing.

Then something stopped him in his tracks. There it was again - the scratching noise he'd heard earlier. He was relieved it wasn't his imagination, but nevertheless wished it was. What was causing it? He felt like an overstretched elastic band, and knew he was near to breaking point.

Fearing he would never get out of this place alive he waved the flame all around to scan as far as he could. Then he turned the flame towards the roof of the portal, only to discover that the light did not reach. He could feel the sweat running down his back.

And then as it continued, he realised it wasn't just sweat. There was something crawling over his body. Bringing the torch closer to his person, he could see insects, hundreds of them. Swiping at them in an attempt to remove them, he soon realised they were not like any insects he'd seen before. The more he tried to knock them off, the more they bit into him, leaving a stinging sensation behind. He slapped his arms and legs furiously, with little effect.

"Get off!" he screamed "Go back to where you came from!" Feeling them running over his body, he screamed, "Leave me alone! Leave me alone!"

Just as he was giving up hope of fighting them off, he realised he was no longer being attacked by them. He shone the flame downwards to see a mass of black and white insects racing away across the floor to disappear into the darkness.

Congratulating himself on getting rid of them, he was about to continue through the passage when he heard, "What's this, yer didn't like yer little visitors, eh?"

As her voice echoed through the passages, Norman was too fearful of calling out her name. He struggled to control the panic that was threatening to overcome him and held the flame close, feeling this was his only protection against whatever lay in wait. Feeling along the slimy wall he continued to wave the flame round him, when he suddenly became aware of a shadow above his head. Bats! He was shocked to see how large they were. The shrill noise reminded Norman of the voice Imelda used in the wood. He tried to ward them off with the flame, but the screeching noise was almost deafening. Then they suddenly took off and flew back up to the top of the portal.

Thinking he'd succeeded in stopping the bats from attacking him further, he was shocked to see when he shone the flame upwards a mass of red gleaming eyes through the darkness. Before he knew it, they were attacking him again. He thrust the flame at them, but many of the bats reached their target. Receiving more cuts and scratches from the bats' long talons, and with the occasional bite from their fangs, Norman screamed at them to leave him alone.

He tried wiping the blood from his face, but it proved to be too painful. Keeping alert for signs of them returning, he set off through the portal. He hadn't gone far when something slid over his foot. He lowered the flame to see what it was and was horrified to see a snake-like creature slithering along the ground. He stood and watched in amazement as the creature raised itself off the ground. This he knew had to be the same creature he'd seen on his way to the village.

Shaking with fear, he tried to creep along the floor, hoping to leave this creature behind. Unfortunately for him this was not to be. Suddenly a smoky green mist encircled the creature, and he was shocked to hear her cackling voice call out. "Leave 'im, me beauties. 'E'll do fer another day." He felt himself go cold with fear. He headed for what he hoped was the portal exit. He continued to wave the flame back and forth in the hope that this would scare off any further attacks from the bats or this creature. But Imelda hadn't finished with him yet.

Thinking he heard a noise, he stopped and listened. In the light of the flame he was horrified to see that the smoky green mist had followed him. Not only had it kept pace with him, it appeared to be taunting him. Now the snake creature began wrapping its body round Norman's legs, then further up his body. Convinced he was going to be crushed to death, he was surprised when the snake-like creature released him.

Taking in gulps of air, he asked, "What do you want?" But the creature let out one long hiss and vanished in a cloud of green smoke.

This was followed by an eerie silence. Norman guessed his ordeal wasn't over, and he was soon proved right. From out of nowhere Imelda's eerie cackle echoed round the portal, "'Ello there, informer!" she hissed.

Nervously he called out, "Where are you? Come and show yourself!" His voice gave away the nervousness he felt.

Then he heard a low growl. He knew that sound – one of Imelda's trofalogues. Where were they? The creatures' overwhelming stench hit his nostrils and he felt nauseous. As the stench increased, Norman became aware how close the trofalogues were, which did little to calm his sick feeling. He had seen how easily her beasts could to rip a body apart.

Now he was even more anxious to be free of the portal. Moving the flame rapidly from side to side, he was startled to see how close Imelda was. But what startled him more was the two snarling trofalogues standing either side of her. Waiting to see what she intended to do, he tried to keep one eye on the trofalogues and one on Imelda. He thought it was odd that her creatures had the same green eyes as she did.

"Yer won't get free of me powers. I don't fink yer liked any of me pets, did yer?" Norman found himself whispering, "What do you want?" Amused at seeing him standing like a statue with the flame just in front of her face, she peered into his face before eerily replying. "Jus' to make sure yer doesn't do anyfing daft. Zanus wants Crocanthus 'ere, and I wants the coloured stone, and don't ferget I needs the woman too."

Norman hadn't been aware she wanted Lottie; he thought they were bringing her to Zanus. Catching his thoughts, Imelda moved threateningly closer to Norman. Spitting as she spoke, she told him, "Yer ter bring 'er ter me." Before he could think of a suitable answer, she added, "Don't fink I won't know if yer got 'er." Norman suddenly felt his legs give way. He fell on the wet floor and remained where he was for a moment, then stumbled back to a standing position. He stammered, "What else do you want? I've got to be on my way!"

The beasts had moved closer to him, and he didn't like the way they showing their bared fangs. Were they about to attack?

"Not now me lovelies, yer can feast on 'im another day," said Imelda. Her words did little to make him feel any easier, especially when he noticed the trofalogues were looking at him and licking their lips. He stumbled along the floor, trying to move away. Observing what he was doing, Imelda warned, "Yer'd best be where yer are. Me pets are 'ungry an' ready fer a meal. P'r'aps yer would like one of me other creatures to 'ave yer fer a meal?" she chuckled. Terrified, Norman aimed the flame towards the beasts and blustered, "I'll burn any of those creatures if they come near me."

"Not good finking, informer. Me pets would get yer long afore the flame 'its 'em," Imelda threatened. As if on cue the trofalogues crouched down, ready to pounce. Norman saw Imelda give them a signal, and thinking this was a signal to attack, he pushed the flame at the nearest trofalogue. It backed away, snarling. Thinking he'd been successful with one, he thought he would use the flame on the other. But, Imelda hissed, "Don't yer dare informer! Yer only safe cos Zanus needs yer to bring Crocanthus. Me pets will tear yer limb from limb if I tells 'em to."

Unnerved by the warning, Norman remained still but checked to make sure there were no signs of the snake creature. Not seeing it, he turned his attention back to the beasts either side of Imelda. Seeing the glare in their eyes and the drool still falling from their mouths he knew they could easily devour him.

"Leave me pets be. I 'as to give yer a potion," said Imelda. She produced a phial from somewhere on her person and pushed it in his face. "'Ere 'uman, yer'll need this 'ere potion to get to Crocanthus."

Norman hesitated. Imelda, reading his thoughts, suddenly cackled, "It ain't poison, we needs yer livin'! Drink it all, or yer'll never find Crocanthus."

Still Norman wavered. Imelda began shaking the phial in front of his face. "'Ere, take it, or else!" Norman reluctantly took the phial from her hand and secured it in one of his pockets.

"How will drinking this tell me where I'm to go?" he said.

Glaring at him through green slit eyes, she replied in a warning tone, "Yer don't need to know, jus' take it when yer leave the portal."

Norman still had doubts about her poisoning him. Just when he thought it was safe to continue through the portal, he felt the hand of Imelda on his arm. "Drink it, or yer'll never find 'im. Crocanthus is not 'isself." With a sudden flash of green smoky mist and a fading growl from the trofalogues, Imelda and her beasts disappeared from sight.

Norman began to churn over in his mind what Imelda had said about the potion. But then, raising the flame to see if there was any sign of the bats, he was shocked to see them hovering above his head. Without delay he set off at a run. When he finally reached the end of the passage he hastily said the words to set the boulder in motion. As he waited for it to move, he wondered what he should do with the flaming torch. Just then he suddenly noticed a hand protruding from the wall; it hadn't been there when he arrived. He gave the torch to the hand and waited as the boulder rumbled away to reveal the light of a wet and dreary day. Stepping out into the light, he quickly uttered the words, "Inkle abble dabble." Then he started away from the portal.

Taking in gulps of welcome fresh air, Norman at last began to feel human again. But now he had no idea where he was. He had never seen this place before, and started to become anxious at the thought of being lost.

As he sat down and pondered over the best course of action, Norman suddenly remembered the potion in his pocket. Taking out the phial, he turned it over and over, debating whether to drink it. Trying to forget who had given it to him, he stood up and placed the phial close to his lips, ready to drink. Then he thought better of it and lowered it again. But then, to his horror he heard the cackling voice of Imelda call out, "Drink it, or else."

Had she left the portal after him? Knowing now that he had no choice, he took a deep breath and drank the liquid down, shuddering as the liquid made its way down his throat. He felt as if his whole body was reacting to the liquid. Certain he'd been poisoned, he waited for what he thought would be his last moment alive.

That moment soon passed. Now he felt something else happening inside him. At first he felt a warming sensation throughout his body, then without any warning he was suddenly struck down with a surging pain searing through his whole body. Doubled over, he screamed and fell to the ground. How long he lay there he didn't know, but eventually he gathered the strength to stand up.

The pain was now beginning to fade, but it still left him feeling as if he'd been given a good beating. It took all his strength to stay upright. But then, looking down at himself, he was shocked to see that his arms had been replaced by feathered wings. His feet were no longer his; they were those of a bird. Shocked at the transformation, Norman wasn't sure what to do. Feeling his face with what had been his arms, he realised that he now had a large beak.

Seeing a large puddle along the pathway, he dared himself to go and see what he looked like. His reflection showed a big, black, raven-like bird. So this was what he had become.

Before he had time to come to terms with his reflection, he heard a voice he hoped never to hear again. "Well, what yer waiting fer? Fly. Flap the wings an' fly," cackled Imelda.

Norman took another look in the puddle and stared at himself in horror. "What has she done to me?" he groaned. "How am I supposed to get back to being myself?" Imelda moved closer to Norman and hissed in his ear, "Fly, 'uman, fly!"

He tried tentatively flapping his arms, with no result. He wondered what he was doing wrong. Why didn't they respond?

"Fly!" shrieked Imelda. He flapped the wings as hard as he could, and then to his surprise he felt himself being lifted off the ground. Before he knew it he was flying through the air.

"Wings, take 'im to, Crocanthus!" screeched Imelda. As

Norman's new wings obeyed the order, he realised he was flying over fields and houses, valleys and waterways. He rather liked the view from up here. But how would he know when to stop, and where?

Some time later, he was surprised to feel he was beginning to descend. Landing behind a shrub he heard again that dreadful voice, "Stay where yer is. Yer'll be 'uman in a while. Over there is where yer'll find Crocanthus."

His concerns turned to Crocanthus, and how he would react to being required back in Dofstram. As he began to transform back into his human self, Norman was painfully aware of his limbs growing in place of the bird features. He was relieved to see his own form return. Standing upright, he stretched his arms and legs to get the circulation moving. Now that the transformation was complete, and the strength was back in his arms and legs, he gathered himself together and stepped out from behind the shrub into a suburban street.

Not wanting to waste any more time, he walked across the road and stood staring at the large wooden door. Guessing this must be where he would find Crocanthus, Norman quivered at the thought of coming face to face with the man who had taken such pleasure in whipping him. He summoned the courage to knock on the door and waited anxiously for someone to answer.

Chapter Twelve

Into the lion's den

As he patiently waited for the door to be opened, Norman was remembering how much Crocanthus had seemed to enjoy flaying him. He could still feel the impact of the knotted whip, and flinched at the memory of his flesh being torn from his back. That was when he had the idea of using Lottie as a scapegoat. Dismissing the memory of how he'd betrayed Jayne and David, he turned his attention back to what he'd been sent to do.

He gave a further knock. With no one answering, he wondered if this was in fact Crocanthus' house. Stepping back to observe it, he noticed an open window and made his way towards it. He cupped his hands and pressed them against the window to see that the room was empty. Disappointed, he removed his hands and contemplated what his next move should be.

He had already decided that if no one answered the door he would take himself off and return later. Beyond that, Norman wasn't thinking. As he gave the door another knock, he felt conscious of being watched.

"Want any help, mate?" shouted a voice. Turning round to see who it was, Norman saw an elderly couple standing at the gate. Surprised at the question, he stammered, "Er, no thanks just visiting a friend."

"We don't have much to do with them inside," said the woman. Wishing they would just go, Norman turned his attention back to the house. He caught the last few words of their conversation. "Bit rude that. Turned his back on us he did," the man was saying.

Norman took a deep breath, raised the handle of the door-knocker again and was about to bring it down on the door when he heard footsteps approaching.

Inside the house, Crocanthus had become increasingly annoyed at the persistent knocking. Having initially decided to not answer it, his temper had now reached boiling point, and not only with the caller. 'Why can't any of those idiot tenants answer the door?' he asked, kicking a nearby bin. No sooner had he thought this when it suddenly it went silent. Not knowing why, Crocanthus found this as unsettling as the knocking. At that moment he had an uncomfortable sense of someone being close by, someone he knew. Not wanting to acknowledge what his senses were telling him, he looked round to see if Imelda was here. He could feel her presence.

"Show yourself Imelda. I know you're in here!" he shouted. Hit by a sudden rush of chilled air, he tried to stave off a moment of panic.

"Yer don't scare me, Crocanthus. Remember, yer needs me fer me potions. Now, go to the door. Yer'd best make sure no one sees yer. Not wiv such a weird disguise on."

"Where are you, Old Crone? Show yourself!" Crocanthus demanded once more. Cackling close to his ear, she uttered, "Yer don't needs to see me. Jus' go to the door." Unnerved, he felt a sudden chill run through him. One part of him was keen to know why Imelda was anxious for him to answer the door, but another part felt it was below him to be the doorman.

"All right, I'll go to the door," he exclaimed. It couldn't be those menials Evoc and Harbin, who he had sent back to Dofstram. So who could it be?

Walking towards his apartment door he swung it open with such force that it banged into the wall behind. Striding angrily towards the main door, he threw it open.

Staring at the man before him, Crocanthus asked in a brusque and rude tone, "Yeah, what do you want?" Alarmed at the aggressive tone, Norman struggled to answer.

Norman recognised Crocanthus' voice, but he wasn't sure what to say. He wondered how this unkempt man could have attracted Lottie. The torn jeans and baggy T-shirt weren't things Norman thought he would ever see Crocanthus wear.

"Well, what do you want?" snapped Crocanthus.

Stammering, Norman finally managed to say, "Er, could you, could you tell me if a man called Crocanthus lives here?" Glaring into Norman's eyes Crocanthus snarled, "Who wants to know?" Norman needed no further evidence that he had found the man he had been sent to bring back to Dofstram. But he thought it might not be advisable at this moment to disclose that he recognised Crocanthus.

"My name is Norman Mansfield and I have been sent with an order from a man called Zanus," he said. "I've been ordered to deliver it directly to Crocanthus. Would you please let me in, and kindly let Crocanthus know he has a visitor?" He took a step closer to the door.

"I wouldn't shut the door if I were you," said Norman, gathering his courage. "You see, I know who you really are. And I don't think you'd like me to say your name out again, would you?"

Without warning Norman was pulled over the doorstep and pushed towards an inner door. Stumbling from the impact, he couldn't stop himself falling onto the floor. He wondered what was going to happen when he heard the front door slam shut. Hoping there were other people around, he glanced round the massive hallway.

Staring at the intruder, Crocanthus looked him over. He had a nagging feeling he should know this person. The only thing on Norman's mind was passing the message on and leaving as soon as possible.

"Could we go somewhere else in private?" he asked. "Then I can tell you what you want to know, and what the orders are." Reluctant to let Norman inside his apartment, Crocanthus stared straight at him.

"You say you know who I am? What do you mean by that? Who are you?" Norman feared what would happen if Crocanthus realised he was the informer.

"I already told you, my name is Norman Mansfield," he said. "Would you mind telling me your name?"

Still with his black eyes boring into Norman, Crocanthus replied, "My name is Jeremy Thackett. Though what business it is of yours I cannot imagine." Norman wasn't too sure if he should tell Crocanthus he knew his true name. It was then he remembered Lottie talking about her friend Jeremy, which made him take a longer look. He decided to remain silent until a more suitable moment.

As if Crocanthus knew what Norman was thinking, he suddenly grabbed him by the collar and pushed him through his apartment door. Managing to stop himself from falling on the floor, Norman picked himself up, stumbled across to a convenient chair and sat down.

"Why haven't you asked me how I came to be standing at your door and asking for a man called Crocanthus?" he asked.

"Why would I want to know how you got here?" Crocanthus asked in a menacing voice. Fearing Imelda would appear from nowhere, Norman quietly replied, "I was given a potion, a potion that brought me straight to you."

Feeling the anger coming from Crocanthus, Norman cowered back further into the chair. Aware he still hadn't passed on the orders from Zanus, Norman thought it might be better if he told Crocanthus everything. In a voice just above a whisper, Norman told him, "As I explained earlier, Zanus demanded I get a certain message to Crocanthus. I know you are the man I was sent to find."

Before he could say any more, he felt a large fist ram into the side of his body. Falling to the ground and gasping for breath, he saw Crocanthus looming over him.

Unable to do or say anything; he felt a rush of cold air go over him making him catch his breath. Was Imelda close by? He glanced round to see Crocanthus standing by the apartment door.

"Get off the floor you idiot, and move over there!" snapped Crocanthus. But before he could get up, Norman felt himself being dragged across the floor, then dropped again. He was surprised to see Crocanthus open the apartment door, look out and then close it with an angry slam.

Norman slowly raised himself up off the floor. Shuddering with fear, Norman felt certain he'd never leave this room alive. Crocanthus was watching his every move. Not wanting to be punched again, Norman made his movements slow and careful as he made his way to the chair he'd sat on earlier.

"So, now you know who I am," Crocanthus hissed in Norman's ear. "I will warn you as I have others, my name is never spoken in this land. My name is Jeremy Thackett. Got it?"

"Got it," Norman replied, wondering how or when he would be able to tell him of Zanus' orders. He was soon to find out. Crocanthus spun round, staring him directly in the eyes.

"What did Zanus send you here for? He's got his birds here. one of them could have brought his orders!" Crocanthus yelled. "Well, what are those orders?" Almost hypnotised by Crocanthus' flared nostrils and cold dark eyes, Norman felt as if his body had been invaded by something nasty. Noticing his shiver, Crocanthus laughed cruelly, and stated, "Scared of me. Eh? Why would he send such a weakling to me?. Now, I've got an early start in the morning. I'm only going to give you a minute. Tell me what Zanus ordered." Norman shook his head in an attempt to clear his thoughts. How had this man managed to remain in this land without giving himself away? He remembered that he was the one who had put Lottie's life in danger. But he wasn't going to worry about that now.

Norman could see Crocanthus was now beginning to change his appearance. He was undecided whether to remain where he was or to try and make a run for it. Before he could decide, he became mesmerised looking at the new person sitting in front of him, who looked every bit the man about town, with his smart clothing and up-to-date footwear. Norman guessed this was how Crocanthus had managed to deceive Lottie into thinking he was a friend. Noticing the thick dark-rimmed spectacles, Norman knew he might be able to disguise himself, but he couldn't disguise his cold dark eyes. There was no Zanuthian odour, which made him wonder if Imelda had given him a potion to hide it.

"So, this is how he was able to befriend Lottie," Norman murmured to himself. Thinking he might have been overheard, he rapidly asked, "How did you do that? Change from looking like one man, to looking like another?"

"Well, now you see Jeremy Thackett sitting here, give me the message from Zanus," said Crocanthus. Startled by the aggressive tone, but not wanting to enrage Crocanthus further,

Norman asked warily, "Are you always like this to visitors? Or could it be you have recognised who I am?"

Staring straight back at Norman, Crocanthus was annoyed at not being able to remember this man sitting in front of him. "If you're one of those nosey neighbours from upstairs, I'll soon sort you out," he said. Norman hesitated, partly because he wasn't sure how to answer.

"Why should I care who you are?" snorted Crocanthus. "Or why Zanus sent you? As far as I'm concerned you can go back and tell him you failed." Managing to stem the fear going through him, Norman stared directly at Crocanthus, then quietly but slowly replied, "You might look like the man you call yourself here, Jeremy Thackett. But I know how cruel and evil you really are."

This made Crocanthus curious. "How do you know all this?" he asked. Observing the cruel mouth as its owner spoke through clenched teeth, Norman feared the consequences if he didn't tell Crocanthus all he knew.

He also noticed that there was a sudden chill in the room, and that he was starting to feel drowsy. Struggling to keep his eyes open, his vision had become blurred. When his eyes turned to Crocanthus, Norman could see the cruel sneer quite plainly. Wondering why it should appear so clear, he guessed Crocanthus was hypnotising him. Shaking his head, and concentrating on avoiding Crocanthus' eyes, Norman failed to see Crocanthus rise from his chair. Gliding noiselessly, across the floor, Crocanthus made his way towards Norman. Terrified, but unable to move, Norman wondered how and when Crocanthus managed to appear next to where he was sitting. Norman now had no power to move any part of his body.

Relishing the power he was wielding, Crocanthus grunted, "I warn you not to go on with this guessing game."

"Release me from your hold, then I will explain," said Norman. "I thought you would have recognised me. We have met before, but not in this land." Wondering if he should continue, Norman was left in no doubt about doing so when Crocanthus raised his hand to bring it down on Norman. Without wasting time, Norman rapidly said, "I'm the one who told your boss about David and Jayne's daughter, Lottie."

Crocanthus said nothing, but Norman was relieved to discover he was no longer being hypnotised. Taking a deep breath and thinking he'd be more comfortable if Crocanthus was away from him, Norman asked, "Wouldn't you like to sit down while I continue?" Much to his surprise, Crocanthus returned to his chair without uttering a word.

Clearing his throat, Norman pondered as to where to begin. So much had happened to him since he'd been captured.

"I haven't forgotten the terrible whippings you've given me," he began. "Do you know you left me near to death? But then you must know, because you had me thrown into a disgusting cell. Luckily for me the other prisoners didn't know who I was, or why I was there. If they had they might not have been so caring." With the face of Jayne coming into his thoughts, Norman slowly added, "Thanks to the care I had from one of the women prisoners, I fully recovered."

Norman felt no remorse at betraying his friend. Waiting to see how Crocanthus would react, he refrained from saying anything further.

Crocanthus disregarded what he'd heard and remarked sarcastically, "So you've come for revenge have you? Perhaps I should have made sure I finished you off when I had you in the dungeons."

As soon as Crocanthus mentioned the dungeons, Norman's mind became flooded with the terrible things that had taken place there. He did not want to be sent back there. All he wanted to do now was pass the message on and get going. He began to explain his reason for the visit.

"I'm only to be here for a short time," he said. "I was ordered to return to Zanus as soon as my task was completed. He demands that you and any other Zanuthians return to Dofstram immediately. The battle with King Alfreston has taken a dangerous turn, and he needs all his people back there."

Pausing for a moment, he added, "There was something else. You have to return with Lottie and some coloured stone, a special stone that glows."

Crocanthus turned to Norman and leeringly taunted him. "So, am I supposed to believe that Zanus would send a grovelling informer to bring me back?"

Noticing the nervous shuffling of Norman's feet, Crocanthus taunted him some more. "Did you think I wouldn't remember that wretched informer who lay on the steps before Zanus?" He took a step closer to Norman, glared at him and uttered in a contemptuous voice, "Look at you! You're nothing but a trembling wreck! Zanus must have been drunk when he sent you. Did you think that telling me your name would make any difference to what would happen to you?" Spitting as he spoke, he laughed loudly as Norman wiped the spittle off his face.

Returning to his chair, Crocanthus began drumming on the arm, impatient at the time it was taking Norman to answer his questions. He was fast losing his temper. Rising from his chair, he moved menacingly close to Norman again. The fear in the man's eyes encouraged him to take advantage of the situation. In a cold threatening voice, Crocanthus demanded, "Tell me everything that's been happening. Don't leave anything out."

Norman knew he couldn't keep him waiting any longer. He summoned as much courage as he could and quickly assured Crocanthus he would tell him everything. He decided to leave out what he considered unimportant. Shuffling his feet in a nervous manner, he started to explain.

"I was told that you, and some others, were sent to this land to capture Lottie and take her to Zanus. He mentioned a coloured stone that glows. The main order from Zanus is that he demands you find the girl and the stone. When you have both in your possession you are to return and take them directly to him."

Taking a sideways glance at Crocanthus, Norman considered it safe to continue. "You know how I came to Dofstram, remember, I was captured in that dreadful cave. I didn't know where I was, but you obviously enjoyed whipping me until I revealed everything I knew."

Tired of hearing about whippings and thinking Norman was withholding relevant information, Crocanthus roared, "What about the bits you missed out?" Staring at Crocanthus, Norman tried to think what he'd left out. He suddenly remembered Imelda telling him that Lottie and the stone were to be given to her. Thinking Crocanthus must have read his thoughts, he nervously added, "There is one thing I forgot. On my arrival at the portal that Old Crone Imelda appeared. Gave me quite a shock I might tell you." Not wanting to relay the next bit, he feared he would be the target for reprisals.

"Well?" shouted Crocanthus. "What's this other bit of information?" Cowering as far back in the chair as he could, Norman reluctantly told him, "Imelda warned me that Lottie and the stone are to be taken to her."

Shocked by what Norman had just said, Crocanthus' thoughts turned to what Imelda had said when he had collected his last lot of potions. Feeling uncomfortable and thinking he could sense Imelda, he started looking round for any sign of her presence. Unaware Norman was overcome by the same feeling, he wondered why he was also peering round the room.

Assuring himself Imelda wasn't around, Crocanthus still felt outraged at having been put in a position to choose between Zanus and her. But he turned his concentration back to his informer. He wondered if he'd heard correctly when he'd heard Norman say, "I know the portal is how you and other Zanuthians travel to and from each land. I know it was created by Imelda. I might add that it's the worst possible way of travelling between lands."

Crocanthus rose from his chair and stood directly in front of Norman. "So now we know why you are here," he said. "And the way you came. What you haven't told me is what else has taken place at the tower."

Not sure he wanted to continue, Norman stared straight into the cold dark eyes and said, "I know Imelda went to see Zanus, but I don't know what was said. David has had several more whippings because he won't say where the stone is. That's when David saw me." A smirk passed over Norman's face when he recalled Zanus' threats warning David not to think about killing him.

Unconcerned about any prisoner being taken to Zanus, Crocanthus was, however, troubled that Imelda had gone to him. This set him wondering if she had gone to give him potions or was there to collect unwanted prisoners.

Striding across the room, Crocanthus cast a vicious blow on

the side of Norman's face. Offering no explanation, he watched with amusement as Norman struggled to remain seated. Feeling a trickle of blood run down his face, Norman was about to ask what he'd done to deserve being punched, when he heard Crocanthus say in a cold voice. "So you think you're clever and know all there is to know about Dofstram? You're not quick enough to avoid getting thumped."

Changing his tone of voice to a threatening tone, Crocanthus continued, "You will learn. Whether I am in this land or Dofstram, I need to know everything. Now, tell me all you know about Lottie and the glowing stone." Trying to ignore the pain coming from his cheek Norman dabbed at the blood. Feeling rebellious Norman felt inclined not to tell Crocanthus any more. However, taking a moment to gather his thoughts he realised if he didn't reveal everything he would get more than one fist.

"I told you before how I know Lottie. I met her through her Aunt Jean, when she took me to meet Lottie's parents." Not wanting to mention Jayne and David by name, Norman continued, "I don't know anything about a glowing stone, only that Zanus wants it back."

Norman slowly got up off his chair. "I think this might be the right time for me to go," he said. He had to report back to Zanus. "Has Lottie returned home, Croc… I mean Jeremy? Have you got the stone?" he asked as he moved towards the door.

The words had hardly left Norman's lips when to his surprise, Crocanthus was standing right beside him with fist raised. Before Norman could move, Crocanthus brought his fist down and smashed it into his face, sending him crashing to the floor. "I already told you, don't ever call me by my name in this land. My name is Jeremy and don't you forget it."

By the time Crocanthus had finished speaking Norman had managed to pick himself up off the floor and was rubbing his sore face. Dabbing at the blood falling freely from his nose and cheek, he missed the signs that Crocanthus hadn't finished with him yet. As he stood looking at his bloody hand he felt the impact of Crocanthus' fist on his ribs. Convinced that several of his ribs must be broken, he tried to remain standing. This proved too much for him and he felt himself drop to the floor.

With a sense of pleasure at having this person at his mercy yet again, Crocanthus couldn't resist giving him several kicks to the body. Then he stepped away from the crumpled figure of Norman and informed him, "I will return when I am ready. And I will let Zanus know what is happening here. I don't need something like you to do that." Noticing Norman was attempting to stand up again, Crocanthus moved towards him, eager to land a few more body punches.

Norman, semi-conscious with shock and reduced once again to a crumpled figure on the floor, only just heard Crocanthus order, "Get up. You're bleeding all over my floor." Doubled up with pain, Norman was unable to comply with the order. Each movement sent stabs of pain through his body. Using the chair for support, he attempted to stand, but was struck by a moment of giddiness. Staying still, he took several painful breaths.

Full of contempt for the crumpled figure on his floor, Crocanthus grabbed him by the arms and pulled him up off the floor. Opening the door, he pushed Norman out of his apartment, warning him of more whippings to come. Then he closed the door with an almighty bang.

Lying trembling on the hall floor, Norman looked round the hallway. Casting his eye on a nearby door he could just make out the word 'CLOAKROOM.' He got to his feet and limped towards the door, wishing Zanus had never sent him to find this brutal man. Facing moments of giddiness he finally reached the door. Dropping back on to the floor, he noticed droplets of blood mingled with sweat lay in a pool beside him.

Inside, he turned on the taps. He was shocked at the reflection in the mirror. Noticing the discoloration round his eyes, he knew it wouldn't be long before they turned completely black. He set about washing the bruising and drying blood from his nose and cheeks. Gingerly touching his painful ribs, he could only surmise that some of them must be broken. The mirror seemed to reflect how his life had changed since that fateful day he'd decided to follow Jayne and David.

He slumped back down on to the floor. How could he have been so stupid and cowardly as to put Lottie's life at risk? He knew the answer - it was his life or hers. Over the course of time he'd convinced himself he'd done the only thing possible, and saw no reason to chastise himself now.

He tried to remember how long he'd been friends with Jean. After what had happened their friendship could never be renewed, he wasn't sure how he felt about that, but passed it off as something to consider at a later time. They had been friends for some time before he was introduced to Jayne, her sister, and the family. With the image of the small rosy-cheeked girl and her long fair hair tied back in a ponytail, he tried to think how Lottie would look today.

He found himself churning over the times of friendship he had once enjoyed with her parents. Listening to David recount some of the adventures he and Jayne had had in the years they'd been exploring old caves, Norman thought he'd like to go with them. At the time he saw no reason not to. Wiping away a streak of blood from his face he wondered now, as he had at the time, how David could have been so quick to dismiss this idea. Resentment bubbled to the surface. Betraying them was justified. How dare David dismiss him out of hand? Wouldn't he have made a good companion?

Even in this uncomfortable position, Norman couldn't resist congratulating himself on having the foresight to plan how he would achieve his goal. Aware Jean took care of Lottie when her parents went on these trips, all he needed to do was discover the date. He didn't have to wait long before David told them when they were leaving. He had just enough time to purchase some necessary equipment.

At the local camping shop, the assistant had been very helpful in guiding him towards the things he would need. Arriving home with his purchases, he had checked the items one by one. Satisfied he had everything he needed, all he had to do now was wait for the day. He wondered now if he would have been so keen to go if he had known what he'd let himself in for.

On that eventful day he had risen early and eaten a small breakfast, then set about packing his car and driving to Jayne and David's house. Even thinking about it now gave Norman a twinge of excitement.

When David and Jayne had finally stepped out of the house, he had watched them wave goodbye to Jean and Lottie. Waiting for them to start their car, he had quickly followed suit. Not sure where the exploration was taking place, he could see they were travelling north. With the persistent rain showing no signs of easing, Norman thought at one time he'd lost sight of them. He had followed at a safe distance and was surprised when they suddenly stopped outside the gate of a small white cottage.

Keen to see what they would do next, he was surprised to see them talking jovially with an elderly man as they made their way further up the lane.

Excited by what he had witnessed, Norman was convinced the caves had to be nearby. Then he was surprised to see an elderly lady driving David's car towards the waiting people. They drove through the open gate, and it wasn't long before the car and the people had disappeared from view. Concerned he's missed seeing where they'd gone, Norman was pleased to see a piece of waste land where he could park his car.

No sooner had he parked than he saw the four people chatting and laughing as they made their way back to the cottage. Jayne and David were laden with rucksacks and other equipment. Now he had some doubts. Should he follow them or not? With what he knew now, he wished he'd remained where he was.

His last pleasant memory was of hearing David and Jayne bidding farewell to the owners of the cottage. Hiding behind a large tree opposite the cottage, he had just managed to hear the elderly man say, "Take care. See you soon."

Waiting for them to set off, he knew he couldn't let them get too far ahead of him or he'd really get lost. Taking care not to be seen or heard, he followed them up the lane, occasionally having to dodge from sight. He recalled the large and beautiful wooded area at the end of the lane. The wood was bursting with life, flowers in full bloom and leaf-covered trees. Not forgetting the birds, which sang throughout the time he was there.

Once again he found himself wishing he could turn back the clock to a time before he'd let envy lead him into trouble. How had they never seen or heard him? He held his head in his hands, seeing everything as clearly now as when it happened.

Wondering why they had stopped walking, he had observed them deep in discussion. David was looking at a map. This almost caused him to gloat, thinking this explorer man David had managed to get himself lost. It was a while later that he realised they were no longer in sight. Panicking, he wondered what he should do. Should he continue or should he go back? Then he noticed Jayne emerge from somewhere further on. Heaving a sigh of relief, he crept as quietly as he could to try and get closer to where they'd stopped.

Before he knew it he was too close, and halted where he was. It didn't take him long to work out that they might have reached the cave they were going to explore. At the time Norman had wondered if he wanted to continue, but then he remembered the rejection from David, which dented his pride.

Expecting them to get on with their exploring, he was fascinated watching them feel the outer cave walls and making notes. A while later they slowly made their way inside. Still unsure if he should follow, he'd hung back, waiting to see if they would come out. Then he moved forward and stood at the entrance to the cave. Staring into the semi-darkness, he couldn't see where it led to, or where the end was. Nervous about entering it, he peered round making sure he wasn't about to bump into them.

He covered the beam of his newly-acquired torch with a handkerchief and began taking small steps, careful not to make too much noise. Soon the daylight outside was completely gone. Noticing how damp and eerie it was, he maintained a safe distance from the explorers.

* * * *

His parched mouth brought Norman back to the bathroom. Making his way across to the basin, he held firmly on the edge and tried to haul himself off the floor. After a few attempts, he finally succeeded. Taking further sips of water and holding onto the basin for support, he could feel the sweat continuing to run down his back. He knew he wasn't strong enough yet to try and leave the cloakroom. He slumped back to the floor, his thoughts straying back to the cave.

He recalled being amazed at how large the cave was. It never occurred to him it could be occupied, or to wonder who the inhabitants were. Shining the torch towards the roof of the cave, he half expected to see a mass of bats hanging upside down. Disappointed that the beam couldn't reach that far, he turned his attention back to David and Jayne. There was no sign of them. Looking round and trying not to panic, he eased a little closer to where they'd been, but still couldn't see them. Thinking they couldn't have gone far, he stumbled on, hoping he would soon catch sight of them.

At last he spotted David in the distance. Something had made him stop. Keeping as near to the cave wall as possible, he eased his way a little nearer to them, and was surprised to see that they were studying a massive boulder. What could have held their attention? Straining his eyes to see what they were going to do next, he noticed David was scraping away at something in or on the boulder.

It was hearing Jayne mutter to her husband, "Please David, just dig a little longer, it's so unusual," which decided Norman against declaring himself. Frustrated at not hearing what the item was, he squatted behind the nearest rock. Without realising it he dislodged a stone, causing it to roll on the floor.

"Who's there?" called David. With only the echo of his voice coming back, he turned to Jayne and asked, "Did you hear something?" He was relieved to hear Jayne reply, "Probably only a stone rolling out of place."

"Are you really sure you want this stone Jayne? It's proving very difficult to remove," said David. But a few minutes later he called out, "There you are," and held it out for Jayne.

"Once it's cleaned, it will be very beautiful," replied Jayne, moving her hands as if displaying a ring. He heard her say, "Just look at it David. It would make a gorgeous ring, or maybe a necklace.

Taking a step into what he thought was another passage, Norman wasn't given time to think about the next move. He was suddenly grabbed by the arms from behind and pushed to the floor. He was aware of two strongly-built, evil-smelling men standing over him.

"Shut yer mouf, or yer'll get some more!" hissed one of the men. Terrified of getting another fist in his face, Norman cowered away. He wondered who these people were, and what they planned to do with him.

* * * *

Shivering now at the memory of the rough treatment he'd received at the hands of these men, Norman began rubbing his wrists as if he could still feel the rope that had bound them together. Rising slowly off the cloakroom floor again, he hoped the giddy feeling wasn't going to repeat itself. Clinging onto the basin, he waited for a moment before washing off the remaining blood from his bruised and swollen face. Not sure if he was yet strong enough to leave, he was disturbed by the sound of voices coming from the other side of the door. He couldn't make out what was being said. Glancing at himself in the mirror he was shocked to see how swollen his face was, but true to his previous prediction his eyes were now almost black.

Hoping the people had gone, he was startled to hear the door handle being repeatedly rattled. Fearing it could be Crocanthus, panic was beginning to set in but then he heard a male voice say, "Damn, the blasted door must have got jammed, I suppose I'll have to report it. I'll give it another try before we go." As the voice faded away, Norman placed his ear on the door to make sure they had really gone.

Taking another look in the mirror at the damage to his face, he just prevented himself from falling onto the floor when he noticed it wasn't his reflection coming back. It was that of Zanus.

Gripping onto the basin, he shook his head and looked in the mirror again. The harsh voice of Zanus boomed out, "So! Yer didn't think I would leave yer alone, did yer? 'Ave yer told Crocanthus to return?"

Staring back at Zanus, Norman was lost for words. The shock of what had just happened had struck him dumb. Annoyed at not getting an immediate response, Zanus bellowed, "Well? 'Ave yer told 'im? Ain't yer got nuffing to tell me?"

Keeping hold of the basin, Norman stammered, "I p-passed the message on. I can't say his name, he doesn't like it said here."

"Yer'd best 'ave news of that stone an' that woman," growled Zanus.

Breathing out slowly, Norman gathered himself together and said, "He will return when he's got them."

"Is yer tellin' me 'e ain't got the stone, nor that woman?"

Zanus' face was now protruding from the mirror. With the black eyes of Zanus boring into his own, Norman stammered "Er, er yes. I, I have told Crocanthus. He said he will return when he's got the girl and the stone."

Watching Zanus stroke his dirty long beard, Norman tried to work out how he was able to project his face through the mirror. Zanus let out a raucous laugh and said, "Don't yer go fergettin', I got meself one or two potions. I can keep me eyes on yer. I'll always know where yer are." Then the face faded back into a reflected image.

"If yer told Crocanthus to get back 'ere, yer'd best get yerself back 'ere too. I 'ave needs fer yer 'ere," hissed Zanus.

Not sure how to answer that, Norman closed his eyes for a moment. As he opened his eyes again he noticed that the image of Zanus was beginning to fade. Relieved to see his own reflection coming back again, he let out a huge sigh and sat down on the floor. The thought of going back to Dofstram brought fresh fears and bad memories.

Holding his head in his hands and willing his shaking body to calm down, he saw flashes of what happened at the hands of those ruffians and feared the same could happen again. Dragged from the cave and roughly tied to one of the horses, he had to run to keep pace with the horse. Where he was going Norman didn't know, but one thing he did remember was thinking his lungs were ready to burst. When at last the horse stopped, he found himself standing outside some enormous wooden gates. A coarse voice demanded to be let through, and it wasn't long before the sound of creaking wood indicated that the gates were being opened.

Dreading what lay beyond the gates, he recalled thinking that there was something evil about this place. He took in the height of the black stone walls and knew he would never be able to escape over them. As the gates were lowered, the creaking and groaning seemed to increase. Finally the horses were urged forward. Hauled up by the collars, they dragged him into the filthy cobbled courtyard. Ordering one of the workers to cut him free from the horse, Norman had thought this might be a chance to escape. Unfortunately not. As soon as the rope was cut he dropped to the ground through weakness.

Seeing his clothes were torn to shreds, he slowly took stock of his sore and painful legs, the skin mingled with blood and torn clothing. He noticed the horse had become unsettled and was shuffling to and fro. Terrified of being trampled on, he tried to move away, but was prevented from doing so. Two of the Zanuthians thought he was trying to escape, and came at him with their fists, landing blow after blow.

He was not sure how long this lasted. He could only remember lying on the cobblestones with fresh pain searing through his whole body. Blinking his eyes to try and remove some of the sweat and blood from blinding him, he noticed a couple of raggedy-clothed stable lads calming the horse down. Lying still, he waited until he felt he could get up without falling back down. That was when he heard coarse voices and raucous laughter and guessed it was at his expense.

It was then that he heard the name of Zanus for the first time. At the time Norman thought this person would help him, but before he could pursue that thought, he noticed several bedraggled womenfolk making their way in his direction. Trying to make conversation with them proved impossible, as for some reason none of the women would talk to him. Even when he tried to thank them for the drink of water, they remained silent.

He did notice that while they were tending him they kept a wary eye on his captors. Somewhat better for the water, he considered the possibility of bribery. Searching through his ragged clothing, he discovered that what he had in his pockets when he had set out was now gone. He cursed himself for following David and Jayne into the cave.

Then a rough hand grabbed him by the collar and hauled him onto his feet. It seemed to Norman the women had scuttled away like phantoms in the night.

Chapter Thirteen

The deserted village

A noise outside the cloakroom brought Norman back to the present. He remained silent and still, hoping it wasn't someone sent to repair the door. He wasn't sure if it was shock or heat causing him sweat profusely, but he did know he was very uncomfortable. Holding his breath and waiting for a knock on the door he was glad to hear the footsteps moving away, followed by a door being closed some way off.

Taking this moment to see what state he was in, he felt disgusted at what he saw. Dried blood on his clothing and his shirt torn, he was not surprised to see his face bruised and battered. The only thing that concerned him now was how he would be able to leave in such a state. What if someone saw him?

Thinking he would try and walk, he took hold of the basin to help him off the floor. Standing still for a moment, he tentatively took a step forward, but faltered. Grabbing hold of the basin, he managed to stop himself from falling back on the floor. He took the towel from the holder and wrapped it round his body. Checking in the mirror, he could see it was only just big enough to cover his tattered clothing.

Exhausted even by such a small action, he sat back on the floor and contemplated the best way to leave. However, his past thoughts hadn't quite finished haunting him, as he was about to find out.

Reluctant to face the consequences of his actions, he blinked several times thinking this would make the memories disappear, instead, he found his thoughts had turned once more to his initial introduction to the Tower of Zorax. Shuddering at the memory of those things hanging off the walls brought real fear to him, as did those horrible screeching black birds. He remembered thinking at the time what a weird place David had come to. Only when he brought David to mind did he wonder where he and Jayne had gone. He couldn't remember seeing them in the tower when he first arrived. But remembering what he witnessed later, he struggled to break free from the memory.

Recalling how roughly he'd been pushed down those slimy stairs, he could still smell the rancid air which led to the dungeons. Not only was he greeted by a stench, there were screams and cries that echoed around the dungeon. This, he was about to discover, were the screams of prisoners being tortured.

Roughly pushed through a steel door, it had taken a while for his eyes to become accustomed to the semi-darkness. With only a couple of small flames sending out light he noticed several guards were sitting underneath them. He was pulled along the floor until he reached a wall. Then he could remember screaming as they strapped his wrists in iron cuffs and left him hanging like a limp rag. How long he hung there he couldn't recall, but he knew the shock he felt when someone ripped the remains of the shirt from his back.

Shouting and screaming did nothing to halt what happened next. His fear was made no less when he heard a harsh voice ordering the guards to get out. It was much later he learned that it was the voice of the hated Crocanthus.

Becoming aware that there were other prisoners in the cell alongside him, he strained his ears and eyes to see if he could discover who else was there. He could remember wondering how many were dead. But then he would hear pitiable groans coming from all sides of the room.

By this time, Norman had given up all hope of ever leaving alive. Suddenly there was the sound of whip being flexed, then a swish of air. At first he thought it was someone else being whipped, but as his back began to sting he realised it was him. He couldn't remember feeling the first impact, but it wasn't long before the pain started to soar through his body. With the full weight of his body being supported by his wrists, Norman felt as if his shoulders were being ripped apart.

With his back raw and burning, he screamed with pain, using what strength he could muster to plead with them to stop. Ignoring his screams and begging, the torturers seemed to increase the pressure. After more lashings from the whip he guessed he must have passed out, as the next thing he remembered was hearing someone whisper, "Hold on, he'll soon tire." There was a moment he could remember wanting to die. The searing pain that travelled throughout his body made him wonder how much longer his arms could bear his weight.

Although he couldn't see anyone, he knew there was a prisoner near him. Attempting to whisper, he found his mouth was too dry and his tongue too swollen to get out much more that a squeak. He wasn't surprised no one answered.

Laying the bloodied whip across the straw floor, Crocanthus stepped closer to Norman's ear and uttered, "You were lucky this time, but there will be another." Hearing him order the guards to release the prisoner and take him to Zanus, Norman knew instantly this was not good. He felt rough hands releasing him from the straps, and fell to the floor. Unable to stand on his own, he shuddered at the memory of the brutal guards who'd taken him through the many darkened passages that led to Zanus' room. All he could think of was getting something to take the pain away. But remembering who had nursed him back to health on other occasions, Norman knew his reception this time would be even less welcoming than before.

The cloakroom suddenly became a blur as he was faced with the memory of Zanus' room. Zanus' seat towered over the room. Not forgetting those terrible black birds that hovered on and around Zanus' chair. The image of their evil eyes peering at him made him shiver. He knew Zanus only had to command them and they would attack. Zanus stood up and flung his cloak of feathers round him, then brought the large stick down on the stone floor with a loud bang, demanding everyone's attention.

"Should we peck 'is eyes out now?" screeched one of the birds. Stunned, Norman had remained absolutely still. He scanned the room without moving his head. He heard the coarse voice of Zanus say, "Not yet. Later p'r'aps if 'e doesn't do what 'e is ordered to do." He feared Zanus was going to place him back in the cell with David. Recalling the treatment Zanus had ordered for David, he was desperate to get free. Then his thoughts turned to Lottie. Hoping this would secure his freedom, he cautiously mentioned her name. Not getting any reaction he added, "She is the daughter of those other two humans." Surely he would soon be free.

He recalled the reaction from Zanus when he learnt of Lottie's existence. Outraged that these people had a kid, he screamed with rage and started snorting like a wounded boar. But Norman hadn't expected him to send Crocanthus to capture her. The next thing he remembered was Zanus demanding, "Bring 'im closer. Let's see what else 'e knows."

"Is 'ere close enough, boss?" asked an uncouth voice. Receiving only a grunt for an answer, Norman was dropped unceremoniously onto the steps. This was the moment he feared those dreadful birds would get their wish and relieve him of his eyes. As if knowing what he was thinking, one of the birds screeched, "Couldn't we 'ave just one eye?" Snorting with amusement, Zanus roared, "What, yer don't wanna lose just one eye?" Leaning closer to Norman, Zanus warned, "Don't yer go finking I don't know what yer finking, cos I do."

Shaking off this memory, Norman now felt he was strong enough to make a move. Quietly opening the door, he opened it just far enough to see if anyone was close by. Relieved to see the hallway was empty he moved as fast as he could towards the front door. Out of breath, he stood for a minute then made his way down the road as fast as he could.

Some time later, relieved he hadn't been followed, Norman was standing outside the gate of the house he had once occupied. Looking round to see if he'd been noticed, he opened the gate and made his way towards the door. He stared in dismay at the run-down property and the garden he'd once lovingly tended, he doubted that anyone lived there. Making a mental note to restore it back to the way it had been, Norman realised he didn't know if he would ever return. He made his way to the side door. Unable to open it, he remembered that the kitchen window at the back would never shut properly. He moved swiftly round to the back and tested the window. To his relief, the window literally fell out into his hands. He made a quick check that he hadn't drawn attention to himself.

It took only a few moments for him to climb in through the window and stand in the kitchen. He was despondent when he saw the state of the damp-ridden walls and ceilings. Making his way to where he'd kept his clothes, it didn't take him long to search through the few remaining ones. Thankful the moths had left a few untouched; he changed into fresh attire, ignoring how damp they felt.

Back in the kitchen, he screwed his nose up when he saw the rust-coloured water coming out of the dripping tap. By now, he was beginning to feel hungry. Not sure what he should do, he knew it was no good looking in here for anything, he guessed the vermin would have made short work of whatever they found. Thinking he might just take a quick look, he began rifling through the dirty and cobwebby cupboards.

On opening the last cupboard, he jumped back in fright. Closing the door with a bang he stood staring at it, then cautiously opened it again.

"Are yer trying to shut me out?" A pair of evil green eyes was staring out at him. Imelda.

"N - no. I didn't expect to see you when I opened the door. What do you want?" But she had disappeared from view.

He felt panic rising. Closing the cupboard door, he made his way back to the chair and heaved a sigh of relief, thinking she must have just been a mirage. Then, from out of nowhere, he heard that eerie voice ordering him to return to Dofstram.

He peered round the small kitchen, wondering where she could have hidden herself. As if she knew what he was thinking, he heard her say, "Yer won't see me but I can see yer. Now, drink the potion on the table an' get back to Dofstram. Yer'll suffer if yer don't. Don't ferget, I needs the woman an' the stone."

Not sure if he should tell her Crocanthus hadn't got either, he was shocked to hear her say, "No needs to worry yer 'ead about Crocanthus. Just get yerself back 'ere."

He was surprised to see a bottle on the table, and couldn't

remember seeing it there before. He lifted it up and stared at the contents.

"Drink it all!" she cackled.

Norman removed the top and put the bottle to his lips. Ignoring the fear that it could be poison, he hesitated no longer and drank the potion in one go. At first, there was nothing to indicate what the potion would do. He wanted to laugh it off as a hoax, but found himself suddenly facing the boulder covering the entrance to the portal. He did not want to enter again, but then he heard her familiar cackling voice urging him to remove the boulder.

"Inkle abble dabble," he chanted.

As he waited for the boulder to move, he wondered if he'd said the words in the wrong order. But just then the boulder began to shift. Overcoming the panic that was beginning to set in, he looked for the flaming torch he'd used previously. As he was about to lift the flame, the voice of Imelda warned, "Don't ferget, I'll be with yer all the way." He started on his way through the portal, ready to face whatever came at him.

* * * *

With a good distance covered and many villages later, DaVendall was troubled by the villagers' lack of response. Wondering what had happened to make these people so reluctant to help, he advised his group to take a rest. He raised his cane to his face and saw that his trusty Gamlon must have been having similar thoughts.

"What can have happened? Normally the Outlanders are ready to help," DaVendall whispered. "Did you notice how scared they all looked? Do you think they could have been threatened by you-know-who?"

"It crossed my mind," replied Gamlon. "There's no knowing what terrors could have been used on them."

"I've had a thought about that. I'm wondering if we dare try and see what's in some of the villager's minds," said DaVendall.

"It would have to be done with some care, we don't want anyone picking up our thoughts," Gamlon replied solemnly.

Then with a slight nod of the head he indicated to DaVendall that he was ready to assist. Checking to make sure they were free of danger, DaVendall asked Gamlon if he was ready. They closed their eyes and felt their minds join as one. Now they prepared themselves to see if they could discover the cause of the fear in the villagers' minds.

After a while Gamlon's mind gave such a jolt that DaVendall quickly withdrew.

"Did you see that?" asked Gamlon.

"Just as I feared, many of their folk have been taken from their homes. It's no wonder they are fearful of helping. Perhaps if they know we need their help to try and rescue the prisoners they might help."

"Trouble is, we don't know where they've been taken them or who has them. We can only guess they are at the tower, but what if…"

Just at that moment DaVendall interrupted. "Don't say the word, Gamlon. I feel a certain person isn't too far away." They wondered what other terrors Imelda had used to instil such fear.

"We'll keep this to ourselves at the moment, and see what happens," said DaVendall as he turned to call everyone to mount up. Settled back at DaVendall's side, Gamlon churned over what he'd seen in other minds. Wondering if the same had happened at the next village, Hesslewick, he couldn't help hoping for a better response.

DaVendall, picking up on Gamlon's thoughts, whispered, "I agree with you, let's hope these Outlanders will offer support. Hopefully the people of Hesslewick will step forward."

"I hope you're right," replied DaVendall, in a vacant voice. "It sure is strange, Outlanders being reluctant to assist. I'm certain they know what terrors will happen should Zanus take over the land. Remembering how his father ruled and the carnage he created, they won't want to return to those dark and brutal days."

Noticing that Themis had ridden alongside him, DaVendall was surprised to see her looking so apprehensive. Before he could ask what was troubling her he felt Gamlon stir. Sensing approaching danger, he asked Gamlon and Themis if they too had sensed something amiss. Thinking it might be better to respond telepathically, Themis stated, “It’s funny you say that, DaVendall, I thought I heard an odd sound earlier. It was coming from some distance away. One thing I do know, it’s coming from within the boundaries of Hesslewick. The troubling thing is, nothing has come into view.”

Having experienced the same thing himself, Gamlon added telepathically, “I can’t make out what it was either. Like Themis, I’m certain the sound is coming from Hesslewick.” Themis asked, “Should I take a quick fly round to see if I can discover what made it?”

Hesitating, DaVendall finally replied telepathically, “I think you should remain here at the moment, Themis. Whatever it is, it could cause you some harm.” Disappointed, but aware of DaVendall’s concern, Themis gave a nod of agreement. Turning her senses to try to discover what the noise could be, she suddenly heard it again.

“Did you hear that? It sounded like a groan to me,” she said.

“I heard it that time. I’ve heard it before,” said DaVendall.

“Me too. And it’s not something I thought I would ever hear again.”

“You aren’t going to tell me it’s you-know-who?” whispered Themis. A look from DaVendall and Gamlon was enough to let her know she’d guessed correctly. Not sure what to say, Themis stared at them with wide frightened eyes.

“Have any of you heard any other unfamiliar sounds?” asked DaVendall. “We’re certain it’s coming from the next village. Or it could be coming from the wooded area just beyond.”

The Ziphers joined minds and telepathically quizzed each other. Themis explained, “Like me, the telepaths heard groaning, but no other sounds. They did agree it seemed to be coming from the village.”

Surprised to hear Themis speaking out loud instead of signing or telepathy, Gamlon commented warmly, “That’s the best of having parents who are from two races. Having a Jasper mother and a Zipher father has proved invaluable to us on many occasions.” Accepting Gamlon’s comment, Themis gently replied, “I am indeed lucky, Gamlon.” Listening to their quiet conversation brought some light relief to the listeners.

DaVendall was about to ask the telepaths to concentrate as one when Cyluc, one of the many male Jaspers, gave a loud shout. "Hide, we need to hide." DaVendall hastily replied, "Cyluc's right, head for that clump of bushes and trees over there." DaVendall and his group wasted no time in heading for cover.

Ensuring their animals were hidden, DaVendall and his group waited in anticipation to see what had alerted their senses to danger. With an eerie silence falling, it wasn't long before a voice whispered, "Even the trees have stopped moving." About to remonstrate with the person, DaVendall decided this wasn't the moment, as the strange silence was suddenly shattered by a terrible screech. Scanning round to try and discover what had caused it, Gamlon whispered, "I bet that's another of…" Before he could finish the sentence, DaVendall raised his cane to eye level and mouthed, "Don't say the name here." Realising how close he had come to saying the dreaded name, Gamlon mouthed, "Sorry."

The sky darkened, and it wasn't long before they saw the reason why; a flock of Zanus' spy birds flying over. Rowena, one of the King's troopers, whispered, "Why are they here?"

Gamlon had been quietly observing Rowena, and noticed how quickly she covered her mouth with her hand. Sensing her anxiety, he watched to see if any of the spy birds reacted. He was amused to see her trying to put her long red hair in order. It wasn't long before his attention was drawn away when he heard a voice whisper loudly, "What's that? Not the spy birds, those other creatures?"

All eyes turned to where the pointing fingers were indicating.

"You know what they are, don't you?" whispered Gamlon. Having seen such creatures on another occasion, DaVendall was reluctant to say anything. Aware they were another of Imelda's creations, DaVendall thought it would be wiser to communicate using telepathy. To ensure everyone would know what they could be facing he asked the telepaths to sign what he was about to tell them.

"It's essential we remain absolutely silent; these creatures are able to hear beyond what the spy birds can," he began. But before he could continue he gasped out loud as did many others. Staring at the grotesque creature that was leading the creatures brought fresh fear to all.

Fearful someone might make a sound which would alert the creatures to their presence, DaVendall repeated the warning telepathically, "Be quiet. Warn the non-telepaths. I will explain all later."

Terrified, the smaller folk quietly and quickly made their way to stand as near to the taller troops as they could. The troops moved closer together to ensure their small friends had extra protection.

Conscious of Imelda's presence, DaVendall knew he would have to place a protective shield around the telepathic minds. He was also aware that while he protected their thoughts they wouldn't be able to correspond with anyone.

Gamlon quickly reached out to Cindra, asking her to let the telepaths know what DaVendall was doing to protect their thoughts. Cindra signed, "Do you think these creatures could be the reason for the other Outlanders' reluctance to ride with us?"

DaVendall responded by signing, "I would say it's more than likely. I'll be able to explain more, once it is safe to do so." Gamlon, sensing DaVendall's concerns with Imelda picking up any telepathic thoughts, whispered, "I'll tell the telepaths to ignore anything that comes into their minds and wait for you to give the OK." Giving Gamlon a nod, DaVendall left Gamlon to explain to Cindra what they'd discussed.

"We don't want anyone in our thoughts, we'll sign until advised," signed Froy, with other telepaths agreeing. Rowena was still curious as to what the other creatures were. Pulling her Jasper companion, Varie, closer, Rowena placed her hands over Varie's and signed, "I wonder what in the blazes those creatures are?"

Varie shrugged her shoulders, then signed, "Didn't Gamlon say DaVendall would explain later?" Nodding her head in acceptance, Rowena felt a tug on her sleeve. Glancing down, she saw it was Froy, the young Zipher who had drawn her attention earlier.

"What's happening?" signed Froy. "Is it all right for us to move?" Realising how alarmed her friend was, Rowena looked her straight in the eye before signing, "Sorry, Froy. I was just asking Varie about those weird creatures. Remember all will be revealed later by DaVendall." Nodding her acceptance of what Rowena had signed, Froy sidled closer to Rowena.

Some time later DaVendall removed the shield from his thoughts and checked for signs of danger before alerting the telepaths that their minds were free. He was keen to make sure it was safe before leading them into Hesslewick. Thinking about the best way to do this, he decided it would be wiser to cloak himself and Cedar, leaving him and Gamlon free to take a closer look at the village. With this decision made, he signed to let the telepaths know that the protective covering had been removed from their minds, but warned them to take care and sign if they were worried. That done, he went on to tell them what he was planning to do. He glanced up at the sky to ensure there were no stray creatures lurking about. Wanting to move on, he wasted no time in cloaking his unicorn and himself.

"I think its all clear," said Gamlon. "I don't sense any danger. But knowing who we saw leading those dreadful creatures, I suggest we wait awhile before moving any closer to the village."

Sensing the same himself, DaVendall whispered, "You're right. We need to wait a while before moving on, just in case you-know-who has become aware of our presence." Returning to his group of people, he uncloaked.

"I don't sense any danger nearby, but we only went a short distance," DaVendall told them. "Nothing appeared to be out of the ordinary. However, I feel we should proceed with caution. Maintain vigilance at all times and keep a check on fellow companions. We have many miles to cover and Alfreston needs assistance."

Relieved to hear they were going to move on, but still curious, Rowena whispered, "What were those creatures with Zanus' birds, DaVendall?" A sea of expectant faces looked straight at him. Without wanting to take up too much time, DaVendall offered a quick explanation.

"Some of you might have recognised the face of the Old Crone. She has somehow managed to create these creatures to imitate her. The only thing I can compare them with is a distorted form of vulture. We have seen them before, which is how I know they have acute hearing. But another of their terrible weapons is their beaks; they are sharper and longer than those of the spy birds. They have long, tough talons at the ends of their wings, capable of tearing strips of flesh off the largest human."

Shuddering at the thought there was something out there worse than the spy birds, Cyluc stammered, "Can, can they get us as well?"

"Not with me here," replied Rowena bravely. There was hushed laughter, but it wasn't long before the other troopers agreed with Rowena and checked to make sure the smaller folk were close by.

The memory of Beauty's captivity came to mind, which made DaVendall mutter, "I wonder if she discovered how to do this after..." Before he could finish, Gamlon interrupted, "I don't think we need to go that far We'll keep those thoughts to ourselves." Thankful his friend had stopped him in time; DaVendall took up from where he left off. "Please take care when you are out in the open, these creatures are evil and will attack anything," he urged. "Right everyone, let's get going. Head for Hesslewick. Remain alert - you never know when trouble will appear."

With much to think about, and the worrying presence of Imelda, it appeared no one felt like saying anything. Slowly they urged their animals to follow DaVendall in the direction of Hesslewick. Remaining silent, they thought over what DaVendall had told them. It was the sighting of Imelda and those awful creatures that had so greatly alarmed them all.

Just then one of the Jaspers suddenly called out, "Look! Isn't that smoke up ahead?" Bringing the animals to a halt, Cedar turned his head and asked, "Isn't that smoke coming from the village of Hesslewick?"

"Lift me up DaVendall, let me see what's happening," said Gamlon. DaVendall did so. "I fear you are right Cedar," he said. "I suggest we proceed with caution."

Observing the animals had slowed their trot to a walking pace, DaVendall wondered what horrendous sights would greet them. Noticing the pained expression on Gamlon's face, DaVendall knew he didn't have to say what he'd been thinking. He wasn't too surprised when Gamlon whispered, "I guess you and I are thinking the same?"

DaVendall decided to keep Gamlon in place, giving him an extra pair of eyes. Sitting proudly beside his friend's shoulder, Gamlon couldn't help grimacing at the sight of the smoke billowing out from the village.

"It wouldn't have taken much to set those thatched dwellings alight," Gamlon uttered.

"Do you think it would be safe for me to fly on ahead?" asked Themis.

Concerned for everyone's safety, DaVendall replied, "No, Themis. I don't think it will be safe enough for you to do that. I want everyone to take a sip of the invisible liquid Beauty gave us. To make sure we don't lose sight of one another, only make it a small sip. That will leave some if we need it later, and it will also enable us to see each other's outline. Have no fear, this liquid will stop others seeing us."

Turning his attention to Cedar, he asked, "Would you and the other unicorns give a little invisibility cover to all the animals? Make sure their hooves are made silent. This will enable us to enter the village unseen."

No sooner had he asked than he noticed the animals were beginning to fade from view. With a last-minute instruction from DaVendall to hold tight to the reins, the group continued into the village. Resembling ghost-like figures, they remained alert to any possible danger. Searching through a veil of invisibility, DaVendall sensed unease coming from the group.

"You don't think she's taken villagers from here, do you DaVendall?" asked Gamlon. About to reply, DaVendall was halted by a groaning sound coming from a short distance away. Raising a hand to halt the others, DaVendall asked, "Can anyone else hear that groaning?" They had all heard it.

"Does anyone know where it's coming from?" asked Gamlon.

"It's coming from the other side of you and DaVendall," whispered Themis.

"I think we had better search over that way and leave the others to search through the village," replied DaVendall.

"I agree," Gamlon whispered back.

DaVendall requested everyone's attention. Waiting for them to gather round, he quietly stated what he'd discussed with Gamlon.

"We need to find any survivors," he said. "Gamlon and I will go this way." He pointed. "I suggest you go in groups and search the dwellings. We really must discover what or who is causing that noise."

"Would this be a good time for me to take a short fly round?" asked Themis. "I might be able to discover more, further into the village." Not wanting to put Themis in harm's way, DaVendall glanced round at the group and told them, "I've tried to pick up where the villagers might be, but for some reason my mind is being blocked." Remembering Themis' request, he turned to her and said, "I suggest, Themis, you take along Cyluc. Keep together and stay close to the others." They watched Themis and Cyluc soar above the waiting group of people to lead the group off on their search.

Glancing over the group below and seeing they were all fairly close together, Themis flew down onto Dylan's horse. "Is everything all right, Dylan?" she asked.

Recovering from the shock of Themis's sudden appearance, Dylan replied "We're all right so far. I wonder why we haven't picked up signs of the villagers. Do you suppose they are in hiding, or do you think they sought shelter in another village?"

"I've wondered that myself," whispered Themis. "Where would the villagers go? Don't forget the terrible carnage we saw in those other villages. I need to join Cyluc. Keep everyone close and let's hope we soon find the villagers."

Having seen Themis with Dylan, Rowena asked her horse to take to her closer to Dylan. As she approached, she called out in a low voice, "Dylan, slow up a bit." Dylan waited until she was beside him, then asked, "What is it Rowena? Has something happened?"

"Nothing, as far as I know. I just wanted to ask what Themis wanted," she replied in a low voice.

"I think Themis wanted a rest. We're concerned there's no trace of the villagers. Perhaps our Jaspers will spot them soon," Dylan whispered.

"That's exactly what we've been discussing at the back. Where could the villagers have gone?"

Walking the horses close together and remaining silent with her thoughts, Rowena suddenly said, "I'll go and join the others at the back. Keep alert my friend." Turning to speak to her horse, Rowena asked, "Take me to the back of the group please." Doing as Rowena requested, her horse commented, "This is so strange. Have you noticed the animals have disappeared too?" Not having noticed that, Rowena asked, "Where do you think they would have gone?"

"I'm not sure. They could be with the people," the animal replied.

Having rejoined Cyluc, Themis asked, "Any luck with finding the villagers?"

"No joy. Is everything all right with the others?" he asked.

"I think so. but I did get a sense of concern from them. Like us, they are wondering if the villagers are in hiding, or..." Themis wasn't keen to add anything extra.

Themis and Cyluc continued flying on in silence until they reached the smouldering dwellings. Shocked by the sight, their concern turned to the villagers.

"Do you think there could be any survivors?" asked Cyluc.

"I don't know. It doesn't look very good from here does it?" Themis replied, in a quiet and thoughtful voice. She was surprised when Cyluc broke into her thoughts and whispered, "Do you think we'll see any of those creatures?"

"I'd almost forgotten about them. I was wondering about the villagers. I still don't understand why we can't pick up where they are. I hope we don't see those creatures, they looked really evil, didn't they?" Themis replied. Glancing down at the group below, she felt some reassurance to see their cover was still in place. How long it would last she had no idea, but she said nothing to Cyluc. Instead she suggested he should fly down and take a rest before they searched another part of the village.

* * * *

As they travelled on, DaVendall and Gamlon sensed each other's mounting concerns. But DaVendall was a little surprised to hear Gamlon whisper, "You'd better draw me from the cane, DaVendall. If we come across any unexpected enemy I'll be ready."

"Good idea," replied DaVendall thoughtfully, but he wasn't giving full attention to what Gamlon said. He withdrew Gamlon from the secured cane attached to his saddle. Grasping the sea-horse handle, which had been neatly secured onto the long-bladed knife, DaVendall's concern was to discover what had made the sound they'd heard. With an idea in mind, DaVendall whispered to Cedar, "Halt here, my friend. I will walk from now on." Dismounting, he led the unicorn to a nearby tree and requested Cedar to listen out for his call.

Giving DaVendall a nudge with his nose Cedar whispered, "Take care, I will come the moment I hear from you." In response, DaVendall gave Cedar a gentle stroke on his nose. "Maintain your cover for as long as possible," he whispered. "I hope it won't be long before I am able to call you."

"Are you sure this is wise?" asked Gamlon. "You might need him."

Bringing Gamlon closer to eye level, DaVendall whispered, "I thought it might be wiser to leave Cedar here, after all we don't yet know what we are going to face. Think what delight Imelda would have in capturing a unicorn."

Gamlon nodded. He couldn't help thinking over what DaVendall had said.

After they'd gone a short distance Gamlon whispered, "Have you sensed danger?"

"I have, but what it is I can't make out," DaVendall responded. "I suggest we use telepathy from now on, until we discover what dangers lay ahead."

Themis now had concerns of her own. Having flown around keenly looking for any signs of life, she noticed how strong the wind had become. As she struggled to fly against it, she could feel her strength beginning to decline. She flew down to join Cyluc and suggested they take a bit longer to rest.

"Good idea," said Cyluc, pleased at not having to fly off too soon. "That wind sure got stronger. It seemed to sap quite a bit of my strength." Hearing the relief in his voice Themis knew he had gallantly followed her, despite battling against the wind and his own weariness.

As they all walked further into the village, the destruction of the dwellings was becoming ever clearer.

Relying on her senses to guide her, Themis struggled on against the wind. Cyluc was finding it more and more difficult to keep up with her. Finally they agreed to join the others back on the ground. But as they were about to descend, Themis noticed an area a little further on that hadn't been covered. Thinking she might just have enough strength to fly over it, she called out, "Fly down to our friends and ask them to wait for me to return. I'll join you in a moment."

Cyluc replied, "Don't go too far." Turning her attention back to where she was headed, Themis summoned what remaining strength she could as she flew towards the unchecked area. Fearful the enemy could be near and feeling her wings beginning to tire, she decided to make a quick flight over and search the remainder on foot. From the air, she could see nothing. Seeing a clear place, she flew down to the ground and sought shelter behind the remains of a smouldering dwelling.

While waiting to get her breath back, she scanned round listening for signs of life. Certain it was safe for her to continue, Themis took one quick look round and prepared to set off. At that moment she thought she heard a noise. She waited for the sound to come again, but there was only silence. Perhaps it was just the wind

She decided to give it another minute. She slowly made her way along the row of smouldering dwellings, quickly checking each one as she passed.

As she approached a dwelling near the end of yet another lane, something caught her eye. She stopped and held her breath. Concentrating her ears for any sound that might indicate danger, she sidestepped along to a smouldering gap and glanced inside.

Was that something stirring in the far corner?

Straining all her senses to understand what she had seen, she tried to ignore the wind. With nothing forthcoming, Themis began to doubt if she'd actually seen anything. Fearful that she had stumbled upon the enemy, she crept stealthily past the remains of the house.

Suddenly, without warning, a piece of smouldering straw fell down from the roof in front of her. Jumping out of the way, Themis realised how lucky she was that it had missed her. Trying to still her rapid breathing, she drew in a deep breath and listened.

Then suddenly, she heard a voice say, "Do you think she's gone?"

Themis took some comfort in knowing her invisibility cover was still around her. Taking a couple of steps further, she hoped to be able to see who was there. She cautiously peered through a hole, seeing a thin beam of light.

She could see a dark mass in the corner, and realised that she was looking at a small group of villagers. Careful not to alarm them, she drew back. Should she reveal herself to these people? She decided instead to go in search of the other villagers.

* * * *

DaVendall had become anxious at not hearing from Themis since she had telepathically told her companions it was safe to continue. He wondered if she was in trouble. After much concentration, DaVendall finally reached her mind.

"We have some idea what was causing that groaning noise, but as yet we can't confirm it," he told her. "We think there is some evil trickery afoot."

"Oh no," stated Themis nervously, "Has Gamlon…?" Before she could finish, Gamlon interrupted telepathically, "Yes, Themis, but we have to make sure. How about you, have you found the villagers?"

Themis assured DaVendall the group were safe and told him about the villager's she'd seen. Gamlon asked, "Themis are you still covered by your invisibility cover? Do you think they might have got a sense of your presence?"

Confirming she was still had some cover, she went on to

explain that this why she hadn't approached the villagers, for fear of scaring them. "I didn't want them to think I was some sort of a ghost," she said. "This wind is making it difficult to tell where sounds are coming from."

"We found that too Themis, that was a wise decision not to reveal yourself," DaVendall replied. "It seems as if everything is under control so we'll let you continue with your search. Please take care, and alert us if you need help."

Chapter Fourteen

Imelda in disguise

With their invisibility cover worn off, Rowena was becoming anxious at the time it was taking Themis to return. Gathering the group together she asked, "Does everyone agree we should continue? I'm concerned that Themis could be in danger."

"Before we move on, perhaps the telepaths could try and contact her," suggested Dylan, one of the troopers. Annoyed she hadn't thought of that, Rowena thanked him for the suggestion then turned her attention back to the group. "Could the telepaths do as Dylan suggested and try to contact Themis? Dylan and I will watch out for signs of any enemy while you do this. We need to know where she is, and above all we need to know she's safe." The telepaths joined minds and concentrated on drawing Themis' thoughts.

It seemed an age to the rest of the group before Froy drew their attention and signed, "We have managed to reach Themis. She's on the ground as her wings are tiring. She says she's all right, but she has something important to tell us. She has come across a group of villagers in one of the burnt-out dwellings. It's some way further on, close to the end of the village. As her cover is still in place she's gone in search of other villagers."

"Themis would like us to go on ahead," said Varie. "We're to follow this lane to the end of the village and turn right after the third lane. They're at the end of that lane. Themis did say to take care as the wind had increased to almost a gale. She will be with us soon."

Content to hear Themis was safe and knowing that at least

some of the villagers had been found, Rowena led the group on. Following the directions Themis had given them, they walked through what was left of the village, edging closer together after facing such devastation and destruction. It appeared the poorly-erected dwellings had taken the biggest impact of whatever had done this.

Slowly continuing up the lane, they searched each and every property hoping to find any villagers. On impulse Rowena went to look in the stables to see if any one had sought shelter with the animals. She shuddered at the deathly silence that greeted her. She soon realised that not only had the villagers disappeared, the animals had too.

"I don't like the feel of this place," whispered Rowena's horse. "Something doesn't feel right."

"Nor me," said Rowena, stroking her horses nose.

"May I suggest the troopers check the outer lanes that will leave the rest of us to check the dwellings?" said Dylan. "I'm not sure what I'm feeling but something's not right."

The troopers agreed to split up and check opposite sides, but they searched to no avail. Joining up again and continuing into another lane, the leader of the group halted them going any further. Thinking they'd seen the worst, they weren't prepared for the number of bodies of dead villagers strewn across the lane and lying beside the ruins.

Dismounting, they slowly moved around the bodies, hoping that someone might have survived. They weren't prepared for the shock of seeing how savagely they had been attacked. Many of them had had their eyes removed. Skin had been peeled off their limbs, and bones broken. The troopers guessed that this was the result of the villagers trying to defend themselves. The lead trooper suggested they move the bodies so the buzzards could not despoil them further. The task seemed to shock them all into silence. At last, and the task completed, the troopers mounted their horses ready to join the rest of the group.

Unaware of what the troopers had come across, Varie had drawn the attention of Rowena and others to something she had noticed ahead. Sickened by what she had seen, she waited a moment before telling her companions what it was. She urged them to follow her as they slowly made their way to see what they could do. Hoping there might at least be one survivor they couldn't believe the amount of villagers lying dead on the ground.

Without uttering a word, Rowena made her way towards a smouldering bundle of straw which had once been someone's dwelling. Stepping cautiously between and around the strewn bodies, she was anxious to discover if anyone had survived. Her companions joined her.

Trying to control her emotions, Rowena felt someone pulling on her arm; it was Froy.

"What is it Froy?" Rowena asked gently. But the fear in Froy's eyes explained what she too was thinking.

"I can't believe what I'm seeing. Who could have done such a thing? Do you think it was those evil spy birds, Rowena?" she signed. Not sure herself, but with a feeling of hatred for those that had done this, Rowena whispered, "I'm certain of it, but we will have to find out who else was involved. It seems a bit too messy for even those dreadful spy birds. It must be those other evil creatures that did this."

Feeling a tug on her arm Rowena turned to face Froy and apologised. "I'm sorry Froy, I guess we need to find out who else was involved in doing this. Stay close by me and we'll continue on together." They could only hope that some of the villagers had survived the attack and managed to seek refuge.

"It looks as if some of these people have been pecked to death," said Dylan. "Look, so many of them don't have their eyes. What could do such a terrible thing?"

They agreed to start burying these people and continue searching. It was with quiet reverence they prepared to bury the bodies. It took longer than they thought, as they set off in sombre mood to gather up their horses.

Then the troopers returned.

"We came across the most dreadful scenes," said their leader. "Not only were the dwellings ruined, there were dead villagers strewn all over the place. It took us a while to take in the brutality. We couldn't find any survivors. It was utter carnage. None of us had ever seen anything so horrific.

"Some of their injuries might have been through them defending themselves. It certainly looked as if the villagers put up a good fight."

Silence fell after hearing this. Then another of the troopers said, "This didn't look like something the spy birds could do. Whatever it was must have been much bigger."

"We found the same thing. Did you bury them?" Rowena asked.

"We couldn't, there were too many for us, but we did move them off the lane," said one of the troopers in a low voice.

"Perhaps we can return and bury them later," Rowena replied. "I suggest we move on or Themis will wonder what has happened to us."

They continued on foot, many quietly talking to their horses. Noticing they were close to the lane where Themis had told them of the discovery of some of the villagers, something made them stop and look around. Cyluc asked if anyone else sensed the danger he was feeling. He felt some relief on hearing nothing had been picked up. Turning to Varie, he asked, "Do you think the enemy is around?"

"Neither Cindra nor I have felt anything." she replied. "I do wish Themis would return. I wonder where she's gone." Ever fearful of the enemy lurking around, it was with some unease that the group decided to continue up the lane.

Finally coming to the end of the lane, Cyluc asked, "Where do we go from here? I thought we would have found Themis' villagers by now." With many thinking the same thing, Dylan suggested they search the immediate area.

Leaving the animals where they were, the Rancouins searched the dwellings and trees while the Ziphers and Jaspers scurried from bush to bush hoping to find any surviving villagers. Then Froy thought she heard a noise. In the process of delving into another bush, she listened to hear if the sound would be repeated. Quietly stepping out from the bushes, she made her way to Rowena. Pulling on Rowena's sleeve, she signed, "I thought I heard something over there. See those bushes all tangled together? I thought it came from there."

Frowning, Rowena wondered why she hadn't heard

anything, but she knew not to doubt Froy's acute hearing. Rowena suggested they make their way back to where Froy first heard the sound. No sooner had they reached the mass of bushes when Froy quickly signed, "There, you must have heard that?"

Calling out to everyone to hush, Rowena told them to listen out for the sound Froy had heard. Suddenly there it was again.

Rowena called out, "Hello? Is anybody there?"

She was surprised to hear Dylan calmly repeat her call. They were all taken by surprise when a timid voice called out. "Who's there?" Dylan parted a couple of the bushes and edged his way in the direction of where he thought the voice came from. Not wanting to scare the person away, he called out, "Hello there, my name is Dylan. Would you show yourself please?" Standing still he waited to see if the owner of the voice would appear.

By this time the whole group had gathered close to the mass of bushes and could only hear Dylan, having lost sight of him the midst of the bushes. Dylan, meanwhile, was waiting anxiously to see if anyone would appear. Fearing it could be one of Imelda's tricks, Rowena decided they'd waited long enough.

Just then they were surprised to see three small figures coming from the rear of the bushes. "You aren't going to hurt us, are you?" asked the child standing in the middle.

"We're not here to hurt you," said Rowena. "We've come to help. My name is Rowena and this is Froy." Not knowing if the children would understand signing, Froy decided to give it a try anyway. "Come with us, we'll take you somewhere safe." The smallest child ran out and hugged Froy. "You're a Zipher, aren't you?" he said.

Smiling down at the little lad hugging her waist, Froy gently released the boy and signed, "Correct. Will you tell me your name?"

Smiling back at Froy, but unable to hide the signs of tiredness and fear the boy replied, "My name is Benin, the other little one is my younger sister Winn, and the one in the middle is my older sister, Dee."

"Can I ask if your parents are with you?" said Varie. Suddenly the boy started to cry, but he managed to tell them his parents had been killed. With his sisters now standing beside him, Dee placed an arm round his shoulders and explained that creatures larger than the spy birds had killed their parents. Trying to stifle her tears, Dee went on to tell them that their parents had died protecting them.

The thoughts they'd had about what could have killed these villagers had just been proved correct. Varie turned to Rowena and asked, "Do you think we should make a move?"

"I think we'd better, but first we'll need to bury the rest of the people," said Rowena. "We can't leave them here for the buzzards." Rowena noticed Dylan had gathered the group and were already doing the unenviable task.

With the task completed, Rowena surprised them by suggesting they gather together to set out a plan of action. A sudden thought crossed her mind. "I wonder where Themis is?" she said. "Have any of the telepaths heard from her since our last message? I thought she might be back by now."

Aware they still had other dwellings to check out; Rowena's horse asked, "Where should we go from here?"

"I think we should continue searching for any other survivors," said Cyluc. "Themis did say she would be with us soon, and don't forget she said there were more villagers at the end of this lane. There might be others wounded, or hiding."

Turning to face him, Rowena agreed. "I think we should continue on foot. If the horses agree they should continue to come with us." she said.

No sooner had she finished when she heard gentle voices of the animals agreeing to assist. Seating the young villagers on the backs of two horses, they were about to set off when the telepaths realised Themis was trying to attract their attention. Signing to let the others know what was happening, the group remained still, but vigilant.

* * * *

Quietly observing the villagers, but unaware of the tasks her other friends had undertaken, Themis concentrated on drawing the minds of the telepaths. Having achieved this, she told them she was back at the end of the lane and was waiting for them to join her. Hearing the expressions of relief from the telepaths, Themis felt guilty at not reaching out to them sooner. With several questions being asked, she suggested it might be an idea to wait until they were all together before relaying what had been happening. An instant decision was made to make haste and join her. Checking to make sure the villagers were all right, the group followed Dylan as he led the way. Dee wanted to ask a question, but wasn't sure if she should. Cindra, sensing this, tugged on her leg and signed, "Is something troubling you?" Smiling back at Cindra, Dee whispered, "You must be a Zipher. I have often wondered how you are able to sense what a person is feeling."

Signing, Cindra replied, "I'm not sure myself. What is it you would like to know?" Dee softly said, "We waited so long for someone to come and help us, but no one came. Those creatures that attacked us were horrible. They were so large, and with beaks big enough to crack a skull. Have you seen any of these creatures?" Cindra just nodded her head. Not keen to discuss what they'd seen and who they'd seen, she signed, "Let's hope we don't come across them on our way to Themis."

* * * *

Meanwhile, DaVendall and Gamlon continued on their way to investigate the strange groaning sound. As they approached the area they thought it had come from, a sudden sense of impending evil came over them. Shivering, Gamlon telepathically said, "I'm getting a terrible sense of evil, DaVendall. I feel we could be near to whatever it is."

"I think we should go over there," said Gamlon

Turning his attention to where Gamlon had indicated, DaVendall told Gamlon he too had felt an evil presence.

"Be ready for anything, Gamlon, I really don't like the feel of this," DaVendall stated telepathically. Putting extra pressure on the knife handle, Gamlon could feel his tension. "I'm ready when you are," Gamlon whispered. Raising his friend to eye level, DaVendall acknowledged Gamlon with a gentle squeeze. Noticing his invisibility cover was beginning to wear off and unsure of what they were about to face, he covered Gamlon and himself with his cloak.

"I wondered if you'd noticed that the cover was fading," Gamlon whispered. Acknowledging the comment, DaVendall continued towards a smouldering dwelling. Recognising it as the home of the leader of the village, he proceeded with great caution. Halting for a moment, he concentrated all his senses, hoping to discover what lay ahead. Gamlon refrained from speaking, but remained ready for action.

With all his senses taut, DaVendall whispered, "Stay alert my friend, goodness knows what perils lay ahead." Cautiously, he made his way to the house. Knowing there could be danger within, he slowly approached the place where a door had once hung.

"Hold on Gamlon, I'm getting a grave sense that danger is close by," DaVendall whispered. Knowing they couldn't be heard through DaVendall's cloak Gamlon whispered, "There's a change in atmosphere. We'd best be prepared."

DaVendall whispered, "Hold it. I've picked up the presence of Imelda. But what's strange is I'm not getting the full sense it's her, this is something different." Their minds joined as one, they slowly entered the property, taking care not to walk on any loose smouldering straw.

Tense but alert, DaVendall noticed a movement out of the corner of his eye. He was surprised to hear Gamlon whisper, "Take a look in the far corner, can you see something that shouldn't be there? Whatever it is, it's not good. There's an evil feeling."

Finally DaVendall decided to approach. With trepidation, he edged closer. He decided to take the initiative and surprise whatever this thing was.

Raising himself off the floor, DaVendall hovered for a moment, waiting to see if there would be any reaction. There was none. He glided quietly over to the corner. They seemed to be looking at a person doubled over. Hesitating before moving any closer, he suddenly caught a glimmer of movement. Gliding a little closer, he saw that it seemed to be Imelda, trying to disguise herself as a victim of the attack. Half was still Imelda, but he couldn't quite make out what the other part was. He could only guess he had surprised her as she began the transformation.

Revolted by what he'd seen, he knew Gamlon would have seen it too. Aware of Gamlon's feelings and sensing his urgency to attack, DaVendall whispered, "Now we know this is Imelda, we need to be wary."

"I'm sure we'll be able to defend ourselves," Gamlon stated. "We'll just have to make sure we don't find ourselves trapped."

"Don't be alarmed by what I'm about to attempt, Gamlon. I'm going to try and draw her out. I'd like to discover exactly what she's become."

DaVendall then transferred his voice outside the cloak and set about making a variety of animal and bird noises. Not getting any response, he sent out a trofalogue howl, but still no movement. Then he remembered the creatures that had flown over earlier. Drawing in a deep breath, DaVendall let out a terrifying screech, resembling that of the creatures.

"Did you see any movement?" he asked Gamlon.

"I think I did. Did you manage to see what she has become? You don't think she would become a trofalogue?"

"When I made the sound of a distressed trofalogue there was no reaction. But when I made the sound of those vulture-like creatures, that was when I saw a glimmer of movement," DaVendall whispered. Catching sight of further movement, he whispered, "Hold on Gamlon. See that, I believe she's about to reveal herself."

Just then a flame erupted from the corner. Jumping back, DaVendall decided it might be better to remain under the cover of his cloak. He watched to see if Imelda would reveal herself.

They stared at the thing as it rose up from the floor. DaVendall placed Gamlon in the cloak pocket. Aware that this was a signal that DaVendall was going to sign, Gamlon kept his head above pocket level, ready to read the message.

"I think we'd better not use our minds as she could pick up our presence," said DaVendall. "Just respond by the blinking of your eyes." Taking Gamlon back in his hand, he pointed his friend in the direction of where he was looking. But now the corner was empty.

Then they noticed something slithering across the floor towards them. At first DaVendall thought it was some kind of reptile, but as the creature drew nearer, Gamlon knew instantly that this was like no reptile he'd seen.

As they concentrated on following the creature's movements, they were startled by a familiar groan. Then a cackling voice called out, "Aah, DaVendall! So nice yer could make it. Come fer 'elpers 'ave yer?" DaVendall looked round, trying to discover where her voice was coming from.

"Can't see me, eh?" the voice taunted, then added, "I know yer 'iding in yer cloak. It's a pity I can't get yer in there." DaVendall and Gamlon were frustrated at not being able to see where the creature had gone. Moving closer to the entrance, DaVendall noticed a movement close by. Slightly unnerved, he remained cloaked. Staring at the creature before him, which he now knew was Imelda, he was alarmed to see part of its huge body lift off the ground. It resembled a serpent-like creature.

DaVendall was shocked to see it looking straight at him and wondered what was preventing him from moving away. She must be trying to hypnotise him through his cape.

"Gamlon, go for its eyes," he signalled.

Lifting himself free of the belt, Gamlon aimed directly at the creature's eyes. Missing on the first attempt, he tried again, managing to stab the creature's forehead. Screeching in pain, it raised the full length of its serpent-like body and aimed straight for Gamlon. He flew away, dodging the venom from the creature's mouth.

Now that the hypnotic state had been removed, DaVendall's concern was for Gamlon. He emitted a low whistle which he knew only Gamlon could hear, and was relieved to feel Gamlon return to his belt.

"Thank you my friend. I wasn't prepared for that. Are you all right?"

"I dodged it just in time, thank goodness. Yes, I am all right, but we need to get rid of this creature, whatever it is," Gamlon whispered.

They stared at the creature as it lowered itself to the ground. The head was huge and misshapen, the face disfigured by a large, ungainly-looking mouth and nose. The bulging green eyes were familiar.

"What a horror!" mouthed Gamlon.

"What yer waiting fer? Scared yer gonna get 'urt?" Imelda taunted. She knew DaVendall was there, but she was obviously angry at not being able to see him.

Sensing the apprehension in Gamlon, DaVendall gave a gentle squeeze on the knife handle to reassure his friend they were still safe. Watching the creature sway back and forth, they were surprised to see wings sprout from the sides of its body.

"What on earth…?" Gamlon whispered. They watched as the creature moved its head from side as if trying to seek out where the voice came from. Realising Imelda had been attracted to the sound of Gamlon, DaVendall decided it was time to remove his cloak.

"I thought you could do better than just groan, Imelda," said DaVendall.

"Watch out!" urged Gamlon" Not asking why, DaVendall moved with miraculous speed to a safer distance.

"Thank you my friend, but what is this thing she's created? I wonder what evil she's thought up this time." DaVendall whispered.

"I can't guess. I've never seen anything quite so grotesque as this before. I think we should try and find a way of getting rid of it before she uses those enormous wings," replied Gamlon.

No sooner had Gamlon said this than the creature flapped its wings and launched itself into the air. Taking advantage of surprise, the creature spanned its wings as far as possible and prepared to swoop down on DaVendall. Using his cloak as a weapon, DaVendall twisted it into a spear. But as he was about to throw the spear, he suddenly found himself unable to move. He heard Gamlon whisper, "Leave it to me DaVendall, it must be something she's done."

Slowly and deliberately Gamlon released himself from the belt. Taking careful note of where the creature was, he aimed the blade straight at its heart. He flew without fear.

Imelda, seeing where Gamlon was pointed, flung out one of her wings and dropped him to the floor. Stunned, but not ready to give up, he gathered himself together and flew towards the creature's throat, striking the leathery skin. He was about to repeat what he'd done when the creature released an agonised groan and rolled its head. Ducking, Gamlon spun round ready to attack again. This time he was met with an unforeseen force. Only managing to stab the creature a few times, he suddenly felt himself being thrown towards the wall.

"Yer not clever enough to get at me, little knife!" Imelda screeched. Ignoring the taunt, Gamlon freed himself from the straw and aimed once again at the creature, not caring which part of the body he stabbed. Gamlon was suddenly hit with searing hot bolts. Falling to the floor, he watched in horror as Imelda's head emerged from within the creature.

"'Arm me creature would yer?" Imelda cackled. "We ain't finished yet!" Moving away from his vulnerable position Gamlon raised himself off the floor, ready to attack her and her grotesque creature again. Ducking and diving, Gamlon managed to avoid the bolts that were directed at him. He flew behind her, took careful aim and attacked. Striking the creature many times, Gamlon was disgusted to see a foul green substance running from the cuts.

Then, without warning, the creature spun round and threw its head straight at Gamlon. Managing to avoid the attack, Gamlon flew speedily out of reach.

Just as he noticed Imelda remove something from within the creature's body, he felt himself being drawn back under DaVendall's cloak. Securing his friend in his hand, DaVendall whispered, "Are you all right, my friend? That was a brave thing to do, but with that creature being one of her creations. She will have full control over it."

Before he could add anything further, the voice of Imelda came at them loud and shrill.

"So, yer don't like me pet, eh? I wonder why?" she cackled. DaVendall knew he would have to do something to stop her before she could do any more harm. Turning to Gamlon, he asked, "Do you know what she had in her hand?"

"No, I never got a chance to see before I was drawn under your cloak."

"That, my friend is the potion she uses to drain the strength and power from her victims," replied DaVendall. Noticing the look of surprise in Gamlon's eyes, he added, "She uses that to subdue those poor unfortunate creatures that hang on Zanus' walls."

Truly shocked by what DaVendall had told him, Gamlon could only manage a whisper. "Wow. That's some horrible thought. Being hung on Zanus' wall isn't for me."

Seeing that the creature was now flying above them, DaVendall knew Imelda would have entered the creature's body to heal its wounds. Drawing his cloak back round himself, he checked once more that Gamlon was all right.

"Ready, follow my lead and we'll try and draw Imelda out of the creature," he said. Watching as the creature circled the room, they noticed the trail of green misty smoke it left behind. DaVendall uncloaked and started to taunt Imelda.

"What's this, Imelda? Got to cover yourself in one of your uglier creations? I thought you could do better than that."

"I'll make yer suffer. I got me some special prisoners 'oo will be given a potion," she cackled. "Made specially fer gettin' rid of interfering enemies."

DaVendall and Gamlon faced each other without uttering a word. They knew their thoughts were as one. Could it be their friends were alive?

Imelda's cackling laugh suddenly stopped. "Yer'll never know!" she hissed. DaVendall feared she must have read their thoughts. Feeling Gamlon stir, he turned his attention to what he was looking at.

Fire bolts were now coming thick and fast in their direction. Quickly dodging the first few, DaVendall soared into the air and glided across to the far side of the burnt-out dwelling. This only served to anger Imelda more, and she sent more fire bolts, hoping that one would set his cloak alight. Furious at not hitting her target she began to send out bolts of fire randomly.

"Move!" shouted Gamlon, just in time to prompt DaVendall to sidestep an approaching missile. Enveloped within the cloak, Gamlon held on while DaVendall ducked and dived round the creature, at the same time managing to dodge the fire bolts.

Lifting Gamlon from his belt, he whispered, "I'm going to distract her by giving her some of her own medicine. You, my friend, will have to use great force in trying to kill the serpent."

Nodding in agreement, Gamlon waited until DaVendall had thrown a few well-aimed fire bolts at the creature, then flew from the cloak to the back of the serpent. Screaming out as each bolt hit its target, Gamlon set about stabbing repeatedly into the serpent's neck. The serpent swung its head round and Gamlon was thrown to the floor. Gamlon warned the serpent "That's the last time you'll do that to me." Lifting himself off the floor, he took aim for the serpent's head and flew towards it. Raising the blade, he brought it down with such force that it brought a loud scream from Imelda. Gamlon watched as the serpent slithered onto the ground.

DaVendall, having seen what Gamlon had done, hoped this would be the end of Imelda. But fearing this could be another of her tricks, he called Gamlon to return. As he did so they saw her withdraw something from within the creature. DaVendall had seen these weapons before; darts with a poisonous tip.

Letting out a shrill screech, Imelda called out, "Die this time, DaVendall. Die!" Then a barrage of tiny darts filled the air. Armed with his cloak DaVendall remained airborne, using his cloak to fend off the darts. His one thought now was how to get rid of them before they could harm him or Gamlon. Taking a deep breath, he released a gale of air, sending many darts back to the ground.

Suddenly they realised that the serpent had risen from the ground and raised itself to its full height. Imelda was screaming at the serpent to get rid of her enemy, and Gamlon decided he must try to kill it once and for all. Plunging his blade in as far as possible, Gamlon took care none of the green substance touched him. Flinging its head in agony, and screaming as Gamlon penetrated its body, the serpent writhed over the ground, trying to spread its wings. Drawing on all their strength, they managed to prevent the creature from lifting itself off the ground.

Deciding a little help would be useful, DaVendall told Gamlon he would seek help from Gorka and some of his reptile friends. It wasn't long before Gorka responded and assured him that the reptiles would help. Soon they arrived, visible to DaVendall and Gamlon but appearing to the serpent and Imelda as flying phantoms. Observing the situation, Gorka looked across at DaVendall before releasing his followers on the enemy.

Unable to see clearly what was attacking it, the serpent screamed in agony as the reptiles' sharp claws and fanged teeth sank into its body. There came a sudden loud screech which seemed to echo round about them. Imelda was shouting, "Kill 'im Kill 'im! Get to DaVendall an' kill 'im! I wants 'is body fer potions."

It came as a shock when Imelda suddenly emerged from within the creature. Still screaming for DaVendall's body, she suddenly vanished from sight. No sooner had she vanished than the creature began to shrink and slump to the floor. Wanting to make sure the creature wasn't able to attack again, the phantom reptiles drifted down to check. Cautiously they circled round the serpent, prepared to lash out with their talons if it showed any sign of life.

Just as Gorka agreed that the creature was indeed dead, a shroud of green mist covered the length of the serpent. When it had cleared again, there was no sign of the grotesque serpent.

"What do we do now?" whispered Gamlon.

"Our moment will come soon. We still have to deal with Imelda, she won't give up just like that. I need to thank Gorka and our reptile friends for their help," DaVendall whispered back.

The phantoms had gathered close by. Thanking them for their help and wishing them a safe journey back, Gorka slithered forward and replied, "Any time, DaVendall. It's thanks to you and another dear friend we still exist, although in a different land to Dofstram." Without another word, the phantoms gradually faded from sight.

"What did the phantom mean when he said it was through you and another friend they still existed?" asked Gamlon. Giving a gentle laugh, DaVendall replied, "These reptiles, along with other species, were almost hunted to extinction. When a certain friend and I discovered the last remaining reptiles we moved them to a place where no one could hunt them. Managing to retain enough strength of will to survive, they made a resolution to help us whenever we called on them. To reach the land they live, we have to cast our minds far beyond their normal range."

"Can anyone summon them to help?"

"I'm afraid not. Only our friend and I are able to accomplish this. In their own land they are free to live their own kind of existence. It took a while for them to accept the assurance that no one would discover where they were."

Gamlon was lost for words. Not having heard much about these phantoms before, he wryly commented, "I guess you must be older than I thought."

"Only by a few years," said DaVendall, laughing. "I guess we'd better be on the move and join our companions. Remember to keep an eye out for you-know-who." Making sure Gamlon was safely tucked in his belt, DaVendall made his way to the lane and stopped to take a look round. About to make his way back to where he'd left Cedar, he halted abruptly on hearing Imelda's chilling voice call out, "I know why yer 'ere, DaVendall, an' I know what yer want. I know them villagers will never follow yer."

Feeling Gamlon stir, DaVendall gripped the knife handle and drew it from his belt. But it soon became apparent that Imelda wasn't prepared to show herself.

"What have you done to these Outlanders?" he called. "You'll never take their land. I'll make sure of that."

Laughing coarsely, Imelda taunted, "With that Alfreston, yer mean?" The malice in her voice as she said King Alfreston's name sent a shiver down DaVendall's spine. "Yer seen what 'appened when they were stupid enough to fight us. Weaklings, they's all weaklings."

"You're wrong Imelda, these people are no weaklings. They will defeat you and Zanus, just as they did before."

Without warning, Imelda suddenly emerged some distance away.

"So Zanus sent you to fight off the Outlanders. Too frightened to do it himself, eh?" Seeing her cruel face twist with loathing, DaVendall took advantage of her annoyance and said, "Well, you'll have to take me on too. I'm not going to let you harm these villagers or take their lands."

Gamlon, no longer able to contain himself, shouted, "What have you done with the villagers? If they are harmed, you and Zanus will suffer for it. We'll make sure you do!"

Imelda charged at them, screeching, "Die, yer friends will jus' like ..."

Sidestepping, and just missing being her talon fingernails, DaVendall warned, "You will not harm me or any more of the villagers."

Furious at DaVendall's response, Imelda was incensed with rage and her longing to kill him. Gamlon released himself from DaVendall's belt and flew straight for her eyes, narrowly missing. Fearing for his friend, DaVendall instantly protected him.

"I'll kill yer, DaVendall, an' that knife thing will be melted in hot fires," hissed Imelda. Then she vanished in a puff of green mist.

Shaken by what had taken place, Gamlon muttered, "She doesn't know I can't be melted." Settled back in DaVendall's belt, he was surprised to see a wry grin on his friend's face. "That information I think we'll keep to ourselves, my dear friend," said DaVendall. Looking round in case she tried to carry out her threat, Gamlon said, "I agree. Now where did she go? I can't see anything but green smoke."

"I guess we'd best be prepared for whatever else she has in store," DaVendall replied. They could still feel her presence, which was soon confirmed by a sudden cackle. "Soon I'll 'ave all the bodies I wants. When I 'ave that stone an' that woman in me 'ands, I'll 'ave all the power I needs!" she shrieked.

"Well you don't have them now, and you never will!" retorted Gamlon.

"Time will tell, Imelda, time will tell," said DaVendall, taunting her. Waiting to see how she would respond, he edged closer to where he had sensed her presence.

"Can you feel her energy? She must have used a potion to hide her odour," he whispered.

"I have felt her presence, but it's strange, I don't feel her attention is directed at us," replied Gamlon.

Then they realised that the green mist was appearing again. Before either could say a word, the mist swirled round like a tornado and vanished, along with Imelda.

"Wow! Did you see that?" gasped Gamlon.

"I did. Now, I wonder, where did it go?" replied DaVendall. Scanning the nearby area, he added thoughtfully, "I can't understand it. I wonder why she didn't try to carry out her threat to kill us again? One thing we can be sure of, she and Zanus will have to defeat us all to get what they want."

"I don't think she will try to get rid of you yet, she'll be hoping she can get you to lead her to our friend," said Gamlon.

"That's something I thought about, but she would have to make sure I was powerless to protect myself and my friends. I think that's what she must have been attempting earlier."

As they were about to walk away from the dwelling, something caught DaVendall's eye. Stopping to take a look, he noticed something clinging onto a length of straw. He thought it might be part of the burnt roofing, but quickly realised this wasn't so. Tapping Gamlon and pointing him in the direction of where he was looking, DaVendall whispered, "Can you make out what that shape is?"

Staring straight at it, Gamlon whispered, "I'm not sure. I hope it's not what's going through your mind."

Wanting a closer look, DaVendall warned, "Hold tight." The next Gamlon knew they were gliding through the air and circling the dwelling. Covering them with his cloak, DaVendall was able to get closer to the object. He didn't like what he saw.

Chapter Fifteen

Rallying the Outlanders

Staring at the shape he had spotted clinging onto part of the damaged roof, DaVendall guessed this could be another disguise of Imelda's. Careful not to let her sense his presence, he remained still. The head of the creature had turned in his direction, and the moment he saw the bulging eyes DaVendall knew for certain it was as he feared. It reminded him of the dragonfly disguise Crocanthus had used on his visit to Bertram's. He wondered what she was planning.

Slowly moving away, he heard Gamlon whisper, "You saw it too, didn't you? It was just like that disgusting dragonfly that appeared at Bertram's house."

"You're right, Gamlon," replied DaVendall. "Let's wait and see what she does next."

"Yer wanna look closer?" taunted Imelda. "'Ave a good look, them villagers will suffer when I gets 'old of 'em." DaVendall placed Gamlon's blade tip on the edge of his finger, and Gamlon knew without being asked that he wanted him to aim for the dragonfly.

Suddenly Imelda screamed, "Kill' im!" Ignoring her, and assured Gamlon was well protected, DaVendall had turned his attention to a wailing noise coming from a distance away. Although he was concerned for Gamlon, he concentrated his thoughts on the noise. Unnerved by the sound, he felt sure it must a villager in distress. He couldn't understand why they had seen no living villagers. Returning to the ground, he called out, "Is anyone there? Please answer. I'm not here to harm you."

Waiting and hoping someone would respond, his concern for Gamlon was increasing. "What if this is another of her tricks?" he wondered.

There it was again, the same wailing noise. He called out again, and again there was no response. Gathering his cloak round him, DaVendall decided to collect Gamlon so that they could search together.

Checking that Gamlon was all right, DaVendall whispered, "Knowing what we are dealing with, I have just the remedy to get rid of it."

"I wish I'd been able to kill it off," said Gamlon. "Each time I aimed for it, it seemed to grow more grotesque, and then the awful wailing noise started."

"I heard it too. I thought it was a wounded villager. When I went to offer help, I got no response. I wondered if it was some trickery of hers. She must have seen me move away and thought she would be able to finish you off."

"Look!" said DaVendall. Something new was heading their way - a swarm of distorted dragonflies. DaVendall pointed Gamlon in their direction.

"Right my friend, this time we definitely need to get rid of them and return to our friends," he said.

Gamlon headed straight for the middle of the dragonfly swarm, swinging his blade in all directions. Shouting with glee each time a dragonfly fell to the ground he noticed DaVendall had made his cloak into a weapon. With DaVendall armed with a two-headed spear and Gamlon swinging at the creatures with his blade, it wasn't long before a great many dragonflies lay dead or dying.

Taking in their distorted features, DaVendall knew this was only the beginning of what was to come. He had decided to call his unicorn Cedar when from nowhere the shrill voice of Imelda called out, "Yer know what to do. Kill 'em. Kill 'em all!"

DaVendall and Gamlon wondered what fresh horrors Imelda was about to unleash on them. Not wanting to bring Cedar into a trap, he raised Gamlon and left him to fly off in the direction of the still-oncoming dragonflies. Imelda was still shrieking, "Kill DaVendall! Kill him!"

Feeling Gamlon return to his hand, DaVendall looked down and mouthed, "Stay still, I have an idea." Summoning his power, he lifted himself off the ground until he was high enough to see the dragonflies at eye level. He raised Gamlon to the same height. Gamlon knew what to do. Concentrating their energies together they sent a burst of flames directly at the dragonflies.

A warning yell filled the air. "So, 'urt me pets would yer? See what yer can do now!" In an instant, green mist had soared over the dragonflies. Dismissing the few remaining insects, DaVendall held Gamlon tight and whispered, "Watch the ground."

Curious, but remaining silent, Gamlon watched as the mist began to vanish. It had left a mass of crawling, scurrying creatures behind.

"Aren't these the creatures she uses in the Forbidden Wood?" he said. "If I remember rightly they devour anything they come across."

"Correct. Now let's see about clearing them, and then we can continue on our way."

"Why would she send these here?" asked Gamlon, staring at the scampering creatures below.

"Because they are like the vultures of the bird world. These creatures do the same thing on the ground. Thankfully they can't fly, so hold tight while I rise above them."

DaVendall raised his cloak over his head and a shimmer of light fell on the creatures below. Screeching as the light fell on them, they began scurrying off in every direction, leaving behind a number of dead bodies.

"What was that all about?" asked Gamlon. "The green mist, and then these horrible little creatures?"

"Do you not remember what happened when we saw a similar green mist before?" replied DaVendall. "That's the mist which almost hypnotised Alfreston's troops on our last encounter with Zanus."

Gamlon let out a huge sigh. "Indeed I do remember it now. It was one time we went on a rescue mission, and didn't these creatures emerge from a mist? If that mist had succeeded in hypnotising us, we would have ended up as Imelda's prisoners. Ugh, the thought of that makes my blade run cold."

"I suggest we move away from here and contact the telepaths and find out what's been happening," said DaVendall. Gamlon hoped they wouldn't have to return. Still concerned other creatures might still be around, he tentatively asked, "Don't you think we should make sure those things have really gone from the house?"

"Not to worry, Gamlon. I have taken care of that. Should there be any remaining creatures; the rays of light I left behind will take care of any inside the dwelling and the surrounding area."

"Thanks for telling me. I'm glad they're not about to follow us," Gamlon replied, with a hint of sarcasm.

DaVendall set about calling Cedar, and it wasn't long before they noticed the unicorn making his way towards them. But once again they had a strong feeling that Imelda was still around. It was soon confirmed. A cackling voice called out, "Come, me lovelies, we 'ave places to go."

Hearing this, they now saw a mass of dragonflies and other creatures flying away from the village.

"Where did all those come from?" asked Gamlon.

"I'm wondering if they were covered by her potions," said DaVendall. "I wonder if that could be why the other villagers were reluctant to help. She knew we were here, and why we came. I wonder what she hoped to gain by exposing herself to us. I wonder how much power she managed to extract from..."

"Don't say it. We don't want her to hear us mention that name," Gamlon urged.

With the arrival of Cedar, DaVendall placed Gamlon back within his cane and set off to join Themis and the remaining group. They sensed that the group were in for trouble.

After walking some distance, and with the memory of the carnage churning over in his mind, DaVendall was about to turn the corner when Themis almost collided with Cedar. "Sorry Themis, didn't see you," said Cedar. DaVendall noticed Themis had been crying. Concerned, he gently raised her from the ground to sit beside him on Cedar.

"What's wrong, Themis? What's happened that's made you so unhappy?" he asked. With more tears threatening to fall, Themis gave a shake of the head, then turned to face DaVendall.

Sensing the sorrow within her, Gamlon asked in a low voice, "You've seen the same devastation we have, haven't you?"

Seeing a reflection of her own sadness in Gamlon's eyes, Themis nodded her head. "It was so awful, Gamlon. It must have been more than those spy birds that attacked these poor villagers."

"You're right," said DaVendall. "I think it might be better if we all gather together, then Gamlon and I can explain everything."

* * * *

Following Themis' directions, it wasn't long before the group came across some of the villagers. Realising these must be the people Themis had told them about, the group were careful not to add to their fears. Varie called out, "Please don't be afraid. My name is Varie and we've come to take you away from here."

At first there was no response, but after a short while a quiet voice replied, "Is it safe?"

"It's safe. Please come and talk to us," Varie asked. Straw began to rustle and they watched as a group of people slowly joined them. By this time Dylan had brought the rest of their group close to the burnt-out dwelling. As the villagers slowly emerged into full light, Rowena was surprised to see that many of them were children. Thinking there could be others close by, she asked, "Are you alone?"

"Yes," murmured a voice.

"Would you like to tell us what happened?" asked Cyluc. There was no reply. Cyluc tried another question. "Do you know if there are any more villagers here?"

After a long silence, one of the older members of the group stepped forward to explain what had happened. What he had to say shocked the rescuers. Rowena commented, "It seems to be the same in all the villages." Froy, catching her words, pulled on her sleeve and signed, "Where are the other villagers?"

"It's possible the others found a place to hide," said the man. "But many of the men and boys were taken prisoner. They were the ones who didn't run fast enough."

Dylan asked, "Did Zanus' troops take them prisoner?"

"Yes. They came just before we were attacked by some enormous creatures which flew with the spy birds."

Another of the older villagers added, "Yeah, they're the ones that killed our friends."

Alarmed at discovering Zanus' troopers had been here, Dylan turned to Cindra and asked, "Can you hear any troopers nearby?" Concentrating her hearing on scanning far and near, Cindra signed "I can't hear anything, but I will remain alert." Seeing what Cindra had signed, Varie asked, "Would you like me to fly round to see if I can see anything?"

"That wouldn't be wise," said Dylan. "It's best if we stay together."

A little disappointed, but accepting what Dylan said, Varie said, "If I hear anything I'll let you know." Wondering what the next move should be, Dylan checked to see if the villagers were settled and ready to move on.

They sat together as one large group. Benin settled himself close to Froy and was telling her about his life in the village before they had been attacked. As the villagers began to feel more secure, it wasn't long before murmuring voices could be heard.

Pacing to and fro, Dylan was keen to move on, but accepting what the others agreed, he continued to make sure no enemy could creep up on them. Halting, he thought he heard a sound and stopped to listen. Wide-eyed and sword in hand, he noticed that many of the people had gathered close beside him. Prepared to fight whoever appeared, Dylan couldn't hide the relief he felt when he saw DaVendall heading in their direction.

Hearing the soft cheer of welcome, DaVendall quietly asked Cedar to make his way over to join Dylan. Dismounting, he lifted Themis off Cedar's back and placed her on the ground. Relieved to see the group were all together, DaVendall was a little surprised to hear calls of, "Where were you, Themis? We're so glad to see you back safe and sound." Several voices soon echoed the same concern.

"I see you found some of the villagers," said DaVendall. "There are certain things I think you should know, and I'm sure there are things you wish to tell us." Seeing so many people, he went on, "Perhaps we should start by letting you know what we discovered. That strange noise we all heard was from a peculiar new creature. I don't need to tell you it was one of you-know-who's creations. To our eyes she'd tried to make it resemble a serpent. She also had other treats in store."

Gamlon added, "Don't forget the encounter we had with her."

"Thinking about that, Gamlon, I'm still not sure why she showed herself to us. One thing I now understand, she's certainly behind the refusal of the other villagers to come to assist King Alfreston. Perhaps if we pay a visit to these villages on the way back, they might be more willing to join us, especially as they will see other villagers here with us. Now, I think Themis should tell us what she discovered. Then perhaps Dylan can tell us what happened to them."

Each party went on to tell of their experiences, with many sighs and exclamations uttered throughout. Finally a moment of silence followed. Gamlon, realising the villagers had sat quietly throughout, turned his attention to them and asked. "Would any of you like to tell us what happened? We've seen the carnage that was left but can you tell us what caused it?"

Gamlon left the villagers to tell their story of how the spy birds had attacked. Although they'd heard the Old Crone's cackle, they hadn't actually seen her. Thinking they had missed out a vital bit, Benin stated, "Don't forget those vicious creatures that attacked and killed so many people, including our parents." Hearing this DaVendall hesitated and considered if he should explain what the other creatures were.

Gamlon, having picked up on the hesitation, whispered, "You will need to tell them what they need to know."

Agreeing with Gamlon, DaVendall asked if they had seen the mass of creatures fly away from the village. Seeing the fear in the wide eyes looking straight at him, he didn't need to ask again. Before continuing, he considered the best way to explain the creatures. Moving himself into a more comfortable position, he started to explain.

"The large attacking creatures are another of Imelda's

creations. We call them Imultures," he said. "We named them that because their faces look like Imelda's. They are cruel vicious birds that are able to tear the flesh off us larger Rancouins. This is something these villagers will have seen."

A villager added in a quiet voice, "They are huge. They have bald heads and massive wings with great claws at the end."

"That's a good description," said DaVendall. "But we must remember, she will have given them powers to attack and kill at her command. I can only guess she had given them a potion to make them more aggressive than the spy birds."

Remembering the monstrous dragonfly on the roof, Gamlon told them, "There is one other creature to be aware of. You all know what a dragonfly looks like. I'm sorry to say that she has created a larger, distorted version. By the way, did you by any chance see a smoky green mist?" There was a murmur of response. "Did it leave behind small creatures which attacked and killed anything that lay on the ground?" he asked.

A loud gasp came from the group. "How did you know about those?" asked a villager. "We did see those creatures, they were like locusts the way they attacked!" He bowed his head, remembering the attacks he'd witnessed.

"Did the mist try to hypnotise you?" asked Gamlon.

"I don't think so. I didn't feel as if she had a hold over me. What about you, did any of you feel hypnotised?" asked Ezran a village elder. The response was negative. "One minute the mist was in front of us, then as it started to go, it left behind some terrible creatures that scattered all over the ground" Ezran continued. "They seemed to be scavenging everything in sight."

"Did you see where they went?" asked Gamlon.

"No, they just vanished in a puff of green smoke," came the response.

DaVendall was now keen to be on his way and he now asked everyone to mount. As the group settled themselves, he warned, "We must keep alert for anything unusual. You've seen what her creatures are capable of, so please be on the lookout for any sign of them."

Having managed to gather a few complete carts, many of the villagers clambered aboard them, while others chose to walk alongside the animals. Quietly and in sombre mood, the group left the village.

Some way on from the village, Gamlon drew DaVendall's attention and asked, "Do you think those creatures will have beaten us to the next village?" With the riders close by hearing this, there were many voices asking the same question. Aware that the next village was almost a day's ride away and with night beginning to draw in, DaVendall encouraged everyone to move as quickly as possible, assuring them they would be able to rest up for the night.

Having given his horse to a couple of the young villagers, Dylan had run alongside a good deal of the way. In between gasps of air, he stated, "I do believe the village is just ahead."

"Thank goodness," gasped Rowena, who had also put a couple of the children on her horse. "I don't think I could have run much further."

Pleased to hear DaVendall call a halt, they took the opportunity to catch their breath. Leaving Dylan to check on the animals, many of the villagers set about preparing a meal, while others searched for kindling for the fires.

Meanwhile, DaVendall's thoughts were a mixture. He was eager to get on and return to Alfreston, but he was also concerned about enemy traps. That was when he decided it would be better to rest so they would be fresh for whatever might happen the next day. With what they'd seen in Hesslewick, he wondered what they would come across in Littlewick, the next village. Exhausted by the events of the day he, like the others, was more than ready for sleep. They enjoyed the prepared meal, and it didn't take long to sort out who should cover sentry duty, leaving the others to sleep in relative peace.

* * * *

As dawn broke, the people began waking and stretching their bodies into life. With food in their stomachs and thirsts quenched, DaVendall still felt apprehensive at what they might face in Littlewick. He decided to leave the younger villagers in the care of a few Jaspers and Ziphers. Although there were groans of disappointment, DaVendall assured them that they would not be left alone for too long.

With the animals ready and having quietly spoken of their own concerns to each other, they waited until their riders were settled. With a few people from Hesslewick, they made their way to Littlewick.

As they approached the village, DaVendall uttered his usual warning to take care and remain vigilant. They searched round periodically for any sign of the enemy. As they were about to enter the village, Rowena suddenly whispered, "Where are the people?"

"I bet they've been taken," said Dee. "That's what happened to our folk." Having heard this before, DaVendall turned to face his friend Blacky, the village blacksmith.

"Blacky, is there any more you can tell us about this attack? We need to know everything if we are to avoid being attacked ourselves."

Stopping his horse, Blacky sat looking straight at DaVendall, unsure where to start. He knew they had had a shock.

"We don't have much time if we are to get back to the King," said Gamlon. With all eyes on Blacky, he began to tell them everything he knew.

"Some folks was busy in the fields when out from nowhere a load of weird creatures and spy birds flew over," he began. "It was real scary. It was as if they come by magic. Then, we hears this horrible cackle and knew it was..." Looking round, obviously expecting to see Imelda appear, he went on, "Before we could take shelter, they started to attack. Soma, my helper, and I wasn't able to help them. They came out the sky like a swarm of bees, only they weren't bees, they was these enormous birds. After seeing this Soma and me, well we hid behind the forge. They was big and strong and looked like they had faces like you-know-who."

DaVendall nodded to show he understood what the man was saying.

"It wasn't long before they came into the village," Blacky went on. "We had no idea if the womenfolk or little ones were all right. It was horrible, real horrible. Those ugly creatures swooped down and started tearing the flesh off the folk that lay on the ground. Worse than that, they… pecked out their eyes." Pausing for a moment, a tear rolling down his face, he continued in a quieter voice, "When Soma and me saw this, we tried to scare them off, but it was impossible. The eyes on those creatures seemed to burn right through us."

"Take heart, my friend," said DaVendall. "There are very few who can stand against her powers." Hearing a sob from the man, Gamlon asked, "Are your family among the villagers?"

The man wiped his face on an old piece of cloth. "My missus is there along with our little ones and Soma, but there are so many of our friends who aren't," he replied.

"Are you saying you didn't see those creatures until the spy birds had attacked?" asked DaVendall.

"That's right. They appeared like a black cloud. We had no time to think. Many of us found shelter behind straw bales and trees, like my family. They pecked out eyes and flesh as if they was nothing. It was terrible. I've never see the likes of it before." He stopped to take a breath and wipe the tears from his eyes. DaVendall gave him a moment before asking, "Is there anything else we need to know?"

"Well, not happy with doing all that, you-know-who sent out these big flames, where they came from we couldn't see but we did see how quickly they burned down our homes. You know what I'm saying, you must have seen what they did to the other houses."

"Is that when the people were taken prisoner?" asked Gamlon. He was still hoping the villagers would appear. Before Blacky could reply, a woman's voice called from the back. "It was them Zanuthians and Gorgonians that took 'em, afore the creatures attacked. You-know-who started calling out they were wanted for treatment. We all know what that means."

"Is that why the other Outlander villagers were reluctant to help us?"

"I guess so," replied the woman.

"But why did they pick on your village?" Gamlon asked, trying to understand what was going on. Another male voice from the group called out, "That's easy. We'd heard there was trouble afoot, and we'd all decided we would gather together and ride out to support the King. I guess this got to Zanus' ears and this is the result."

"But that doesn't explain why she attacked with such force, or why she took people away," Themis signed.

"I think it does, Themis," said DaVendall. "She must have managed to gain control over them, possibly by hypnotising them. I think it must have been an invisible spraying. As soon as the villagers faltered, this enabled her to set those creatures loose."

Stroking his beard, DaVendall thoughtfully continued, "That must have been the reason why the other Outlanders were against fighting Zanus. It must have really angered him to hear these villagers would help Alfreston."

"You don't need to worry about telling us what she wants them for, we all know what happens when she gets her claws into you," said the woman. "I think we should visit the other Outlanders on our way to the boundary. After what happened to us they might offer their help now."

Giving the signal to ride on, DaVendall continued to go over in his mind what he'd heard. He wondered if any other Outlanders would ride with him now. Entering the village of Littlewick, DaVendall indicated to the people to slow down. Doing as requested, they stared round anxiously, fearing this could be a trap. Continuing slowly into the village, Gamlon whispered, "Do you think we'll find any survivors?"

"I was wondering that myself," said DaVendall. "Let's hope we're not too late." Reaching the centre of the village, they were shocked to see many mutilated bodies strewn around where the market stalls usually stood. The group dismount in silence. Joining the people on foot, they quietly and reverently took whatever implements they could find and began to bury the fallen. It soon became apparent that there were few if any survivors.

DaVendall called out, "Outlanders of Littlewick, I have come to seek your help."

"We're here, come forward," came a voice.

"Show yourself. Then we will proceed," called DaVendall.

DaVendall was delighted to see a large man stepping

forward from a wooded area, with a beaming smile on his face. DaVendall dismounted and walked across to shake the man's hand. "Gressard my dear, dear friend, how good to see you." DaVendall warmly greeted him.

"DaVendall, it's so good to see you too, and that young friend of yours, hello Gamlon! Are we pleased to see you! I'm sorry to say that only some of us were able to take refuge in this here cave. As soon as we got wind of the Old Crone being close, we gathered as many people as we could. We'd seen the smoke from the other villages and knew it wouldn't take her long to reach us."

Taking in the sad faces of their other friends, Gressard added, "Some of the people in the market square were taken prisoner by Zanus' bullies. You probably saw what happened to the ones who didn't get away. It was those dreadful birds that left the carnage."

Distressed by what he was hearing, DaVendall told Gressard they had seen similar destruction in the other villages. "As you are aware, these are not good times," he said. "King Alfreston needs help. He's determined to rid Dofstram of Zanus and his bullying companion Sizan. There is fierce fighting taking place at the borders of your Outlander grounds, but there are too many enemies for the King and his people to fend off."

"I see you have taken care of our fallen, for which I thank you deeply," said Gressard. "We will ride with you. But what of our women and children? We can't leave them unprotected."

"They should come with us. We will take them to a place of safety along with the other Outlanders," called a woman. Considering the distance they had to go, and aware of the danger these folk could face if left alone, Gamlon drew DaVendall's mind to his. "We should collect the people who can't fight and place them in that big cave, near to where we sheltered the animals earlier," he said. DaVendall agreed.

Turning his attention back to Gressard, DaVendall explained there were other Outlanders waiting in a place of safety. Noticing the look of concern on Gressard's face, he added, "With Cedar's powers, we will be able to cover the area with a cloak of invisibility. They will remain safe so long as they don't step outside and break the cover."

Having been told what was happening, the Littlewick villagers gathered behind Gressard and waited anxiously for his decision. Clinging onto the few animals they'd managed to save, Gressard called out, "Carts - bring carts for the weak and the children. We have enough horses for the others."

Watching the villagers attach the carts to some of the waiting horses, one of the horses asked, "Will everyone who's going by cart please climb on board. We know there could be danger, so let's get moving." It wasn't long before the carts were full and the remaining horses ready for moving on. Leaving the people to sort out who was riding where, and arranging food and clothing on the carts, DaVendall was telling Gressard what had taken place in the other villages. Shocked at what he'd been told, Gressard realised DaVendall was explaining how Zanus had sent Crocanthus to capture the daughter of David and Jayne.

"What are you saying? This evil man has been sent to the humans' land?" Gressard asked. "I thought our land had been discovered by accident. How has Zanus managed to find a way?"

"One way Gressard, and I'm not about to say the name," stated DaVendall. Knowing of human involvement in the last big battle, Gressard struggled to contain his anger. "Did he get her?" he asked.

"No. She is being protected by some special friends."

"Does this mean David and Jayne have returned?"

"I'm afraid David and Jayne never reached their own land. We are unsure if they are being held prisoner again or were killed during the escape. That's a task that has fallen to our friends. A number of helpers have gone to try and free the prisoners of the tower. We decided this was the best time to try, owing to Zanus removing many of his troopers to the battlefield."

By this time the villagers had accumulated all they could carry, and with the carts laden with people and goods, DaVendall gathered them together. Seeing fear and anxiety on their faces, DaVendall gave the signal for everyone to walk on.

"Are these all the Outlanders from the other villages? There don't seem to be many here," said Gressard.

"The other Outlanders were reluctant to help, but now we

know what caused it we will call on them as we make our way to the King," replied DaVendall. "We need all the help we can get. I think we should ride hard to the shelter and take a short rest before continuing."

On the way to the shelter they revisited the villages on the way. As soon as the folk of Fettlewick saw the party, they ran to greet them. Gressard was telling leaders from the other villages to join up with him and his people and ride to help King Alfreston. Heartened by the villagers now being prepared to help, DaVendall assured them their families would be safe until they returned.

Attaching carts to the horses and placing the smaller folk on board, DaVendall checked to make sure everyone was ready and gave the signal to set off. Catching the odd sentence here and there and learning what they'd gone through, DaVendall felt proud to be counted as their friend. It was at this moment he declared he would get the King to send troops to help these people restore their homes and their villages.

Much of the remainder of the journey was travelled in silence. On reaching the cave the children jumped from the carts and ran towards awaiting friends. DaVendall began getting everyone busy collecting firewood and buckets of water.

DaVendall assured the villagers that they would be covered with a veil of invisibility, and the entrance to the cave would be sealed. "With Cedar assisting, no animals or birds will be able to pick up your scent," he told them. "The veil will only be able to protect you if you all remain inside. Should anyone break the seal to venture outside, it will allow the enemy to sense your presence." He then asked Cedar to place a veil from the back to the front of the cave. Following behind, he added a layer of invisibility cover.

Taking a last-minute check to make sure the people inside were all right, DaVendall and Cedar sealed over the front of the cave, making sure it was thick enough to keep even Imelda out. Then they wasted no time in setting off to where King Alfreston and the Outlanders were in battle.

* * * *

Taking a moment to try and reach Beauty's mind, DaVendall found himself facing the same block he had experienced before. "I guess our friend must be near the tower," he whispered to Gamlon. "Something's preventing me from contacting her." Having tried a few times himself, Gamlon whispered, "That blocking can only be from one person, and I don't need to say who. If our friend is close to the tower, I hope she takes great care."

With their thoughts on Lottie and Beauty near the Forbidden Wood, Gamlon shuddered at the thought of what would happen if they were caught. Eager to get to where the battle was taking place, DaVendall urged everyone to ride faster. They would rest overnight, leaving only a short ride to reach the King.

Chapter Sixteen

Into the Forbidden Wood

Having tried on many occasions to reach DaVendall's thoughts, Beauty was unaware that DaVendall had been having the same problem contacting her. She was fast becoming concerned about her friend's safety. Considering the dangers she and her friends could face once they enter the Forbidden Wood, Beauty reached out with her thoughts and was relieved no enemy presence was picked up.

"When we leave here, please remain as silent as possible," she said. "We will be faced with many dangers. Our first encounter when we enter the wood will be with the trees. They are not like any other trees. They are in Imelda's control and will inform her the minute anyone enters her wood. At least they can't tell her who or where the trespassers are. Their branches will rip into any part of the body they touch. Please watch out for them.

"The next hurdle will be the creeping vines. They slither constantly along the ground and will wrap their tendrils round anything that moves, including your legs and feet. Then they will use their power to drag you to the ground. If this happens, please shout out loud. Imelda will show immense anger at anyone who dares to enter her wood. If her trees and vines aren't successful in getting rid of the trespasser, she will send out ghastly little earth creatures which scurry along the ground gnawing at anything and everything in their path. These are to be avoided at all costs. The Old Crone places drops of poison on their teeth."

"Don't you have a potion of your own, my friend, just in case this happens?" asked Letswick. Smiling across at him, Beauty reassured everyone that she did indeed have a potion of her own. Sensing mixed emotions from the group, she refrained from going into further detail.

They set off at a steady pace. After a while Dandy turned to tell Beauty, "I believe that's the edge of the wood. Do you want me to continue?"

"Please stay alert," whispered Beauty. "I just want to have a quick word before we enter. As you can see, we are about to enter the wood. Please be as quiet as possible. Don't forget, the trees will alert Imelda. She will send other creatures to discover where we are. But if we remain as quiet as possible we might be able to venture close to the tower before her creatures find out where we are."

Taking a last look round the group, Beauty waved her tail and asked Dandy to walk on. Binro looked across at Nain and signed, "Here we go again old friend. I wonder how long it will be before she sends out her trofalogues."

"Not too soon I hope," replied Nain. "But we have to be prepared for whatever unearthly creature she sends out."

"This is going to be a very dangerous task, so the sooner we get to the tower the better," signed Letswick. With nods of agreement from the others, they followed Beauty into the wood.

* * * *

It soon became apparent that the trees of this dark and eerie wood were aware of the intruders. Swaying their spindly branches, they gave the impression that they were stretching out for something to touch and trap. As the wood moaned and groaned around them, Lottie couldn't help shuddering. She stared round at her companions, wondering if any of them were thinking the same.

Drawing Penny's attention, Lottie attempted to smile at her, but then she saw how large and frightened her eyes were. Lottie gave Penny a thumbs-up sign, which Penny acknowledged.

Keeping an even pace, the animals were taking great care

not to make too much noise. The silence which had surrounded them was brought to a close when an eerie cackle echoed through the wood. Disturbed and frightened, Penny clung onto Letswick's arm, "What was that?" she whispered.

"That was Imelda letting us know she is aware that someone's in the wood. She doesn't know who it is," Letswick whispered.

Just then a cackling voice called out, "I knows yer in 'ere, an' I'll find yer!" Letswick whispered to Penny, "Are you all right?"

"Not really, but I'm not going to let some old woman scare me," Penny whispered, trying to sound more confident than she felt. Proud of the way Penny had shown courage when needed, Letswick knew she wouldn't shrink from what she would face this time.

"It's all right to be fearful of this one Penny, she's not like any old woman. This one is evil," he said. Penny gave him a shaky smile, which he acknowledged with a squeeze on her arm.

As they made their way further into the wood, it appeared to Lottie that it was getting darker and mistier. Struggling against the cruel branches as they tore into everything they touched, many of the group were left with red weals on their limbs and bleeding faces.

Then Nain gave Rista a nudge and whispered, "Can you hear that?"

"What did you hear?" said Rista.

"I'm not sure. There it goes again. Do you think we've been discovered?"

"Was it that rustling noise?"

They were surprised to hear Eram whisper, "I heard it. I hope it's not those trofalogues on the prowl."

Keeping the animals to a steady walk, Beauty whispered, "Dandy, have any of the animals picked up on what's causing that rustling noise?"

"Not so far, Beauty. But Doran says whatever it is has been following us for some time," Dandy told her.

Alarmed to hear this, Lottie whispered, "What does that mean, Beauty? Who's following us?"

"We'll soon find out. If it's her trofalogues we'd have smelt them, and they would have attacked by now," Beauty replied.

Before anyone could say another word, the animals came to a sudden halt. Picking up the same sense of danger as they had, Beauty told Lottie, "Stay calm, Lottie. I'll still be here." Then she gave herself a light covering of invisibility, becoming only just detectable to the eye. Keen to protect her brooch, Lottie adjusted the lapel, leaving just enough of Beauty clear.

It wasn't long before the dreadful cackling voice shouted out, "I know yer in me wood. I'll soon find yer! Now, 'oo do I feel is 'ere? I 'as a feeling it's someone useful to me." As she finished, the wood seemed to have become encased in silence. The group started to edge closer together. Then, without warning, Imelda continued. "Aha, I know 'oo is 'ere. 'Ello me glowing stone, I guess yer being 'ere must be to do with certain prisoners, eh? Yer won't 'ave any luck, they's all bin taken care of."

"My friend, we need to do something to stop this taunting. We need to get to the tower as soon as we can," Letswick whispered. Hearing his voice, Beauty came into full view and whispered, "Thank goodness. I thought for one moment she knew where we were."

Still shaking after what she'd heard, Lottie wondered why Imelda had referred to Beauty as a 'glowing stone'. Did it mean she didn't know what form the stone had been carved into?

"This is something we've managed to keep from the enemy," said Letswick. "They have been searching for years to find the stone that glows. They don't know why it glows. This is what has kept our friend safe."

"I didn't know that, Letswick," Yemil whispered. "Looking for years I mean."

"It doesn't matter how long they've looked for it, they certainly won't get their hands on it now," Lottie stated in a stern whisper. Smiling up at Lottie, Beauty asked, "How long can we avoid …" But Penny suddenly shouted, "Look. Look over there, what's that coming out the ground?"

"So," stated Nain, "Now the terrors start. I wonder what the Old Crone has sent to torment us with."

"Don't say that, Nain. I've seen some of her terrible treatments," Rista whispered.

"I'm sorry Rista, but we knew it wasn't going to be easy coming through here," Nain replied, looking round.

While they'd been paying attention to Rista and Nain, the dark cloud seemed to have gathered momentum, and was slowly beginning to encircle the group. Suddenly they realised that the vines were wrapping their tendrils around the animals' legs. Dandy turned to Beauty and whispered, "We'll need to do something to stop this."

Wanting to avoid Imelda picking up where they were, Beauty whispered, "Try to use a few lightning bolts. I'll seek Letswick's help to deal with this sudden darkness. We still have some way to go, so we don't want to reveal ourselves to anyone."

Dandy and Doran prepared themselves to throw out rays of lightning bolts. Raising their heads, they saw that the other unicorns were ready to follow. Wasting no time, the unicorns lowered their heads and shot blue lightning rays along the ground. After they had repeated this a few times, the vines started to scream out. Drawing their tendrils from the animals' hoofs, they quickly disappeared into the ground.

Beauty meanwhile had turned her thoughts to Letswick.

"We need to clear the cloud," she said. "I can't help feeling a sense of evil from within. We won't be able to move it too far in case it alerts her, but we must prevent it from advancing on our people."

Letswick murmured his agreement and they joined their minds together. Creating light within the cloud, what they saw inside horrified them. At first they were unable to make out what the creature was, but with their minds as one, they knew it wasn't good. They pushed their minds further into the cloud and were shocked to see a gigantic crab looking at them. They managed to remove their minds before the crab's claw could penetrate it.

Letswick and Beauty withdrew their minds from each other and sat looking at each other, knowing they must tell their friends what the cloud had hidden inside it.

"Are you all right, Letswick?" asked Yemil. "What did you see?"

"Tell us, Letswick, we need to know," a chorus of voices

whispered. Agreeing they should know, Beauty asked Letswick to tell all. Leaving Letswick to explain about the cloud and the creature, Beauty transferred her mind to seeking help. Still shocked at seeing the monstrous crab, she wondered how many more would appear. Quietly chanting, she knew none of her friends here would be able to hear.

Feeling her energy begin to waver, Beauty chanted the same words again. She sent her thoughts to the sea-horses in the lagoon, hoping the message would get through.

She was in luck. Back in the lagoon, Coral, one of the older sea-horses, picked up the familiar distress chant and knew who had sent it. She let Beauty know she was listening.

"Good to hear you, Coral," replied Beauty. "We could do with a little sea-horse help here. We are having a problem with a cloud. This is no ordinary cloud, as you might guess. This one has a huge black crab inside it. As yet I am unsure if there is more than one. Letswick and I only just managed to remove our minds when it attacked. We need to move this cloud and its contents far away so we can continue our journey."

"I'll bring some helpers," replied Coral. "Give us a signal so we can arrive unseen." Listening to Coral summon the sea-horses, Beauty remained within her thoughts, ready to give the signal.

Anxiously waiting to move on, the group were unaware of what Beauty had been doing, so they were amazed when they saw that the dark cloud had become surrounded by a transparent bubble. Mesmerised and unable to take her eyes off the bubble, Penny whispered, "It looks like the mass is being moulded into something." They watched wide-eyed as the cloud and the inner black mass disappeared.

With the dark cloud and its contents safely in the bubble, Coral and friends removed it. It wasn't long before Imelda was screeching her anger as she tried to discover who had removed her cloud. Ignoring her shrill voice, Coral encouraged the sea-horses to continue on their way, assuring them that Imelda couldn't harm them.

In response to Imelda's screeching, the crab clawed again and again, but to no avail. Once they had carried it away to safety, Coral pierced the cloud with the end of her tail, bursting it and leaving the crab to fall. Before it could scurry away, the sea-horses attacked it as one. The crab soon lay dead on its back. A terrible wailing noise echoed round the wood.

Gathering all the sea-horses together, Coral told them, "We need to get away from here, it won't be long before this creature is discovered." She immersed them in a watery bubble, and the sea-horses blew the bubble back to where Beauty was waiting.

It seemed to the waiting group that no sooner had the bubble disappeared than it was floating back. They were able to see floating round inside it a number of sea-horses. Stunned at the sight, Lottie whispered, "They weren't hurt by that Old Crone, were they?"

Assuring Lottie they were all safe and that the creature had been taken care of, Beauty set about placing a protective cover round the bubble to ensure a safe journey home. After a short conversation with Coral, Beauty bid her friends a fond farewell. In response, the sea-horses gave a wave of their tails. Thanking them again for their help, Coral replied, "We will help any time, Beauty. Take care on your mission." Then the sea-horses departed.

Certain that Imelda wouldn't let them get away with killing one of her creatures, Beauty suggested they move on. They had only gone a short distance when Imelda issued her warning.

"Yer'll pay fer what yer did to me lovely. I'll make sure yer do!" she cackled. Giving the signal for everyone to continue, the unicorns covered the animals with a light veil of invisibility. "We don't want her capturing any of us," Dandy told Beauty telepathically.

"How did all those sea-horses get inside that bubble?" asked Lottie. Penny, equally stunned, whispered, "Where did that light come from?"

"I asked my friends from the lagoon to help," said Beauty. That was how we moved the cloud before the creature inside could harm us. To answer your question Penny, those blue flashes were released by our trusty unicorns. That was the only way to remove the vines from their hooves."

"I remember now, we saw other unicorns do that when those birds flew over the Queen's coach," said Lottie.

Beauty suddenly felt danger. Sniffing a foul but familiar stench, Beauty knew at once that somewhere close was at least one trofalogue. Not wanting to alert them to their presence, she whispered to Dandy, "Keep going. I expect you've smelt them too. Keep your eyes open for them, we don't want to alert them to our presence, they could just be out searching for Imelda's crab."

Flicking his tail, Dandy sent out a danger signal to the other animals. As the smell of the trofalogues wafted past, Lottie said to Yemil, "I know that horrible smell – trofalogues!"

Beauty asked Yemil and Lottie to look round and let her know if they could see any sign of the creatures. It wasn't long before they noticed a movement coming from a group of nearby shrubs. Tapping Lottie on the arm, Yemil whispered, "Did you see those bushes move?"

Observing the same movement, Beauty whispered, "Hold on, let's see what it is." The whole group had halted and were now gathered together close to Letswick. The rustling of the bushes seemed to cease. Then, unexpectedly, a grotesque creature emerged from within. The group were mesmerised.

"What is that?" asked Penny. About to reply, Letswick saw that the creature was making its way along the path. Staring back at it, Penny was trying to think where she'd seen something like this before.

"That looks like some kind of dragon, but without the long face," Lottie announced.

"That's where I've seen it. In one of those history books in the library. I'm sure they were supposed to be extinct," Penny commented. Seeing the scared look on Lottie's face Penny called out, "Are you all right, Lottie?"

"I don't know, I think so," Lottie replied. Then turning her attention to what Lottie was pointing at, Penny grasped Letswick's arm and held on tight. "What's happening?" she whispered. Before he could respond, they suddenly heard a familiar cackling voice.

"I know yer've got the stone, so I know the woman is with yer," said Imelda. "This is me new pet, pretty ain't it? Give over the stone an' the woman an' I may just let yer live."

Making his way slowly towards Letswick, Eram whispered

"Got any advice, my friend?" Staring at the 'dragon' and convinced it had moved closer, Letswick whispered, "I think we will have to wait and see what Imelda does when we refuse to do as she says. Perhaps this poor malformed creature will be set on us, in which case I suggest you quietly get everyone to arm themselves." Penny whispered, "How could she do that to another creature? She's wicked."

Halted by the appearance of a huge whirlwind, they noticed it was driving the dirt from the ground into the creature's eyes. Lottie was frightened of the creature before her, but she also felt some pity for it. Beauty, sensing this, entered her thoughts and said, "This wind will not hurt the creature, only scare it off." Looking at her brooch, Lottie realised the wind must have been created by Beauty to move it out of the way.

Penny, having seen the whirlwind at the same time as Eram, grabbed Letswick by the arm and hid her face. Letswick knew this was not something to fear. "It won't harm you, Penny. Look, can you see what the wind is doing? It's drawing the creature away from us." Staring at the cloud of dust which was now circling round the creature, Penny watched as it seemed to push the creature further into the wood. The trees had stopped swinging their cruel branches and the creeping vines were no longer crawling along the ground. The group hoped someone would have the answer. As if on cue, Beauty, raised her head above Lottie's jacket and said, "Sorry, everyone, I had to stop the creature from attacking us."

"Is that why it's gone so quiet?" asked Lottie. "Where did it go?"

"I could see Imelda had just sent an image to stand beside the creature," explained Beauty. "If it had been real she wouldn't have hesitated releasing the creature on us. The whirlwind created enough force to remove the creature to the farthest end of the wood. Imelda will soon know what's happened and will use her powers to get it back to her."

Binro signed, "Do you think she really knows you are here? Or do you think she is guessing, hoping we will give you away?"

"I have no doubt she knows. What will annoy her is not knowing where to find what she wants. She will stop at nothing to get it."

"She will do everything she can to track us down," Letswick said, in a solemn voice.

"Do you think it has confused the trees as well?" asked Yemil. "See how still the wood has gone."

"Imelda will have created the stillness in the wood," said Beauty. "She will be searching for the dust cloud holding her creature."

Glad to know Imelda would be out of action for a while, they prepared themselves for continuing on. Rista was still curious as to what the creature was. Letswick whispered, "You might not have seen anything like this before, Rista, but it's a kind of dragon. I have seen this poor creature a couple of times. I will have to ask Lottie for a book from her library and show you what a real dragon looks like. Unfortunately this poor creature has been distorted to suit the Old Crone."

The group had now travelled some distance into the wood, but they were soon brought to a standstill. Wondering what could be the problem, they watched as Eram signalled them to wait. Eram suddenly felt Binro tug on his arm and saw he was pointing ahead and holding his nose. It was only a matter of moments before the stench of the trofalogues reached everyone's noses.

"Trofalogues!" Eram called out.

Alarmed at having to face another attack so soon, Penny and Lottie stared at each other and shrugged their shoulders. They turned their attention to the direction where the trofalogues were coming from. Picking up the nervousness of the group Beauty whispered to the unicorns, "Dandy, Doran, please surround the group with a veil of invisibility. Lottie and I will deal with the trofalogues."

Not sure she heard right, Lottie whispered, "How can I help with these creatures, Beauty?"

Beauty had concentrated her senses to see exactly where the trofalogues were and was shocked to discover how close they had come. With not a moment to lose, Beauty joined minds with Lottie to create a barrier between the group and the trofalogues. Leaving Lottie to maintain hold on the barrier, Beauty called her friends the silkworms. She asked them to reinforce the barrier, making it thick enough to stop the trofalogues from coming any nearer. As soon as they heard Beauty's call for help the silkworms started to weave a silken barrier, ensuring it was thick enough to prevent an attack. Waiting until the silkworms had finished, Beauty assured them they were cloaked in an invisibility cover which would remain long enough for them to get away.

Beauty advised the group, "We will be protected from the creatures for a while. Our friends have created a barrier which will give the trofalogues a bit of a headache. Remain still and quiet, everyone. It's possible they haven't seen us, they probably picked up our scent."

Knowing what the trofalogues were capable of, Letswick telepathically asked, "Do you think we should move on? Who knows how long the silkworm barrier will keep them at bay."

"The silkworms have made the barrier thick enough to halt them for some time. Like you, I want to reach the tower as soon as possible. Before we move on there's something I want to do," Beauty told him.

Beauty concentrated on seeing if her friends the silkworms were safe and the barrier still in place. Silva, the leader of the silkworms, assured Beauty the web would hold for a while. Thanking her Beauty told them not to stay any longer and to be aware that the cover would only last long enough for them to return to their habitat.

The trofalogues were now snarling and leaping at being prevented from continuing on their way. Letswick and Beauty agreed that more would have to be done to get rid of them. Seeing how fiercely the trofalogues were attacking the barrier, Lottie was alarmed at how much fiercer they had become since the last time she had encountered them.

Penny, terrified of being attacked, grabbed hold of Letswick's arm. He gently placed his hand over hers.

"All will be well, Penny," he whispered, giving her a warm smile. Taking some comfort in what Letswick had said, Penny was pleased that he didn't remove his hand from hers.

The more the trofalogues tried to break down the silken web barrier, the more aggressive they became, clawing at it with their sharp claws and trying to tear it away with their teeth. The group could only hope they would soon tire and leave. Beauty told Letswick that she was going to try to rid the area of the trofalogues. He knew she had more powers than he, so he turned his attention to the group.

Terrified they would succeed in getting past the barrier, Lottie couldn't help but stare at the trofalogues, which reminded her of wild wolves. They were certainly like no other wild animal she'd ever seen, even in books. Noticing one of the larger animals open its mouth and growl, she was shocked by the size of its fangs. She was disgusted by the drool that fell from their mouths as they continually threw themselves at the barrier.

After the trofalogues' last attack, Beauty reinforced the barrier with a covering of spiked mesh. They began flinging themselves against the barrier, only to reel back in agony as the spikes pierced their skin. It wasn't long before the impact of these spikes stopped the trofalogues from trying to break through the barrier. However, it hadn't stopped their snapping and snarling. The stench they emitted had a nauseating effect on the entire group. Sensing this, Beauty entered Lottie's thoughts and stated, "Now is the time for you to join with me, Lottie." Their minds entwined, and Lottie noticed a glimmer of light emerge a short distance away. As the light grew brighter and larger, Beauty asked her to concentrate on it. Doing as Beauty asked, Lottie saw something come from the light, but couldn't make out what it was.

As the image began to take shape she was delighted to see four beautiful sabre-toothed tigers. Remembering the first time she had seen them, she guessed why Beauty had sent for them. Watching as they slowly transported down, she heard Beauty say, "Hold the light still, Lottie. Our friends the tigers will need it to shield them from the sight of others."

Pleased to be called once again to help their friend, Manga, leader of the tigers, called out, "Hello Beauty. I take it you are in need of a little help."

Lottie was fascinated to see what would happen now. Maintaining her hold on the light, she heard one of the tigers say, "So, hopefully we're free of the Old Crone for a while."

"I'm not so sure," said Manga. "I think I heard her voice calling out to these beasts telling them to kill the trespassers. I take it she means you?"

"That's what I heard too," replied Beauty, "But have no fear, as yet it is only her voice that can reach us."

"That's a relief, it will make dealing with these trofalogues a lot easier," replied Manga.

Beauty and the tigers set about getting rid of the trofalogues. For such large animals, Lottie was impressed at how speedily the tigers moved. As they lashed out at the trofalogues, never missing, Lottie couldn't help feeling these disgusting animals were no match for Beauty and the tigers. Not able to see who or what was attacking them, the trofalogues growled and snarled as the tigers' teeth and claws sank into their bodies.

Lottie felt that these were the most aggressive and vicious animals she had ever seen. Obviously wanting to get rid of the trofalogues as soon as they could, the tigers began attacking them with a vengeance. Soon many of the trofalogues lay dead on the ground, leaving others to limp slowly away.

Listening to the ear-splitting screams as the trofalogues were attacked, Beauty was fearful Imelda would appear. She was well aware of what some of Imelda's potions were capable of. Making her way across to the tigers, she saw that many of the silkworms had come back to join them. Although the barrier was now broken, the silkworms asked if Beauty wanted it replaced. Beauty assured them that their work was done.

Waving farewell to her silkworm friends, Beauty asked the tigers, "Would you please stay for a short while? With the barrier now removed we could be faced with more trofalogues. We're on our way to the Tower of Zorax to free the prisoners, and we want to get as far as possible before we face any more trouble." Delighted to help Beauty, Manga agreed they would stay for as long as needed. One of the younger tigers asked, "Is this Zanus' tower?"

"It is. There are many of our friends held there, and we want to free them," Beauty replied sadly.

"That's a very bad place to go to, Beauty. Can we help?" asked Manga.

"I agree with you but I think it would be safer for us to go on alone. If I need your help I will not hesitate to call on you. I am however, a little concerned about King Alfreston. He has taken many people to help the Outlanders, who are in a fierce battle with Zanus and Sizan."

"That'll be the younger Zanus," said one of the older tigers. "I guess he's thinks he should control Dofstram just as his father did long ago, before he lost it to King Alfreston."

Manga suggested, "I think we might just journey back that way. You say the King is on his way to the Outlander border?" Giving them a warm smile, Beauty added, "He is, but please take care if you really mean to go that way. Those spy birds are about, as are possibly other creatures we don't know about."

Wanting to return to the group, Beauty bid the tigers farewell and a safe journey. As she prepared to draw her mind from Lottie's, she heard Manga say, "We'll be with you until you are sure it's safe to continue without us."

Content with what had taken place, and with the knowledge the tigers would be with them for a while, Beauty waited for a moment before drawing her mind free from Lottie's.

"That was fantastic, Beauty," whispered Lottie. "I don't know how you do it. Will they be able to help King Alfreston?"

"They will. Moff and Kestron will soon pick up on their presence."

"But why can't I see the tigers?"

"They will stay protected by those white clouds. If we can't see them, they won't be visible to others. But they'll be watching over us until it's safe for us to continue alone."

"What happened?" asked Penny. "One minute those ugly beasts were trying to find us, the next half of them were dead."

"I called on other friends of ours, the sabre-tooth tigers. It was they who dealt with the trofalogues. That's what the screams were. The tigers are going to stay with us for a while to give us a chance to move on, then they will leave. Manga and his tigers will go via King Alfreston. Knowing Manga, he and his friends will get involved with the battle."

"That's great, Beauty," said Letswick.

"Hoorah for the tigers," called out the others.

"We need to get going before we come across any more dreadful creatures," said Eram.

"Hold tight, here we go," whispered Letswick. "Stay alert, Penny." Giving Letswick a nod, she settled back and wrapped her arms round his waist. Maintaining silence and keeping to a steady walk, Yemil whispered, "Beauty, can you hear that scratching noise?"

"Yes, it's been with us for a while. I can't quite make out what it is, but stay alert," Beauty replied. Not waiting to see what was making the scratching noise, Beauty reached out to the telepaths and asked them to join minds with her. With all minds joined, Beauty sent out a high-pitched signal. Screams soon came from where the scratching noises had been heard. Some of the creatures had left the shrubbery and were now standing in the open. But then the cackling voice of Imelda drowned out the signal. As soon as the telepaths heard her voice they quickly released their minds.

"Now I knows yer in 'ere, me pretty stone," Imelda chuckled. "Why don't yer come an' see me? I won't 'urt yer. If yer don't come ter me, I fink some 'arm may come ter yer friends."

"You might have some of my powers, Old Crone, but you will never take them all," warned Beauty. "I still have enough of my powers to deal with you. Be warned."

"Be warned yerself, me glowin' stone, I will 'ave you an' yer friends afore yer can get to Zanus' tower. Don't ferget, I still got some of yer powers, enough to seek yer friends out. Soon I'll 'ave all yer powers. Don't ferget." Her screeching cackle sent cold shivers through the listening group.

Alarmed at hearing the Old Crone's threats, Letswick drew Beauty's attention and signed. "Take care my friend, she hasn't discovered where we are yet. We don't want to give her any help." Waving her tail back and forth, Letswick knew Beauty had understood what he was signing.

The same could not be said for Lottie and Penny. While Letswick had been signing, they had been sitting rigidly on their animals staring at each other, wondering if either would speak. Eram gave the signal for them to walk on. Noticing the cover had disappeared from the animals, he whispered to Binro, "I dread to think what horrors she has in store." He tapped Eram on the arm and signed, "Should I take a quick flight round, just to make sure it's safe?"

"Not at this stage, Binro. If there is danger we will face it all together," Eram whispered. Accepting this, Binro concentrated his hearing on what could be waiting ahead. As they ventured further in to the wood, Beauty asked the telepaths to concentrate their hearing on what might lay ahead.

Nain and Rista were discussing what direction they should go to reach certain prisoner cells once they got into the tower. Overhearing the last bit of their conversation, Binro signed, "That's going to be a very dangerous adventure. I just hope we find the prisoners quickly so we can get out." Nain replied, "That's going to be the worst bit. We know many of the cells where he keeps special prisoners. We can only hope he still uses the same ones."

Then they were shocked to hear Eram call out, "Over there, what's that?" Letswick held onto Penny and whispered, "Stay still, let's see what's worried Eram." Eram seemed to have been concerned by the rustling of the trees. As he was about to urge everyone to walk on, he suddenly noticed a purple haze rising in front of them. He heard loud gasps come from his companions, and knew instantly they had seen it too.

Wondering if this was another trick Imelda was using to try and discover where they were, Letswick rode close to where the group had gathered and whispered, "Don't move. Let's see what it does." They sat still and watched. At first it appeared to be lingering where it was, then without a sound it began swirling in and out of the trees. Beauty whispered to Lottie, "We need to move away from here, this is another of the Old Crone's tricks." Lottie looked down and whispered, "What can we do?" Then she looked up to see the haze moving down towards them.

On instruction from Beauty, Lottie stated, "Our friend says you must be ready with your armour to take on whatever might come from the haze. She will make sure no harm comes to us." Turning to draw Beauty's attention, Dandy used the method of communication Beauty had arranged for the animals to use in such times as this. "Should we cover ourselves? Are we in immediate danger?" he asked.

"Not at the moment, we need to save some of your strengths to help when we reach the tower," Beauty told him. Dandy soon relayed to the other animals what was about to take place. No sooner had Beauty finished her conversation with Dandy than the leaves on the ground started to swirl round as if caught in a whirlwind. Beauty drew Lottie's attention and asked her to once more relay what she was about to be told. Gaining everyone's attention, Lottie whispered what Beauty had told her.

"This is a specially-created wind. It's been sent to find out exactly where we are. We need to move beyond it. Eram, this is for you, will you please lead? Try and stay in the direction where we first saw the haze. I am assured it won't return there."

Letswick gained Eram's attention and whispered, "We're ready to move on. We don't want the wind catching up with us." Eram gave the signal for the group to ride on.

Suddenly Penny tapped Letswick's arm and asked, "Look, is that the tower? I can just see the tip of something beyond that hill."

Lottie wondered anxiously if she could be seeing her parents again.

Looking at how much of the wood they still had to go through, she couldn't help feeling they'd never make it. Occupied with her thoughts, Lottie hadn't noticed Penny was looking at her. Turning to Letswick, Penny whispered, "Do you think…?" but before she could complete her sentence, Letswick placed his hand over hers and whispered, "Careful Penny, we mustn't build up anyone's hopes." Settling back into position, she felt Doran being urged forward.

Chapter Seventeen

The Tower of Zorax

Having seen how close they were to the tower, Beauty was keen to discover if she would be able to contact any telepath within. Closing her eyes and concentrating her thoughts directly on the tower, she was met with the now familiar grey mist surrounding it. She searched to see if there was anywhere she could break through, knowing she would have to be very careful not to risk alerting Imelda to her presence.

Disturbed by the turmoil in Beauty's thoughts, Lottie joined her mind to Beauty's and asked if she could help. Beauty responded, "We've got to break through this mist. It's been created by Imelda, so we must be very careful not to let her know we're here. I must do everything I can to reach a telepath."

"Just tell me what to do and I'll follow," Lottie replied, trying to control the butterflies in her stomach. With the other telepaths in the group picking up on their thoughts, it wasn't long before a surge of energy encouraged Beauty to continue. They listened carefully as she explained the best way of succeeding.

"Now we are much closer to the tower, if we concentrate as one mind we might manage to break through the mist. At the same time, we must be careful not to alert Imelda. It would help if the person who had the compass would open it just for a moment, that way I would be able to trace where it was coming from. If I feel Imelda is aware of us I will let you know, then we must withdraw from each other's thoughts immediately."

"Beauty, I don't think you will miss me if I withdraw my

thoughts now," said Yemil. "I'm thinking about the non-telepaths who won't know what's taking place. They will need to know so they can protect us from anything Imelda sends to harm us."

"Good idea, I will leave it in your capable hands. Please alert Eram and ask everyone to take care," Beauty replied. No sooner had they felt Yemil's mind leave theirs than Beauty asked them to bring their minds together.

Yemil made her way to Eram and told him what the telepaths were going to attempt. Eram gathered the non-telepaths together and relayed the message, urging them to be extra vigilant and advise if there was any immediate danger. No one had to ask why, as some of them had heard Yemil talking to him.

As Beauty approached the mist and felt the strong energy from their minds, she hoped it would be enough for her to finally break through the barrier. What surprised her was the strong resistance coming back. She decided to risk using her powers to make the final break. Aware she would need the strength of the telepaths' minds to hold the mist still, she set about explaining what she was going to do.

"Please hold the mist for as long as you can," she said. "I am going to use a bolt of energy to try and get through. I'll use Lottie's mind to keep watch over my thoughts, as I won't be able to sense the presence of a certain person once I go deeper into my mind."

The she set about concentrating all her power on breaking through the mist. Feeling a fresh surge of energy as Beauty went deeper into her mind, the telepaths only just managed to hold the barrier in place. As she concentrated on keeping watch over Beauty's mind, Lottie was amazed at how dense the mist was. There was something about it that gave her an uneasy feeling. But knowing Beauty was trusting her to be guardian over her mind, Lottie remained observant.

Beauty struggled to find a way through the barrier. At first she thought she might have to give up, but on her last attempt she suddenly managed to create a small gap in the mist. She took the opportunity to call out to the telepaths within the tower. She was anxious to hear a response, as she knew this couldn't last long or Imelda would sense what was happening.

"Whoever has the compass, please open it," she called out.
Exhausted from using her extra power, Beauty checked that Lottie was all right and then told her to release her mind to join the other telepath minds. Then Beauty rejoined the group, asking them to release their minds so she could let everyone know what happened.

One by one, Beauty could feel their minds withdrawing. Feeling somewhat fatigued after using the extra energy, she whispered, "Are you all right Lottie? You did very well in guarding my mind. I could feel the unease you were feeling. Do you have a little water you can put on my face please?"

Lifting the water bottle from the saddle, Lottie whispered, "I'm so pleased I could help in some way. You used an awful lot of energy. Are you really all right?" Pouring the water into the cup from the top of the bottle, Lottie lifted the bottom of her jacket and dipped it into the water. Gently wiping Beauty's face, Lottie was concerned that Beauty hadn't replied to her question.

"Are you all right?" she whispered again. "I could feel the strength of your mind and it's far greater than mine will ever be. Perhaps when you feel refreshed you can tell us what you were doing."

Anxious to be on her way, Beauty asked Eram to bring everyone closer. Keeping a constant lookout for the enemy, she quickly explained what she had done. Then she added, "Look out for a beam of light. If any of you see it please let me know at once. I just hope my message got through. Now I suggest we make our way to the tower. Keep watch for the unexpected and hopefully we should be there in a couple of hours."

Settling back on the lapel of Lottie's coat. Letswick and Penny joined Eram and Binro as they set off towards Zorax.

* * * *

Crocanthus, raging with anger at being ordered back to Dofstram, stomped round his room, having removed his potions from their secure hiding place. Selecting the potion he wanted, he drank it down in one gulp. As he waited for it to take effect, he wondered how he was going to explain to Zanus why he was returning without Lottie or the stone. Knowing the punishment for not obeying Zanus' orders, he had to think of a good explanation.

He took a look in the mirror and was relieved to see that the transformation was almost complete. As he watched the rest of the disguise develop, he knew that he had become a dragonfly like no other.

With the transformation complete, he fluttered his wings to test them. Satisfied he could fly without too much discomfort, he flew out of the window and made his way to the portal.

As he spoke the words to uncover the portal, his lack of patience was increasing. Seeing a space small enough for him to enter, he flew straight into the portal. His one aim now was to get free of it as soon as possible.

He looked anxiously around to see if Imelda was there, feeling in no mood to put up with any more of her tricks or weird creations. He flapped his wings and set off, making sure he stayed well away from the bats. But he hadn't gone far when he heard Imelda call out, "Yer can't fool me Crocanthus. Don't ferget it was me that give yer the potions."

He was suddenly confronted by a pair of green glaring eyes, and realised he was not going to escape Imelda after all. He found he could not move. She laughed as he struggled to get free.

"So, yer thinking yer might jus' get away, eh?" Imelda cackled. "I don't see no woman. But yer might just be hidin' the stone - are yer? Be warned Crocanthus, potions means payments! I will 'ave yer life fer payment if I 'ave ter. Many lovely creatures can be made from that body!" With another cackle she released him, sending him falling to the ground.

He lay waiting to see if she was going to return for another attack. Not sensing her presence, he crawled along the ground to find a place to rest. Securing himself in a small crevice, he waited until he felt strong enough to continue. His malevolent thoughts about what he'd like to do to her were interrupted by a call of, "Don't even think about it Crocanthus! Yer'll always be mine."

He crawled out of the crevice and set off for the end of the portal. Once safely outside, he set off in the direction of the village to retrieve his horse.

As he walked arrogantly into the village, his disgust was obvious. How could Zanus trust his horses to these revolting people? Shouting for someone to bring his horse, he kicked several villagers who got in his way. Mr Tinks, the man he knew to be the stable master, stumbled across the courtyard with his horse, quickly followed by Mrs Tinks.

Mr Tinks said breathlessly, "'Ere 'e is, all fed an' watered. All fed an' watered".

"You don't need to say it twice, fool!" snapped Crocanthus. "Get out of the way, I've a long way to go." Pushing past the elderly couple and just missing treading on other folk nearby, he raised himself into the saddle and set off away from the village.

"I'm glad 'e's gone," said Mrs Tinks. "I 'opes 'e never comes agin. I don't like 'im. 'E's a cruel one 'e is."

Worried in case his wife had been heard, Mr Tinks took her by the arm and muttered, "Come on in an' mek us a pot of tea. I 'opes the Old Crone didn't 'ear yer." Tutting and moaning, Mrs Tinks allowed herself to be jostled into the crumbling shack to make tea.

* * * *

Leaving the village far behind, Crocanthus was soon well on his way to the tower. He had devised a story and convinced himself Zanus would accept it. He was going to tell him that he had discovered that the stone and Lottie were together, and in Dofstram. He pushed the horse into a gallop. He wanted to get to Zanus before Norman Mansfield did.

* * * *

Meanwhile, Norman was unaware that Crocanthus had got to Dofstram before him. Arriving at the edge of the village, he noticed Mr Tinks and was relieved to see that he was leading a horse.

"Is that my horse? I need to get going," he said. "I have a long way to go."

"Yer can 'ave this 'orse," replied Tinks. "'E's bin fed and watered, so 'e'll get yer to where yer needs ter go."

Norman waited for Mr Tinks to check the saddle was secure, then mounted the horse and set off down the muddy trail in the direction of the Tower of Zorax. Riding the longer way round, Norman hoped to avoid being seen by the other folk in Dofstram. Not having taken much notice of the land or the people who lived there, he couldn't understand why Zanus wanted to control it.

Norman thought of their first meeting. Zanus had been was the dirtiest, most unkempt man he'd ever come across. His filthy long hair seemed to flow down from his face to join up with his equally long and straggly beard. Then he remembered what it was that had caught his eye; Zanus' cloak of feathers, as filthy and matted as his hair. It did cross his mind to ask how many birds had lost their lives for him to have a cloak like that, but he was glad now he hadn't. Feeling a shiver of fear run down his back, he felt as if he was once again facing Zanus' evil scowl.

It wasn't until he stood up that Norman realised just how big a man Zanus was. The image that came to mind was that of a brown bear, except that instead of fur he had feathers.

Norman pulled his own coat around him, grumbling about the cold, damp weather. He noticed that the people he passed were maintaining a safe distance. He was also aware that the warning birds were twittering amongst themselves as they tried to see who the rider was. After sighting Crocanthus and now this stranger riding in the same direction, the warning birds were keen to see where they were going.

The birds weren't alone in spotting Crocanthus and the stranger. Both men had also been seen by the Jaspers and Ziphers on guard duty. Sounding off the warning horn, the smaller folk sought cover in their underground dwellings.

Surprised at how quickly Crocanthus had disappeared, the birds guessed he would be going to Zanus or the Old Crone. They all agreed they would follow only as far as it was safe. Flying a little further, the warning birds were soon joined by a number of Jaspers. After greeting one another, they turned their concentration back to the rider. Mistaking the Jaspers for another kind of bird, Norman ignored them and continued on his way. Glancing up, he saw a flock of birds overhead. He thought for a moment they were following him. But why would a flock of birds want to do that?

Observing him heading in the direction of the Forbidden Wood, one of the warning birds said, "I don't think we should go any further. We all agreed not to enter the wood. We could wait here for the Jaspers to return."

"Let's fly down to the people and let them know the latest," suggested another bird.

Knowing Crocanthus had returned, the warning birds were eager to inform the Queen. The warning birds thanked the folk for their hospitality and set off for Castle Urbone. Flying past the sentries, they called out their farewells and warned them to take care.

Norman, fearing what could be waiting for him inside the wood, slowed the horse to a walking pace. Looking round, he wasn't sure what he was looking for. The memory of how he'd been unceremoniously dragged through the wood on the way to the tower did little to make him want to continue.

When he had gone a little way in, he suddenly brought the horse to a halt. He thought he had heard the Old Crone's cackle. He very much hoped he was wrong. Terrified that she would suddenly appear, he urged the horse to walk on, remaining low into the saddle.

It dawned on him how quiet the wood had gone. Then out of the stillness he suddenly heard Imelda call out. She seemed to be talking about a "glowing stone". Thinking he must have misheard, he stayed where he was to hear if she would repeat herself. It wasn't long before he heard her call out, but this time she was inviting the stone to go to her. Relieved she hadn't picked up on his presence, he heard her familiar eerie laugh again as it echoed round the wood.

Continuing on his way, Norman tried in vain to avoid the attacking branches, while his horse had the vine tendrils to deal with. As he approached the tower he was wondering what kind of reception he would get. Taking in its vast black walls and the enormous solid wooden gates, a sudden flash of memory reminded him of what had happened the first time he had entered the courtyard. He had been tied to the horse's saddle and dragged through the Forbidden Wood before being unceremoniously dropped on the muddy pebbled courtyard, where his captors had taken great delight in kicking and thumping him.

As he reached the entrance he plucked up his courage and asked for the gates to be lowered, knowing he couldn't postpone his entry any longer. Calling out, he demanded to be let in.

"'Ere's the 'uman. Zanus' informer," the gatekeeper sneered, turning to face Norman. "I 'ope's yer 'as good news fer 'im, 'e's in a right mood today." Disliking these brutes and their bullying techniques, Norman was not prepared to pass on any information to them.

He called for a stable-hand to take charge of the horse, dismounted and handed the lad the reins. As he was about to speak to the stable-hand, he was stopped by a terrifying roar from inside the cave. He knew it was Zanus. Alarmed, but aware he had no choice, he gingerly made his way inside.

Avoiding the poor unfortunate creatures who hung on the passage walls, Norman walked through to see that Zanus' door was wide open. Taking a deep breath, and wishing he didn't feel so nervous, he stepped into the room. Seeing the state Zanus and the crowd surrounding him were in, he guessed they'd been drinking.

"What yer waitin' fer!" roared Zanus. "Get 'ere." Norman slowly walked to where Zanus was pointing, failing to notice Crocanthus watching him from a darkened corner. Stuttering, he tried to explain to Zanus what he'd done to try to find the glowing stone.

"I l-looked everywhere," he said. "I know you told me it glowed, but I never saw any glowing stones. Then I started to think, perhaps it was taken to my land."

Cowering back as Zanus rose from his seat, Norman tried another tactic. "I could return and have another look, but I wouldn't know where else to look. I covered everywhere I thought it could be. I ransacked Lottie's house, but no luck."

I know where she an' 'er bleedin' friends are, yer idiot," said Zanus. "I demand someone finds this stone or there will be many 'oo will face severe punishment!"

Norman stood trembling and waited to hear his fate. Then

he was terrified to see Crocanthus step forward. The memory of how this man had appeared to Lottie was still a shock.

"What you looking at? Did you think I hadn't come back?" said Crocanthus. Edging closer to Norman, he laughed cruelly to see him stumble backwards. With Zanus and the others in the room joining in the laughter, Norman felt his anger rising. Managing to stop himself from falling completely onto the floor, he asked, "How long have you been here?"

"Long enough to hear you explain about going to Lottie's house. If you didn't know what you were looking for, why did you think it was there?" Crocanthus asked in a sneering voice. Not having a ready answer, Norman turned his attention to where the vicious birds had flown, on the back of Zanus' chair. Would they attack him? As if Zanus knew his thoughts, Norman was surprised to hear him say, "Not yet, 'uman. Their turn will come."

* * * *

Meanwhile the warning birds had arrived back at the castle and were busy relaying to the Queen who they'd seen and where they'd been. Dismayed by the news, Queen Matilda thanked the birds and told them to take a rest and have a little extra refreshment. As they flew round to the stable, they weren't surprised to see many of the castle folk waiting for their arrival.

"I think we'll let the birds have a bite to eat and then they can tell us what they have seen," said Igorin. He got the stable lads to put out extra seeds and nuts, and it wasn't long before the birds had had their fill. With stomachs full and thirst quenched, the birds flew down to reveal what they had seen. Just as the Queen and her friends had been horrified to learn of Crocanthus returning, so were the listening folk. Taking a deep breath, one of the senior Jaspers asked, "Were they both going towards the wood?"

"I guess Crocanthus would have gone straight to the tower, but we're not sure about the stranger, we didn't want to follow him into the wood," replied one bird.

"I hope DaVendall is on his way with more Outlanders," said Igorin. "We have already had a few casualties brought in."

"I think we should be prepared for anything to happen,"

said one of the Jaspers. With heavy hearts, they returned to where they'd come from. Turning to walk into the stables, Igorin called everyone to come closer.

"Well my friends, I guess we might need to make sure you are ready for riding at short notice," he said.

"We heard, Igorin," said one horse. "We are ready for whenever the time comes."

"Just say the word," shouted another. Turning to the stable-hands, he asked, "Please make sure there is food and water available."

After discussing what they had learned from the warning birds, Queen Matilda suggested it might be a good idea to try to trace the whereabouts of Alfreston, DaVendall and Beauty. They all agreed it would be a good idea. Lucy and Frances made their way to the table holding the maps. The Queen asked the marker if it could show where the three groups were. The marker move from area to area and finally came to a stop just in front of the Queen.

"I'm sorry, Your Majesty, I have been unable to trace them," it reported. "The King's group is possibly hidden by those hills on the other side of the wood. I can't see into the wood without alerting the Old Crone. I guess it might be a while before DaVendall will appear. As for Beauty and her group, they must be very near the tower, so I won't try and reach them. I will stay on the map and as soon as anything appears I'll call you."

"Thank you," replied the Queen. "I know what you say is true, but as you live on the map I know you will be aware sooner that I when something does appear."

As they walked back to their chairs, Lucy brought up the subject of the stranger. "Frances, you remember the warning birds said there was a stranger who followed soon after Crocanthus?"

"What made you think of him?" asked Frances.

"I've had a horrible thought," Lucy replied. "I wonder if this stranger was the informer."

"Whatever made you think that?" Frances replied. "Why would such a person be allowed to ride free in Dofstram?"

"I was wondering that myself," said Queen Matilda. "What if the informer had been sent back to your land to try and find Lottie and our friend?"

Back at the castle, Queen Matilda and friends were discussing the informer. "That's scary, Matilda. How could the informer travel between lands?"

Suddenly Marmaduke's voice interrupted, "That's easy. The same way it was possible for all the other Zanuthians to get to Lottie's land, through a portal created by Imelda."

"That's a terrible thought, Marmaduke," said Lucy. "But, if that is the case, how did the informer get to Dofstram in the first place? How would he know of the portal?"

"I can only guess he must have found a similar way to Dofstram as Jayne and David," Marmaduke replied.

Then Winston spoke up. "I was just remembering that Lottie's parents are cave explorers," he said. "What if the informer followed them on an expedition, only this time it went wrong? Instead of their usual discoveries, they found a way into Dofstram. That would make it possible for the informer to follow."

"Wow, Winston!" said Marmaduke. You know what, I bet that's exactly what happened."

Frances rose from her seat and went over to Winston and gave him a gentle hug. "I think you might just have answered a question we'd all been asking," she said. Turning to Matilda and Lucy, she added, "Such a lot to think about. I think I'll just check up on the patients and see if Frenkal needs any help. Perhaps I can prepare a few more bandages."

"Wait for us, we'll join you," called Lucy and Queen Matilda.

"What if we join the marker and see if we can spot something?" said Marmaduke. I'm still amazed at how you worked all that out, Winston."

"So am I, I couldn't think what to say, Winston, but well done to you and your thoughts," Rubie commented, making Winston turn slightly red. Moving across to join Marmaduke and Winston at the map table, Rubie added, "Good idea, Marmaduke. I can't sit here wondering what to do."

"Nor me," replied Winston, hoping his red face would soon go.

Chapter Eighteen

A voice in the darkness

David edged closer to the door of the dungeon. He could hear the guards muttering together, and wanted to know what they were saying.

"I 'ears Crocanthus and that informer 'ave returned," he caught one of them saying. "I bet they came to ride with Zanus and 'is crony Sizan." Paying closer attention, David heard another remark. "I 'ope 'e tells us we can go an' fight off those Outlanders." Another coarse voice added, "We needs ter get Zanus' land back. Then we can 'ave some fun."

David knew they had to get free, and soon, if they were to prevent that from happening. He waited until they had moved away and then when all was quiet, he crawled towards the back of the cell, urging the other prisoners to be quiet. Nodding their heads in agreement, they quietly followed him. As he relayed what he'd heard, there were gasps from the others. As he finished speaking, a solemn silence fell over the cell. A few moments later, Bacjo whispered, "I suggest we let the other prisoners know what David heard."

Norda added, "Everyone needs to know there could be something about to happen. Does this mean....?" but his suggestion of a possible rescue was interrupted by the sound of the guards outside the door. Crouching close together, the prisoners sought comfort from one another as the guards started their cruel taunting, hammering on the cell doors and calling out coarse threats of what punishments the prisoners would get. Then the guards and prisoners alike were shocked to hear the bellowing voice of Zanus. A moment later he appeared in front of them, glaring at the guards through his black, cold eyes.

"What's this noise fer?" he bellowed.

"It's them prisoners. We was jest givin' 'em a warnin' to be quiet," one of the guards replied nervously. The other guard added, "Yeah, p'rhaps they was finking they was gonna be rescued."

Laughing raucously, Zanus stomped closer to the nearest cell door and shouted loud enough for all to hear, "None of you scum will ever escape!" Then he swung round to the guards and shouted, "Why would they think they might?" Glaring from one guard to another, he saw the usual look of fear in their eyes.

"Secure these dungeons and get ready to ride to battle!" he ordered. "We don't want them escaping like before, do we?" he asked menacingly.

"'Ow we gonna make sure them prisoners don't get free?" grumbled one of the guards. "Specially when we's out fightin'."

"We'll be back soon, and Dofstram will be mine," Zanus thundered on. "See what 'appens to yer all then! And what yer mumblin' at? Keep them prisoners quiet or yer'll be joining 'em!"

Angered to think that the prisoners could be thinking of a possible escape, Zanus wondered if, like last time, someone had gained access to the dungeons. He decided he would make Imelda put more protection round the tower. That way, he convinced himself, if there were any rescuers here he would have them trapped.

Walking round the dungeon, his thoughts turned to leaving the tower and how many troopers he could leave to guard it. Wanting to ensure Zorax was fully shielded from any attacks King Alfreston might have planned, he went over to the cowering guards and warned them, "Make sure all prisoners are secure. If yer fail, I will kill yer. Be warned, it will be a very slow and painful death."

Hearing one of them grumble something about it not being fair, Zanus turned on them and gave each a crack across the face with his stick. Leaving them to nurse their wounds, he stomped up the slimy dungeon steps in the direction of his room, satisfied that his demands would be carried out.

With the threat of Zanus hanging over them, and with renewed hatred for him, the guards took their anger out on the prisoners by threatening what they would do to them while dragging the cell keys along the rusted metal bars.

Just then they heard more guards approaching. "What yer 'ere fer?" Ain't yer s'pposed to make sure them cells is secure?" shouted the guard. A coarse voice replied, "Ours is secure. But yer'd best make sure these don't escape. Don't ferget these are Zanus' special prisoners."

"Yeah, they's well safe," another voice added. "I s'pose yer waitin' fer them lackeys to come." Gloating over the possibility of the 'special prisoners' escaping, a voice called out, "What yer gonna do if they 'scapes?" The offended guard turned on the caller and warned, "Watch yer mouf, or yer'll get a fumpin'." Suddenly the guards started arguing and punching each other.

One of the more senior guards was concerned that the prisoners might escape. He had seen many other guards killed as a result of the last attempt. Shouting above the noise, he finally drew their attention, and scathingly told the guards, "Yer can torment these prisoners if yer want, but remember what Zanus will do if any gets away."

At the mention of Zanus' name they stood staring at each other, wondering who would be the first to make a move. Noticing one of the cell doors had been opened the other guards yelled at the offender to shut it.

"You idiot, they could 'ave got free. I'm not gonna be punished fer yer being so stupid." Frustrated at not being able to carry out his plan to torture at least one of the prisoners, the guard slammed the cell door shut, making a show of turning the big rusty key.

The prisoners were listening to hear if anything of interest would be said. With so many guards gathered outside the cells, they knew something was about to happen, but what?

* * * *

Making his way back to his room, Zanus suddenly heard a coarse voice bellow, "Open the gates, idiots!" Recognising the voice of his brutal ally Sizan, Zanus wondered what had brought him back from the battlefield. Turning to Crocanthus he ordered, "Get the troopers ready to leave for battle. Don't ferget some will 'ave to be 'ere to guard the tower an' the prisoners."

He spun round to face Norman and snapped, "Yer'll ride with me." Shocked to think he would riding out to battle, Norman stuttered, "M - me? I've never fought, especially not in a battle."

"Yer'll learn," laughed Zanus.

Anxious to see why Sizan was not on the battlefield, he ordered Norman to stay where he was. Leaving Crocanthus to carry out his orders, Zanus made his way to the courtyard. The yard-workers were scuttling to open the large wooden gates. Moving clear of the entrance, they wanted to make sure they wouldn't be on the receiving end of Sizan's fury.

"Where've yer been? 'Ow dare yer keep me waitin'!" Sizan shouted, glaring at everyone in sight. Realising he hadn't seen Zanus present did little to calm his anger. "Where's Zanus?" he roared.

"'Oo's 'e?" muttered Lema to Vigo, his fellow stable-hand

"That's Sizan, the leader of the Gorgonians."

"What's 'e doin' 'ere?" whispered Lema.

"We'll soon know," Vigo whispered.

Continuing with their task of sweeping the courtyard, but keeping a wary eye on Sizan, Lema suddenly pointed towards the entrance. An army of Gorgonian troopers was making its way through into the courtyard. What gave them an even bigger shock was seeing the grotesque animals they were riding.

Forgetting he'd summoned Sizan to Zorax, Zanus was enraged at seeing so many Gorgonians in his courtyard. "What they doin' in my yard?" he bellowed. "Get 'em out! Make 'em wait ready outside."

Sizan, annoyed that he was being ordered to remove his troopers, demanded to know why they couldn't stay. Zanus approached him and stared with furious black eyes, Sizan ordered his troopers to leave the tower.

"Come on, we'll 'ave a flagon of ale," said Zanus. "I wanna 'ear 'ow yer 'ave taken the lands."

Vigo's hatred for Zanus was as intense as it was for Crocanthus. He murmured, "One of these days I'm gonna get me own back."

"Let me know when, an' I'll 'elp," said Lema.

Watching their overseer, Brennard, approach across the courtyard, Vigo moved away from Lema, sweeping as he went. Brennard was heading straight for Lema. Vigo was horrified to hear the swish of the whip and see it come down on Lema's back.

He was determined to stop Brennard hurting his friend. "Boss, don't ferget them 'orses," he urged. "Zanus will go crazy if they's not ready, jus' like 'e was afore, 'member?"

Brennard paused, whip still in the air. He was thinking of the treatment he'd received from Zanus on a previous occasion.

"Ger on wiv it den," Brennan shouted back, putting down the whip. Lema wasted no time in making his way to the nearest stable. Lema was huddled in a corner.

"I fought 'e was never gonna stop," said Lema. Despite how sore his back was, Lema knew it would have been much worse if Vigo hadn't mentioned Zanus. He whispered his thanks.

"Don't never let 'im 'ear yer talking, ever, 'e don't like us to talk," Vigo explained, then gently taking hold of Lema's arm he added, "Let me 'ave a look, p'r'aps a bit of 'orse lotion will 'elp?" Without waiting for Lema to respond, Vigo collected a bottle of lotion and prepared to smear it on his friend's back. Aware this would be a painful process, Vigo whispered, "Try not to scream, I knows it'll be kinda sore."

"I won't scream," promised Lema. He stuffed his fists into his mouth as Vigo laid a handful of lotion on his friend's sore back. No matter how gently Vigo tried to rub in the lotion, he could feel his friend flinch on impact, but true to his word he never let a scream leave his mouth.

"All done. Yer was very brave, Lema," Vigo quietly told his friend. Taking the lotion back to its rightful place, Vigo made certain Brennard would never know it had been used on his friend.

Taking in the pale face and the thin body of his friend, Vigo decided to give Lema some of his gruel, hoping it would give him some extra strength. Once Lema had sipped the gruel he began to pull himself into a sitting position. Pleased to see some of the fear had gone from his friend's eyes, Vigo set about grooming the horses.

* * * *

Meanwhile Sizan and Zanus were talking in Zanus' room.

"Why aven't yer sent more troops?" asked Sizan. "We bin fightin' off them Outlanders wivout yer help."

Spinning round, Zanus glared at Sizan and uttered, "I bin waitin' fer Crocanthus to return. Now 'e's 'ere we can round up the troops and go. First we'll 'ave a flagon of ale an' a morsel of food." He shouted for ale and food to be brought immediately, sending the servants scurrying in all directions.

Leaving Sizan to stand in the middle of the dark and gloomy room, Zanus shouted, "Get a seat, but don't fink of sittin' 'ere by me." Taking a seat from a corner of the room, Sizan looked round to see where he could put it. Thinking he might try and join Zanus, he was stopped from going any closer as Zanus ordered Sizan to place the chair some way from him. Pointing to where Sizan should sit, Sizan was furious at the treatment, and angrily demanded, "Why can't I sit there?"

"Cos I says yer can't," Zanus replied, offering no further explanation. Sizan was about to retaliate when he heard Zanus give a low whistle. He noticed that the birds had become restless. Fearing they were about to attack, Sizan warned, "Don't do it, Zanus. I'll cut down any bird afore it gets me." He drew his sword

"Leave the weapon!" warned Zanus. "Any 'arm to me birds will mean 'arm to yerself." But he signalled the birds to stay where they were. He knew Sizan and his brutes were needed to help him take Dofstram.

Cowering in a darkened corner, Norman was finding it difficult to take his eyes off Sizan. He knew this man to be just as cruel as his master. With his matted hair joining the equally matted beard, it was the distorted features that shocked him most.

Feeling someone staring at him Sizan scanned the room and spotted Norman's figure cowering in the corner.

"'Oo's 'e?" he asked Zanus.

Zanus gulped down a mouthful of ale and wiped his hand across his mouth.

"'E's me informer. 'E was s'pposed to find a certain stone, and a 'uman brat. 'E failed, so 'e's gonna 'ave to 'elp me get my lands." Giving off a raucous laugh, Zanus adds, "Course, 'e might get killed 'isself." As he finished talking both men started to roar with laughter, not caring that Norman was shivering with fear in the corner.

Hearing this, Norman knew any idea of returning home would depend on his living through the battle. With the stone still in his mind, Zanus ordered the guards, "Bring me the 'uman. 'e will 'ave to tell me 'oo 'as the stone."

* * * *

Back in the cell, David wondered if there was some way the compass could show them a way out. He sensed someone approaching, but in the darkness he couldn't see who it was. It wasn't long before he noticed Norda easing himself down beside him. Before David could say anything, he heard Norda whisper, "David, was it the compass that gave us that glimmer of light?"

David replied, "It was indeed the compass, Norda. I was hoping it would show us a way to escape."

Suddenly another prisoner called out, "Guards, guards coming!" They heard the sound of stomping feet and raucous laughter. Shuffling their tortured bodies along the grimy floor, the prisoners tried to get as far from the cell doors as possible. The prisoners listened for the inevitable turn of the key. Suddenly a coarse voice shouted, "Come on 'uman, boss says yer need some 'elp with findin' a glowing stone."

Horrified, Jayne took hold of David's arms. "Can't you see, he's still bleeding from the last time!" she pleaded. Ignoring her pleas, the guards pushed Jayne away. Grabbing David by his arms, the guards made their way to the door. As they did so many of the prisoners called out to leave him alone. Annoyed at the noise the prisoners were making, one of the guards retorted, "We'll take all of yer if yer don't shut up."

The prisoners sat in shocked silence as they watched the guards pull David towards the door. With what little strength David could muster, he shouted at the guards to leave his wife alone. Although his body wanted to scream out in pain, he was determined not to give the guards the satisfaction of knowing how much they had hurt him. Concentrating on Jayne and not wanting her to be harmed, he demanded again they leave his wife alone. This only served to encourage them to taunt the prisoners and laugh more raucously.

With the strength of the guards and his own weakened state, David found it impossible to free himself from their grasp. Then he remembered the compass. He wondered how he could remove it from his pocket and drop it on the floor. He concentrated every effort on managing to free one of his arms. Finally able to reach the compass, he removed it from his pocket and dropped it on the floor.

His one fear now was that the guards had heard the muffled sound as the compass hit the straw-covered, grimy floor. He would have to do something to take their attention away from the sound. Without a second thought he swung his fist at the nearby guard and called out, "Come on then, if you keep your boss waiting he'll give you a whipping."

David knew he'd succeeded in distracting them when he saw the clenched fist coming straight at him. Managing to move his head to one side, he avoided the impact. Annoyed at missing his target, the guard yanked David up by his arm.

"Get on!" one of the guards shouted angrily, as they dragged him through the door and let him drop to the floor before slamming the door shut.

Ignoring the pain and cuts to her hands, Jayne clawed at the door screaming at the guards to leave her husband alone. She was unable to stop herself from sliding down the door and landing in a heap on the floor, where she began sobbing into her hands, feeling totally dejected.

How long she sat there she didn't know, but suddenly she felt an arm being placed round her shoulders.

"Jayne it's me, Petra," said a voice. Not able to talk, Jayne remained where she was. Then she heard Petra whisper, "I think the guards are coming. They could be bringing back a prisoner. I don't know if it's David or not."

"Did you say David was coming back?"

"I don't know. It might be one of the other prisoners, but I'm sure I heard them dragging someone along the floor," Petra whispered.

Holding her breath, Jayne lifted herself off the floor and strained to hear if she could discover what Petra had heard. She was desperate to know what was happening to her husband. Pressing her ear to the door, she listened for any sound, but failed to hear anything.

Suddenly she heard a shuffling noise from the other side of the door. Thinking it might be David, she called out his name.

"Shut yer noise or 'e'll be killed, fer sure," grunted a coarse voice.

Shocked to see how swollen Jayne's eyes were, Petra urged her friend to go with her to the back of the cell. As they settled themselves on the floor they were surprised to hear Norda say, "Jayne, I took the opportunity to fly up to look through the bars. I just caught sight of David being dragged up the steps. I guess he's being taken to Zanus. But guess who the guards were? Evoc and Harbin."

"That's who I saw," said Norda. Gripping onto Petra's hand Jayne murmured, "I'm sure they were the ones who were sent to kidnap Lottie."

"That's what I heard too," said a voice from somewhere in the cell. Recognising the voice as belonging to Bacjo, Jayne edged across to where he was sitting, but was surprised to see others from the cell were already there.

"What does this mean?" whispered Petra, "Does it mean they succeeded, or they're back because they failed?" Jayne turned to Mittoy and asked, "Have you heard why they've returned?"

Mittoy signed, "I managed to catch some of what was being said when the guards were moaning about being made to guard the cells. Crocanthus and the informer returned a while ago. This struck the guards as being funny, seeing Zanus had attacked him for not returning with the stone and the woman."

Not able to read everything Mittoy signed, Jayne apologised

and asked Bacjo to fill in the bits she missed. Norda added, "This must mean they haven't discovered what the stone looks like now. They must never know!"

"It might be safe for now, but with the Old Crone and Zanus wanting it found it will have to be a very brave person to keep it shielded," signed Sanso. Jayne surprised them by whispering, "You don't think the stone could have found its way to my land, do you?"

"If that's what's happened, it might be wise not to talk any more about the stone," said Petra. "You never know if a spy bird is hovering about." Thinking about spy birds, it was a natural instinct for them to look round and make sure they were free of them.

David was still not aware of what was happening. He recalled dropping the compass on the floor at the cell door, and being anxious it hadn't been discovered by the guards. He was aware of being unceremoniously dragged up cold slimy stone steps, and with each bump struggling to stay conscious. He wondered if he had actually managed to utter, "Where am I going?" or if it had been someone else saying it. It was some time later when he heard one of the guard's say, "Yer'll find out when yer gets there."

Continuing up more steps he wasn't sure he was relieved to hear a voice say, "We're 'ere."

David knew instantly who this guard was – one of the Zanuthians who had been sent to kidnap Lottie.

"It's a pity you failed to kidnap the person you were sent for," he said.

"'Ow do you know?" Said one of the men. "'Oo says we didn't get 'er?"

"Yeah," the other one said, "'Oo says it?" Evoc moved closer to David and said, "We 'ad a good time scaring 'er."

"We did lots of scaring," said Harbin. "One time, we tried to run 'er off the road."

"Pity we never succeeded, Harbin," said the other man. They continued to reveal more of the things they'd done and the scares they'd given her, taunting David about how scared Lottie had been.

Listening to this upset David, knowing he hadn't been there to protect his daughter. Controlling the rage that was fast bubbling to the surface, he wondered if they would let slip anything about Crocanthus. Then he realised Evoc had called Harbin by name. Punching Evoc on the arm, Harbin warned his partner, "We was told no names. We've not to say names."

David now knew these were the men who had been sent to kidnap his daughter. He would get his revenge when he could. With his mind on what he would do to these two creatures, he realised they were at Zanus' room.

"So, 'is mightiness 'as gone to 'elp them Outlanders," David heard Zanus say. The room was filled with raucous laughter.

"We needs ter get rid of 'im an' 'is 'elpers," said Zanus. "This land is mine." Slumping back into his seat, he shouted for more ale, oblivious that half the previous mug was now on the floor.

Ignoring David, who was being supported by the two guards in the doorway, Sizan shouted back, "'Oo's it belong to? Cos I wants my share." Gulping down the ale and wiping his arm across his mouth, Sizan stared at Zanus and added in a coarse voice, "What parts am I gonna 'ave?"

"Land, lots of land from the furthest parts..." began Zanus, but before he had had the opportunity to finish he noticed open door. Could it be Imelda?

"'Oo dares interrupt me?" he roared. Glaring round the room, he cast his eyes on David, supported by the guards.

"'Ow long yer bin standin' there? Bring 'im 'ere, closer to me."

"I know who these ugly mugs really are," said David. "I also know who they were sent to kidnap. Dofstram will never by yours! King Alfreston and his friends will make certain of that."

At that, Evoc and Harbin punched and kicked him mercilessly. Unable to stop himself from falling onto the stone steps, David became aware of Sizan's presence. Through half-closed eyes, he tried to see who else was in the room. He could see no sign of his daughter.

Zanus was near to exploding after what David had said. Desperate to get his hands on the stone, he had to order the guards to stop. He was eager to vent his own rage on David, but he knew he could do this once he had the stone and the woman safely in the tower. His mind was filled with wanting to gain control over Imelda, so he was determined to make David tell him where the orange stone was hidden.

Stomping down the steps, Zanus demanded, "Where 'ave you 'idden the stone?" Giving David a harsh kick in the ribs, he ordered David to get up. David tried not to think of the pain which had shot through his body; his only thought was in protecting the stone and Lottie.

"Get up. You interfering 'uman's 'ave bin nothing but trouble!" shouted Zanus, giving him another hard kick. "Get up! I want answers."

Struggling to rise from the floor David stopped halfway. He had just realised that Crocanthus was standing by Zanus' chair. He felt a sudden jolt of fear. Was Lottie here? Was she in this dreadful tower?

He was doubly shocked to see Norman Mansfield, the man he knew had betrayed his daughter. Seeing him standing smugly next to Crocanthus gave David the strength to get up.

Zanus was quick to notice where he was looking. "Yer can 'ave 'im later. Tell me where yer've 'idden the stone. What if that brat 'as it?"

Stroking his straggly beard, he moved closer to David, glaring at him through black eyes.

"We know she's in this land," he said. "We only need to get 'er, then we can make 'er tell us where it is."

David struggled to clear the words in his mind. When he realised the full implication of what Zanus had said, he felt a rush of adrenalin run though his body. The next he knew he was charging up the steps to get to his enemy. Before he could reach him, he was halted by Crocanthus. Beyond caring about himself, he fought to free himself of Crocanthus' grasp and dived at Zanus.

Zanus, convinced David couldn't get to him, was shocked to see his cloak being grabbed and feel himself being pulled off his seat. David and Zanus ended up rolling down the steps. As they reached the ground, David aimed a fist at Zanus' face, making contact with his nose. He got in a couple more punches before the guards grabbed him.

Roaring at the guards to remove David, Zanus gathered his cloak around him and tried to stand up. However, David was determined they were not going to take him away and pushed the guards off. Fuming with rage, Zanus hit out with his staff, not caring who he hit.

"So 'uman, yer fink yer can kill me eh?" he taunted.

Out of breath and exhausted, David warned, "I will get you one day, and it will be a day when you least expect it."

Terrified at what had just taken place, Norman feared David would turn his attention to him. He was relieved to see David restrained by the guards, and returned to his previous position to see what punishment Zanus would inflict on David. Instead, he was horrified to see Zanus turn his attention to him.

"He's gonna kill yer. P'r'aps I should let 'im do it now." Zanus goaded Norman.

Dumbstruck, Norman looked from Zanus to Crocanthus, wondering if this was really what they intended.

"Not just yet informer, but soon," said Crocanthus. "Perhaps Zanus will make a gift of you once he discovers where the stone is."

Cowering away without taking his eyes off David, Norman knew Crocanthus had not succeeded in finding Lottie or the stone.

David had been observing Crocanthus and was aware he was about to get some kind of punishment. Walking threateningly close to David, Crocanthus bent towards his ear and uttered, "Your daughter and I got on very well. We were good friends until others decided to interfere. Unfortunately for Lottie, she discovered who I really am. That became dangerous for me. I had to get rid of her. Unfortunately I first had to make her tell me what she knew of a glowing orange stone."

Listening to Crocanthus, Zanus jumped up from his seat and shouted, "Find it, and find it soon! I 'ave to go and kill some 'umans."

Pushing Evoc away from David, Crocanthus took David's arm and twisted it up his back. Giving him a punch in the stomach, he warned David it would get worse in the torture cell if he didn't give them the answers they wanted. Doubled over in pain, David heard the guards laughing at his treatment until Zanus told them to shut up.

"Where have you hidden the stone?" hissed Crocanthus. "Could it be you sent it to your brat?" To Zanus he said, "Perhaps it might help him remember if his woman is brought up here."

Realising he was talking about Jayne, David shouted, "Leave her alone! My wife knows no more than I do."

"What about yer brat?" roared Zanus. "Where's she?" Angered at the way they were talking about Jayne and Lottie, David lunged at Crocanthus, only to be rewarded with a whip striking him across the face. With the original cut re-opened, it wasn't long before blood was running freely down his face. Holding the wound, David warned, "If you harm my daughter or any of my friends I'll make sure you suffer." Losing the strength to stand, David dropped to the floor. With his memory of Crocanthus' thirst for torture, he feared Lottie had come to harm.

Shaking his head and trying to remain conscious, he noticed Zanus approaching. He held his breath, waiting for the inevitable kick. As Zanus' boot made contact with his sore ribs, he was unable to prevent himself from yelling out.

"I might just let yer watch when yer brat's tortured," Zanus grinned. "I will 'ave that stone. If yer won't tell me where it is, we'll enjoy finding out our own way."

David's defiance was beginning to get to Zanus. He leaned close to David's face.

"Yer won't like what we will do ter yer friends," he snarled. He nodded to Crocanthus to continue beating David into submission. Blow after blow rained down on his body, with Zanus yelling all the time, "Where is the stone? 'Oo did yer give it to?"

Finally he ordered Crocanthus to stop, adding menacingly, "I wonder. If yer brat 'as it, we need to get 'er, then we' will 'ave both."

Concerned for his daughter's welfare, and feeling certain he was about to die, David was filled with an overwhelming desire to kill Zanus. Not later - right now. Despite the pain racing though his bleeding and bruised body, he attempted to stand, but as he managed to lift himself into a kneeling position he was suddenly attacked by Zanus' birds, pecking and biting into any part of his anatomy they could reach. Drawing as much strength as he could, he forced his arms to swing out in an attempt to push the birds off.

"One day Zanus, you and your disgusting birds will pay for this," shouted David, as loud as his lungs would let him. Cruelly amused at what David said, Zanus urged his birds to attack harder. Sinking back onto the cold stone floor, David tried to curl himself up, trying to prevent the birds from attacking his sore body. But try as he might, he found it impossible to avoid them. David felt his body go numb as they tore into his body with their cruel beaks.

By now, David was in despair. Faintly he heard Zanus taunt, "Yer'll never live to see me dead, 'uman." He heard Zanus summon the guards to remove David back to the cells. Banishing his birds to the rafters, Zanus now noticed how pale Norman's face had gone.

"Be warned 'uman, this could 'appen to you," Zanus warned him.

Slumping down on his seat, Zanus watched the guards drag David's bleeding body from his room. Far from his anger abating, it only seemed to have increased

"If yer don't tell where the stone is, yer'll never leave 'ere alive!" he roared But David could not hear. He had slumped into unconsciousness.

* * * *

In the cells, the sound of sobbing reached the prisoners' ears. At first they thought it was coming from Jayne, but they soon realised it was not. Wondering how they could discover the source, Jayne asked Kira if the Ziphers could contact other Ziphers in the cells.

Kira carefully drew many of the Zipher minds to hers. Urging them to take care, she asked them to join her in trying to discover where the sound was coming from. Concentrating their thoughts as one, their minds travelled round the cells in search of who was weeping.

Kira sensed a number of thoughts from people in pain. She asked cautiously, "Is anyone there telepathic?"

At first there was no response, but then a voice entered her thoughts. "I am, but only if the other mind is close enough," it said. Not wanting to expand any further until she had support, Kira drew Sanso's attention and signed, "Could you whisper a message? A voice has responded, but I'm nervous it might be a trick. Please ask the telepaths to join their minds to mine and I will ask another question." Signing he would do that, Sanso set about whispering to the telepaths to join Kira's mind.

Feeling the strength of the other telepaths minds linking with hers, Kira asked, "Who are you?"

"My name is Kolen, and I'm from the village of Hesslewick," said the voice.

"Kolen, my name is Kira. Was that you we heard sobbing?" Kira asked. Taking a breath, Kolen explained that many of his friends from the other villages were being held prisoner. He explained how the Zanuthians and Gorgonians had managed to capture them.

Shocked to hear this, Mittoy interrupted, and telepathically asked, "Why? What did they want with you?"

"None of us are too sure why we were taken. It's our guess we are to be kept for Imelda. That's why we weren't put in with you other prisoners. The Old Crone took great delight in burning down our dwellings, leaving her vicious birds to attack. They killed many of the people who tried to flee. We're certain we are here for the Old Crone's experiments."

Giving Kolen a moment to recover, Mittoy quietly and telepathically explained to him of the many prisoners throughout the dungeon. Then he added Kolen, "Tell your friends we will keep you informed if we hear anything. Perhaps you would do the same for us?" Assured by Kolen that he would, Kira gently explained that she and her friends would be withdrawing their minds, but they would return.

Minds withdrawn, the telepaths sat looking at each other, hardly daring to believe what they'd heard. Norda, impatient to be told if they'd found the source of the sound, asked, "Well, did you find out what it was?" Signing, and leaving others to relay what was signed, Kira explained about Kolen and where he was from. Noticing the rapt attention, Kira went on to sign, "And he's not alone. There are many captured village folk, and guess what, they've been brought here for the Old Crone to experiment on."

"Oh no!" Jayne exclaimed, then quickly added, "Are there very many, Kira?"

Kira nodded. "Lots," she signed.

Jayne was surprised to see Mittoy making his way towards her.

"Jayne, I saw David drop something on the floor," he signed. "I think it might have been the compass. I've tried to find it, but I can't."

"Let's both go back there and see if we can find it," Jayne suggested. Following Mittoy, they made their way back to where he had indicated. Feeling round the grimy floor and hoping it was the compass David had dropped; Jayne stifled the tears that kept threatening to fall.

"We can't afford to lose it. Where could it be?" Jayne whispered.

The prisoners hunted through the filthy straw in silence for a while. It seemed an impossible mission. They were about to call off the search when Jayne felt a hand placed over hers and turned to see who it was. Before she could say a word, Norda held something up in front of Jayne's eyes. It was the compass.

"Well done Norda," whispered Jayne. "Perhaps you should put it safely in your pocket until David returns."

Not sure he wanted the responsibility of securing the compass, Norda took hold of Jayne's hand and whispered, "You have it." Grasping the device tightly, Jayne whispered, "Norda has found the compass, but we'll have to find somewhere to keep it safe."

Settling herself beside her friends, Jayne wondered where she could secure the compass.

"Can't you hide it on yourself, Jayne?" Thinking Bacjo must have read her thoughts she turned to him and replied, "I was just thinking that. But what do I do if one of those dreadful guards comes to get me?"

"Do what David did, drop it on the floor," Petra whispered. "We'll find it, just as Norda did."

Jayne ran her fingers over her now shredded garment, in the hope of finding a bit of material that would make a suitable hiding place. Feeling around, she discovered a piece of material that might just do. Taking two ends of the material, she tied them together and managed to make a safe pocket in which to hide the compass.

Meanwhile Petra had been thinking of a rescue attempt, while Mittoy and Eva had other thoughts; they wanted to try to reach David's mind. Deciding this would be the best time to try, they sidled over to Sanso to sign their intention. Relaying their intentions, Sanso replied telepathically, "I'm ready when you are."

"I think you must have read our thoughts, Sanso," signed Eva, with a wry smile. Then, in a more serious voice, she stated telepathically, "I suggest we sit close together and prepare our minds for reaching out to David." Shuffling closer to each other they gave the nod indicating they were ready. Blocking out any other thoughts, they prepared themselves to reach David's mind. But some kind of barrier was preventing them from reaching David's thoughts.

Eva suggested they withdraw their minds. Norda whispered, "I don't understand it, why can't we get through to David?" Drawing Sanso and Mittoy's attention, Eva signed, "That's a weird barrier. You don't think…" Before she could finish signing Mittoy took hold of Eva's hands and mouthed, "Don't think it." Then telepathically he said, "I suggest we give it one more attempt and if we fail we'll have to think of something else."

Sorry she'd even thought David might not be alive, Eva eagerly agreed they should try again. They concentrated harder, but they were still unable to break through the barrier between David's mind and theirs.

"Knowing where we are it could be the work of you-know-who," Mittoy signed.

"Careful, we don't want any repercussions or more punishments," Eva telepathically warned him. Just then they heard guards' voices.

"'Ere, this is where we got 'im from," said a coarse voice.

Bringing her knees under her chin, Jayne bent her head forward and clasped her hands round her legs. Hoping it was David, her hopes turned to fear as she wondered what they'd done to him this time.

It wasn't long before the cell door was opened with such force it hit the back wall, making the prisoners jump. Raucously laughing and yelling at the prisoners, the guards threw someone inside.

As soon as the sound of stomping feet had disappeared, Jayne hurried over to see how her husband had fared. Although the cell was very dim, she could see the fresh cuts and bruises on his face. She felt a moment of panic, thinking he had stopped breathing. She held her face close to his mouth until at last she caught a gentle breath of air on her cheek. She sat beside him, tears of relief flowing freely down her face.

Finally, realising she had wounds to tend, Jayne gathered up what cloth she could from his tattered clothing and began gently wiping his face. She was alarmed at the number of fresh weals on his body. She knew they were the results of harsh whipping.

Jayne leaned closer to David and whispered, "David, can you hear me?" It was a few moments before David lifted one of his hands. She placed her hand in his.

"It's all right David, you are safe with us now. I need to treat these wounds. You know it will be sore, but I'll try not to hurt you any more than I can help." Feeling his hand squeeze hers gently, Jayne continued carefully wiping the blood from his face before tending to his body. It took some time to treat his wounds. Quenching his thirst from the stale water bucket, David slowly began to come round.

How long he'd lain on the floor David didn't know, but he knew that each movement he made was extremely painful. Glancing round at the faces looking back at him, he tried to give a smile, but discovered it hurt his mouth.

"Are you ready to tell us what happened?" asked Jayne. He nodded and asked them to give him a minute. Then he leaned against the wall and began slowly relaying what happened, starting with his visit to the torture room.

"We know those guards who took you were Evoc and Harbin," said Jayne. "You must remember them. They were two of the cruellest. They took great delight in whipping us."

"I do," said David. They didn't like it when I told them I knew who they were," David replied. Taking a few breaths of air he continued, "I was taken to Zanus' room. He was discussing Sizan's demands for land." There were gasps from the other prisoners. "They plan to divide the land up between them," he went on. "Zanus annoyed Sizan by telling him Dofstram belongs to him. This caused an argument. Zanus told him he would get the lands at the furthest parts of Dofstram. We must all be aware that for this to happen they will need to get rid of King Alfreston and his family."

A voice from one of the other cells called out, "We've got to get out of here. King Alfreston will need all the help he can get."

David jumped - he had felt someone take hold of his hand. He looked to see who it was and saw Norda staring at him.

"Sorry to make you jump David, but I thought you should know Mittoy saw you drop your compass," he whispered.

"Yes, I believe you dropped this," said Jayne, handing the compass to him, "Norda found it."

"I forgot about that," said David. "Well done Mittoy. I saw someone huddled in the corner, but I didn't realise it was you. I just hoped whoever it was would see what I'd done." Turning the compass over in his hand he turned to Jayne and whispered, "I'm still hoping this will offer us some way of escaping."

A moment later, Bacjo noticed a familiar face peering through the bars - Harbin. Why would he be looking in on them? He told the others what he had seen.

"David, you don't think Zanus has Lottie do you?" said Jayne. Easing his painful body closer to Jayne, he took hold of her hand and replied, "I don't think so, Jayne. I didn't see any signs. He took delight in telling me I could watch when he deals with Lottie, so I have to hope she's still safe."

"Oh David! However did she get involved?" said Jayne. "If they failed in what Zanus wanted, is that why those two brutes have returned?"

"Remember Jayne, we know how Lottie got involved.

Thanks to the informer, who we know is Norman Mansfield. I just hope he hasn't involved your sister Jean. What worries me is, Lottie probably doesn't know this so-called friend of her aunt's is the one who gave her away. There is one thing I am sure of - if she has certain friends with her she will be well protected."

Jayne suddenly remembered that David hadn't been told about the other prisoners. Taking hold of his hand, she told him, "There's something you might not know, David. There are many new folk being held prisoner here. After you'd been taken we could hear sobbing. A telepath among them called Kolen told us they had been brought here by those brutes to be held until Imelda sends for them to be used in her experiments."

Taking hold of her arm, David whispered, "Did I hear right - there are prisoners here from the Outlander villages?"

Jayne nodded. "That's not all," she said. "Their homes have been burned to the ground by Imelda. They were attacked by those devil birds. A lot of them were left for dead."

"Are there many villagers here?"

"I think so."

Suddenly a timid voice entered David's thoughts. "Are you all right now. David? These brutes sure know how to torture." Turning to where he thought the owner of the voice came from, David whispered, "Was that you, Mittoy?" When Mittoy confirmed it was, David, in a low voice, responded, "I'm all right now. Just a bit sore."

"Will all telepaths join with me to see if we can discover what they're planning?" asked David telepathically. "We can be certain of one thing, whatever they are planning it will be big and evil. Especially with Imelda and that dreadful Sizan involved."

Just then Mittoy signed they had picked up thoughts from Zanus' room. "There's no mention of your daughter, but we did hear the word informer," he told David, telepathically. David pulled Jayne closer to relay what he was told.

"That's Mansfield," said David. "He was there with Crocanthus and Sizan. All telepaths please try to find out what they're planning." The telepaths concentrated their thoughts in the direction of Zanus' room.

David thought for a moment, then took the compass from his pocket and twisted it round. He still felt that somehow it held the key to their escape.

He flipped the lid open and turned the dial. Thinking he heard a faint voice, he looked round to see if any of his companions had spoken, but one had.

There it was again – a voice.

"Listen, can't anyone hear it?" said David. They all listened for a moment.

"You don't think it could be...?" murmured Jayne.

"Hold on, I'll give it a try. Leave me to concentrate and I'll see if you're right," said David.

Closing his mind to everything around him, David concentrated all his thoughts on reaching Beauty. He was about to give up when he heard a faint voice say, "Leave the compass open." Shaking, he slowly called out telepathically, "Is it - our friend?"

Waiting anxiously for the answer, David was delighted when he caught the word 'rescue'. He looked up to see many anxious faces looking in his direction. "Come on, David, don't keep us in suspense any longer, tell us what happened," said Jayne.

"I spoke to her. I really did. And guess what I heard, the word rescue, just before our minds disconnected. She said I have to leave the compass open. I won't be able to do that all the time, but I will every so often. I guess we'd better be ready for whatever is required. Please, think before you say anything, and I suggest we don't use our telepathy for this. Remember, the Old Crone is able to pick up on thoughts if they are strong enough. Sign to our friends, and get them to pass the message to all the others." Breathless, David was relieved he'd managed to relay everything.

The prisoners concentrated on getting the message to everyone, at the same time urging them not to use telepathy. While they were doing this, Jayne suddenly thought about the other prisoners. David assured her they would be told. Then he said, "I'm also concerned our thoughts might be picked up by Crocanthus."

"I forgot about Crocanthus. But couldn't you on your own

reach out to Kolen? You don't have to give the whole thing, just say there is hope of being rescued. Make it short but give him the same warning you gave us."

Smiling at his wife, David took her hand in his and said, "You're a whiz, Jayne. I could do that and withdraw my mind before anyone can pick it up."

David sought out the mind of Kolen and told him a little of what had taken place. Kolen told David he would make sure everyone was ready for whatever was about to happen. Then Kolen set about relaying to his friends, what David had told him.

"Well done, now we will have to be very careful we don't arouse suspicion that something is going on," Jayne warmly told him when he had finished.

* * * *

Norman hoped Zanus had forgotten him, but no such luck. He was ordered to follow Sizan into the courtyard. He reluctantly stumbled down the steps and followed through the passageways. Listening to the thumping noise of the heavy boots, and mindful of the beasts which hung on the passage walls, Norman wondered how he was ever going to escape his nightmare.

He suddenly recalled the first time he had walked down this passageway. Watching Sizan recoil from Zanus' creatures, Norman could remember doing the same thing. But unlike Sizan, he hadn't been given the chance to ask anything about them.

Having been dragged from the cave through the Forbidden Wood, he had been pushed along these passages. Unaware of where he was being taken, it had been a shock to be thrown unceremoniously in front of Zanus. Cringing at the memory of lying prone on the hard steps, he could still hear himself stammering like some simpleton as he told Zanus what he knew of David and Jayne.

"They are a husband and wife team who go on expeditions, exploring old caves and things. They hope to discover other..." Before he could finish what he was saying, Zanus had leapt straight at him waving a large staff in a threatening manner. Not prepared for the cold menacing voice, he had shivered in fear when Zanus demanded, "An' jus' what did these 'ere 'umans discover?"

Norman had been too terrified to resist. He had told Zanus how he had seen David take something from a large boulder - a shiny stone.

His attention brought back to where he was, Norman stared ahead, wondering how much further they had to go to reach the courtyard. Stumbling over something on the floor, he wanted to see what it was but his attention was caught up with listening to Zanus and Sizan discussing ownership of the land. Not caring who had what, Norman drifted back into his thoughts.

He remembered looking through a gap in the wall into Zanus' room to see the evidence that David and Jayne had been horribly treated. He recognised the clothes he had last seen them in, was now soaked with blood. Unable to hear all that was said, he'd been shocked to see Crocanthus whipping their still bodies. Thinking they were dead, he was shocked to hear the terrible screams that came from Jayne.

Norman had thought up a possible plan to get away. When he had been fetched back in front of Zanus, he told him, "If I return to my land, I could discover everything you need to know." Zanus, intrigued but irritated by the whining voice, told him, "Any lies an' yer'll go back to the room of torture. Yer best 'member, I will know."

Norman had been startled to hear a terrible screeching voice call out, "Oo we got 'ere, Zanus? Is this one of yer creatures to torture?" Staring round and not able to see who had spoken, he had seen a green mist swirl up from the floor.

Recalling how scared he was at the time, he clearly remembered that his eyes felt as if they were burning. Drawn irresistibly to the creature's green eyes, he thought for a moment that they were sending him into a hypnotic state. He could see what the creature reminded him of. Facing him was a fully-grown lizard, complete with scaly skin and green slit eyes. Without warning it opened its mouth to reveal two large fangs hanging inside as it released a loud warning hiss.

He wasn't sure what would have happened next if Zanus

hadn't warned, "Leave 'im. 'E's gonna go an' bring back their brat. Yer'll 'ave 'im later."

Then in a flash of light the creature had gone and in its place was a person, but not like any other he'd seen. It looked like a gargoyle with its unkempt hair, pointed nose and wrinkled skin. All he felt she needed was snakes coming from her hair.

Zanus must have noticed the look on his face, because he roared with laughter and said, "Be wary of the Old Crone, she 'as magic yer won't like!" Dismissing Norman with a shake of his staff, Zanus warned, "I ain't finished with yer yet. Don't even think of running away. Stay 'ere in this room, over in that corner."

"What you wanna do wiv 'im?," asked Imelda, slowly walking round the chairs, and stroking the birds close by. Keeping his eye on Imelda, aware she could use some kind of trickery, Zanus replied, "'I ain't gonna do anything to 'im yet. E's gonna get the brat of those interfering 'uman prisoners an' bring 'er to me. I need yer to get this informer back to where 'e came from."

"So, they 'as a brat, do they?" Scratching the end of her nose with an offensive-looking fingernail, Imelda spun round and asked tauntingly, "I'm thinking she'd 'ave to come to me. I need to know if she 'as the stone."

"She's not gonna be your prisoner, yer old 'ag. She's gonna be brought to me!" Zanus shouted. Without warning or any obvious sign of movement, Imelda appeared straight in front of Zanus and stood over him as she warned, "Be very careful Zanus. We ain't got our land yet, an' yer needs me 'elp to do it."

Now, fearing Imelda could have reached his thoughts, he broke away from his memories and searched up and down the passage to see if the Old Crone had appeared. Wondering how much further they had to go, he noticed a light at the end of the passage. Guessing they were reaching the courtyard, he hoped the grotesque creature that had emerged from the mist wasn't about to reappear.

"Get the weapons and troopers ready!" Zanus was shouting. Norman felt fear stealing over him again. Was this the day he was going to die?'

Chapter Nineteen

Into the Tower

As they arrived at the hill close to the Tower of Zorax, Beauty wanted to make sure everyone was prepared for the dangers they would face once they entered. It would be safer if they could discover how many enemy were within, so Beauty told Eram she would try to break through the mist before they continued. Settling down and keeping constant vigilance, they waited to see if Beauty had any luck with her task.

With the assistance of Lottie, Beauty concentrated on breaking through the mist. Urging Lottie to keep her thoughts on the mist, Beauty struggled to make even a small gap in it. Lottie, picking up on the difficulty Beauty had, was using as much energy as she could to hold the mist in place. Realising this, Beauty turned her thoughts to where Lottie was concentrating hardest.

At last Beauty was overjoyed at seeing a small opening in the mist. Digging deeper into her thoughts, she called out for any telepath to reply. Not sure if she heard a faint whisper, she called out once more, "Would any telepath tell the compass holder to keep it open?" Sensing Lottie's grip on the mist was beginning to wane, Beauty called out one last time, "Keep the compass open!"

Releasing Lottie's thoughts from hers, Beauty turned her attention to discovering how many troopers were inside, and where they were. Alarmed at the number in the courtyard, she continued searching the stable and other outside areas.

Having checked that Lottie was OK, Beauty went on to tell

her friends how they'd managed to break through the barrier. Informing them she'd relayed a message to the telepaths inside, she said that the only thing that concerned her was not knowing who had received the message. She was concerned that the compass could be in enemy hands.

Beauty suddenly became alert to danger. Quickly throwing an invisibility cover over her companions, she whispered. "Please remain quiet! Sizan has arrived with a large army of Gorgonians."

Just then a coarse voice demanded to be let into the courtyard. Watching through their protective cover, the fear they felt prevented anyone from making a noise. Seeing so many Gorgonians tramping close by sent shivers of fear through the people.

As they watched the last of the Gorgonians enter the courtyard, Letswick whispered, "So many enemies. I think we should be careful there are no stray Gorgonians."

"What do you think they are here for?" whispered Penny.

"They've come at the command of Zanus. They must be going off to battle against King Alfreston and the Outlanders," Nain explained nervously. Emerging from her cover Beauty whispered, "We must wait to see what happens. Sign or speak in a low whisper, don't use telepathy as our thoughts could be picked up." With the cover removed, it wasn't long before they all had the same idea – to hide.

Eram, eager to know when they could proceed, asked, "I wonder how long we will have to wait. I want to free the prisoners as soon as possible so we can leave this horrible place."

The group suddenly fell silent at the sound of cursing and swearing coming from the courtyard. The gates were being slowly lowered. Holding their breath, the group waited to see what the next move would be. The booming voice of Zanus followed. "Get out, an' wait outside."

Horrified to see just how many Gorgonians had emerged, Beauty wondered where Sizan was. Attracting Dandy's attention, she whispered, "Dandy, please give a light invisibility covering to the animals, it's more difficult for them to hide." Pleased to see the animals were beginning to fade from view, Beauty asked Lottie, "How are you now, Lottie? Your help with the mist was surprising. We have more power together than I thought possible."

"I would do anything to help you and your people, my friend. It was a bit scary though, especially seeing how eerie that mist kept trying to join together," Lottie whispered.

Penny was about to ask a question when Letswick placed a finger to his lips and mouthed, "Hush, just for a while." She gave his arm a slight squeeze to acknowledge his request. Still holding onto Letswick, she was alarmed to hear a number of coarse Gorgonian voices moaning and groaning at being thrown out of the courtyard. The observers were shocked to see a group of Gorgonians heading in their direction. Sheltering herself into Letswick's back, Penny felt his hand take hold of hers. Although she felt slightly calmer at the touch of his hand, she was still aware of the danger they were in.

Eram whispered to Binro, "I wonder how we can distract them away from here?" Taking hold of his hand, Binro signed, "Perhaps Letswick could do that." He noticed Letswick and Penny had moved closer to them. Signing, Letswick said, "I was wondering that myself. I won't be able to go far because of the protective covering, but I'm sure Yemil would come with me."

Eram asked Penny to stay with them. Seeing the fear on her face, Binro made his way to stand beside her. Passing Penny's hand into Binro's, Letswick whispered, "I won't be long. Stay here with Binro and Eram, they will keep you safe."

Satisfied that Penny was settled, Letswick made his way to Lottie and Yemil. Stooping down close to Yemil, he signed, "Would you come with me? I want to distract these brutes from coming any closer." Slightly alarmed at the request, Yemil didn't hesitate to agree. Placing her mouth close to Lottie's ear she whispered, "I'm going with Letswick to try and divert these brutes." Then she disappeared from view.

Following Letswick's lead, they flew over the enemy to see how many there were. Confident they would be able to divert this number, they began buzzing like flies between and around the Gorgonians. Amused to see the enemy's fruitless attempts to swat them away, Letswick took to blowing air on their faces, while Yemil took pleasure in tugging at their ears. Noticing a lone trooper, Yemil was about to give a tug on his ear when the trooper shouted, "Why yer doin' this? We'll soon get yer." Quickly flying back into the air, Yemil was surprised to hear another trooper call out, "Shut yer mouf. What if it's the Old Crone? We don't want no punishments from 'er."

Realising the trooper wasn't shouting at her, Yemil flew to Letswick and whispered, "They think it's the Old Crone tormenting them. There are a couple of troopers down there moaning at each other at being attacked."

Amused at the troopers as they stomped back to join their fellows, Letswick thought about the times his friends had been terrorised by these brutes and wondered if he dared give the same annoyance to the waiting group. Gaining Yemil's attention, he indicated where he was going to fly to. Flying to his side, they flew straight at the group, who were still moaning at being banned from the courtyard.

Aiming straight at the Gorgonians' faces, Letswick managed to catch their attention. Following close behind, Yemil completed the torment by flapping her wings. Unsure of what was attacking them, the troopers began waving their hands in front of their faces and yelling at whatever it was to leave them alone. Taking Yemil's hand, Letswick flew onto the leader's back. The trooper screamed out, "What the 'ell is goin' on 'ere? 'Oo's punching me?" One of the troopers yelled, "We can't see no one."

Not believing this, the second trooper turned to the first and lunged at him ready with his fist. Missing his target, he screamed, "I'll get yer fer fumping me." Screaming back that it wasn't him, another trooper stated, "It could be that Old Crone."

Landing a well-placed punch on the trooper's ear, Letswick only just avoided being hit by the waving hand. Yemil flew closer to Letswick and whispered, "I think we should go back now. These troopers are truly unsettled." Wanting to do more, but realising Yemil was right, he gave the trooper one more punch, leaving him yelling abuse at his invisible attacker.

Landing beside Eram, Letswick whispered, "Mission

complete." With a low laugh, they settled back to see what was going to happen. Pleased to see Letswick had returned unscathed, Penny gave Binro a hug and thanked him for his company. Penny and Letswick remained quietly with Eram and Binro. Meanwhile, Yemil had taken her place back with Lottie.

Yemil was a little surprised when Beauty whispered, "Well done you two. That will give them something to think about. Now I think we had better remain quiet and see what happens." Humbled by Beauty's praise, Yemil whispered quietly, "Thanks, my friend." She settled down beside Lottie to wait and watch events about to unravel.

Aware something had taken place, Lottie was about to ask what when she felt a slight movement from her brooch. Drawing the lapel up near her mouth, she whispered, "Is something happening?"

"There's movement coming from deep within the tower," whispered Beauty. "Zanus and Sizan are approaching the courtyard."

No sooner had Beauty said this than they all heard the demanding voice of Zanus order his menials to lower the gates. An army of troopers filtered through, some on horseback and many others on foot. As the mass of Gorgonians and Zanuthians stomped their feet, the ground trembled from the impact.

Squeezing Letswick's hand, Penny didn't need to tell him of her fear; he had already sensed it. Desperate to ask a question, Letswick calmly said, "Later, Penny. Watch and see what happens." No sooner had he spoken than loud screams and shouts were heard coming from beyond the tower walls.

Lottie and Penny glanced across at each other, then slowly lifted their heads above the shrubbery. With the stench that came from the troopers and animals, Penny and Lottie had to pinch their noses.

They were horrified to see that some of the Gorgonians were riding these beasts. Staring at the creatures, they noticed many were pulling huge carts of weaponry. The cargo looked heavy even for those beasts to pull.

Penny stammered, "Are they tàking those weapons to where the battle is?" As horrified as Penny, Letswick solemnly replied,

"I'm afraid so, Penny. This means we will have to get to King Alfreston very soon."

Lottie was transfixed. "Were they really Gorgonians on those beasts?" she asked.

"Indeed they were," replied Nain. "I'm not sure which are the uglier, the beasts or the Gorgonians."

Looking at the Gorgonians, Lottie was surprised to see how dark and foreboding their eyes were. They were sunk far back into their heads, giving the impression they were empty sockets.

Lottie whispered, "Are you all right, Penny? I've never seen such horrible things as these."

"I'm all right, just a little scared. They don't half smell, I bet they can be smelt a mile away," replied Penny.

"Why are these creatures so misshapen? What are they?" Lottie asked Beauty.

"Many of these beasts are mutations of a prehistoric species," said Beauty. "No one is quite sure what, but I suppose they would have been around at the time when dinosaurs roamed your land."

"I didn't think a dinosaur could be that grotesque," said Penny.

Lottie turned her attention back to watching the enemy. With the invisibility cover now evaporated, Eram whispered, "How long before we can make a move?"

"Not long now. I still sense movement within the courtyard, let's wait and see what's going to happen," Beauty whispered. No sooner had Beauty finished speaking than another army of Zanuthians stormed through the gates, armed to the hilt with assorted weapons. Lottie leaned close to her brooch and whispered, "There's so many of these brutes. That's not including those Gorgonian weirdies." Keeping her eyes peeled on the long line of troopers, she stared and stared again. Was she seeing things or was that really her Aunty Jean's friend?

Unable to stop herself, Lottie suddenly let out a loud gasp. "Did you see Jeremy – I mean Crocanthus - riding alongside Zanus?" she asked.

"I did," said Beauty. "I guess you've seen someone else. Am I right?"

Lottie's mind was in such turmoil it took her a while to answer. "Yes. That man riding behind Crocanthus. His name is Norman Mansfield. He's a friend of my Aunty Jean. I can't think why he's with them. How does he know this land? Did he know Crocanthus was Jeremy? I wish I knew the answers."

Guessing this must be the informer, Beauty concentrated her thoughts on him. Eager to get a feel of what sort of person this is, she took great care not to alert Lottie or the other telepaths to what she was doing. Picking up Norman's thoughts, Beauty was aghast at what she discovered. Listening to him express his uncaring excuse for giving Lottie's identity to Zanus, Beauty decided this person would never get close to Lottie again. Continuing to express his fury at Crocanthus for not finding the stone and Lottie increased Beauty's dislike and anger at how callous a person he was.

Beauty became more alert when Norman mentioned David by name. She was shocked to hear him jeer at the memory of seeing David whipped. As she travelled through his mind, she was able to see the dreadful state the prisoners were in.

Beauty decided to treat Norman to some of her own thoughts. She began to create hallucinations. Norman, unaware of what was happening, suddenly saw flying creatures coming straight for him. Screaming out, he watched them get nearer and nearer. Then they began attacking him, biting and stinging every part of his face and neck. Screaming out loud, he tried to fend them off, but in vain.

Annoyed at the screaming behind him, Crocanthus turned and raised his whip ready to come down on Norman. As the whip fell on his arm, Norman screamed louder.

"Shut yer noise!" shouted Zanus. Angered by this treatment, Norman whined, "I'm being attacked by weird creatures. Can't you see them? They're flying all round me."

"Shut up or you will feel my whip again," snarled Crocanthus. "There's nothing flying round, you must be imagining it."

Satisfied with this outcome, Beauty thought of one more thing before she removed her thoughts from Norman's. Knowing it wouldn't be long before his hallucinations would cease, she set about giving him a rash which would make him itch. Before he knew it, Norman became aware of an intense itch on his face and neck. At first he thought it was through being hit with the whip, but as it continued he had to disregard that. Not aware he was giving cause for alarm, he was shocked to hear Crocanthus shout, "Now what's the matter with you? Have you gone mad? Stop squirming around, you'll spook the horse."

By now, it seemed to Norman that the itch was all over his body. He couldn't make out why none of the others were scratching. Then the thought of being poisoned crossed his mind, which made him shout, "Someone must have put something in my food. I'm itching all over. Have I been poisoned?" By this time, he was covered in blotches where he'd scratched so hard. With the troopers jeering and laughing at him, Norman's anger rose inside him. He vowed to himself he would get his own back at some time, and return to his own land.

"It won't be so easy, 'uman," called out Zanus. "The Old Crone will make sure yer stay 'ere." Shocked to think Zanus had picked up his thoughts and fearful of Crocanthus and his whip, he looked down at the ground. Turning his thoughts once again to David, he placed the blamed squarely on his shoulders for getting him into this dreadful situation.

Content with leaving Norman with his torment, Beauty settled back on Lottie's lapel. Yemil meanwhile had been giving some thought to what she'd heard Lottie tell Beauty earlier. She hesitated for a moment, then plucked up the courage and asked cautiously, "Do you think he could be the informer?"

"I hadn't thought of that. But it's possible."

"I wonder how he knew of Dofstram and Zanus," said Lottie. Turning to Yemil, she added, "Do you think he knew Jeremy as I knew him? If he did, I wonder why his name was never mentioned." Taken aback by these comments, Yemil considered the best way to ask what she wanted to ask next. Beauty sensed Yemil's dilemma.

"Ask the question, Yemil," she said. Not surprised that Beauty had sensed her thoughts, Yemil whispered, "Lottie, do you think he knows where your parents are, and if they are still alive?"

"Do you think he might know, Yemil?" asked Lottie. "I bet he wouldn't tell me anyway."

Although Beauty had been listening to the conversation she didn't want to raise Lottie's hopes, so she remained quiet about what she had seen in the informer's mind. Turning her thoughts to the amount of armoury and troopers that had left the tower, Beauty was aware of their destination, and was becoming anxious to join King Alfreston. About to give the all clear for them to move, she noticed more carts and weaponry being rolled out. Aware this weaponry was heading in one direction, the Outlander barrier, Beauty hoped she would get to King Alfreston in time.

Letswick was quietly observing this himself, and had become aware of the urgency to get this mission completed and join King Alfreston. As they waited for the gates to be closed, it seemed an eternity to the observers.

As soon as he considered it safe to talk, Eram said, "We need to gain entry to the dungeons as quietly and quickly as we can." Turning his attention to Nain and Rista he asked, "Can you show us the safest way to enter? It might be you will remember which passages are close to the prisoners." He asked the unicorns to shield all the animals, and asked, "When we move from here, will you be able to find somewhere close to hide?"

"We can do that," replied Doran and Dandy together. Taking a look at where Eram was facing, Doran added, "We'll seek shelter amongst those trees. We'll use our protective covering to get as close as we can." Turning to Letswick, Doran continued, "Just give me the signal and I'll bring the others along with me." Letswick whispered, "Will do. Take care, we don't want that Old Crone getting her hands on any of you."

Eram beckoned to Nain and Rista to go with him. Nervous and apprehensive, Rista concentrated on listening out for the enemy while keeping close to Eram. Recognising the area he was looking for, Nain turned to Rista and whispered, "We're here. Rista, would you keep watch for the enemy while I show Eram the entrance?" Rista agreed to keep watch, but asked them not to be too long. Lying flat on the top of the bank, she concentrated on listening for the enemy.

As she watched them prepare to make their way down the slippery bank, Rista thought she heard a noise and thought it best to alert Nain and Eram. She slid down to join them. Surprised to see her, Nain asked, "Is there trouble?"

"I heard a noise and thought it best to let you know. I'm sure it was enemy troopers." Pointing to a place they could hide, Nain led Rista and Eram towards it. On reaching the place, Nain realised he hadn't considered Eram's height. It was a secure place for him and Rista, but Eram would need a bigger place. Looking round, Eram noticed a convenient place big enough to hide. Securing Nain and Rista in their shelter, he made his way to his. He shuffled down inside the hole and removed a little more dirt, making it easier for him to keep out of sight.

They all remained silent and waited anxiously for the approaching voices to fade away. Fearful they might be seen, Nain and Rista huddled closer together.

"I hope Eram is safe," whispered Rista. Not expecting an answer, Nain held Rista close to him while they waited anxiously for the troopers to leave.

How long they had been there no one knew, but it was some time before they were relieved to hear the voices fade off in another direction. Making sure it was clear, Eram crept over to Nain and Rista.

"I don't think we should waste any more time. Let's go," he said. Having gone about halfway down the muddy bank, Nain pointed to something at the bottom of the bank. Rista whispered, "It's the entrance to the dungeon. Follow him down, and I'll climb back to the top and keep look out."

Not able to see what he was looking for, Eram suddenly noticed a large area covered with branches and debris. He slowly descended down the bank. Continuing on, Nain indicated excitedly for Eram to follow. Slipping and sliding down the muddy bank, it didn't take long for Eram to join Nain. The nearer they got to the bottom the muddier it became. With only a short distance to go, they took great care not to slip.

Suddenly Eram noticed that Nain was standing beside a large wheel. Conscious of Rista at the top of the bank, he checked with Rista to make sure there were no enemy around. Assured by Rista it was all clear, he quickly joined Nain. Brushing aside the debris, they soon exposed the entrance to the dungeon. Aware the wheel was to be used to gain entry, Eram realised this was too small an entrance for the larger folk to get through.

Seeing the look of despair on Eram's face, Nain said, "Don't worry, we can ask our friend to make it larger." Replacing the debris back over the entrance, they began clawing their way back up the bank and collapsed on top of it. Nain, having got his breath back, said, "I'll go and bring the others to join us."

"Take care, we still don't know where the troopers are," said Rista. She watched as Nain set off.

Nain approached the rest of the group and told them about their discovery. "Could you make the entrance larger for our taller friends to get through?" he asked Beauty.

"I can, but come, we must make haste," Beauty whispered. "Would you lead the way, Nain?" Walking alongside Lottie, Nain whispered, "It will be very scary inside, the dungeons are black and smelly."

"Now - now, don't go scaring everyone. We'll take it carefully and do our best to avoid the guards," Beauty whispered gently.

"Sorry. I was speaking my thoughts out loud," Nain said. Taking hold of Lottie's hand, Nain pointed to a high bank a little way ahead. "That's where we are heading," he said. "Eram and Rista are lying low just behind those shrubs." In silence they continued until they reached the top of the bank.

Having noticed the group approaching, Rista and Eram came forward. "It's OK at the moment, we haven't seen any enemy," Eram told them. Attracting Lottie and Letswick's attention, Eram pointed to the entrance, then went on to explain that it was covered by debris. Now Lottie was close beside him, Eram explained the difficulty the larger folk would have getting through the entrance. Assuring Eram she had been made aware of the problem, Beauty saw Binro sign, "Can you make it larger now? We don't want to be caught by any of the enemy now we've got this far."

"Will do," Beauty replied without hesitation. Beauty concentrated her thoughts on enlarging the entrance. Turning to Rista, Eram asked, "Would you and Binro mind being at the end of the group?" With a sign of agreement from Binro, he heard Rista say, "I'm sure Binro wouldn't mind being with me." Getting into position, Nain asked Lottie to follow him, leaving Eram to follow behind her.

They made their way through in single file, leaving Binro and Rista at the back. They were all thankful the rain had stopped. It had, however, left a slippery and very muddy bank, which caused a bit of a problem for the smaller folk as they struggled to stop themselves from sliding to the bottom.

Reaching the entrance, Nain began scraping away the debris he and Eram had placed over it. With help from Eram it was soon clear enough for them to enter. They set about turning the wheel to slowly reveal the entrance to the dungeons.

Now the entrance was large enough to take them all, Nain suggested Eram should enter first. Stepping inside the darkened passage, Eram hesitated before continuing. Seeing Lottie was close behind him, he was encouraged to move on by Beauty's calming voice. As he moved further along, his one wish was to get this mission over. Letswick drew closer to Beauty, who whispered, "Please warn the folk the entrance will revert back to its normal size and the wheel will secure it once we've entered." Doing as Beauty requested, Letswick stopped Rista and Binro from going any further. They waited to hear what he was going to say.

"Sorry If I scared you, but just a word of caution. You might not have heard when I was telling the others," Letswick whispered. "As soon as we are safe within the passage the entrance will return to its original size, and the wheel will secure the entrance." With everyone inside, he noticed the entrance was beginning to shrink. Knowing many of the pitfalls within this place, Letswick gained their attention once more to let them know of his plan.

"Just to check we aren't walking into a trap, I think it might be better if we continue in single file. Perhaps Nain and Rista will come behind me. Give us a couple of moments before you follow on. Then it might be best if Lottie and Penny lead the remainder. That way if any of us are caught...." He left the rest unsaid, but they all knew what he meant. "If you hear the enemy, press close against the wall, that way the dimness of the passage will give us some protection."

Trying to adjust their eyes to the dimly lit passage, Letswick whispered, "If everyone is ready, we will set off." Hearing the murmurs of consent, he led the way through the passage. At the end, Letswick stopped to take a look round. He whispered to Nain and Rista, "I can't see or hear anything. I think we can proceed."

As they were about to turn into the next passage, Rista drew their attention to the still-open entrance. Thinking it should have closed by now, Rista was about to suggest she should go and see why it hadn't when she noticed Yemil was making her way back. Not happy to leave Yemil on her own, she went to join her.

Butterflies were going round in Lottie's stomach. "It's been so long since I've seen my parents," she sighed. "I can't help wondering if…"

"Careful Lottie, remember we don't want our thoughts to be heard," whispered Beauty. It won't be long now."

As they prepared to make their way back to the rest of the group, Rista and Yemil were suddenly stopped in their tracks when they heard a voice say, "E's a real devil, that's what I say, I means it, Vigo." Then they heard someone reply, "One day, Lema, one day we'll get a go at 'im."

"With 'is own whip I 'opes!" said the other voice. Gentle laughter followed. Binro signed to Beauty, "It sounds like these folk don't like Crocanthus."

Yemil was about to suggest they would need some light when Rista jumped back.

"'Ey, 'oo's down ..." Before he could finish asking the question, they heard a sound come from inside the entrance. Thinking it was guards, Lema and Vigo ran and took shelter behind a clump of shrubs.

Unaware they had scared the two stable-hands, Yemil indicated to Rista that she was going to take a look. Rista, fearful Yemil would be seen, crawled closer to the entrance, just as Yemil called out, "Who are you?"

"I'm Vigo an' I'm with me pal, Lema," replied Vigo nervously.

"Don't tell 'em our names, we don't know 'oo it is!" Lema urged his friend.

"This is my friend Rista," said Yemil. "We really won't hurt you." Slowly edging her way out of the entrance, she was greeted by two scruffy and dirty-faced stable-hands.

"Cor, is you two Jaspers?" said Vigo.

Landing close beside them, Yemil asked, "You won't give us away, will you?"

"No way, we don't like any of 'em 'ere. Cruel, they are all cruel," said Vigo.

Stepping in front of his friend, Lema told them, "I'm Lema. Vigo saved me life, so I'm gonna 'elp 'im when 'e needs it." The pair stood as straight as they could, trying to give the impression they were taller than they really were.

"What yer doin' 'ere, Yemil?" Vigo asked cautiously. Chuckling at the way they were staring with eyes wide open. Rista and Yemil felt a moment of uncertainty. Neither was sure how much they should tell them. Turning to telepathy, Yemil requested advice from Beauty. After explaining who she was with and why they were there, Beauty replied, "Make sure they really are to be trusted. Don't reveal any more than is necessary. If they are really keen to help, try and find out what help they think they can offer. Remember Yemil, we need to make sure they don't shout for the troopers."

"Yeah, I bet she was doin' that 'ead thing, yer know where they talk without movin' their lips," said Lema. Laughing, Yemil surprised Rista by turning serious and asking if there was somewhere they could go out of sight.

"We could go where we 'id," stated Lema.

"Yeah, over be'ind them broken down shrubs," added Vigo.

Amused at how they always seemed to speak after each other, Yemil nodded. Once safely hidden in the shrubs, Yemil told Rista what had taken place between her and Beauty. Yemil noticed the two pairs of eyes staring in her direction and wondered if one of them had anything to say.

"We really will 'elp yer," whispered Lema.

"Yeah, we really will," added Vigo. "Is yer alone?"

"'As yer got lost?" asked Lema. "We can 'elp yer to find a way out."

"If I tell you something, will you promise not to give us away or call for the guards?" said Yemil. Seeing the shocked expression on their faces, she apologised and offered to tell them something of why they were there.

"Some of my friends have been taken prisoner, so we have come along with a few of our other friends to try and rescue them," she said. "We know Zanus will be on the battlefield, so we thought this would be the best time."

Yemil thought the men might have some questions; instead they took turns in telling her what they'd gone through. They also shared their eagerness to deal out their own punishments. Shocked to hear of the rough treatment they'd been dealt, Yemil felt it was safe enough to ask if they really could help find a way out. Suddenly the two lads understood what she'd said. Vigo stammered, "Yer, yer gonna go down in them dungeons?"

"Cruel things 'appen down there," said Lema, in a nervous voice. But just then Vigo grabbed his arm and turned him round so he could see the approaching troopers. Terrified they must have been seen, Lema began to shake. Noticing this, Yemil was convinced she'd made the right decision to trust them.

"Wriggle down that trofalogue hole," she said. "I know it's smelly but it's safe. Rista and I will find a place to hide. With the smell from the trofalogues, they won't know we are here."

Not having to be told twice, Lema edged his way behind a tuft of grass and slid quickly into the trofalogue hole, followed by Vigo. Shivering with fear, they left Yemil and Rista to secure themselves in another trofalogue hole. Keeping their breathing to a minimum they pressed against the wall and waited for the guards to pass by. With the stench from those dreadful beasts, Rista hoped the guards wouldn't stay long.

Unaware of the frightened folk hiding not too far from where they were, the troopers peered over the bank edge, not really expecting to see anything or anyone. Fearful of the consequences if they were discovered not searching properly, one of the troopers said, "Let's get back. There's nuffin' 'ere."

The troopers turned and went back in the direction from which they'd come.

Rista and Yemil, cautiously left their trofalogue holes and made their way over to where Vigo and Lema had hidden themselves. Pleased and relieved to get away from the stench, the two lads wasted no time in scrambling out into the fresh air.

"I jus' 'ad a fought, if yer sure yer want to go down the dungeons, Lema an' me can show yer a good way out, one not even them bullies knows," Vigo told them.

"But, we'd 'ave to come down an' join yer to get to it," Lema added.

Not too sure that was a good idea, Yemil hesitated before replying. "You promise not to give us away to the guards? And you will remain quiet and do what is asked?" Without answering, Vigo and Lema nodded emphatically. Glancing round to ensure it was safe to continue, Yemil led the way to the entrance. Moving aside the cover they'd put in place earlier, she felt the same nervous feeling she'd had on her previous entry. Peering into the dimness of the passage, she urged her companions to move quickly and quietly. Vigo and Lema were taller than her, which caused Yemil some amusement as they squeezed their bodies through the small space. Waiting for Rista to enter, Yemil telepathically asked Beauty to secure the entrance.

"Come on," she whispered. Making their way down the darkened passage, Yemil was relieved to see her friends hadn't gone too far down ahead.

"We were waiting to make sure you were all right," Lottie whispered. Noticing they weren't alone, Penny whispered, "Who are they? Where did they come from?"

"This is Vigo and Lema. They have offered to help us," said Yemil. Beauty remained silent while waiting to make sure they really did want to help. She hadn't sensed anything unpleasant about them, but she was aware Imelda could have created these folk to be her spies.

Lottie suddenly became anxious. What if they mentioned her brooch? Drawing the lapels closer together, she noticed the warm smile Beauty gave her. Meanwhile, anxious to get back to Letswick and Nain, Rista told them she was going to return to the front.

"Where did you get to?" Nain asked Rista.

"Yemil and I noticed the entrance hadn't closed, so we thought we would go and see why. We found two stable-hands who say they know a safe way out of here. They told us how badly they'd been treated and offered to help us."

"I hope they aren't spies of Imelda's. I suppose we will just have to wait and see," Letswick muttered.

Now everyone was back together, Letswick checked it was safe to continue. Aware of some cells being close by, he checked to see if anyone was in them before giving the signal for everyone to follow. They passed through a number of grim, dank passageways before coming upon more slippery steps which he knew led to more cells. There were scurrying rats to avoid, and it had taken the group longer than they thought to get this far. Lottie feared they must be lost after trekking through so many passages.

At last they found themselves in a passage which Letswick recognised as the one where he'd attempted his last rescue mission.

"Are there any folk in these cells?" he called softly. There was no response. He decided to give it one more try. "Can anyone hear me? It's Letswick," he said.

A voice suddenly entered his thoughts. "Hi Letswick, it's me, Kira." He recognised her voice immediately. "Hi Kira, so nice to hear your voice. How many prisoners are there?"

"There are many of us," another voice said. Not sure who it belonged to, he wondered if the Old Crone was up to her tricks. Then another voice entered his mind - Beauty.

"Hello. Can you tell us who you are?" Beauty asked.

"Hi, it's Mittoy." Suddenly hearing a sound outside his cell door, Mittoy quickly withdrew his mind from Beauty and Letswick. Turning to Kira he signed, "I wonder if they heard the same sounds we did?"

"It's possible, don't forget Beauty has the power to hear things many of us can't hear," signed Kira. Aware Letswick had been in telepathic conversation with someone, Rista clasped Nain's hand. Thinking something must have unnerved his friend, he whispered, "Are you OK, Rista?"

"I'm OK," she replied, trying to hide the way she was really feeling. Not convinced Rista was being honest, Nain assured her they would be all right so long as they stayed together. Slightly assured by this, Rista whispered, "I'm just being silly, its being back in here again."

Maintaining silence and keeping a look out for guards, and the odd rat or two, they were about to start off towards the cells when they heard a coarse voice shout, "Is the 'umans in 'ere, or is they in yer cell?"

"They's bin moved from 'ere. They's in 'is special cell," came the reply. This seemed to amuse the listening guard, as loud guffaws of laughter sounded round the dungeon.

Signing, Binro asked, "We'd best not use our minds or whisper. We don't want to alert anyone we are close by." Tapping Yemil on the arm, Vigo was about to ask what he had signed, but Yemil placed a finger on his mouth and shook her head. They stood waiting for the next instruction.

With the sound of the guards moving further away, Beauty flicked her tail to let Lottie know she needed to say something. Placing her ear as near to her brooch as possible, Beauty whispered, "Would you please let Letswick know we will release these prisoners before we continue." Lottie whispered, "What about the keys, won't they need them to open the doors?"

"I will see they open Lottie, we need to make sure it's safe and then everyone will have to move very quickly. We still have many more prisoners to save." Knowing Beauty would do what she said, Lottie made her way to Letswick and quickly passed on Beauty's message.

Cautiously they made their way along the passage until they finally reached the door. Listening for any sound which would indicate the enemy was approaching, Penny and Lottie jumped when the cell door gave a loud clunk.

Hearing the sound of coarse voices, followed be the sound of stomping feet, Letswick knew the enemy weren't too far away. Nervous and scared, Penny looked at Letswick and mouthed, "Can you hear them?" He nodded and motioned to them to move back away from the door.

Disgusted at the slime they could feel on the walls, they

knew the only way to keep safe was to press themselves as far into the walls as possible. With only a glimmer of light coming from the flaming torches, they waited anxiously to see if the guards would notice them.

"Why we gotta stay 'ere?" moaned one of the guards.

"Cos we gotta make sure them prisoners don't get away," replied his companion.

"We'd best make sure they're still safe, I don't want no punishment if they gets free," added another guard.

"Let's go an' make sure them useless guards still got 'em 'uman's safe," uttered the first guard.

"What about these? I'm sure I 'eard a noise come from 'ere," moaned another of the guards.

"Don't matter about these, it's those 'uman's we gotta make sure don't get away," one of the guards commented. The guards' voices drifted off in the distance.

Hearing this, Beauty thought it might be a good idea if Nain and Rista took Eram to search the remaining cells for other prisoners, leaving their other companions to help Letswick with these prisoners. Passing this thought onto Letswick via Lottie, he hesitated before agreeing. But he soon realised this would be the best way of discovering where all the other prisoners were on this floor. Giving Beauty a nod, he set off to fetch Eram, Nain and Rista.

Drawing Penny's attention, Beauty asked, "When Letswick returns with Eram, Nain and Rista we will need to split up. Eram and his group will need to go down that passage where the guards have gone. As soon as they do, I would like you to go and bring the others to help with these poor people."

"Won't that be dangerous? Going after the guards, I mean?" whispered Lottie.

"It's dangerous down here too, Lottie. Don't forget we've had lots of scares before and survived them," Penny whispered.

Seeing Letswick, Eram, Nain and Rista coming close, Penny went to meet them and pass on the plan Beauty had told her. Penny whispered, "We need your help. Beauty would like you three to search the rest of the cells around here. You'll have to be careful, because it's the way the guards went. We overheard them talking of special prisoners. We don't know who, but our friend is sure they will lead you to them." Remembering the last part of the message, she asked Nain, "Keep us in touch. Use telepathy carefully, as thoughts can be picked up." Turning to Letswick she said, "I'm just going to collect the rest of the people, Lottie is waiting for you by the cell door."

Not sure if she was more nervous of the rats or being caught by the guards, Penny made her way back to where the remainder of the group were. If it hadn't been for the scampering rats Penny felt sure she would have reached these people sooner. Relaying Beauty's request, she went on to tell them where Eram and friends were and what they were doing. Gathered together, Penny led them to join Letswick and Lottie.

Chapter Twenty

The rescue begins

Leaving Lottie with her mission and Letswick to his, Eram set off with Nain and Rista. Having gone some way through the passage, they began to hear faint coarse voices were heard in the distance. They slowed down, wanting to maintain a safe distance from the guards. Rista assured Eram they must be heading towards the place where Zanus kept his special prisoners.

Being taller than his companions, Eram had to avoid banging his head where parts of the dungeon ceilings were lower. Maintaining silence throughout and remaining alert, Rista had somehow found herself just a little in front of her companions. Turning the corner, she was shocked to see a group of guards sitting and supping ale. She tugged on Nain's and Eram's arms and whispered a low warning.

Aware they were close to their destination, Eram and Nain cautiously poked their heads round the corner. The sight of so many guards confirmed to them that they had gone in the right direction. Not sure what the next move should be, they crouched down and waited, hoping the guards would move away.

Just when they thought the guards would never move, one of them called out, "I'm gonna check those damn 'uman's is still alive, we don't want no trouble from 'is lordship when 'e returns." Eram watched to see which way the guard went. Thinking he would go straight to a certain cell, he gave them a moment until he felt it was safe for him to follow.

They could hear cruel taunts coming from the guards. Glancing at his two companions, Eram whispered, "This must be where some of the prisoners are being held."

"Who do you think might be here?" asked Nain.

"I don't know. Let's just see if we can free these prisoners," Eram whispered. They began edging their way closer to where the guards were standing, taking care not to knock any loose flakes off the wall.

Eram drew Nain and Rista close beside him. "I'm going to have to do something to make the guards move or we could be here for some time," he said. Nain grabbed hold of Eram's sleeve and shook his head. "Wait a while and let's see if they will go off. They'll soon get tired of taunting the prisoners," he whispered quietly.

They waited. As the shouting and cursing continued, a voice shouted, "I 'opes 'is special prisoners is gonna give 'im the right answers," which brought forth loud guffaws of laughter.

Then another of the guards shouted, "We'd best check they's still in there. P'raps we'd best check on them Outlanders too." The laughter suddenly stopped when one of the guards said, "They's not fer 'im, they's fer the Old Crone, she wants 'em fer 'erself. We'd best keep 'em safe too." Recoiling at what they'd heard, Eram, Nain and Rista just looked at one another, not saying a word.

Relieved to hear the sound of the guards' boots fading further down the passage, Eram decided he would take a look to make sure it was clear. Thankful he couldn't see any enemy, he turned to his two companions and beckoned for them to follow. Nervously they joined him, then all three crept further on into the passage. Faced with a line of cells and thinking the guards would return soon, Eram called out in a low voice, "Hello is anyone in these cells?"

Astonished to hear Eram's voice, the prisoners within the cells were unsure if this was a cruel trick. Sanso edged his way close to the door and listened. Following close behind, Bacjo drew his attention and signed, "I'll see who's there." Before he could agree or disagree, Bacjo flew up to the height of the bars.

"It wasn't a guard, but I couldn't see who it was," said Bacjo.

It had been a shock to see a face looking back at him through the bars. Just as they were absorbing what Bacjo had told them, voices were heard approaching. Nain only just managed to draw Rista and Eram out of sight to prevent them from being seen by the approaching guards.

"I can't 'elp finking there's somefing goin' on. I feels it in my bones," said one. Laughing at his partner, the other guard said, "Don't be daft. 'Ow can somefing be goin' on? The Old Crone 'as got this 'ere tower covered by some kind of mist. 'Sides, we'd soon 'ear anyfing odd cos Zanus left some of 'is spy birds 'ere. They can 'ear fer miles."

Discussing a variety of ways in which to distract the guards, Eram, Nain and Rista were relieved to hear a guard order everyone back to their posts. With much moaning and groaning, they stomped back. As soon as the last guard had gone, Eram seized the opportunity to make his way to the cell door. Not sure what to expect, he stood as tall as he could in the hope of being able to see through the iron bars. The cell was so dim that he wasn't able to see much, but what he did see shocked him.

Nain whispered, "How many are there?"

"Lots," Eram whispered and then added, "Can you ask our friend to release the locks?" Nain concentrated on raising Beauty. Responding to Nain telepathically, Beauty asked, "Do you need help?"

"Can you release the cell doors, please?" said Nain. They heard the lock clank open. Thinking this would be the right moment to open all the cell doors, Beauty turned her thoughts to releasing all the locks and bolts. Terrified the guards might have heard the sound of the locks, Rista cautiously entered the cell.

"I thought it would only be one cell," whispered Eram. At first they thought the shuffling sound was rats, but as their eyes adjusted to the darkness they realised it wasn't rats but prisoners.

With the dim light from the passage flame, Rista strained to see if there were any of her friends in there. Noticing a couple in the far corner she approached slowly and whispered who she was. There was no response.

Rista jumped as something touched her arm. It was Norda. He was staring at her in disbelief, thinking she must be a ghost.

Staring into the dimness, he shook his head, wondering if he was hallucinating.

"I didn't know you were being held in here," Rista whispered. Taking in their shabby appearance, she could only guess what these people had gone through.

"Will you help me to get these people out?" she asked. "I'm not sure how near the guards are."

"Is it really you, Rista, or am I having a dream?" asked Norda. But he knew that soft laugh could only belong to Rista. Recovering from the shock, Norda agreed to help and began moving from one group to another.

In a calm and quiet voice, Rista urged everyone to follow Norda and make their way from the cell. As they left the cell, Rista whispered, "Stay very quiet. Don't let the guards hear you. Oh, and stay close to the wall, it will make it harder for the guards to see you."

Slowly the cell began to empty of people. Hoping no one had been left behind, Rista went to check. Approaching the back of the cell she noticed there were several people leaning against the wall or lying on the rotting smelly straw. Moving closer, she could see these prisoners were in no state to walk on their own. Attracting the attention of Eram and Nain, she quickly informed them of the plight of the remaining people. Shocked by what he saw, Eram assured them they wouldn't be left behind.

One by one the weakened prisoners were helped out of the cell. With a few stumbling, Eram gathered these folk into his arms and on his back. Placing other weak prisoners with the stronger ones, they began making their way along the passage. Listening for guards, Nain quickly searched each cell to make sure no one would be left behind. Having accumulated a number of prisoners from other cells, they maintained a slow and steady pace away from their cells. Eram whispered, "Stay as close together as you can."

* * * *

Nain suddenly realised that there must be other cells they had missed, as their other friends and the Outlanders weren't among these people. He suggested they take the freed prisoners back to join Letswick and the others so they could go back to search for their other friends.

At times a distant coarse voice could be heard which alarmed them, but slowly and quietly they continued on behind Eram. With Nain and Rista remaining at the back and encouraging the weaker ones to keep moving, they turned in fearful silence into another passage.

Thinking he saw something, Eram halted them abruptly. He wanted to make sure it wasn't the enemy. Going down on his knees, he crawled along the cold stone floor, keeping close to the slimy wall. Fearing he could end up facing a guard, he suddenly noticed a pair of feet in front of him. Stopping where he was, he slowly looked up and breathed a sigh of relief.

Letswick, who had seen Eram crawling towards him, couldn't help grinning at the expression of relief on Eram's face. "Hello there Eram, what are you doing down there?" grinned Letswick.

"What a relief it's you," said Eram. "I couldn't make out what I saw. I have many people waiting for me to give the all clear signal."

Letswick looked at the group. "No sign of David and Jayne?" he asked.

"No, they weren't in the cells we emptied. There are many weak people here. Once we get them away from here, I'm going back to search for them and the Outlanders," Eram whispered.

Letswick was left wondering what the next course of action should be. He had felt certain David would be with Eram. Making up his mind to go with Eram, Letswick began jostling the people along. "Hurry along now," he whispered, helping several of the small weak folk.

Fortunately it didn't take long for the group to reach the place where Letswick had placed their friends. As they arrived, they exchanged greetings. Thinking they might be heard, Eram reminded them to remain quiet and take a rest. Tired and weary, the people eagerly accepted the opportunity. Yet the fear of being recaptured was never far from their minds.

Noticing Eram was preparing to leave, Letswick approached

him and whispered, "I'm coming with you, but I think we have to plan our way. We know they aren't in the passages we've covered, so I guess we had better try that one over there." He pointed to a passage which was a little way away from where they were.

Eram felt a shudder of danger run through him. Noticing how much darker this passage looked, he wasn't keen to enter it. Letswick sensed his thoughts. "We'll all be together," he whispered. "I suggest we take Lottie, then our friend can help when needed."

* * * *

Turning to face Beauty, Eram whispered what he and Letswick intended to do. Pondering for a moment, Lottie asked, "Does this mean you didn't find my parents?"

"I'm hoping that if we search that other passage, we will come across our other friends, and possibly our Outlander friends."

"You aren't going without us," said Lottie. She looked down at her brooch and saw Beauty smile. "After all, you may need assistance from a certain someone."

"It seems Lottie is getting certain powers of her own," said Letswick.

Sanso signed, "How come we've got those two stable-hands? They aren't going to give us away, I hope."

"They say they know a way out where we won't be seen," Letswick told them. "Don't mention our friend. They know nothing about that."

"We'll make sure they don't give us away," Sanso signed. Still not ready to trust them completely, and wanting to move on, Eram turned to Norda and asked, "Would you stay with these people? Even with their protective covering they will need to remain silent. They have had some pain-reducing treatment from our friend. Leave them to rest. We have a long way to go before this is over."

Beauty announced, "Covering in place." Then, asking Lottie to give Norda the phials, she added, "Please use them sparingly.

They will take the worst of their pain away."

Noticing the people fade from view, Norda and Sanso promised to take care of the folk and ensure everyone stayed quiet until they returned. Turning to Sanso, Norda said, "Come on, let's go and make sure everyone is settled."

Sanso ran to Letswick and signed, "Don't forget the Outlanders. They might not be in with our other friends. We know one of them is called Kolen."

"We won't forget them," whispered Letswick. Waiting for Sanso and Norda to re-join the group resting close by, Penny had moved to stand beside Lottie.

"Don't forget me," she whispered, taking hold of Lottie's hand. Lottie smiled back at her. "Where would I be without you, Penny?" she whispered.

Fearing the return of the guards, Nain halted Letswick and stated, "I'm coming too. I can help discover what other cells Zanus has his prisoners in." Giving him a smile, Letswick gave the signal which set his friends following him. Setting off to the dark and foreboding passage, he realised he wasn't the only one who was wondering how successful they would be.

They hadn't gone far into the passage when they heard running feet behind them and turned to see the two stable-hands approaching.

"Yer'll never find yer way wivout us," said Vigo.

"Come on then, but keep quiet," said Letswick. "You'd best keep just in front of us. Don't get any ideas of running off and leaving us to the guards."

"We won't, mister, we'll be wiv yer all the way," Lema whispered. Urging his friends to stay close, they continued through the mouth of the passage.

Letswick was beginning to have concerns about the state the prisoners would be in. As this thought churned over in his mind, he suddenly halted and listened. There it was again, stomping feet in the distance. Aware his friends had halted behind him, he signalled to them to seek shelter in the crevices of the walls. Clinging on to the slimy walls, they could only guess how close the guards were.

Fearing they were about to be discovered, Penny grabbed

Lottie's hand and squeezed it. "We'll be all right," she mouthed. Penny gave her a weak smile. "They're too close for comfort," signed Nain.

Letswick drew Lottie's attention and pointed to her brooch. Signing, he asked, "Is there anything we can do?" Concentrating on where the voices were coming from, it didn't take Beauty long to discover exactly where they were. She was horrified to see how close they were to danger. Determined to make sure her friends remained safe, she gave a flick of her tail. It wasn't long before an army of small, invisible creatures began to nip and torment the guards.

"What's that?" shouted a coarse voice.

"What d'yer mean what's that?" asked another. Hearing another moan, the guards swung round ready to attack each other. Thinking it was the trooper next to him, one of the troopers shouted, "Get off. If yer don't keep that sword away from me, I'll kill yer." Another shouted, "It ain't any of us, yer idiot. It's somefing coming from the air. I can't see nuffing, but I can feel the damn things biting me." They all began scratching and tearing at their hair and clothes trying to free themselves from whatever it was. Panicking, a coarse voice called out, "Yer don't fink it's the Old Crone, d'yer?"

"Don't never say 'er name. We don't want none of 'er 'orrible spells in 'ere," warned a nervous-sounding guard.

As the creatures increased their attack on the guards, a coarse voice shouted, "'Oo is it? 'Oo's doin' this?" Hearing the guard's screams, the group wondered what was happening. The guards had removed their swords and were swatting the air at random. Eram and his group stifled their laughter in fear of being heard. Relieved to see many of the guards had made their way further down the passage, the group wondered if the remaining guards would follow.

"What were they aiming at? I didn't see anything," said Penny. Trying not to laugh, Letswick assured her she and her friends were in no danger. "Just a little assistance from a certain friend," he explained.

Letswick urged everyone to move quietly through the passage. Vigo and Lema hurried quietly to join the others. On reaching a corner they heard voices. Letswick took a few steps to peer round and see who it was.

"Guards," he whispered. "They're sitting drinking at a table."

Hearing this, Beauty joined her mind to Lottie's and said, "We won't be able to use our telepathy for long, so please concentrate on what you can see in my mind. There are more guards we need to be rid of." Feeling Lottie's mind merge with her own, Beauty continued, "Good, now I know you have them in your mind hold on to them."

Lottie felt an involuntary shiver run through her as she saw the guards' filthy state. "They can't hurt you, Lottie," said Beauty. "Keep them where they are, I'm going to send them away. This will need to be done quickly, as we don't want our own minds to be entered."

Lottie suddenly noticed a peculiar shape hovering over the guards' heads. She watched as the shape began to take the form of a floating cloud. Slowly and menacingly, a ghostly human image emerged from it and descended to where the guards were. Absorbed in watching, Lottie realised the ghost-like apparition was not alone; more ghosts began descending to join it. They floated down in front of the cowering guards. The guards looked up, petrified, as the ghosts began circling round. Then, quick as a flash, they lined up to make a barrier between the guards and the rescuers.

The guards stood staring at the now perfectly formed people. As a guard attempted to move, the people joined up as one and barred the guard from moving. Just then a coarse voice roared, "They're ghosts! That's a bloke who died in the torture room the other day." The guards began yelling and screaming in horror. "Get away! Yer can't 'urt us." They had drawn their swords and tried to attack the ghosts, but their swords had no effect on these people.

How long this went on Lottie wasn't sure, but then she heard the gentle voice of Beauty asking the ghosts to remove the guards far away from the cells. On hearing her request, gusts of icy wind swirled round the guards. Losing their balance, they fell flat on the floor. Stumbling and falling over each other, they finally managed to get up off the floor and fled to the far end of the passage until they were out of sight.

In place of the people, the ghosts now reappeared. Making their way to Beauty, their leader said something to her which only she could hear, then bid farewell to her and her friends. Seeing the cloud forming above them, Beauty thanked them for their help and bid them farewell.

Letswick smiled at the puzzled looks on the faces of Vigo and Lema and went to check on Penny.

"You seem very quiet," he said quietly.

"I have so much to ask, but I think it should wait until later," she replied. "These Zanuthians really are the ugliest and cruellest people I have ever seen. How could anyone want to harm the people of Dofstram? They are such gentle folk." Seeing the pained expression on Penny's face, Letswick took her hand in his and quietly assured her all would be well, in time.

"We need to get away from here as soon as we can, then we can have many talks," he said. Giving his hand a squeeze, Penny knew that if she said anything more she would end up crying, and she knew this wasn't the time.

Letswick urged everyone to follow now that the area was free of guards. He was surprised to see that some of the cells here were empty. Eram called out, "Can anyone hear us?" At last he thought he heard a sound.

"I'm not sure what you heard, but I heard something like a very quiet 'yes'," Lottie whispered.

"Eram, call out again and ask the prisoner to keep making a noise so we can follow the sound," said Beauty. Eram called out again in a low voice, passing on what Beauty had requested. After a short pause, a voice called out, "How can you let us know if you're our friend?"

"A piece of my property could be here, and I've come to claim it," called out Letswick. No sooner had he finished speaking than a number of voices could be heard shouting for help.

"Lottie, move to the front, I'll lead you to the cell," said Beauty.

"Our friend knows the way," Lottie told them. She was quickly joined by Letswick and Penny as Beauty guided them through the passage. Seeing steps leading down to another level,

Beauty said, "Down here - the cells are round the corner."

With Eram and Letswick taking the lead they slowly made their way, making sure they didn't slip on the slime-covered steps. Peering round the corner, they saw many more cells, all heavily guarded. Letswick whispered, "I think we are going to need a little expert help again on getting rid of these guards." Leaving Eram to keep an eye on the guards, Letswick went back to speak to Beauty. Explaining the situation, Beauty assured him everything would be taken care of.

Imitating the voice of Imelda, Beauty ordered the guards to get ready for battle. To convince them the demand was real, she sent out an ear-splitting scream, just like one of Imelda's.

Then they heard a voice call out, "Who's out there?"

"I know that voice, Bemar, is that really you?" called out Letswick.

"It is, and we want out of here," Bemar called out. By this time the group had assembled closer together, so when they heard Bemar call out, Lottie was unable to contain herself any longer. She called out, "Are my mum and dad with you? David and Jayne?"

A loud gasp came from within. "Lottie, is that you? We heard you were being sought by Crocanthus."

Lema leaned across to Vigo and whispered, "Ain't those two the ones 'e moved?"

"Hush Lema, we don't want to go making mistakes," replied Vigo. "Let's see 'oo's in these 'ere cells."

As the lock of the first one clicked open, the prisoners edged away. After hearing the Old Crone, they weren't sure this wasn't another of her tricks.

The rescuers were busy trying to adjust their eyes to the dim light of the cell. Lottie however, was busy trying to see if her parents were inside. Beauty, sensing the panic coming from the prisoners, gently whispered, "Come forward friends, we are here to help you."

They were surprised to see several people huddled together at the rear of the cell. In the time it took Lema and Vigo to reach the people, Letswick and Eram had joined them. Quickly assuring the prisoners who they were and why they had come, in no time everyone was busy getting ready to go. Many prisoners needed assistance to get away. Turning to Eram, Letswick whispered, "These people are in no better state than those other prisoners."

Gathering the fittest together, Eram and Letswick asked the stronger to help their weaker friends. Gathering the weaker ones together, Eram and Letswick looked at each other, both wondering how many more there would be.

"I'll go ahead with these two stable-hands," said Eram. "We'll check the cells as we come to them. We'll keep an eye out for enemy guards."

"Good idea," replied Letswick, "We'll follow close behind." Calling Lema and Vigo to go with him, Nain explained what they were to do. "We need to check those other cells, and make sure it's safe for the others to follow." Taking a look at one another, Lema and Vigo went and stood by his side.

"Come on, let's get going. Don't forget to check carefully, we don't want to leave anyone behind," Nain told them. The three set off down the passage, checking cells as they went.

Lottie felt certain she would soon come face to face with her parents. Not knowing why, she suddenly felt nervous. As she reached the cell door, Lottie called out, "Mum, Dad, are you in here? I can't see you, where are you?"

Letswick waited to see if there would be any response. Not hearing anything, he was about to call again when he felt a tap his arm. He looked down to see Bema looking at him with tears in her eyes. Expecting the worst, Letswick changed to telepathy and quickly asked, "Are they alive?"

"Yes," Bemar whispered. "Before Zanus rode off, he had them moved to a different cell, along with some others. We have tried to reach David telepathically, but a barrier has been put round their cell. Do you think our friend can break through the barrier?"

Beauty interrupted gently, "You say they are in another place, Bemar?"

"Yes," Bemar replied. Hearing the response, Beauty stated, "I think Lottie and I try should try to get through to David. While we do that, would you continue caring for these folk? Eram will be taking these good people to join their friends."

"I'm coming with you," stated Penny, in a firm voice. "Lottie is my friend and I said I would help keep her safe."

"Come along, Lottie's friend," said Letswick, in an amused voice. "We wouldn't think of leaving you behind!"

"Will you see if Petra is with them? She was taken from the cell at the same time," said Bemar.

"Be assured, we will not return without all the prisoners," Letswick told her in as assured voice. Nain, Lema and Vigo were now coming through the passage with more prisoners. Letswick was busy churning over in his mind how Eram could get these people back with Sanso and Norda safely.

"Where did all these people come from?" asked Penny. A voice replied, "We've been prisoners for so long. We never thought we'd be freed."

Eram warned all the prisoners to be quiet, for fear of alerting the guards. Turning to the gathered group of people, Letswick told them what he had considered.

"Some of these people are not so strong, so I suggest you all join the other people we have secured," he said. "A small group of us will go in search of any other prisoners. We will have to be very quick, as it won't be long before the guards will realise what's going on. You will need to take great care, guards could be anywhere. Remember, silence!"

While they had been organising themselves, Beauty suggested to Letswick that he should include Lema and Vigo. "One of them might just know where these other cells are," she said.

Noticing Bemar was standing beside Eram, Beauty asked, "Do you have any idea where our friends might have been taken?" Bemar was able to tell Beauty she knew the direction, but not the cell. Pointing to a different passage, equally dark and foreboding, Beauty recognised this as one they had not yet tried. It seemed more foreboding than the others. She thanked Bemar, then went on to say, "Nain and Eram will lead you back to where the other people have been secured."

Letting Vigo and Lema know they would be going with Letswick's party, Eram made his way to the front ready to lead them on, leaving Nain and Bemar to bring up the rear. Giving his group a light cloak of invisibility, Beauty suggested Eram should move quickly to join the other people. Looking round to see who had mentioned his name earlier, Vigo looked at Letswick and asked, "'Oo said my name? I fought we was gonna go with these 'ere people." Giving Vigo an amused look, Letswick assured him he would soon know.

Waiting until Eram's group were out of sight, Letswick and Vigo set off in the opposite direction, with Lema close on their heels. Facing the dark passage, and nervous of not knowing what to expect, Penny took hold of Lottie's hand and gave it a squeeze. Lottie, having similar feelings herself, looked gravely at Penny.

With a glimmer of light from the flaming torches, the shadows that reflected back off the walls scared them at times, even though they knew it was only their own shadows. Penny continued to scan the floor for rats. She had heard their squeaking and scratching, but she felt she could cope providing they didn't come into view.

Treading carefully and trying not to make a noise, they made their way down the passage. Thinking she saw something, Penny pulled on Letswick's arm and whispered, "Did you see that?" Letswick could see nothing.

"It was like a black shadow," said Penny. "Perhaps it was just my imagination."

"OK, Lottie," said Beauty, "This is the moment when you are going to have to be very strong. We are going to join minds with Letswick and try to break through the barrier Bemar told us surrounded the other prisoners. If one of them has the compass, they might just think to open it."

Lottie drew in a quick breath. "I'm ready when you are," she said.

"Ready fer what?" asked Vigo.

"What's happening?" whispered Penny.

"That's what I wanna know," interrupted Vigo.

"An' me," added Lema.

Leaving Lottie and Beauty to join minds, Letswick explained briefly that they were going to try and find out where the remaining prisoners were. Assuring Vigo and Lema they were in no danger, Penny placed a finger to her lips. Vigo whispered, "'E's a Jasper, one of those people 'oo can talk wiv 'is mind."

Joining minds, Beauty sensed the struggle Lottie was going through. To calm her fears, Beauty telepathically said, "It will be all right, Lottie, just stay calm. Whatever you do please don't call out, not even if you recognise a voice, or you will give us away."

Letswick added, "As soon as we are away from here we will all be able to talk more freely. Are we ready? Then let us concentrate our thoughts to the telepaths." Nervous yet excited, Lottie struggled to control her feelings, remembering what Beauty had said about not shouting.

With all minds together and concentrating their thoughts towards any telepath, the gentle of voice of Beauty called out. "If there are any telepaths here please respond." Remaining as one mind, they hoped to hear some response. Recalling the depth of the mist surrounding the tower, Beauty wondered if Imelda had created a similar mist around these other prisoners. Calling out one more time and getting no response, Beauty summoned her silver spear to come and break through the mist. With the barrier resisting the attack, Beauty threw orange powder towards the mist. At first it appeared nothing would happen, but then the barrier seemed to dissolve. The spear then began to make the break larger. Leaving Beauty with this task, Letswick removed his thoughts and whispered to Penny, "Any sign or sound of guards?"

"No," Penny replied. "But I did see that black shadow again. It wasn't my imagination. Vigo and Lema saw it too." The two lads were bursting to say something.

"I saw it. 'Orrible it was. It slid across that wall," said Lema, pointing. It didn't look real, it was an 'orrible creature. We seen somefing like this afore."

"Where, Lema? Where have you seen this before?" asked Letswick.

"Just afore the Old Crone appeared. Remember Vigo, the day that other 'uman was captured?" Recalling that awful moment, Vigo nodded in agreement.

"When are we gonna get goin'?" asked Vigo. Only half

hearing what Vigo had said, Letswick was eager to let Beauty know what Lema and Vigo had told him. Realising this wasn't the right moment; he would wait to see if Beauty had been successful in raising the attention of a telepath. Noticing Vigo staring at him, Letswick quickly assured him it wouldn't be long before they would be on their way.

Reaching the minds of Lottie and Beauty, Letswick was surprised to see that the barrier was slowly dissolving into thin air. Fascinated by what was taking place, Lottie felt she was becoming hypnotised, until they heard a blood-curdling scream fill the air. "'Oo 'as touched my barrier? You will die in agony fer this!"

Recognising instantly who the voice belonged to, Beauty told Letswick and Lottie to remain calm while she tried to send out a message. Ignoring Imelda's warnings, Beauty concentrated her mind on contacting a telepath.

"I know yer still 'ere!" the shrill voice called out. "Could it be me stone 'as come to rescue 'er friends?" Terrified of what might happen, Lottie felt certain this person must be talking about her parents. Wondering if there was anything she could do or say, she heard Letswick telepathically say, "Careful Lottie, we don't want our thoughts picked up."

"Give yerself to me and yer friends will be freed," called Imelda "I only 'as to see yer glow an' I'll know where yer are." Letswick suddenly feared for his friend's safety. He surrounded Beauty's mind with more energy from his own. He knew this was the only thing he could do.

Chapter Twenty One

Reunion

Anxious that Beauty might be harmed, Lottie knew from the sudden burst of thought energy that Letswick had done something. Although Beauty knew Imelda could cause her friends' minds harm, it couldn't stop her doing what she had to do. With the extra energy from Letswick, Beauty released a low sound which she knew only David would hear, followed by a message: "If you have the compass, leave it open." Not hearing a response but feeling Imelda's power had become stronger, Beauty quickly released their minds.

Still aware of the presence of Imelda, Letswick whispered, "That was really something. But be aware, I feel a stronger presence around us. You know who I mean."

"She must have been alerted to someone being in the dungeons," said Beauty. "Once her barrier had been broken, she would know it had to be a power strong enough to break through. Now we need to discover if she is in the tower. I guess not, or she would have sent one of her creatures to search for me."

"She might be here," said Letswick. "Penny told me she saw a black shadow earlier. Then when you were in telepathic mode, she said she'd seen it again. But this time, these two lads here saw it as well."

"Just afore the Old Crone appeared, that was when that other 'uman was caught," said Lema.

"'Oo was that other person speaking? I ain't seen no one else wiv us," asked Vigo. Hearing a gentle laugh, he spun round and asked Lottie, "Is yer laughin' at me? I know someone is." Quickly apologising, Beauty assured him he wasn't being laughed at. Watching the two lads spinning round searching for her voice, Lottie whispered to Beauty, "Should we tell them?"

"In a little while Lottie. I need to try and discover if that certain someone is here," Beauty whispered. "She is desperate to get her hands on me, and by taunting me she hopes I might reveal myself. She won't know I sent a message which only David would understand."

"What message?" asked Lottie.

"I asked him to leave the compass open. Keep watch for a beam of light." Suddenly Vigo uttered, "Like that one?" Staring at Vigo, they noticed he was pointing to the ceiling.

"That's like the beam I saw when we were on our way here," Penny whispered.

"That's the compass beam," Letswick replied. Looking across at Lottie, he caught the flick of Beauty's tail. Wondering if something was wrong, he made his way closer to her. "I think we should let these lads know it's me they can hear. They are terrified it's something to do with... her."

By this time, the two stable-hands were completely lost as to what was going on. Recounting the events that have taken place, Vigo uttered, "First I 'ears voices, then 'orrible silence, then an eerie cackle. I know 'oo that was. Then a light shone over our 'eads."

"It's nothing to worry about," said Penny. "Our friends will make sure no one can hurt you while you're with us." Giving them a warm smile, she was pleased to see their concerned expressions leave their faces.

Taking this moment to reveal herself, Beauty whispered, "Lema, Vigo, would you come and stand by Lottie?"

"Oo said that?" whispered Vigo and Lema, almost with one voice. Grabbing hold of Vigo's arm, Lema whispered nervously, "Can yer see 'oo said that?" Amused at their thoughts, Beauty tried once more. "Would you please came and stand by Lottie? Then I can introduce myself to you."

"Cor blimey, the voice wants to meet us," whispered Lema. Wanting to discover who it was, Vigo took hold of his hand and pulled him close to Lottie. He wondered if it was she who possessed the magic. As he stood staring at Lottie, Beauty surprised the two lads by asking, "Take a look at the brooch on Lottie's jacket." Staring at each other, fearing it was one of the old Crone's tricks, Vigo whispered, "'Oo are yer?"

"Don't be afraid, no harm will come from any of us here," said Beauty.

"Cor, did yer see that, its mouf moved," whispered Vigo. They found themselves staring stared straight into Beauty's face.

"Does yer 'ave a name?" asked Lema. "My pal 'ere give me my name. 'E could give you a name too." Listening to the conversation between Beauty and the lads, Letswick said he would explain.

"You asked about strong magic," he said. "This brooch is a good friend of ours. It has certain powers which no one can explain. One thing to remember, no harm will come to you so long as the brooch remains safe."

Staring wide-eyed at Letswick, Vigo asked, "What do yer call it?"

"That's easy. We refer to the brooch as our friend," Penny replied. Gazing back at the brooch, Lema whispered, "'Ow can yer speak?"

"Like you, Lema, with my mouth," said Beauty. She was amused to see Lema jump back.

Sensing something was wrong, but not sure what, Letswick saw a look of alarm cross Beauty's face. Then he felt his arm being tugged. Seeing that it was Penny, he was surprised to see the look of fear on her face. Staring at the far wall, he suddenly saw what had caused her fear, a darkened shadow.

"What's that?" whispered Lema.

"Stay still and quiet," whispered Beauty. "I'll find out what's going on."

While the shadow seemed intent on clinging to the wall, to the surprise of the watching people a different shape suddenly appeared - not a black shadow, but a spear of light. Letswick put a finger to his lips and mouthed, "Our friend." Watching the spear of light enter the dark shadow, they were surprised to hear an eerie voice say. "So, me lovely, where yer been 'iding? I knew yer'd come back to me."

Letswick knew the shadow was trouble, and his alarm increased when he heard Beauty say, "I warned you before, Imelda. Any harm comes to my friends and you will answer to me."

Letting out a screeching cackle, the black shadow moved across the wall. What they heard next made them more fearful.

"Don't ferget stone, I got some of yer power, so yer know I will be able to find yer," Imelda warned in a venomous tone. Lottie saw that the black shape was beginning to change. Increasingly concern for her brooch, she tapped Letswick's arm and alerted him to what she was looking at. Taking in what Lottie was showing him, Letswick struggled to make out what the shape was. He asked everyone to remain calm and still. As he said this, he noticed the spear of light release itself from the shadow.

The next moment he found himself facing a pack of snarling trofalogues. Quickly drawing his sword, he noticed his friends were doing likewise. He was glad Queen Matilda had given the ladies weapons. The two stable lads had their own weapons ready. Looking across at her friend, Penny whispered, "I didn't think we'd have to use these."

With swords in hand, Penny and Lottie stood close to Letswick, while Vigo and Lema stood shoulder to shoulder, armed and ready. All eyes were on the creatures. The drool which dribbled from their mouths made Lottie feel sick.

Suddenly she realised her brooch had gone. Panicking, she went down on her knees and began searching the grimy floor. With only a dim light coming from the distant flame, all thoughts of any weird creatures had left her.

"What are you doing, Lottie?" asked Penny.

"My brooch has gone! I can't find it anywhere down here," Lottie told her, tearfully.

"Where are you? Please tell me how to find you!" pleaded Lottie, still sifting through the dank straw. Letswick knelt beside her and whispered, "Our friend will return. There is a problem that can only be dealt with by our friend. Come and stand beside me and Penny, and before you know it your brooch will be back."

Desperately hoping this was true, Lottie gave one more

brush over the floor, then stood up, wiping the tears from her face. Her attention was back on the trofalogues. They were snarling and their eyes were glaring. She braced herself to fight off the horrible creatures.

Letswick whispered, "Right friends, this is the moment." Then everything seemed to happen at once. As the nearest creature prepared to lunge out at them, a silver sword flew through the air and plunged deep into the trofalogue's side. Accepting this as the signal, Letswick led the charge towards the creatures. The stench the creatures gave off made the fighters feel sick. While the silver spear continued to claim a few more of the trofalogues, they could hear the screeching voice of Imelda, warning them of dire consequences for hurting her creatures.

Penny and Lottie wielded their swords as if they had done this before, much to the surprise of Letswick. Busy with their own creatures, Vigo and Lema fought for some time before they managed to kill any. Checking over their cuts and scratches, Vigo drove the blade into one trofalogue's stomach with a vengeance. Satisfied, he turned to Lema and said, "We soon got rid of 'em didn't we?" A number of trofalogues were now lying dead on the floor, and an eerie silence fell over the passage.

It wasn't long before a loud and piercing scream filled the air. "Yer'll all suffer fer this! Kill me pets would yer? Glowin' stone, let's see yer shine! Let me see where yer are. Yer can't hide from me forever!"

Looking round to see where the spear had gone, Lottie was surprised but relieved when she saw her brooch safely back on her lapel. Beauty whispered, "Take care Lottie, she's not finished with us yet."

Beauty now tried to discover where Imelda was hiding. Not sensing the Old Crone, she thought about the arrival of the trofalogues, which made her wonder why these creatures would be accompanied by Imelda. Or had she sent them by portraying an image of herself?

"I know you are not here, Imelda," said Beauty. "I can see that's only an image on the wall, that's why you appear as a shadow."

Staring into the darkened part of the passage from which the creatures had emerged, Lema drew their attention to a black shadow crawling over the wall. It slithered down the wall and disappeared into the floor.

"It's all right, Lema, it's gone now," Vigo whispered to his shivering friend.

"So it was her? Is she really not here?" said Letswick.

"Not at the moment, but now she knows I'm here we need to move quickly and get these people out of here," Beauty whispered. Putting her lips to her brooch, Lottie whispered, "I don't know how you did that spear thing, but it was great. It sounds as if she still thinks you're just a stone." Seeing the warm smile on Beauty's face, Lottie placed a finger on Beauty's back and gave her a gentle stroke.

Noticing the pale faces and wide eyes looking in his direction, Letswick's impatience to move on was increased. "Keep quiet, we don't want the guards to know we are here," he urged them. Quietly moving to the front, he led the group cautiously along the passage. Many of the cells were empty, and he wondered if he was leading the group down the wrong passage. Deciding it would be better to continue to the end, he sensed an element of unease coming from within the group.

Then, from somewhere further along, a man's voice called out, "Is someone there? Who is it?" Jumping back in shock, Beauty calmly told Lottie to remain quiet. She added, "We need to make sure it's not the Old Crone playing with our minds." Lottie froze. Could that have been her father?

Inside the cell, David was having concerns of his own and hoped this wasn't some trick of Imelda's. Turning to telepathy, he cautiously asked, "Who created you to be what you are today?"

"Well done. That's a good question. I was created by a friend who rescued me from a boulder a long time ago. Without this friend I wouldn't be here today," Beauty answered.

"It's good to hear your voice," replied David. "I knew it was you asking for the compass to be left open. Now the guards have gone, I can open it and let the beam lead you to our cell."

He opened the compass, and it wasn't long before a long

beam of light lit up the ceiling and the passage. Observing where it was coming from, Beauty telepathically told David, "Thank you for the beam, I know where you are now so please close the compass again. We don't want to alert the guards to our presence."

Thinking this was the longest moment of her life, Lottie wondered how much longer she would have to wait to be reunited with her parents. Beauty, having picked up on her thoughts, whispered, "Not long now, Lottie."

Back in the cell, David knew their escape was only a short time away. Then he heard another voice enter his thoughts – Letswick.

"It's a relief to hear your voice," said David.

"Me too," said Letswick. "I wondered what had happened to you, when we freed the other prisoners. Bacjo told us you and some others had been moved to another cell. How many are with you?"

Anxious to let her father know she was there, Lottie couldn't wait any longer. Without waiting to hear a response to Letswick's question, she called out nervously, "Are David and Jayne Montmerencie in there?" Trying to stem the tears that were threatening to fall, she called again, "Please say they are." Then she heard a familiar voice call out, "Lottie, is that you? Oh Lottie, I can't believe you are here. How is that possible? We thought we'd never see you again."

"Mum, I can't believe I'm really talking to you. There is so much to say," Lottie said, trying to control her sobbing. She gathered together then asked, "Are you and Dad in the same cell?" With tears now freely rolling down her face, she had for once forgotten the guards.

Meanwhile excitement was mounting inside the cell. David was holding onto Jayne's arm. "I can't believe Lottie is here!" he gasped. They were delighted that they had spoken to their daughter but remembered where they were, and knew what could happen if the guards caught their daughter and her friends.

"No more talking now," Beauty told David, "We need to get you all out of here. Oh, just to let you know, Lottie has the same ability as you. Like father like daughter."

"So Lottie can communicate telepathically," said David to his wife. "I guess this is the result of a certain someone going to our land."

"I wonder how they came together?" replied Jayne.

David turned to his fellow prisoners and told them it wouldn't be long before they would be free. But he urged them to quell their excitement, reminding them not to alert the guards. The prisoners stood wide-eyed and shivering with apprehension. Was this really happening?

Giving David a smile, Petra said, "We are ready to go. I can't believe we are going to get out of this horrible place."

"We must leave as soon as the door is opened," said David.

Lottie had become anxious that the guards would return before they freed the prisoners. Sensing her thoughts, Beauty told her, "We must now unlock the cell doors and free the prisoners."

Standing still and silent, they waited to hear the door unlock. David pulled the door open. For a second the rescuers and prisoners stood looking at each other, not sure they could believe their eyes.

Jayne stared in disbelief at the woman who stood before her. This was a grown woman, not the child she had left behind years before. Gathering herself together she shuffled over and took Lottie into her arms. "Lottie, my dearest Lottie, I thought I would never see you again." With tears streaming down both their faces, David wasted no time in putting his painful arms round the two women. Just for a moment they all seemed lost for words.

Feeling herself being squashed, Beauty whispered, "Please don't squeeze me any harder or I might drop off." David stepped back and was somewhat surprised to see the brooch he'd created pinned to Lottie's jacket. Just for a moment he wondered how he'd not seen it sooner. Seeing the wink come from the brooch, he knew Beauty must have protected herself with an invisible cover. Unable to take her eyes off Lottie, Jayne felt a tug on her arm. She saw that David was pointing at the brooch on Lottie's jacket.

"I don't know what to say," said David, staring warmly at

his daughter. "You were just a child when we left, and now look at you, a fully grown woman. Come and let us have another hug before we move." Lottie flung her arms round him.

"I thought I would never see you again. I've missed you so much. There's been so much happening I don't know where to start," Lottie said, through sobs.

Observing the reunion, Vigo whispered to Lema, "I ain't got no family. Or if I 'ave I don't know 'em."

"Nor me," said Lema. "But we could be family, just you an' me." Smiling a weak smile, Vigo whispered, "I'd like that."

Having heard what the lads said, Beauty whispered, "You have many good friends here." The lads turned their attention to the brooch. Vigo whispered, "Does this mean we 'ave more friends?"

"It does," said Letswick. "And friends look out for each other and give help when it's needed."

"We can do that, mister. We does that already, Vigo and me," Lema whispered.

"I think we'd best see about moving on," said Letswick, smiling.

Eager to introduce Penny to her parents, Lottie drew her close. Shaking Penny's hand, Jayne felt for a moment she'd seen this face before. Realising this couldn't be possible; she turned her attention back to Lottie. Lottie was explaining how good a friend Penny was, and saying she didn't know what she would have done without her.

"I feel I have seen you before," said Jayne. "I know that's impossible though, I've been held here for so many years."

"I wonder, are you in some way related to Bertram and Frances Barker?" asked David.

"They are my parents," Penny replied, with pride sounding in her voice.

Lottie was shocked to see the terrible state her mother and father were in. Many cuts and bruises were visible on their grimy faces and arms. Their clothes had been torn to shreds and they were barefoot. Feeling her eyes well up, Lottie turned to look at the other prisoners and saw that they were no better. She wondered if these people would be strong enough to escape.

Letswick interrupted with a cough. "We must move on, you never know when a guard might appear," he said.

"Do you realise that some of these people won't be able to make it on their own?" Letswick whispered to Vigo.

"We can't leave anyone behind, the guards will whip 'em to death," replied Vigo. "We'll 'ave to 'elp them get away. Isn't that what friends do?"

Seeing Vigo in a new light, Letswick warmly assured him he was correct. With the flame in the passage being the only source of light, it was very difficult to see where all the prisoners were. The more able were waiting by the cell door. Remembering how the weaker prisoners had stayed at the back of the cell, Lottie and Penny carefully made their way there. Owing to the darkness, it was very difficult to see how many prisoners were there.

Turning to Penny, Lottie uttered, "I dread to think what awful treatment these people have had."

"No wonder they were moved from the other cells," whispered Penny, trying to prevent stray tears from falling and concentrating on how she could help these people. Beauty, seeing the plight of the prisoners, knew that without help they wouldn't survive the rest of the journey.

Beauty asked if there was any water close by. Lottie looked round and saw a pail of dirty water in the corner. Going to fetch it, Lottie asked, "Why do you want this filthy water?" Without responding, Beauty asked her to place it close to the prisoners. "This will take a moment, Lottie. Place my tail into the water, please." Doing as Beauty asked, Lottie waited to see what would happen.

Drawing on her power, Beauty slowly cleaned the water. Satisfied it was clean enough she released a liquid from her tail, turning the water blue. Then Beauty asked Lottie to scoop up the clear blue water and give it to the prisoners. Lottie did so.

Penny returned from leading a group of able prisoners out of the cell to see Lottie scooping up the clear blue water and giving it to the weaker prisoners.

"Can I help?" she asked. Without looking at Penny, Lottie said, "Not with this, but we will need help with these people.

This liquid was made for them to drink. I suppose it's a kind of tonic." Beauty smiled to herself at Lottie's explanation.

Penny, thinking she would let Letswick know what was happening, made her way to where she had left him. Tapping on his arm, Penny said, "Lottie needs help with some very weak prisoners. I know we ought to get going, but we can't leave these people behind." Agreeing with Penny, Letswick left David to gather everyone together and to wait by the door. Going to the back of the cell, he saw Lottie handing out the last of the liquid. "So this is where you all are. Are you feeling a little better now?"

There were murmured responses from some of them that they were. Letswick told them they had to leave, but they would be assisted. Turning to Lottie, he gave Beauty a wink and said "Well done, these people will be able to make it, with help." Suddenly there were a number of people offering to help. Some of the prisoners limped across to the door. Some of the weaker ones stumbled, but the relief of getting free gave them the strength to continue.

Noticing Lottie standing quietly beside her, Penny whispered, "Are you all right? It must have been a bit of a shock to see your parents after so long." Observing her friend's tear-streaked face, she placed a comforting arm round Lottie's shoulders. Beauty, aware it would be a long and hazardous journey out of the tower, kept her thoughts to herself, hoping Imelda wouldn't make a sudden appearance.

"I suggest we get on with helping these people out," said Penny. "We don't want to get caught by the guards, or we'll be taken prisoner ourselves. Let's hope this is soon over." Not responding for fear of crying, Lottie gave Penny's arm a gentle squeeze. Remaining close to each other, they made their way to join the others.

"I think we should be the last to leave," said Beauty. "Letswick will guide us." Murmuring their agreement, they settled in behind the group, which was by now were slowly making its way through the passage. As they shuffled along, Penny wondered what tortures these people must have suffered. As he led them along the dimly-lit passage, Letswick felt Beauty's presence.

"Do you sense danger?" he whispered. In an equally quiet voice, Beauty assured him he was safe to continue. Then to Lottie she said, "Please move closer to Letswick." Adjusting the person she was carrying to a more comfortable position, Lottie took hold of Penny's arm. Wondering if something was wrong, Penny realised Lottie wanted her to go with her towards the front of the group.

"I think it might be better if I stay at the back, Lottie. I might be able to help some of these people," Penny whispered. Disappointed, Lottie whispered, "If you're sure. If any help is needed I'll return." Once again Lottie realised how lucky she was to have such a good friend. Smiling at Penny she added, "Please take care of yourself as well as the people. It's difficult to see much in this light."

Content to leave Letswick to lead, David noticed Lottie had moved closer to him and wondered if was at the request of Beauty. Feeling Lottie squeeze his arm, he heard her whisper, "I'm going to join Letswick." Smiling down at his daughter, he said, "Take care." Noticing Penny was remaining behind with him, he checked to make sure she was OK. "Are you all right, Penny?" he whispered. "If you need a rest I'll take over."

"I'm all right, thank you. I just thought I could be of more use at the back. Lottie will be with Letswick," Penny told him. "We'll make it, Penny. Our friend will keep us safe." Never having been a person who suffered much with nerves, Penny wondered why she felt nervous now.

In single file they continued along many dark and foreboding passages. Fearing the guards must by now have realised that their prisoners had escaped, they were all desperate to get as far away as possible. Deciding they should take a rest, Letswick noticed Beauty give a flick of her tail, and guessed she was agreeing with him. He gave the signal to halt.

David made his way to Lottie and broke the silence by whispering, "How did you two come together? I take it you've been with Lottie for some time, my friend. I have to say it's so good to see you again. I don't suppose the enemy are aware of your new shape."

"Not yet, but I think this is a conversation for later. Everything can be explained then," Beauty said. David returned, and Letswick gave the signal for everyone to continue.

Lottie was still coming to terms with actually being back with her parents. To check it wasn't a dream, from time to time she glanced back to make sure they were really there.

At last Vigo and Lema beckoned them to go down a flight of steps, previously unseen by his new friends. Vigo whispered, "Its safe fer now. Come this way." Walking a little further on, he stopped and whispered, "Careful, guards could still be 'ere. This is where them Outlanders 'ave been put." Quietly and cautiously they continued to follow Vigo and Lema, some of them wondering if they were being led into a trap. Letswick edged this way closer to the lads.

"Are you sure this is where the other prisoners were brought?" he whispered. "I can't hear anything." Having thought the same himself, Vigo wondered if they'd been moved somewhere else. But just then a strange sound came from further along the passage. Halting, they looked at each other wondering what it was.

"There's an Outlander here called Kolen," David whispered. "I have spoken to him many times. He can only use telepathy over a short distance, but as he knows my voice perhaps I should try and reach him."

"Go ahead," said Letswick.

"Kolen, are you there?" asked David telepathically. Almost immediately a reply came back, "We are all here. You sound a lot closer in my thoughts than you did before."

"Please get everyone together and stand away from the door. We are here to take you all with us," said David. Hearing the sounds of surprise and relief coming from the other side of the door, Letswick telepathically asked Kolen to keep everyone quiet.

"I think this is something for me to do," said a gentle voice. They heard the cell lock clunk open. Pulling the door inwards, many Outlanders began leaving the cell. Shocked to see so many, David sought out Kolen. Shaking hands and clasping each other to their chests, David whispered, "At last, my friend.

All the other prisoners have been freed. Are all your friends in here with you or were others taken somewhere else?"

"This is all the Outlanders," replied Kolen. "We were captured by those dreadful goons when our villages were attacked and burnt. We were taken for Imelda's purposes. You know what that means."

"Are there many weak people here, Kolen?" asked Letswick. Assured they were all well enough to get away, Letswick called Vigo and Lema to lead on and take the quickest way to where their other friends were waiting. Just as they were about to leave a voice called out, "Some of our friends were taken to the torture room. I haven't seen them return."

Shocked to hear this, Letswick turned to Vigo and asked, "Is there some way we can get to that room? "We can't leave anyone behind."

For once in his life, Vigo felt very important. He told Letswick, "I'll 'ave to go the long way. It's the safest. The short way means goin' past them guards."

Letswick, knowing he was putting his trust in these stable lads said, "Right lads let's get going. Penny, might I suggest you stay with Jayne at the rear, and Lottie perhaps you and our friend will stay close behind us. David and I will go on ahead with Lema and Vigo. No telepathy, only very low whispers or signing." Letswick touched Vigo and Lema on the shoulder and indicated they should walk on.

Following close behind, the group remained silent as mice. The only sound to be heard was the mouldy straw crunching under their feet, and rats squeaking as they scurried away. Not recognising where the lads were leading them, Letswick whispered, "Are you sure this is the right way?"

"I said it was gonna be the long way," said Vigo. "We ain't seen no guards, 'ave we?" He suddenly felt a tug on his arm. "We are near to 'em now" whispered Lema. "Jus' 'ave to be extra quiet."

Hearing this, Letswick signed to those near him telling them what he'd been told. Certain these folk would be in a sorry state, David eased his way forward and offered to search the cell. Letswick asked Jayne to make sure everyone remained quiet. Lottie whispered, "Is there anything we can do?"

"Not at the moment, we will need to see how badly they have been treated," Beauty whispered.

Vigo had seen many prisoners killed during torture but didn't want to tell his newly-acquired friends that. Beauty, having picked up his thoughts, silently whispered, "Thank you, Vigo." The voice was so quiet Vigo wasn't sure he'd heard it, but seeing Penny smile at him he guessed she must have heard it too.

Meanwhile, David and Letswick were creeping towards the door of the torture room. Wondering why there weren't any guards, they took the opportunity to open the door and quickly close it. With only a glimmer of light from the flame outside, they waited until their eyes had adjusted before moving any further. In a low whisper, Letswick called out, "This is Letswick from Castle Urbone, who is in here?"

A faint rustle of straw caught their attention. David and Letswick moved slowly to where it came from. As they approached the area, they were shocked to see several people lying on the floor. They were clearly already dead.

"There are four in here, and one strung up on the wall," said a voice. "He's had a whipping, and we don't know if he's still alive."

"You see if you can get those people out," said David to Letswick. "I'll go over to the other one. Even if he is alive, he won't be able to get out on his own."

Letswick crawled towards the others and whispered, "Can any of you walk?"

"Just about. We were left for dead after the guards had finished torturing us," replied the original speaker. Letswick suggested they crawl to the door.

David, meanwhile, was making his way to the prisoner chained to the wall. He knew from experience that the guards had left him there to die.

"We have come to take you away from here," he said. "Can you try and brace yourself for when I release the handcuffs?" There came only a faint murmur. He started trying to loosen off the handcuffs as gently as he could. As he gave the chain a final tug, cuffs and chain fell to the floor, followed closely by the man. David bent down to reassure the man he would be all right. Realising he couldn't stand, David, although still weakened himself from his torture, started to drag the person along the floor. The man soon lost consciousness. Relieved to be free, the other prisoners stood, unsteadily, trying to show they could walk despite the pain.

David meanwhile, was determined he wasn't going to let this man die. Whispering a few words close to the man's ear, he said, "Hold on my friend, we will get you out of here. Please believe me." Having somehow, between him and Letswick, placed the man on David's back, they urged the prisoners to try and walk a little faster.

Fearing he'd heard stomping feet, Letswick didn't want to alarm these people any more than they already were. Keeping a steady pace and helping any who needed help, it wasn't long before they were reunited with the others.

Kolen was quietly scanning the new arrivals. When he saw the man on David's back he let out a groan. "What have they done to you, Relek my friend?" he said, "You are safe now, you must rest".

Asking Lottie to make her way to where Relek lay, Beauty asked, "Please release me and place me on this man's forehead." Once there, Beauty started to hum in a quiet tone, while gently waving her tail. Then she asked Lottie to place her back on the lapel.

"He will sleep for some time, so we will have to take turns in carrying him," said David

"I will carry him first," stated Kolen, helping to lift Relek off the floor. Now everyone was ready, the weaker being supported by the stronger, Lema and Vigo prepared to lead them back to where Eram was waiting with the other people.

As they turned into yet another passage, Norda came forward.

"Hi, my name is Norda," he said. "I think you must be Lottie?" Taking in the smile and nod from Lottie, he continued, "We weren't so many until the Outlanders were captured. They are here because of Imelda." It soon became apparent to all the people why Imelda had taken the Outlanders prisoner.

Realising David and Jayne were standing quietly at the rear of the new group, Petra and Sanso made their way to join them. Clasping hold of their hands, Petra whispered, "We were so worried when they came and took you all out of the cell."

"Yes, we thought they'd come to take you for more punishment," signed Sanso.

Kolen and his friends began explaining what had happened at their villages and why the Outlanders had been brought to Zorax. Horrified to hear what had taken place, Letswick was keen to know if any of them had seen DaVendall.

"He was riding out to seek help from as many Outlanders as he could get," Letswick explained. "We know King Alfreston has taken troopers and helpers to assist the Outlanders at the boundaries, and DaVendall was going to bring along more help."

"We knew it," said Petra. "We guessed there must be a battle going on. Sizan and Imelda have been here shouting about troubles at the boundaries. Then we heard the guards moaning at having to stay behind when they wanted to go to battle."

"Did any of you see DaVendall?" asked Beauty.

"Nah," said a villager. "We 'ad no idea what was 'appening. We was captured by those brutes and brought straight 'ere. The last we saw was our houses being set alight and that Old Crone flying along with these big ugly birds. They was the ones that attacked the folk on the ground."

Thinking they should move on, Eram whispered to Vigo and Lema, "Right you two, time to show us a quick way out of here. No tricks, I'll be right behind you." Facing each other and fearful of worse torture if they failed, Vigo whispered, "Yer'd best keep up. Guards will soon know yer've escaped."

With so many prisoners, progress was slow. Thinking it might be an idea to split the group in two, David reasoned that he could use the compass to find the way out they'd used before. Letswick agreed.

"If we continue being all together, we stand a good chance of being caught, but if we split up at least we can be sure some of us will get out," David pointed out.

"Perhaps it might be a good idea to take Petra and Norda,

along with Jayne and Lottie," said Letswick. "I expect Kolen will come with you, then you can take turns carrying Relek."

"What about Penny?" said Lottie. "I want her to be with me."

Aware of how protective of each other these two friends had become, Letswick added, "You're quite right, Lottie. But on this occasion, how about asking Penny?" Letswick caught Penny's attention and beckoned her to his side. Wondering what was wrong, Penny made her way to join the group, just in time to hear David say, "I agree. Penny should decide." Still not sure what the conversation was about, Penny suddenly noticed how like her mother Lottie was. She studied their faces before asking, "Let Penny decide what?"

Letswick told her what they had been discussing. Penny hated being put in these situations. Part of her wanted to stay with Lottie, but the other part of her wanted to remain with Letswick. Feeling a little self-conscious she looked at the company then said, "I would like to stay with Letswick, if that's all right with him."

"Most assuredly young lady, most assuredly," Letswick replied, beaming across at her. He moved across to take Penny's hand. Comforted by the strength of Letswick's hand, Penny gave it a gentle squeeze. Smiling at her, Letswick whispered, "Well done, little lady. Decisive, just like your dad." They were smiling at each other like a couple of conspirators.

"If everything is settled, I'd like to make a move," said Eram.

With everyone informed of what was going to take place, it wasn't long before each had settled with their selected groups. Making sure there were enough strong people to support the weak, they made ready to move out. Just before they set out on their different paths, Lottie went across to Penny and gave her a hug.

"Take care, Penny, my very good friend. I guess we'll meet up soon," she said.

"I will, you take care too," said Penny. "And yes, we'll get together again soon."

Prepared to leave, Letswick made one more request to Beauty. "Is there anything you can give these people to ease their pain?"

"Oh dear, with everything happening at once, I forgot," replied Beauty. "Lottie, would you hand Letswick some of the phials in your pocket?" Turning to Letswick she added, "These will last for a while, but use them sparingly. We need to make them last until more can be made. Take care and we'll meet up again soon."

"Thank you, my friend," whispered Letswick. Giving Lottie and Beauty a wink, he set off to give the wounded a sip from the phials.

As he was doing this, he suddenly felt someone enter his mind. Handing over his phials to Rista and Yemil, he asked if they would continue without him for a while. Now free to open his mind to whomever was trying to contact him, he recognised Bacjo's voice.

"Is everyone ready?" asked Bacjo. "Nain has checked, and it appears the guards have moved to another part of the dungeon, so may I suggest we make a move? Eram has everyone together now."

Yemil and Rista were now approaching the last few people waiting for medicine from the phial. Seeking out the ones who needed assistance, Letswick asked the stronger people to come and help with their friends. Noticing Mittoy and Eva were busy helping their friends, Penny asked him to lift an injured prisoner onto her back. Making sure they were settled, he placed another on his own, then sent a message along the line for Eram to move on.

Letswick then whispered to his companion, "Hold tight. We'll soon have everyone out of here." With Penny at his side, Letswick remained at the back of the group with Bacjo and Sanso. Leading the group forward, Eram urged Vigo and Lema to move on. Eram secretly hoped they weren't being led into a trap.

Just then, they heard what they had feared most - the sound of stomping boots and coarse voices. Fearing the arrival of enemy guards, Eram brought everyone to a halt. In a quiet solemn voice he asked, "Do any of you know which direction the guards are coming from?"

Letswick asked Yemil, "Can you make out if they are near

us?" Taking a moment to listen, Yemil signed, "They seem to be a short distance away. We'd best stay still for a while and I'll let you knew when it's safe." Signing to let her know he agreed, Letswick edged his way closer to Eram and whispered what Yemil had told him.

Letswick placed his charge on the floor, then went to check on the rest of the people, who assured him they would be able to keep up. Wondering where the guards were, Eram poked Vigo and Lema in their backs, and muttered, "This isn't a trap I hope." Staring up at Eram, Vigo stated indignantly "No. We wouldn't do that. We wanna get away too."

Lema whispered, "Do yer know which way?" Noticing the pale face of his friend, Vigo replied, "I bin down this 'ere tunnel many times. I 'ides down 'ere when I don't wanna get caught." Taking Lema's hand, Vigo continued down the familiar passage.

Settling his charge on his back, Eram urged them to continue on their way. Rista, fearing the appearance of the Old Crone, heard Nain say, "Don't think about her, Rista. We'll be all right." Feeling only slight encouragement from Nain she took a deep breath and continued. Looking at him and observing his calm manner, a feeling of tenderness came over her. She was thinking how lucky she was to have such a good friend.

They set off, taking short rests whenever they thought it was safe to do so. After passing down many dark and grimy passages, Vigo at last spotted a

faint glimmer of light. He pointed it out to Eram and Letswick. Relieved to see daylight, Eram said, "Let's go and get everyone else, then we can get out of this horrible place."

Leading the way, Eram was soon joined by Letswick and Vigo, but Vigo soon stopped them from going any further. Drawing Eram's attention, Vigo told him, "See that op'ning in the wall, that's where them guards sits an' 'as their food. We'll 'ave to be very quiet, in case they've come back." Staring at the area Vigo pointed out, Letswick asked, "Do they often come here?"

"Sometimes they're 'ere when I comes through, but sometimes they're not," Vigo whispered.

"Well I guess we'll have to make sure everyone remains silent."

Eram was restless. “I’m for fetching those others and making my way out of here” he said.

“I agree,” replied Letswick. They went back to collect the injured and check everyone else was ready to go. Letswick gave a gentle warning, “No noise. We must be very quiet from now on.”

As they passed where Vigo had warned of guards, Letswick urged everyone to get as close to the wall as possible and quietly follow. Terrified of being heard or seen, the people filed slowly and quietly past. But there was no sign of any guards. Letswick urged everyone to walk as fast as possible and aim for the light ahead.

Chapter Twenty Two

Escape from the Dungeons

Proud that he'd brought these people safely to his secret exit, Vigo grinned at Lema and said, "We'll 'ave to lead 'em along those bushes." With the people huddled in a small cavity in the wall, Letswick was keen to know how they were going to get to the other side of the tower.

"Some are too sick to run," whispered Vigo. "Yer'll 'ave to do what I 'as to do, crawl along the ground. Stay close to the bushes, an' only a few at a time mind, or we'll all get caught."

Lema added, "Yer'll 'ave to stay quiet as a mouse. Guards 'ave big ears."

"We understand," replied Letswick. He relayed this to Eram, quietly adding, "I think we'd best sort out who is able to leave without assistance. We'll take anyone who needs help."

"I can help," said Penny. "Just tell me what to do and I'll do it." Proud of how Penny was always ready to assist; Letswick gave her hand a squeeze, and replied, "Your help will be invaluable. Thank you."

Letswick and Eram were both concerned at the number of people who needed help.

"We're not out of danger yet," said Letswick. "Vigo has assured us that this is where we exit. We will need to be extra quiet as there are guards close to it. Once we reach the exit point, we will have to cross an open space. However, there are a few sparse shrubs from which we can get some shelter. We will need to crawl under them on hands and knees. The most important thing to remember is to remain silent. No whispering or telepathy, or we will give ourselves away. The fittest will go first and the rest will follow with assistance from the rest of us. We will possibly have to make a couple of runs, but be assured, everyone will get out."

"Would you sort out who will go first?" said Eram. "Vigo and Lema will take you on from there. Good luck everyone and remember, quiet as church mice." Nervous and fearing they would get caught, the people tried to remain calm while sorting out who would go with who. With that sorted, Letswick asked Bacjo and Sanso to bring up the rear.

"Cor, I 'ope we don't see no bullies," whispered Vigo to Lema.

"That's what I 'ope too," whispered Lema in reply. "'Ow does 'e know where to go?"

"Here we go," whispered Bacjo. "Vigo and Lema are already on their hands and knees. Good luck friends." In complete silence, Vigo and Lema led the first group past the guards and onto the point of exit.

"Give them a moment to let their eyes adjust to the light," said Bacjo. He could see some of them were having difficulty.

"Only a moment, we don't wanna get caught," Vigo replied. As he and Lema set off with their group, Letswick chanced contacting Beauty to ask if she would give them a moment's protective cover. Beauty took a quick glance to see how many people there were. Surprised to see so many, she explained the cover wouldn't last long. Thankful to have heard from Letswick and knowing they were nearing the end of their journey from the dungeon, Beauty turned her attention to what was happening to her group.

Meanwhile, unaware of the protection Letswick had arranged, the people continued to make their exit. After completing several trips across the muddy ground, Penny was beginning to feel weary, but she was determined not to let these people down. Noticing the warm encouraging smiles from many of the Ziphers and Jaspers, she could only guess they must have picked up how she was feeling. Acknowledging their smile, Penny soon found extra energy to continue.

Observing Mittoy and Sanso busy helping others to cross

and having done a couple of trips himself, Letswick also knew the difficulty of trying to get through the muddy ground. Eram noticed many of the smaller folk were in need of help as it appeared they were getting sucked down. Gathering a group to take across, Letswick met up with Eram, who had just pulled a Zipher free of the mud.

Some of the remaining folk tried to persuade Letswick to leave them in the dungeon.

"I have explained no one is going to be left at the hands of those bullies," he told them. "Now, you will have to be very quiet and crawl on your bellies if you have to. We need to pass the guards. The exit point is not too far from there. Keep as near to me as possible, and please be quiet." All eyes were on him, eager to get going.

Eram and Penny approached. "Penny and I are going to make one final return to the dungeon," Eram told Letswick. "We just want to make sure we haven't left anyone behind." Yemil offered to go with them. Letswick urged them all to take extra care. As he watched them set off, he turned to his friends and said, "Ziphers stay alert for any sounds indicating the enemy is near."

Vigo, fearing they would get caught and be tortured into giving everyone away, went across to Letswick and asked, "'Ow long afore we can move? What 'appens if they get caught? " Taking in the wide open eyes and the scared look on the questioners' face, Letswick whispered, "It won't be long now. Do you know of a way to get us safely outside the tower walls?"

"I know a way, it's not a nice one, but no one else knows it," Vigo told him.

"We're worried about the ones who went back into the dungeons," said Rista. "Do you know if they're on their way back?"

"I haven't heard from Yemil that anything is wrong. Perhaps she hasn't been able to contact me," Letswick replied. "I'll go back and see if they are waiting. Tell everyone to stay where they are and not to make any noise. We aren't free of the tower yet."

Setting off to re-enter the dungeon, Letswick managed to keep himself covered by the sparse shrubs. This was one of those times he was glad he was a small person. Reaching the area where he knew Eram would exit, he looked round to see if there was any sign of activity, either from his friends or his enemies. With nothing apparent, he decided to wait rather than enter the passage.

At last he was delighted to see his friends peer out of the exit. Beckoning them to continue, he watched out for the enemy while they crawled towards him. Ready to greet his friends, he saw more prisoners crawling slowly behind.

"Hi Letswick, it's so good to see you there, I wondered how we were going to find new hiding places," whispered Eram.

"Where were these people? I thought we had freed everyone," said Letswick. "There are prisoner's that have obviously been tortured and left to die," Eram explained.

"So where were they, Eram?" Letswick asked.

"Beneath the torture room floor. It seemed none of them had the strength to call out, or at least they couldn't raise their voices above the noise of the guards. At first we couldn't work out where they were, but after Penny explained we were friends who had come to help, one of the Ziphers managed to attract Yemil's attention through telepathy. After that, it was matter of finding the right stone to lift. Of course we weren't prepared for the state of them, but between us we raised them onto the cell floor, and here we are." Seeing many more prisoners advancing, Letswick asked, "How did you manage to avoid the guards? Surely one of them must have heard you?" Letswick asked. Giving him a broad smile Eram replied, "Don't forget we knew the way out, so we avoided bumping into them. They might have heard something, but they probably put it down to rats."

Letswick was anxious to get these people to a secure hiding place. Gently lifting one of the prisoners, Eram gently placed her into Yemil's arms. Then lifting another he placed him in Letswick's arms, and then did the same for Penny. Able to support two of the Jaspers, he asked the remaining few to follow him and Letswick. Without a murmur from any of the prisoners, they followed slowly behind.

Penny placed her charges safely under the shelter of the nearby shrubs and sat down beside them. Thankful to hear

Letswick and his group were free of the dungeons, Beauty agreed with Letswick to let Vigo lead them outside the tower. They left the freed prisoners in the care of the stable lads. Her mind withdrawn from Letswick and Yemil, Beauty suddenly sensed danger close to where Letswick had said they were. She soon saw that it was a pack of trofalogues. Aware that they would be able to smell fear, she wasted no time in putting into place a scent mask, while sending a message to some friends who she knew would come to her aid. Closing her mind to all incoming telepaths, including Lottie, she concentrated on reaching out to their leader, Septin. Then she warned Letswick that a pack of trofalogues were heading his way, and told him she would take care of them.

David meanwhile was eager to get going with his group. Having asked Kolen to stay close to him so they could take turns in carrying Relek, they prepared to leave. Lottie, grasping her mother's hand, whispered, "Come on, Mum. We'll stay together." Jayne was beginning to feel the results of many beatings, and was hoping Lottie wouldn't notice.

Looking at the brooch attached securely to Lottie's jacket, Jayne whispered, "It's so good to be together at last, especially with our friends." Giving Jayne a warm smile, Beauty, having picked up on how weary Jayne had become, whispered, "We have so much to tell, it will be good to get away from here." At that moment, David signalled he was heading off.

Unable to shake off the feeling that Imelda could be around, Beauty wondered if she had sensed the prisoners escaping from their cells. Just then her fears were borne out. Imelda's shrill voice echoed round the dungeon. "Guards, there are prisoners free! Find 'em, find 'em! Whip 'em all an' lock 'em up! If yer fails me, the whippings will be fer you."

Beauty set about trying to discover if she was in the tower. Taking care not to let Imelda pick up on her thoughts, she wasn't too surprised when Imelda's voice changed from a shrill screech to one of warning. "So! Me stone 'as come to set the prisoners free. Be warned, stone, they'll never get away!" Changing her tone from a threat to a taunt, she added, "Come to me an' I'll let yer friends go free." Lottie clasped her hand over her brooch and whispered, "She'll never get you! I'll never give you away." Meanwhile

"I can sense yer in 'ere!" snarled Imelda. "Don't ferget, I 'as part of yer in me 'ands. I'll soon find yer."

Thinking Imelda could have already sent creatures to attack her friends, Beauty called out, "You might have taken some of my power, Imelda, but not enough to do what you threaten to do. I will give you a warning. Harm any of my friends and I'll make sure you really suffer."

Noticing the glow from Lottie's brooch, David edged nearer his daughter and whispered, "Keep our friend covered. The Old Crone might see her." Lottie pulled the lapel inside, leaving no trace of a glow.

It suddenly went silent. Gone were the screeching voice and the sound of approaching guards. Lottie felt even more anxious to get out of this place.

Beauty's thoughts were concerned with how King Alfreston was faring. Wishing she could have reached him, she just had to hope it wouldn't be long before they met up again.

Norda had now gone on ahead at the request of David. Using the dim light from a single flamed torch to guide him, it was with increased urgency that he made his way to the end of the passage. Finally reaching it, he sat for a moment to get his breath.

He had promised David to keep a lookout for any sign of the guards. Seeing a group not too far from where he was hiding, he was tempted to take revenge on them for what they had done to his friends, but he knew he would have to wait for another day. Little did he know how soon this would be.

David considered the next move. Binro signed, "Keep your eyes on the compass light ahead, it will show us the way out."

"Right David, no stopping until we reach the end of this passage," said Beauty. Giving the signal to move on, David set off in a more positive mood. He opened the compass to give a little more light, urging his group to move as quickly as they could. Beauty, having picked up on David's concern about the lack of light, concentrated her thoughts on a dim flame coming from a torch on the wall. Gradually she increased the flame, which gave the group confidence to move faster and provided enough light for everyone to follow.

At last they reached the steps which indicated that they were close to the end. Advising everyone to take care, as the steps were covered in slime, David checked to make sure they had all kept together.

Norda's attention was suddenly drawn to a dark mass approaching from the sky. Transfixed at the sight, he blinked a couple of times to see if he could see what it was.

"I wonder if the area has grown over?" David asked himself. Taking it slowly, the group edged closer together. Noticing the light coming through the end of the passage, they knew they had reached daylight. On seeing Norda's head above the cover, David closed the compass and whispered, "Hi Norda. We're here at last, have those guards returned?"

Scrambling out from cover, Norda crawled over and grabbed his arm. David crawled out from the passage to see what had got Norda excited. It appeared to be a swarm of locusts heading for the tower. As they drew closer, it was clear that these were no ordinary locusts. They had exceptionally large heads, with large bulging eyes, and they were bigger than any other locusts David had seen, the size of birds. Seeing the panic these creatures were spreading among the troopers, David realised these locusts must be something to do with Beauty.

Making his way to where Lottie and Jayne were standing, David was concerned to see how much more weary Jayne had become. Thinking he would stay with her for a while, he turned to Beauty and calmly said, "I think there are some friends of yours out here. Lottie, would you take our friend to have a look?" Smiling down at her brooch, Lottie crawled towards the top of the passage.

"Thank you, Lottie, but on this occasion we needn't worry," said Beauty. "My friends would never harm us. They will, however, keep our enemies occupied while we make our escape."

Beauty, aware of Jayne's weakened state, knew why David wanted to stay behind. She quickly drew his mind to hers. "This will have to be quick, David. I just want to let you know

Letswick's group are close to the end. Try not to worry too much about Jayne. I will give her something to help." Pleased to hear how far the other group had got, David asked, "Is that why the locusts are heading to Zorax?"

"That's right, but I also sensed a pack of trofalogues heading in Letswick's direction. The locusts will take care of them, which will help our other friends to continue on their way," Beauty replied.

The people were delighted to see the havoc the locusts were causing among the guards. What they couldn't see was the torture the locusts were treating the trofalogues to. "It looks as if those bully guards have met their match," said Norda.

Thinking it might be a good idea to go ahead and find shelter, Petra whispered, "Would you like Binro and me to go first? If we go together we will soon find the safest places to hide."

"That would be a good idea, Petra," whispered David. "Are you all right with that, Binro?" Binro nodded. Leading them to the exit point, David checked it was all clear, then gave the word to go. Expecting to be caught at any time, Petra took hold of Binro's hand and flew across the open space. Turning to the Zipher standing beside him, David said, "Kira, please prepare a group of people and be ready to run across to join Petra and Binro. I will check on the others so this will give everyone time to prepare."

Staring at the stretch of ground they had to cover, Kira knew it would be fraught with danger. Moving across to David, Kira signed, "I think we had better be moving soon. Is it safe to leave?"

Taking a quick look out of the passage and seeing that the guards were still preoccupied, David gave Kira the signal. The group wasted no time in gathering close to Kira. Fearful of the dangers involved, they were ready to follow her to where Petra and Binro were waiting.

There was a moment when some of the escapers thought they had been seen. The crouched low on the muddy ground, remaining still until Kira gave the signal for them to continue. Arriving safely on the other side, they fell on the ground, panting. It was a while before anyone could speak.

Petra made her way to Kira and asked if she was fit enough to do another run. Kira told Petra she would leave as soon as she'd got her breath back. "I will return and bring some more across. It's good to know you and Binro have found safe places for them," she said.

Leaving them with Petra and Binro, Kira decided that the quickest way back was to fly. Remaining vigilant, she flew back to where David was waiting with another group of people. Relaying to David what Petra had told her of the safe places, she then signed, "Warn everyone to take care when they set off. They must run as fast as they can. It's quite a distance between here and safety."

David was pleased to hear that Petra and Binro had found enough secure places to hide all the waiting people.

"Perhaps the Jaspers would like to go next?" said David. "Take care when you fly, watch out for any guard that might notice you. Petra and Binro will have found places to hide, so make for where they are. Once the Jaspers have left, the rest of us will make our way across two at a time. When you reach the exit area, check to make sure it's clear, then run as fast as you can, and don't stop until you are safely on the other side."

As the group paired up ready to go, David checked each time before giving the all clear. It was then David's thoughts turned to Letswick and wondered if they were nearing the end of their journey from the dungeons.

Gathering a group of people, Kira prepared them for their escape. She warned them that it was a fair distance to cover and they would have to run like hares to get across. It was a group of very nervous people who waited for David's signal to follow her. Not wanting to worry them any longer, he turned to Kira and said, "Ready." Kira gave the signal for everyone to leave. As they scrambled out of the passage, the sudden unfamiliar daylight caused many to hesitate. It had been some time since they had seen daylight, but with fear driving them they were soon running to safety.

Supporting each other and with Binro leading the way, they were led to their place of safety. Binro covered them with branches from the nearby shrubs to make sure they could not be seen. Satisfied they were safe, he made his way back to where Petra and Kira were in hiding. Now they had to wait for Jayne and David's group to arrive.

Back at the exit area, David told the prisoners to be aware of any unexpected movement from the guards. Jayne gave a weak smile and whispered, "Ready everyone? Don't forget we must run as fast as we can. It will be difficult because the rain has turned the ground to mud." Soon after, David gave the all clear for them to leave.

Jayne was thankful for whatever it was Beauty had given her as she felt some of her weariness wear off. Emerging from the passage, she was shocked to see how close the guards were. She kept as low to the ground as possible, envying the small folk as she tried to stoop level with them.

Suddenly one of the Jaspers called out, "Down quick, guards approaching!" Terrified of being caught, they fell to the ground and hid in the muddy furrows.

Remaining quiet and hardly daring to breath, despite their breathlessness, many were sure this was the end of their freedom. The guards were still cursing at the continual attacks of the locusts, and it seemed an age before the noise died down.

Jayne peered over the furrow. "It's time to go. Stay low and quiet, not too far to go." They didn't need any more encouragement to run for their lives. Finally reaching the other side, they fell to the ground, just as their friends had done previously. Binro sat down beside them and waited only a moment for them to catch their breath before urged them to their hiding place. Making sure they were safely there and well covered, he made his way back to where Jayne was waiting.

"Did you see what happened?" she said. "I thought we were going to be caught. Thank goodness those locusts kept them occupied. We had a lucky escape."

Worried by what she'd seen, Petra made her way to join Jayne and Binro and checked that everyone was safely hidden.

"I hope David and his group are here soon," said Jayne. "We have all been held prisoner for too long." Feeling a tap on her arm, she turned to see Petra looking at her. "I think you had better stay here with us," Petra told her. Settling close to Binro and Petra, Jayne couldn't stop thinking about David and his group still having to cross the open ground.

Admiring the tenacity and bravery of his friends, David started to prepare the last group which was leaving with him. As the group shuffled themselves into position, he suddenly became anxious for his daughter. He couldn't help recalling Zanus' leering voice when he had told David he wanted Lottie for himself. Knowing how cruel he and his sidekick Crocanthus were, he was aware Lottie wouldn't stand a chance against these evil men.

Moving closer to Lottie, he suddenly heard Beauty enter his thoughts. "Now is not the time, David. We will keep Lottie safe. Just concentrate on getting everyone to safety."

"Please come as near to the exit as possible," he said to Beauty. "We have no time to lose. Once or twice the guards seem to have been disturbed by something other than the locusts."

They were about to leave when they were halted by a warning from Beauty. Having become aware of approaching guards, she waited and concentrated her senses on discovering where they were going. Hardly daring to breath, they waited anxiously for the all clear. As soon as it came, he gave the word to go. They dashed across the open ground between the furrows as the previous groups had done. Fortunately they managed to achieve this without any disturbance from the guards, and when they finally reached their destination they fell to the ground panting for breath. Jayne made her way over to Lottie, while Petra assured David that everyone was safely hidden away.

The rescued prisoners were pleased to be out of the dungeon, but aware there was still a long way to go. "I suggest we wait here for a while and plan our next course of action," said David. But even as he said it, he was wondering how they would manage to get to the other side of the tower walls. He wasn't keen to go through the courtyard. Deep in thought, he was surprised to hear Norda ask, "Do we have any unicorns nearby?"

Hearing the mention of unicorns gave Beauty an idea. Attracting David's attention, she explained that there were many badly tortured people with Eram.

"I know they are free of the dungeons," she said. "This happened a while ago. Vigo has told Letswick he knows of a way under the tower walls, so he is going to lead them through." Drawing Lottie's attention, Beauty explained her plan. "This is a deed for us to complete," she said. "We have done this a number of times, calm and quiet is all that is needed. Letswick is possibly outside the tower, but we will need to reach his thoughts to confirm this."

Remaining silent, David could feel Lottie and Beauty trying to reach Letswick's mind. Still amazed to have discovered his daughter was telepathic, he said nothing, but concentrated on hearing Beauty's plan.

Within a matter of moments Letswick replied telepathically, "I hear you. I hope you are all safe. We are about to send the last of the people through the tunnel, then we will gather together outside the tower. Vigo has used this exit many times. I guess you have a plan for us?"

"This will take much courage, Letswick," said Beauty. "As soon as you are away from Zorax, make sure everyone is in a secure place. When that is done, contact Doran. As you have many injured people in need of care, ask Doran to come and bring the other unicorns. Guide him to you, but most importantly don't forget to remind him to make sure they have protective covering."

As soon as Beauty had finished speaking, Letswick let her know his group were clear of the tunnel. Waiting to enter the tunnel himself, he added, "I will send a message as soon as I am through, then I can direct Doran. As soon as the unicorns arrive please let them know I have asked Queen Matilda to prepare to receive them."

"Do you think it would be possible for more unicorns to be sent from the castle?" asked Letswick.

"That's a good idea, I will ask Matilda to send reinforcements. Now back to where we were. As soon as the friends are ready to depart with the injured, I will give them some protective covering of invisibility. It should last long enough to get them away from the wood."

Absorbing all that had been said, Letswick replied, "I am

now going to follow Vigo through the tunnel and then send a message to Doran."

He got down on all fours to enter the tunnel, then had a sudden thought which he quietly relayed it to Beauty, "Take care when using telepathy, we are on dangerous ground," he said. With that he withdrew his mind and urged Vigo to lead on.

Coming to the end of the dark and grimy tunnel, Letswick decided to gather everyone together to explain their next move. Before doing this, he sent out a message to Doran. As they gathered together and waited for the arrival of the unicorns, it was proving very difficult to keep everyone from coughing with the dust and filth clogging up their noses and mouths. Thinking this was never going to end, Lema nervously asked Vigo, "Is we gonna go with 'em?" Letswick, seeing the lads huddled together, crawled up closer to Vigo and whispered, "What's wrong?"

"I 'eard a noise," Vigo whispered. Just then a loud rumbling sound came from overhead. Letswick knew this was the sound of troopers, and guessed they were reinforcements for Zanus. Holding onto Vigo and Lema, and signalling for the others to remain still and quiet, he whispered, "Give them a while. As soon as the noise stops we must quickly move to a safe hiding place. Vigo, is there a good safe place for all these people to hide?"

Unnerved, but feeling important to be asked this, Vigo said there was. Crawling side by side, Lema and Vigo tried to climb the bank, but the rain had made it treacherous and it was a struggle not to fall down to the bottom. Seeing Letswick and Eram were having similar difficulty didn't make Vigo feel any better. Reaching the top, Vigo turned to Letswick and explained they needed to go down the other side of the bank and get as near to the bottom as possible. Getting his breath back, he took note of how far they had to go.

Sitting beside Vigo and gasping for breath, Letswick asked, "Is there something we can use for cover until we reach the bottom?"

"Leaves an' sticks is about all," said Vigo. "Not much growin' down 'ere, but I guess we can scoop up enough for now."

"That would be good. I'll leave you and Lema to collect as much covering as you can." Leaving the stable lads to their task,

Letswick explained to Eram what Beauty had planned, then left him to finish making his way to the bottom.

Looking after the injured, Penny and Yemil had taken it in turns to help many of them down the muddy sides and into the safety of Eram's arms.

Having reached Doran, Letswick explained where they were hidden, in a deep ravine outside the tower walls, where he told Doran there was ample room for them. They would be able to fly close to where everyone was in hiding. Warning the unicorns to cover themselves with a protective cover before entering the wood, they agreed on the signal Doran should give to announce their arrival.

Still feeling important at being asked to help shelter these people, Vigo whispered just loud enough for all to hear, "There's cover fer some, if yer follow me an' keep quiet, I'll show you where to 'ide." Taking hold of Lema's arm, he pulled him down to join him on the ground. Signalling for the others to crawl, he made his way towards a gap surrounded by dead-looking shrubs. He and Lema moved the shrubs aside and ushered the people into hiding.

"Cor, this must have been a trofalogue hole. It still stinks," said someone.

"Well the trofalogues won't find us," said Lema. "This is a good place to 'ide." That said, they fell quiet as they waited for Letswick and Eram to join them.

While Letswick's group were settling down and waiting for the next move, Beauty was attempting to reach Queen Matilda's mind. Discovering something was blocking her thoughts, she reached out to David's mind and told him the trouble she and Lottie were having. Joining his mind to theirs, he said, "OK, now we have our minds joined we will need to concentrate hard to break through whatever is blocking our minds and try to reach Matilda."

They then concentrated all their thoughts on getting through to Matilda, but with no response. Beauty was concerned; she felt that the concentrated energy from the other two minds should have been enough to break through.

Then Beauty realised what was preventing them from

getting through. She had come across this barrier before, and now she wasted no time in searching for one of the weapons she'd seen in the courtyard, a large ball covered in spikes. Closing her mind to David and Lottie, she concentrated on lifting the weapon. As it spun round, she threw it against the barrier. It created little damage, so she tried again. This time it made a gap large enough to allow their minds to travel through.

Joining her mind back to David and Lottie, Beauty tried again to contact Queen Matilda. At last she heard a faint response. A familiar voice replied, "My friend, is that you?"

Excited at hearing Matilda's voice, Beauty knew she had to make this message short and to the point. "It is. We can't talk long, Matilda, but I need your help. Many prisoners are badly injured and in need of attention. We could do with a couple of coaches with unicorns. Dandy and Doran need help with the injured. Letswick is with Eram, safely hidden from the enemy. He has asked Doran to guide the unicorns to where Letswick and friends are. I thought you might like to know that David and Jayne are safe and with us," Beauty explained.

"Hello Queen Matilda, it will be so good to speak to you again, but it might a little while yet before we are all back together," David added telepathically.

"David, I can't believe that after all this time we will be together again" replied Matilda. "We have been so worried not knowing if you were alive or not. I am looking forward to being with you and Jayne once more. Take care."

The barrier was now beginning to block their thoughts. With their minds now parted, Lottie clasped her hand in her father's and whispered, "I never thought we would be using telepathy together with our friend, did you?"

Giving his daughter a warm smile, he replied, "No, Lottie. I did not." Meanwhile, Beauty was concentrating on sending a signal to Doran to let him and his companions know help would soon be arriving. Then in a sombre voice she reminded him to make sure they were well protected against the evil within the Forbidden Wood.

* * * *

Overcome with joy at the news from Beauty, Queen Matilda turned to Lucy and Frances.

"That, my friends, was Beauty. David and Jayne are alive. She has asked for carriages to be sent to bring back the injured. Thank goodness we prepared all those beds and bandages."

"How are they?" asked Lucy. "Are they injured?"

"I don't think so. Beauty couldn't stop the barrier from blocking our minds, so I guess we'd better be prepared." She turned to Frances and murmured, "I wish we could hear from Alfreston."

Having thought the same herself, Frances rose from the chair and walked towards the door.

"We will in time, Matilda. But as you said, we'd better be prepared."

Just then Krast appeared at the door. "Is anything the matter, Your Majesty?" he asked.

"We are expecting a lot of wounded people to arrive, Krast. I want you to run round to Igorin and ask him to send carriages with unicorns to bring them back. They are with Letswick in a ravine outside the tower walls, so remind them to give themselves protection against being seen. The marker will show the safest way for the unicorns to go. I suggest you ask cook to prepare some broth and pots of tea."

Approaching the table on which the map was laid out, he asked the tortoises to hold the corners still. Watching the marker make out a route, Winston whispered to Marmaduke, "I love watching the marker. It's so magical."

The marker moved slowly and carefully, seeking the safest way for the unicorns. Satisfied with the route at last, the marker turned to Krast and said, "This is the safest. But they will still have to be careful when flying over that part of the wood."

"Thank you, marker," said Krast.

"Haven't you forgotten something, Krast?" said the marker. Krast turned to see a parchment on the marker's back and picked it up. It was a copy of the route.

"How can the marker do that?" asked Winston in wonder.

"How would the unicorns know the way if they didn't have a map?" said the marker.

Krast left the building and ran hastily round to the stable, calling out for Igorin as he did. He explained Queen Matilda's request, and it wasn't long before carriages and unicorns were ready to leave. As they said farewell, voices were calling out, "Take care!" Then the unicorns and carriages soared into the sky.

Chapter Twenty Three

The evil of Imelda

Hearing there were unicorns with carriages on the way, and having assured Beauty they would ensure their companions would be well covered, Doran thought over what all that Beauty had told him. Turning to face his companions, he relayed what Beauty had told him. Giving them time to absorb the latest events, he asked the animals to gather together, then asked Dandy to join with him by giving everyone a protective covering. Looking at each other as they gathered together, they were a very quiet group, each with their own thoughts of the dangers ahead of them.

Making sure the covering was complete, Doran quietly suggested, "If we are ready, we should be making our way." They suddenly noticed how dark it had gone and looked up to see that the sky was filled with Zanus' spy birds.

"I think we had better stop," said Dandy. "We don't want them to hear us." Slowly the light returned as the spy birds flew on their way.

"I suggest we stay with the horses, Dandy," said Doran. "We are near to entering the wood and we might need to reinforce their covering." Before Dandy could speak, one of the horses replied, "I wondered if you were going to fly over, Doran. I'm glad you think it would be better to stay with us. None of us want to be captured by that Old Crone."

Dandy moved closer to the horse and whispered, "Try not to think of her. Concentrate on reaching Letswick."

As they approached the wood, it was only the thought of

helping their friends that gave them the courage to continue. They walked slowly and cautiously to avoid being tripped over by the vines and struck by the swaying branches.

Now they could see a darkness sweeping across the ground. Their immediate fear was that Imelda knew they were there, but then Doran spotted another flock of spy birds flying past. Ready to defend themselves should the birds fly near to them, they soon realised it wasn't them they were searching for. It was a relief to all when a voice said, "We're nearly there."

Thinking of what lay ahead, Letswick was surprised to hear a low whistle come from close by. In an instant he knew it was Doran. He responded, and it wasn't long before he felt a damp nose on his arm. Delighted and pleased to know the animals had arrived safely, Letswick gave Doran an affectionate stroke on the side of his head.

"You weren't harmed coming through the wood, were you?" he asked. Nuzzling close to Letswick's ear, Doran replied, "We had a bit of a scare when a flock of spy birds flew over, but they went straight on. We brought the horses. I thought you might need a bit of assistance with some of the people."

"That's a good idea. Many of the people are weary and need help," Letswick replied. The animals were still invisible to the human eye, so Eram put out a hand to feel for them. Dandy nuzzled up close and whispered, "How many injured are there, Eram?" Jumping at the touch from Dandy, Eram whispered, "Quite a number. How many do you think you and Doran can carry?"

"Quite a few, we brought the horses along to help," Dandy told him. Penny nudged Eram's arm and pointed to a shimmering image descending close by. As it landed, it was soon followed by another. Realising what it was, Letswick beckoned to Eram and Penny. Curious as to what the shimmering was, they moved closer to Letswick and were surprised when he said, "This is more unicorns, with carriages to carry the injured to the castle."

Fascinated at what was taking place, Penny edged closer to Letswick and put her hand out to see if she could feel one of the carriages. Smiling up at her, Letswick asked the unicorns, "I take it they are from Queen Matilda?"

"They are," said a unicorn. "The Queen sent us to help carry the ones who need it. We can't wait too long, as the cover will only last a short while. The Queen was delighted to know the prisoners are free."

Eram began to put the weaker prisoners inside the carriages. Vigo and Lema were fascinated to see the people vanish from sight as Eram let them go. Making sure the weaker and injured folk were safe inside the carriages, Eram placed others onto Dandy and Doran's backs. Keen for the carriages and unicorns to be on their way, Eram told Doran everyone was ready to go.

"Do you think we should go round the wood?" whispered Dandy. One of the other unicorns replied, "We thought we would go back the way we came. We'll have enough cover for that."

"Carry on my friend, we'll follow you," Doran whispered. Checking his riders were holding tight, they flew fast behind the carriages. Relieved, but sad to see their friends leave, the remaining people were anxious to know when and how they were going to rejoin them.

"'Ow did yer make 'em vanish?" asked Vigo. Letswick laughed. "Nothing to worry about, lads, just a friend giving a hand." Not sure that this was the answer he was expecting, Vigo looked at Lema and gave a shrug of his shoulders.

* * * *

Beauty had known Matilda would do as she requested. Turning her thoughts back to the current situation, her first concern was with the locusts. Seeing that they were still busy keeping the enemy occupied, she was keen to join up with Letswick's group. She contacted Septin, leader of the locusts, and thanked him for all the help he and his kind had given. "You are free to leave when you are ready," she told him.

"We have enjoyed being able to torment these bullies," said Septin. "Although they killed many of our friends before we found a place of safety. I think we will stay a little longer just to make sure you and your friends are safe." Giving Septin a warm smile, Beauty accepted the offer. Turning her attention to Lottie, she began to explain what she planned to do.

"I never thought of locusts as friends," said Lottie. "Coming here has made me think differently about all the creatures and animals back in my land. I wonder how many would love to live in a land like this."

"Like before, Lottie, I am going to create a huge bubble," said Beauty. "When that is done, I would like you to hold it. It will be large enough to carry everyone here to join Letswick. Don't worry, it will be shielded from the eyes of the enemy."

Almost immediately Lottie saw the most beautifully coloured bubble appear from nowhere. She watched it grow larger and larger until she feared it would burst. Fascinated, she heard Beauty telling David, "Please get everyone inside this bubble as quickly as you can. Time is not on our side."

Noticing how quickly the people responded, Lottie soon realised that as the people stepped inside the bubble they vanished from sight.

"Take care, Lottie," said Beauty. "Don't release the bubble from your mind until I make sure everyone is safe. As soon as everyone is in the bubble I will transport it to where Letswick and his people are."

Assuring Beauty she wouldn't release it until she was told, Lottie watched the bubble floating over the tower wall. She couldn't help wondering how far it had to travel. Seeing it slowly move away from the wall and float off into the distance, she wondered where it would land. She lost sight of it for a moment, but just then she was surprised to see it gently float to the ground. It was further from the tower than she had expected.

Lottie heard Beauty telling the people it was safe for them to leave the bubble. Seeing them hesitate, she added, "You will be shielded by a protective covering for a while, so please hurry across to Letswick. Your friends are waiting for you."

Waiting until the last person had left the bubble and was safe with Letswick, Beauty told Lottie to release her mind from the bubble. "We need to join Letswick and his friends," said Beauty. Before Lottie had time to ask how this was going to be achieved, she was surprised to see that she was standing beside her parents.

"How did you do that?" whispered Lottie.

"Just a little touch of magic," Beauty whispered, giving Lottie a wry smile. Wondering how she was going to explain her sudden appearance to her parents, Lottie noticed her father looking directly at her.

"Are you all right, Lottie?" asked Jayne. Not sure how to explain what had happened, Lottie smiled and assured her mother she was fine, then wondered how it was she hadn't noticed before how weary her mother looked.

Gathering everyone around Beauty whispered, "Lottie, would you take me closer to Letswick?" Edging herself through the people, it wasn't long before she was standing close to him and drawing his attention.

"Is there something I can do?" asked Letswick.

"Would you please let these people know their injured friends are safe at the castle?" said Beauty.

Lottie gave Penny a hug. "It's so good to see you, Penny," she said. "We must try not to get parted again."

"Excuse me," said Beauty, "Would you mind if I had a little space to breathe? Hello Penny, it's so nice to be with you again."

"Hello. We had a few nasty shocks but we came through it," stated Penny

"Are you ready for some more danger, Penny?" Beauty asked.

"After what has happened, you'd better not try leaving me behind," Penny replied firmly. Hearing this, Letswick laughed and said, "Well done, Penny." Then in a serious voice he added, "You have been so brave, but there will be dangers even we can't foresee."

Placing her hands on her hips and trying to look indignant, Penny replied, "I don't care. If our friends are in danger they will need all the help they can get." It was obvious that no one was going to stop her from going.

Beauty, full of admiration for the courage these humans had shown, feared the repercussions if they failed to rid Dofstram of Zanus and Imelda. Letswick, picking up on Beauty's concerns, uttered, "I don't think we can leave them out."

Lottie meanwhile was talking to her father. "It's great to know the injured people are now safely at the castle" she said. "Do you think it will be long before we will head out to help at the battlefield?"

"Not long," said David. "Please take great care, Lottie. They will show no mercy, so don't hesitate to defend yourself." Remembering his time in the dungeon and the cruelty he and others had suffered, he murmured, "I never thought my daughter would be involved with fighting off these devils."

Lottie looked at her father. Taking hold of his arm, she whispered, "I'm so sorry, Dad, I never noticed how tired and weary you and Mum are. Are you sure you are up to more fighting?"

"I'm sure we are all weary," he replied. "It was a case of survival. We never gave up hoping we would be rescued, it just took a little longer than we thought. Little did I suspect my daughter would be one of the rescuers. As for fighting, neither your mother nor I would leave this beautiful land without doing all we can to rid it of that evil Old Crone and Zanus. I guess that's how most of the prisoners feel. Some of my friends have been held in the dungeon for so long that they just yearn for the day they can reclaim their lands."

"We must plan the best way to proceed" said Beauty. "Before we discuss that, there is just one thing, David. Remembering your last encounter with them we must ensure they don't capture you or Jayne again."

"That's been one of my concerns, but now I have Lottie to watch over too," replied David. "At least Lottie will be able to help us keep track of where she is through her telepathy. But I'll need to ensure Jayne is safe."

Penny was standing quietly by Letswick's side. She too had noticed the state of the prisoners, but was glad to have been part of their escape. As she was about to say what she was thinking, a picture of her own mother came to mind. Remembering Frances' answer to every problem, she murmured, "Perhaps a mug of tea might help?"

Hearing Penny mention tea, Jayne moved across and gave her a hug. "That's exactly what Frances would have said," she smiled. Then in a wistful voice Jayne added, "I am so longing to see my friends again."

David looked round to see where the others had gone. Surprised to see many people standing close to Eram and

Letswick, Lottie felt her surprise must have been reflected on her face as Eram whispered, "They know where we are going and they want to come with us."

Beauty had been looking at the number of folk who had offered to come and help. She knew they would be aware of what they would be facing, but that hadn't stopped them from offering their help.

She began to wonder about the two stable lads. "Are Lema and Vigo ready to go into battle?" she whispered to Letswick. "Do they realise that if they are caught Zanus will punish them mercilessly?"

"They'll be all right, Beauty," said Letswick. "They want to attack the enemy as much as we do. They made it quite clear they weren't going back to the tower, they'd already made up their minds to join us."

Thinking of the journey ahead, Beauty advised a well-earned rest while they discussed the best approach to King Alfreston once they reached the Outlander border. She left Letswick to explain their plan. He explained that they would be given a protective cover, and quickly assured them it would last long enough to get them well away from the wood and the Tower of Zorax. Picking up worried thoughts coming from Vigo and Lema, he edged closer to the two lads. Having become fond of these two lads, he was keen to reassure them that they would be given the same cover.

"All will be fully explained when we are free of this place," he said. "When you see the cover being placed over us, don't be alarmed. You'll be able see your friends, but it will cover us from enemy eyes."

"Will it 'urt, this cover?" whispered Vigo.

"No, it's not heavy. Now, once the cover is in place you will soon be getting a chance to give the Zanuthians a beating."

"That's what I want. Chance ter give 'em bullies some of their own treatment," stated Lema. But Letswick was concerned at what carnage they might find on reaching the battlefield.

King Alfreston had become anxious at the time it was taking him to reach the Outlanders. Guessing the map marker would have lost track of where they were, he concentrated on their destination. Aware of the distance they still had to go, he decided this would be a good time to take a short rest. He sent Pointer to fetch Drewan and suggested everyone should dismount and give the animals a rest.

On their return, Pointer and Drewan made their way to the King. Drewan dismounted and asked the King. "Is everything all right? We have been a while checking round for signs of any enemy." Pointer made his way to speak to Drewan's horse. "I think we should join our other friends and have a rest" he said.

Soon it was time to resume the journey. Calling Gazer and the other animals over, King Alfreston announced that he had something to say.

"Before we continue, I think everyone should know what is planned," he said. "We'll continue until nightfall, then take a short rest before going on to find the Outlanders." Turning to Pointer, he asked, "Would you take a quick look round to make sure there are no approaching enemy? Jaspers, would you take a short fly round just to make sure it's all clear?"

The Jaspers and Pointer set off to make sure it was free of any enemy. Leaving the Jaspers to fly overhead, Pointer made his way on the ground. On the way, he was surprised to come across a few stray rabbits. Concerned they would be caught he asked, "What are you doing so far from home? Have you seen or heard the enemy?"

"Gosh Pointer, you gave us a fright," said one of the rabbits. "We did see those devil birds flying round earlier, but we were too quick for them to grab us."

"You were lucky this time, but you might not be next time. Now, may I suggest you get back to your family? I wouldn't want the birds to get a second chance at grabbing you."

"You're right, Pointer. Take care and good luck on your mission," replied the rabbit. "Come along now, we don't want to be seen by those devil birds, or worse the Old Crone." With flicks of their tails, the rabbits turned and set off in the direction of home.

As they turned away, Pointer was surprised to hear Moff enter his mind. "Any sign of the enemy, Pointer?" he asked, telepathically.

"None round here," replied Pointer. "What about you?"

Just then Pointer's attention was drawn to Farren, one of the female Jaspers, who told him they hadn't seen any sign of the enemy during their fly over. Making his way to the group, and remaining alert to any presence of the enemy, Pointer thanked Farren for letting him know and then suggested she and her friends return to the King.

Having ridden some distance with no sign of the enemy, King Alfreston turned to Moff and asked, "I wonder why we haven't seen any enemy activity?"

"Like you, I feel they are at the Outlander border," replied Moff.

Suddenly the sound of stomping feet sounded in the distance. "I wonder how close they are," said Kestron.

"Not far, I would guess," replied Moff. "There will no doubt be many enemies, especially now Zanus had made up his mind to rule the land." Malla, one of the younger Ziphers, riding along with Moff, signed, "I will try to hear how far away they are." She was surprised to hear Kestron's voice in her thoughts.

"Thought two minds might be better than one, Malla. Have you discovered where they are?"

"Not yet, but they don't seem to be coming our way. I have picked up the sound of carts. Do you know what they use them for?"

"I'm afraid I do," Kestron replied. "They use them to carry their weaponry. I hope we will soon move on." Releasing their minds, Malla turned to King Alfreston and signed what she and Kestron had discovered.

Remembering how weapons had been used during other battles, Alfreston was aware of the damage and harm they could do. With a renewed feeling of energy, he was keen to get to the Outlanders as soon as possible. Suggesting they take a short rest, he urged them to be ready to ride out on his command.

King Alfreston asked Kerez, "Please give the animals a cloak of light invisibility to ensure they are well protected. If you look over there at the small copse, that would be a good place to make for." Kerez led Gazer and the other animals to the copse and laid a veil of invisibility over them.

King Alfreston sat beside Pointer and asked, "Well, Pointer, sense any enemy around?" Giving his full attention to the King, Pointer told him it was all clear at the moment, then went on to tell of his meeting with the rabbits.

"I hope they don't stop on the way home. You never know when danger will strike," the King commented. Feeling thirsty, Pointer leant over to Veber and asked, "Any chance of a drink and a morsel of food?" Signing, Veber replied, "I'll fetch you some, Pointer. We put your share separate."

Pointer sat looking round at the large group of people, wondering how many of his friends would return. Shaking off this thought, he noticed Bertram massaging his buttocks. "Lack of practice," explained Bertram with an embarrassed grin. "It's been some time since I last had to ride so hard."

"Same here, Bertram," commented Sam. Grinning at his companions, Sam asked Peter how he was coping. Drawn into the somewhat embarrassing conversation, Peter shyly replied, "I go riding quite a bit, so it's not so hard on my system."

"Don't worry, you'll soon have more to worry about than sore buttocks!" laughed Moff.

Peter took the opportunity to ask Moff, "Where did those birds go, the ones that were flying with Drewan?"

"You mean the warning birds," said Moff. "They will only fly so far, just to ensure it is clear of devil birds, then they will head back and report to the Queen." Concerned at the birds being on their own, Peter asked, "Will they be all right?" Moff gave Peter a reassuring nod. Turning his attention back to the group, Peter was surprised to see what was being signed. They wanted to know what he did in his land.

"I am a full time student at attend the local college close to the library, where I work part time with Penny and Lottie. Penny is a student as well; it's only Lottie who works there full time, with a lady called Ms Beckett."

"What's a college?" one of the group asked. "What's a library?" asked another. With a gentle laugh, Moff stated, "You've started something now young man, they won't be happy until you've explained it all to them."

"Quite right," Bertram added, "You'll need to tell all now,

Peter." Seeing a lot of faces waiting to hear what he had to say, Peter said, "I'll sign as I speak, it will be good for me to practise. If I go wrong, you will have to correct me." He was about to start when King Alfreston suggested, "I think before Peter continues, the telepaths should join their minds and try to contact Queen Matilda. I'd like to know if any of the other groups have been in contact." An instant silence fell over the group.

Peter was fascinated by seeing so many expressionless faces in place of the excited ones. Sensing his thoughts, Pointer tapped him on the arm and whispered, "Don't worry, Peter, they will have closed their minds to all other sounds and will concentrate on trying to reach Queen Matilda's or possibly Marmaduke's mind."

"I thought you were trying as well, Pointer?" Peter whispered.

"There are enough telepaths to get through, if it's possible. I am going to keep my senses free in case any enemy approach. I guess you will have to tell them later what a college and a library is," Pointer whispered.

"I don't mind, this task is much more important than what I do in my land," Peter whispered. Just then, they noticed Kestron was signing and whispering, "We're not having any joy getting through to Queen Matilda. I guess we are the wrong side of the hill and it's blocking our thoughts."

"That's what happened when Lucy tried to contact me," said Sam. "We weren't able to finish what we were saying. Everything went blank."

King Alfreston asked everyone to gather their animals and get ready to move on. Reminding everyone to stay alert, he asked the Ziphers, "Please use your hearing and report any sounds to me."

Now the animals were free of their covering and everyone was ready, the King signalled them to walk on. Noticing Drewan just ahead, Pointer ran to join him, fearful of what they were heading into. Peter suddenly noticed that Sam and Bertram were riding either side of him. Bertram leant towards Peter's horse and said, "Try not to worry too much, Peter. Keep your wits about you and your eyes open for attacks, and we'll come through this all right." Giving Bertram a faint smile, Peter wasn't sure what he meant, but he wasn't going to query it.

Riding hard, and with the ground still soft from the downpour, they appeared to be making good progress. Sam commented, "The one good thing about this soggy ground is it will keep the dust from giving us away."

With time short, King Alfreston decided to chance going through a small part of the wood and called Rouand and Drewan to tell them of his plan. They were alarmed at the idea.

"Are you sure, Your Majesty?" said Drewan. You know the Old Crone will know the moment someone has entered."

"We need to get to the border as quickly as possible," said the King. "Time is most important. If we take care going through a small part of the wood, we will reach the Outlanders much sooner." Not about to argue with the King's decision, Rouand asked, "Should I lead with the troops through first?"

"That would be a good idea. I'll ride alongside you. I am aware of the dangers of the wood, but we don't have a lot of choice."

Peter leaned towards Moff and asked, "Is this the horrible Forbidden Wood I have heard about?"

"This is no ordinary wood, Peter," said Moff. "I don't know what you have been told, but it's controlled by Imelda. Anyone who dares to enter does so at their peril."

"Is there anything I should look out for?"

"Watch out for the trees, they like to attack you with their spindly branches, and the vines. But I hope the unicorns will take care of them."

Just then Kestron rode up to him and said, "Keep your eyes open and stay close to me." Thanking Kestron, Peter asked Pinto to keep alongside Kerez. Picking up the tension in Peter, Pinto turned his head and whispered, "It is nasty in there Peter, but the unicorns will take care of us horses. I will keep close to Kerez and Kestron, so keep hold of the reins and we'll soon be through." Peter gave Pinto a gentle pat on the neck and thanked him.

King Alfreston joined Rouand at the front of the troops. "Let's hope we don't meet too much evil on our way," he said. Raising his arm, Rouand gave the signal to move on.

Kestron approached King Alfreston telepathically and asked, "Are you sure we should be going in the wood?"

"I need to get to the Outlanders soon or they will all be killed," replied the King. "I don't see any other way of getting to them. If we continue on our original route we will be too late. Please make sure everyone stays close together. Perhaps you would ride with Moff at the rear. I am aware we have others here who are new to the wood, but our task is too great for us to waste time."

With Peter now joining him, Kestron told Peter he was going to ride back to join Moff at the rear of the group. He felt Pinto walk a little faster to keep up with Kerez. Easing Kerez beside Moff's horse, Kestron asked, "Do you think this is wise?" Surprised to hear Kestron speak, Moff replied, "This must be really worrying you, it's not very often you speak."

"I am worried, Moff. Remember, we have a young lad here who doesn't know what can happen in this wood," Kestron stated. Realising they were falling behind, they urged their animals to ride on and catch up.

Listening to the conversation between Kestron and Moff, Kerez turned his head a fraction and asked, "I think we should make sure the creeping vines don't wrap their tendrils round the animal's feet. Gazer and I could send appropriate protection across the woodland floor in advance of us going in."

"That would be a good idea, Kerez" said Kestron. "With a bit of luck we won't suffer too much. If the vines do become thick and strong it might mean you and Gazer will have to repeat the treatment to get rid of them."

Suggesting Peter stay with Moff, Kestron left Kerez to make his way across to Gazer. Coming alongside the other unicorn, Kerez told him what Kestron and he had been discussing. When King Alfreston heard this he urged Gazer to do whatever needed to be done.

Approaching the wood, the unicorns stopped. Peter, having seen Bertram making his way over, whispered to him, "What's happening?"

"Not sure yet, but I'm sure we will soon find out," said Bertram

Just then, Sam attracted Peter's attention and pointed. Before he could stop himself, Peter shouted, "Wow, where did those blue flashes come from?" Sam warned him not to call out. Whispering his apologies, Peter sat quietly watching the unicorns complete their task.

With so many people to get through the wood, King Alfreston asked everyone to be ready once the unicorns had finished. Fearful of Imelda sensing their presence, he was relieved to hear Gazer say, "The ground is free. If everyone is ready we should move on before the vines repair their tendrils." The King gave the order for everyone to move on.

The wood gave each rider a sense of foreboding. They knew it was waiting for them. The branches soon began reaching out to scratch the faces and arms of the intruders, leaving red weals wherever they made contact.

Trying to ignore what the branches were doing, Peter had become alarmed at the blackness facing them ahead. Noticing Kestron was close to the King, he asked Pinto to take him closer to Sam and Bertram. With only the sound of sound of crushed leaves beneath the animals' feet, they wasted no time in moving deeper into the black wood.

Alfreston glanced back from time to time to make sure everyone was keeping up. He could now see vines noiselessly creeping along the ground. Gazer assured him Kerez had already warned him what was happening.

"We are holding off from dealing with it at the moment," he said. "We fear it will alert you-know-who to our presence."

"Don't let them get too thick and strong, or they will stop the animals," King Alfreston whispered.

Kerez noticed that in the distance the change the King had feared was taking place. Seeing how thick and dense the vines had become, he carefully gained Gazer's attention. Gazer waited for Kerez to give the word that would enable to stop the vines from reaching them. Then they threw blue flashes across the ground. As the flashes burned the vines, they screeched in pain.

Aware that Imelda would now be alert to someone being in her wood, King Alfreston and Drewan urged the friends to ride hard and as fast as they could. Startled at what was happening, Peter suddenly realised Moff had joined them.

"Keep going everyone, and don't stop for anything," warned Moff. Making sure Malla was holding on tight, he looked across to check Farren was OK. Keeping pace with Moff, and seeing Sam and Bertram just behind, gave Peter the courage to continue.

Just when they thought they thought they had escaped the attention of Imelda, they heard her cackling voice echo round about them. "Who dares to enter me wood? Attack me trees and me creepers would yer? Me beauties will make yer all suffer. Yer bones will give a tasty meal. Be warned, me beauties will eat well this day." Halted in their tracks, they feared she would appear before them. For some reason Peter felt the wood had become darker than when they entered. "Sam, do you think it's darker now?" he said.

"I was just thinking that myself," replied Sam in a low voice. Now the atmosphere surrounding them seemed to change. Shocked at how dense the vines had become, they were aware that something else was happening. Their minds were being drawn into a hypnotic state. They seemed unable to take their eyes off the vines, which were closing quickly upon them.

Pointer, not affected by what was happening, wondered at first why the group weren't attacking the vines. Then, noticing the stillness of their bodies and the glazed look in their eyes, he knew what it was. Having seen this before, he knew he had to bring them out of this as quickly as possible.

He tried barking, but that didn't work. The next thing was to try and rouse the unicorns. Approaching Gazer, he raised a front paw and began stroking the unicorn's nose. There wasn't a flicker of recognition. Next he moved across to Kerez, with the same result.

Pointer was beginning to panic, wondering how he was going to bring his friends round. Then he tried Deena. "Can you hear me, Deena?" he asked. At first there was no response, but then he noticed a flicker of movement.

"Deena, Deena!" he called, "Can you hear me?" At last he heard a faint murmur in response. He began pawing her arm and calling her name. "Deena, please free your mind to everything other than my voice," he urged. Sensing her struggling to do what he asked, Pointer urged, "Keep trying, Deena. You are almost free of whatever trapped your mind." After what seemed an eternity to Pointer, he was rewarded with a smile from Deena and a croaky voice asking, "What's happened to me?"

"Deena, I need help in bringing the others round," said Pointer. "Would you fly from one to the other and keep calling their names until they answer? I will do the same with the animals. Take care though, I know this is the work of the Old Crone."

"I will do that. I'm not very strong but I will do what you ask," Deena assured him. As Deena began her mission, Pointer set about working on the unicorns. Taking longer that he'd hoped, he finally achieved his goal. As the unicorns shook their heads to free their minds, they each asked the same question, "What happened?" When Pointer explained, he asked the unicorns to take control of attacking the vines, which by this time were so close that some of the tendrils had started to wind round the animal's legs.

As Pinto came round, he asked Pointer, "Was this something to do with the Old Crone?"

"It was, but hopefully Deena has managed to bring round the other people," said Pointer.

Suddenly the voice of King Alfreston shouted, "How did that happen? Where did the time go?" Pointer explained. "This is the work of the Old Crone. She managed to hypnotise you and the animals. However, there is something in my system that prevented the same happening to me. She didn't keep you under long enough to do any real harm, but she will know she has lost her power over you. We must all be extra alert to anything that will occur."

Shocked by what they'd heard, Sam asked, "What do you think she will do?"

"I don't know, but it will be something malicious," Pointer replied.

"The vines are under control," said Gazer. "They are too dense to destroy completely. May I suggest we move on?"

"Good idea, Gazer," said Alfreston. Let's move quickly out of here." Turning to the animals, he added, "We trust you to take us out us here as quickly as you can. Take care not to trip on any stray undergrowth."

With a murmur of agreement, the animals started on their way. Peter, moving closer to Kestron asked, "Have you had that happen to you before?"

"No, and I don't want it happening again," Kestron signed. Reading his response, Peter acknowledged he understood. Then Rouand let them know they were near to the end of the wood. Comforted by the news, the animals didn't need to be asked they increased their walk to a trot. But just then they heard an ear-splitting howl.

"Trofalogues!" shouted a voice. King Alfreston ordered them to draw arms and prepare to fight off the devils. Taking up the sword Moff had given him on leaving the castle, Peter wondered what kind of creature a trofalogue was.

He soon found out. A pack of the weirdest animals were charging towards them. Terrified, Peter lunged out at one of the creatures as it tried to leap onto his horse. Pinto kicked out with a hind leg, sending the trofalogue howling.

Catching a glimpse of the fear on Peter's face, Pinto whispered, "We'll soon disperse these beasts, Peter. Just be ready with your sword."

"Thank you," whispered, Peter, seeing a pack of snarling animals close by. He lashed out with his sword, not caring where the blade fell as long as he was able to prevent the creature from harming him or Pinto.

The stench the creatures emitted did not stop the group from displaying great bravery and fortitude. Some were luckier than others; some of those at the back sustained terrible bites on their legs and arms. Their fear that they would not be able to keep up with the others was picked up by the telepaths. Drewan turned his horse round and made his way back to where the injured were. "How injured are you?" he asked.

"Some worse than others I'm afraid, Drewan," one of the injured stated.

"You can't stay here or you know what will happen. We need to get you out of here along with the others, so please try and hold on." Alarmed at their riders being so badly injured, one of the horses said, "Hold on tight to the reins, we'll get you out no matter what happens." Drewan led the way back to where the others were still fighting off the trofalogues.

They suddenly noticed that the trofalogues were no longer attacking. King Alfreston took a deep breath and suggested, "Be aware this could be another one of her tricks." Now there was only an eerie silence.

"I wonder why they vanished like that. There's some weird goings on here," stated Sam.

"Whatever it was, I don't think we've seen the last of them. We will need to ride hard and fast to get free of the wood," Drewan told them. He turned his attention to the rest of the group and commanded the animals to set off for the end of the wood. They made good progress. With the edge of the wood now very close, they galloped as fast as they could, still trying to avoid the crawling tendrils of the vines.

They were only a short way from the end of the wood when they were suddenly aware that they had not seen the last of Imelda's tricks. Barring their way were a crowd of disfigured zombies, moaning threateningly at them.

Moff had seen these strange beings before. "These poor figures are her failures," he explained. "She uses them to prevent anyone from escaping from the wood." Sympathy for the zombies didn't take away the fear they created as they stood across their pathway. In an attempt to confuse them, Drewan suggested they split into two groups and made their way round them. Unfortunately, each time a member of either group moved it seemed as if the zombies knew in advance what they doing and beat them to it.

Realising they were in need of assistance, Kestron and Moff joined minds and called out to the thoughts of any telepath who could hear them. On their third attempt they were delighted to hear Letswick respond.

"Hi, Letswick, it's Kestron and Moff," replied Kestron. "We're in a spot of trouble. We were about to exit the wood when a crowd of zombies decided to stand in the way."

"Could you ask our friend to send a bit of help," added Moff. "We're so close to reaching the Outlanders. We don't want to waste time here with these sorry creatures." Understanding the gravity of their situation, Letswick made a short reply. "I will. We are on our way."

Beauty, having heard the request, wasted no time in reaching her friends the sabre-tooth tigers and explaining what had happened. Manga and the other tigers flew swiftly to the aid of the group. Aware that Imelda would be delighted to capture one of them for experiments, they were very wary of approaching the wood without a form of protection. Using their special scent glands, they matched their own scent to that of her trofalogues.

On arriving at the wood the tigers could see where King Alfreston was and where the zombies were, but they did not realise the consternation the trofalogue scent was causing to the group below. Thinking Imelda had created a new breed of flying trofalogues, King Alfreston told his group to be prepared to fight off the offending creatures.

"Don't fire Moff!" said Manga telepathically. "It's me, Manga, with some of my trusty friends. We have come to offer support at the request of a special friend." Anxious to prevent the tigers from being harmed, Moff called out, "Please lower your weapons and concentrate on the enemy on the ground. We have friends here to help."

"Is that right, Moff? Friends have arrived to help us?" called out King Alfreston. But Moff concentrated on watching the tigers descending close to the zombies.

At first it appeared to the onlookers that the zombies were untroubled by the presence of the tigers. Then, as if hypnotised, they slowly turned round to face them. The onlookers realised this would be the right time to make their escape. They were soon past.

Watching the battle between the zombies and the tigers, it was quite clear to the onlookers the tigers were winning. But now they heard the screeching voice of Imelda echo round the wood.

"Attack an' kill, me beauties!" she howled. "Kill 'em all, you zombie idiots. Kill 'em an' bring their bodies back 'ere."

Imelda's orders seemed to put new life into the zombies. But they could only lash out randomly with their arms, failing to injure the tigers. As Imelda's voice faded, Sam turned to Bertram and whispered, "I'll be glad to be out of this evil wood."

Grinning at Sam, Bertram replied, "Not just your nerves, Sam, I think I can safely say she does that to all who dare to enter her wood."

"Shouldn't we call the tigers off?" said Peter. "I know these poor creatures are our enemy, but wouldn't it be right to let them go?" But then he realised that the zombies had indeed disappeared, leaving the tigers in control.

Satisfied they'd completed their task, Manga said, "We'll take ourselves off now, Moff. If we are needed again please let our friend know and we will return. See you again everyone. Take care." Then the tigers soared into the sky and disappeared into the clouds, just as King Alfreston called out, "Thank you for your help."

With the tigers now out of sight, he turned to his companions and urged them to take this moment to ride out of the wood. The group followed his orders without delay.

"Hold tight, Peter," said Pinto. Peter stood up in the stirrups and looked to see where Sam and Bertram were. Catching sight of them not too far ahead, he asked Pinto, "Would you mind taking me to join Sam and Bertram?"

"Hold on. At least we don't have to rush this time," Pinto replied. Coming alongside the two men, Peter asked, "Have you ever seen anything like that? At one stage I wondered if we should all run for our lives, or just keep swiping out with our swords."

Giving Peter a lop-sided smile, Sam replied, "We wouldn't have got very far if we'd tried to run. However, you did the right thing, hitting out at anything that attacked."

"You were very brave back there," said Bertram, "But the battle we are heading for is going to be a lot harder. Just keep your feet on the ground and the sword in your hand, and as Sam said, strike anything that attacks."

Settling down to continue on their way, Kestron surprised Peter by tapping on his arm and signing, "Some scary moments, eh young man?" Releasing the reins, Peter signed, "Hi Kestron, I wondered where you were. I don't think I want a repeat of what just happened." Riding beside Kestron, Peter felt how lucky he was to have friends like these.

After discussions with Drewan and Rouand, King Alfreston told the remainder of the group they were going to set off for the last part of the journey. Aware they still had a way to go, the animals paced themselves while their riders were keeping an eye out for any approaching enemy.

Peter whispered in Pinto's ear, "Where did those zombies go?" Half turning to Peter, Pinto replied, "Back to Imelda. She will have other uses for them."

Chapter Twenty Four

The Battle at the Barricades

As they rode on, they began to see a strange dust cloud approaching. Fearing it was enemy troopers, Rouand warned, "This could be more Zanuthians, coming as reinforcements to Zanus." Straining to try and make out what was causing the dust clouds, Drewan decided to ride on ahead.

At last Drewan reappeared, eager to tell his news.

"As we feared, it is more reinforcements," he told the group. "There must be hundreds of Zanuthians and Gorgonians. They are heavily laden with weaponry that will knock the barricade to pieces." He refrained from mentioning the damage the weapons would do to people.

They discussed how best to approach the barricade. Aware they would have to go through the courtyard, Drewan told them, "We need to make sure the gates are open. I think this is where the telepaths could help." Turning to the telepaths he asked, "Would you try and contact your friends in the courtyard and ask if they will make sure they are ready to open the gates?"

"Our animals must be hidden. Imelda would dearly love to get her hands on the unicorns," Kestron signed. King Alfreston turned to Gazer and stated, "That will be something you and Kerez could take care of. Make sure all the animals are well protected."

"Will do, your Majesty, just give the word," replied Gazer and Kerez with one voice.

"Knowing there is an army of reinforcements coming to Zanus, it's important we find out what weaponry the

Outlanders have," said the King. Looking round the group, he added, "That I will leave to Rouand and Bertram. The rest of us will place ourselves strategically where most support is needed." Turning his attention to the archers, he added, "Archers, you will place yourselves around the balustrade and be ready to fire on my order."

Acknowledging the roles that had been placed on them, they were not surprised when King Alfreston said, "Now, I suggest we move on. The Outlanders will not be able to stop the Zanuthians from breaking through."

Peter felt a moment of uncertainty. Never having been in a fight, he was concerned at letting his new friends down. He glanced across at Sam and Bertram, wishing he could be as confident as they looked. Moff, picking up on Peter's concerns, made his way over to try and reassure him.

"Try not to be too afraid, Peter. There will be many of us, but as yet we don't know the full extent of Zanus' army. Just remember, these are brutal and ruthless men, so don't hesitate in taking a life. They won't hesitate to take yours."

Breathing hard and trying to calm down, Peter had offered his help and he wasn't one to go back on his word. "Thank you, Moff. I feel ready now, I won't let you down," replied Peter, worried that his voice gave away his nervousness.

"I know you won't, young Peter. Protect yourself well, and take down as many of the enemy as you can."

* * * *

Alerted to the arrival of the King and his helpers, the sentries on guard duty were quick to tell the gatekeepers to watch for the signal before opening the gates. Relieved to hear who was approaching, they waited anxiously until the signal came. Then, still wary of any possible nearby enemy, they removed the large baton that had been placed across the huge gates. Pulling on them, they opened them just far enough to see the arrival of their friends. As they came closer, the keepers swung the gates full open.

With greetings over, the group set about their appointed

tasks. After being introduced to Vical and Petrona, Rancouins in charge of the armoury, Rouand and Bertram went with them to take stock of what was there. They were shocked at the onslaught these people had suffered.

"Have all your homes been destroyed?" asked Bertram. Petrona replied, "I'm not sure. We came from Hesslewick some time ago, when these villagers were first attacked. What about you? It couldn't have been a pleasant journey here."

"It could have been better, just a few scary moments," said Rouand. Smiling at the two faces looking at him he went on, "I suggest we find out what weapons you have here." Rouand and Bertram noticed the pride these people showed in the weaponry they'd accumulated.

"We have made plenty of arrows and spears," murmured one of the people. "With help from Vical and Petrona we have prepared some buckets of tar. We can't wait for the opportunity to pour it over them devils." They set about quietly placing the various weapons ready for action.

Pointer had gone with the horses and unicorns to find a secure place for them to hide. The shimmering protection from the unicorns made it easier for the animals to follow Pointer. Gazer turned to Pointer and said, "When we are needed, please let us know." Assuring Gazer he would do that, Pointer made his way back to join the others.

As he walked the short distance to where the King was standing, Pointer couldn't help noticing the destruction that had already taken place. Sad that many of his friends weren't around, he wondered how many more of them he would lose in the forthcoming battle. Reaching the King, Pointer let him know the animals were secure. Not knowing how much time they had, Sam set off to gather a number of men, women and children and set about repairing the worst parts of the barricade.

Making light of it, so the children wouldn't be any more frightened than they already were, Sam said, "We don't want those bullies coming in and stealing our food, do we?" A chorus of young voices responded, "No we don't. We don't have much for ourselves." The children set about gathering anything that would help secure the barricade, and it was eventually restored to almost new.

Just then they were shocked to hear the coarse voice of Zanus call out, "Get all the weapons 'ere!" Sam and his friends looked nervously at each other, but didn't feel they needed to say a word. Having suffered at the hands of Zanus and Sizan previously, they knew it wouldn't be long before Zanus ordered an attack.

Curiosity got the better of Peter, and he glanced over the balustrade. He was not prepared for the sight before him. Shocked to see so many huge, malformed beasts, he saw that some of them were pulling great carts behind them. Although he had never having seen anything like this before, he knew what destruction such weapons could do. He had read about them in books at the library, but the books had not prepared him for the enormous size of these weapons.

Peter turned to see if his friends on the balustrade had seen the same. It was obvious from their expressions that they had. Feeling a moment of panic, he recalled what Moff had told him earlier: 'Arm yourself well and don't be afraid to kill as many of the enemy as you can.'

Turning his attention to the other side of the barricade, Peter now saw that the enemy were dragging ladders behind them. Aware of what was intended, he tugged at Moff's arm and pointed. By this time, Moff had been alerted by the telepaths to what Peter had seen, and asked them to make sure their friends were aware also.

Meanwhile, King Alfreston had checked with the archers and told them to be ready when he gave the signal. Pleased to see his archers had been joined by many other friends, he could see that everyone was now on full alert. The people down in the courtyard were just as prepared. Busy filling the buckets with tar, they then placed them on carts ready to be taken to the firing points. This left the children busy running to and fro with bundles of arrows and other weapons.

The scene brought back memories of David and Jayne being recaptured. This in turn gave them the courage and energy to continue. After several carts of tar had reached their destinations, Bertram noticed some of the children watching with wide scared eyes. "We don't want the enemy to think we've only a small supply," Bertram said, as he turned to remove buckets of tar off the cart. "How many more buckets are there?" Being told there were another two cartloads, Bertram said, "Come on Rouand, if we go back with these carts we can soon load the buckets."

Amused at the number of folk that had joined them, Rouand replied, "Right, with everyone here, we'll soon load this cart," They wasted no time in stacking the buckets on the cart. Bertram's respect for these people increased as they worked diligently, two to a bucket and making sure nothing got spilled.

While this was taking place, there was much activity taking place in the courtyard. Many Outlanders had been busy arranging makeshift fires, on which they placed the buckets of tar. Seated by a crumbled dwelling, a number of children and older folk were busy sharpening arrowheads. Once completed, they were placed against the wall ready for delivery wherever they were needed.

Peter couldn't believe how quickly everything seemed to be done. Keeping an eye open for any stray ladders being positioned, his fears had been replaced by anxious waiting. Kestron, who had been silently standing close by, gave Peter a tug on his arm and signed, "We all share the work, especially when it comes to fighting off these brutes." Realising Kestron must have read his thoughts, Peter felt a little embarrassed and thought he owed him an explanation.

"That is what happens most of the time in my land. Not fighting off brutes like these, but helping with different things," he said.

"I know what you mean," said Kestron.

Surprised to hear him speak, Peter asked, "Why don't you speak all the time?" Grinning, Kestron signed, "What would I do with my hands if I didn't sign?" Peter gave him a wry smile and turned his attention back to the other side of the barricade, just as Drewan made his way to join them.

"I thought I would come and see what was happening up here," said Drewan. At that moment, a flock of spy birds flew over the balustrade, to be quickly fired on by the archers. Zanus now called on several of his troopers to attack the barricade. The defenders, fearing they wouldn't survive this attack, were prepared to give everything they had. Sensing this, Moff and Kestron made a point of walking round the balustrade to bring calm back to the people.

"Remember, we don't want to be ruled by him and his cronies," said Moff. "Make every arrow and lance count."

Somewhat assured by those calming words, the defenders stood tall ready for the onslaught. Having given the archers the signal to fire at will, the folk on the ground had been busy helping Bertram and Rouand to fling the buckets of tar over the barricade and onto the enemy below. In another part of the barricade, a number of folk had armed themselves with lances and were busy defending the area where the injured had been placed. The battle continued, leaving many injured and dead on both sides. Amid the sorrow of seeing their friends dead and injured, the defenders' excitement grew as they saw many of the enemy creatures fall from the sky.

* * * *

Meanwhile DaVendall and an army of Outlanders were well on their way to the King. Periodically DaVendall would try to reach the minds of the telepaths. Now he encouraged them to urge their animals on. It wasn't long before the people recognised where they were. Knowing their destination was close at hand, they suddenly became aware of a foreboding presence, and they knew who it must be. Gamlon felt certain Imelda would make her presence known when they least expected it.

It was a relief when the pouring rain which had accompanied them for most of the way began to ease off. Being wet through did nothing to deter their eagerness to reach King Alfreston. Before they knew it they were engulfed in a grey mist.

"We need to be aware that our presence has been noticed, just as we sensed her," said Alfreston. "We must be very near our destination for her to try and halt us now." Having had a similar thought himself Gamlon replied, "I wonder what devilry she will create against us."

"That, my friend, is something I have no doubt we will soon find out," DaVendall responded in a thoughtful voice. Moving closer together, they kept a wary eye on the mist. Then Gamlon pointed to a flock of Zanus' spy birds overhead. At first, they feared they were about to attack, but then their attention was turned to the larger birds flying after them, and their huge wingspan and long pointed beaks. Watching as they flew overhead, they were shocked to see the larger birds staring at them through dark eyes. Benin suddenly shouted, "Them's like the creatures that killed our parents."

The voice of Gressard added, "The lad's right. These creatures are like the ones who attacked our fallen friends."

"We know who created these, don't we?" said Gamlon. "I think we should do something about these vultures before they start attacking any more of our friends. They are known by some of the Outlanders as creatures of the damned."

"That's indeed what they are. Now let's see if we can't get rid of a few. If we join our powers together, I'll ask Cedar to deal with the spy birds. It will take a lot of our energy to deal with those other creatures," DaVendall replied. As he lifted his cane above his head, Cedar whispered, "I'm ready when you are. Just say the word." Then DaVendall hissed "Now!"

DaVendall rose in the air and released Gamlon from his cane. Attacking the larger birds by throwing energy bolts from his fingers, DaVendall was soon joined by Cedar, who threw lightning bolts at the spy birds. Taking a quick look to see if Gamlon was all right, DaVendall saw the glint of Gamlon's blade as he brought it down on another bird.

Squawking in terror as the lightning bolts caught them, many of the birds tried in vain to avoid the attack. Unable to cope with the onslaught from DaVendall and Gamlon, the larger birds turned and flew off, to where DaVendall did not know. The repercussions would no doubt be cruel and bitter, but that was something they would have to face later. Their immediate attention was on the enemy.

With the mist still hanging over them, Rowena thought she saw a flash of light. "What was that?" called out Rowena. Dylan, having seen flashes like these before, drew alongside her and said, "Nothing to worry about, Rowena. Where those spy birds went I'm not sure, but I wouldn't mind betting they've gone to alert Zanus of our presence."

Shocked by the sight of so many birds on the ground, Rowena thanked Dylan for the explanation then went on to say, "If they have gone to Zanus it won't be long before he sends his bullies to deal with us."

"That's what concerns me too. We'll just have to be extra alert," replied Dylan. Rowena suddenly grabbed Dylan's arm and whispered, "Did you hear that voice?"

"I did, but I'm not going to think about her, she has a habit of appearing if you give her too much thought," Dylan whispered. Suddenly the mist seemed to disperse as quickly as it came. Taking his opportunity, DaVendall urged everyone to ride hard and fast.

* * * *

With the battle becoming more intense and the rain easing off, King Alfreston couldn't help thinking that without help, Zanus could soon achieve what he wanted - control of Dofstram. But he knew everyone would give their all before that happened.

Standing on the balustrade, he looked down to see Zanus and Sizan retreating and drawing their troopers back with them. Convinced they would be preparing for another attack, he looked to see what was happening beyond. Not able to see clearly what it was, at first he thought it was a mirage. The came a flash of light, quickly followed by another. He knew this wasn't lightning.

"Did you see those flashes, Bertram?" he asked, Bertram turned his attention to where the King was pointing.

"I thought I saw something but can't make it out. Is it possible it could be DaVendall?"

"It must be him, who else could send out such bright flashes? If it is, I should be able to break through to his thoughts. Would you stand cover?"

As he concentrated on reaching DaVendall's mind, it wasn't long before King Alfreston was greeted warmly by DaVendall. Fearing Imelda would pick up their thoughts, he went on to explain, "Can't stop for long, my friend. We've had a bit of spy problem. No names, but we will soon be with you." Then in a more serious tone he told DaVendall how desperately they needed help. "I saw the flashes of light and hoped it was you," King Alfreston said. They released their minds just as Gamlon uttered, "Sounds as if we've arrived in time."

"It sure does, Gamlon. That means we need to get moving," DaVendall replied. Delighted to know he and his friends were close, the King quickly passed the good news along. With the enemy's constant attack, they were relieved to know help was close at hand.

Entering a valley between two large hills, DaVendall halted the group. Pacing to and fro, Gamlon remained silent, aware that DaVendall was planning the best line of attack. He began strategically placing the army of people ready for attack. Waiting for the appropriate signal, they armed themselves ready.

With volleys of arrows pouring down on their friends at the barricade, DaVendall's attention was brought to the carts being pulled along by huge creatures, the like of which many had never seen before. Checking everyone was armed and ready, DaVendall shouted, "Attack, attack!"

The group began to gallop as fast as their animals could carry them and were soon upon the enemy. Releasing Gamlon from the cane, DaVendall told him "Time to do battle my friend. Do what you need to do to stay safe." Encouraged by the sight of DaVendall and the Outlanders attacking the enemy from the rear, the King gave the order for the archers to fire.

As friend and foe mingled in desperate battle, the voice of Zanus could be heard shouting, "Kill! Kill all! Leave DaVendall, he's mine." Continuing to battle on, a group of his troopers ran towards the barricade, intent on capturing the King. The sound of horses squelching in the mud soon reached the ears of the defenders at the barricade. Fearing it was the enemy, they were armed and prepared to fight them off. That was when Bertram called out, "Look, its DaVendall, and our friends behind him!"

Battling their way through the enemy, they fought hard, killing and maiming as many as they could. Sadly the losses didn't apply to the enemy alone; many of their friends had also lost their lives. Quick to notice what was happening to his friends, King Alfreston ordered the archers to fire their arrows in the direction of the enemy. Turning his attention to the gates, he then sent Deena down to tell the guards to open them on his order.

On the battleground it was fast becoming a bloodbath. A mass of fallen bodies, enemy and friend, fought close together, each determined to kill the other. More and more bodies were piling up on the ground, along with those who had been badly injured.

Gamlon, having been removed from DaVendall's cane, went in search of his own enemy to dispose of. Flying through the air, he avoided the flying arrows and lances as he made his way to where he had seen a group of Zanuthians making their way in DaVendall's direction. Flying back to DaVendall, he noticed he had not escaped injury. One of the enemy managed to spear DaVendall's thigh, and laughed thinking he had finished him off. As he rode off gloating at what he had achieved, it hadn't occurred to this trooper to check DaVendall was dead.

Gamlon, seeing DaVendall slumped over the saddle, asked Cedar to make his way to the gates. Noticing how injured DaVendall was, Dylan called out to the riders, "Make for the gates." He was relieved to see his friends following DaVendall. Fighting off the enemy as they went, it wasn't long before they were near to the gates.

The people on the balustrade couldn't wait to greet their friends. Some of the defenders noticed that DaVendall had been injured. Failing to capture any of his enemy, Zanus had demanded all weapons be aimed at DaVendall. Ordering Sizan and his Gorgonians to break down the barricade, he called for his spy birds to attack from the above.

At that moment there was a warning shout from someone on the balustrade - "Take cover, demon birds!" Calling on the archers to fire at the birds, King Alfreston turned his attention to the people in the courtyard. Whilst admiring the courageous way they were fighting, he was aware many of his friends would not survive. He looked to see how far DaVendall and his group were from entering the courtyard. Seeing how near to the gates they were, he noticed that many of the enemy were closing in on them. Without delay, he gave the order for the gates to be opened. Then Dylan shouted for everyone to make for the courtyard.

By this time many of the folk in the courtyard had armed themselves and were fighting off any enemy. Keen to close the gates as soon as possible, they were relieved when the last person entered. The guards on gate duty quickly closed the gates again and secured them with heavy bars.

Pointer had also made his way to join DaVendall, stopping in his tracks when he saw DaVendall's injury. Gamlon came across and explained what had happened. Then Moff and Bertram came across to join them. "I thought a little help was needed," Moff said kindly.

"We ought to help DaVendall off Cedar first," Bertram stated quietly. Kneeling down, Cedar was keen to do his bit to help DaVendall. Easing him out of the saddle, he was concerned that DaVendall had lost consciousness. Placing him gently on the ground, Pointer made his way to Cedar and said, "Perhaps you would like to take the animals over to the stable. I will let you know how DaVendall is. The folk at the stable are ready and waiting to feed the animals and give them a well-earned rest."

At first Cedar was reluctant to leave DaVendall, but after an assurance from Moff that he would be well cared for, he rounded up the unicorns and horses and led them to the stables.

While this had taken place on the ground, Sam had been fighting off the enemy alongside Peter and Farren, on the balustrade. "Right people, this is the time to vent your anger," stated Sam. Wondering how much worse it could get, Peter had secretly feared this moment, but now it was here he was ready. Catching Sam and Drewan looking in his direction, he was nearly caught by one of the Gorgonians who had managed to silently climb up a nearby ladder. Turning round, Peter raised the sword and aimed it directly at the stomach of the enemy. He was rewarded with an ear-piercing scream as the Gorgonian fell to the ground.

"Well done there, Peter," called the King. "Keep it up, we want to make it safe for everyone to get settled." Keen to make sure Peter remained as safe as possible, Pointer made his way to Peter and placed himself in a position to bite any trespassing leg that came over the turret. Amused by the way Pointer was handling the enemy, Peter and Farren continued to deal with any trooper who tried to get over the balustrade.

* * * *

As he came round, DaVendall was surprised to see he was sitting on a bed of straw in one of the stables. Assured by friendly voices that he was safe now, he drew on his strength to give them a warm smile. Wanting to speak to the King, he tried to get up off the floor but fell back. Moff and Rouand gently helped him back on to his feet. Taking a deep breath, DaVendall fought off the pain and listened to what Moff was saying. Learning of the events that had taken place through the wood and the welcome arrival of the sabre-tooth tigers, he was relieved to hear that most of King Alfreston's group had come through alive.

Gamlon quietly asked, "Does that mean our other friends are safe?"

"It does, but that's not all," said Deena, "We have managed to reach Letswick and his friends. They reckon they are about half a day's ride away." With delight and relief showing on his face, DaVendall whispered, "Well done." Standing and getting his bearings, DaVendall glanced down at Gamlon as if to reassure his trusty friend he was all right.

"Are you ready to walk?" Gamlon whispered.

Desperate to speak to the King, DaVendall replied, "I'm fine, Gamlon. But we have a battle to fight and I must speak to Alfreston." Following behind DaVendall, Moff noticed everyone was busy relaying their experiences. He knew the most important thing would be knowing their families were safe.

Seeing DaVendall approaching, King Alfreston went towards him and clasped him in his arms. "It's so good to see you, my friend. I hope you're wounds have been treated?" DaVendall confirmed that they had

"We have suffered many attacks," said the King. "Thankfully we have managed to keep them out." Recalling the grotesque creatures they had seen, he added, "A little before you arrived we were attacked by some weird creatures. If you look in the distance you might just be able to see them. Then of course there are the inevitable spy birds."

No sooner had he said those words than a flock of spy birds flew up from nowhere and hovered close to the barricade. The defenders were quick to see that these weren't just spy birds; they were the terrible vulture-like birds. Without waiting for orders to attack, Gamlon joined the archers as they sent out a volley of arrows. Flying over the balustrade, Gamlon attacked every bird within reach. He was delighted to have the opportunity to do something constructive and wasted no time in bringing down his blade on many of the birds, while being careful not to be hit by a stray arrow.

Below he saw enemy troopers lined up and ready to charge. Making his way back to DaVendall he told him, "Those birds must have been sent as a diversion. If you look over there, there are enemy forces approaching the other side of the barricade, leaving that line of troopers to attack this part." Trying not to show the pain he was feeling, DaVendall removed his hand from the King's grasp. Taking a look round the barricade, he noticed the balustrade was lined with well-armed people, including many of the womenfolk.

At that moment their attention was drawn to the sound of approaching enemy troops. As the stomping feet came closer, they were horrified to see leading the charge a pack of trofalogues, snarling and growling as they bared their cruel fangs. From nowhere, the shrill voice of Imelda screeched through the air, bringing Zanus and his army to a halt. Aiming her threat at the King and the defenders she screeched, "So, yer think yer've won? Yer've 'armed some of me creatures. I know why yer 'ere and I know yer'll not succeed."

Knowing this would have unsettled the defenders, King Alfreston shouted, "Ignore her threats, and keep your eye on the enemy." Looking round at each other, the defenders could see their own fears coming back at them.

Ordering his troopers to attack, Zanus shouted, "Alfreston is mine!" Wielding their armour, they galloped to the barricade. On another side of the barricade, Sizan was following the trofalogues, ready to destroy the barricade.

Following the troopers, Zanus broke away from the group and made his way to where the trofalogues had managed to tear down a small part of the barricade. Having left his horse just far enough away not to be detected, he crept stealthily along the bottom of the barricade. Keeping an eye open for anyone seeing him, he stayed low to the ground and stepped inside the barricade. Still unnoticed, he clung to the side of the barricade and made his way to the balustrade steps. Hiding under the steps, he looked round to see where the King was. With hatred overriding any other thought, he eased himself away from the cover of the steps and raced to where King Alfreston was standing.

Having been to check on the people in the courtyard, King Alfreston was unaware he was about to be attacked. Holding his sword above his head, Zanus roared, "Time to die, Alfreston!" But just as he was about to plunge his sword into the King's back he was halted by a horde of descending spectres. Screaming at them to get out of his way, he became even more irate when they stood between him and the King.

Hearing the screams from Zanus, Sizan ordered the trofalogues to tear down the barricade. Frantically tearing away at it, the troopers shouted to let Zanus know they were coming. They slew many of the defenders, who in turn were killing and maiming the trofalogues and troopers. There were screams of chaos in the courtyard.

The troopers were shocked to realise what had prevented Zanus from killing King Alfreston. "Spectres! Look out fer the spectres!" a trooper shouted.

Alarmed to see how close Zanus had got to the King, many defenders left their posts to fight off the enemy and to stop them from getting to the King. With so much blood from friend and enemy alike, it wasn't long before the ground had become a muddy bloodbath. Overcome by so many defenders, Zanus decided he would have to wait for another moment and shouted for his troopers to follow him. The defenders whooped with joy when they saw Zanus and his troopers retreating.

Shocked by what had happened, King Alfreston wondered how the spectres had known he needed help. He was surprised when they told him "A friend asked us to drop in." Giving a wry smile, King Alfreston thanked them warmly.

Many of the defenders had gathered around the King, wanting to know if he had been injured. Assuring his friends he was all right, he turned to the spectres and suggested they return to their own land. Then he wished them a safe journey home.

In the shock and horror of what had happened, the defenders were surprised to hear the sound of trofalogues snarling close by. Forgetting Sizan was still on the other side of the barricade, DaVendall called out, "Stand your ground my friends, and then let them have everything you've got. Aim for their necks or eyes."

King Alfreston made his way to the balustrade. Pointer, looking straight at him, wasn't surprised to see him standing tall and bold with his sword ready in hand. He was, however, surprised to hear him say, "Just the thing, DaVendall. Now we need the archers to prepare their bows and leave them to take care of anything in the sky." Turning to Pointer, he asked "Can you get a message to a certain friend? We could do with a little of our own magic".

* * * *

About to concentrate on drawing Letswick's attention, Pointer was surprised to hear his voice enter his mind. "Hi old fella, would you tell the King we're not too far away? Be with you shortly," Letswick said. Pointer was so delighted to hear his friend's voice that he was unable to answer for a moment. Shaking his head, Pointer said, "It's funny you should enter my thoughts just now; the King said we could do with a bit of magic in beating the enemy back."

Alarmed that things were worse than he thought, Letswick asked cautiously, "What's up, Pointer?" Pointer told him what happened. Turning to defend himself against an intruder, he then turned to the King and told him their other friends would be there shortly.

Sensing someone coming closer, Pointer turned to see Peter and Sam making their way towards him. Waiting until they were close enough, Pointer whispered, "Letswick and our friends are not too far away." Relieved to hear this, Gamlon said, "Having seen the way Zanus released his army of troopers to attack the barricade and his attack on Alfreston, I hope our friends don't leave it too late."

Witnessing the effect the archers were having on the enemy, Gamlon said, "Let's hope every arrow finds its target." Feeling Gamlon raise himself free of the cane, DaVendall whispered, "Take care my friend, remember it's not just him and those bullies. Many of our friends will be injured or killed."

Kestron drew their attention and signed, "We are ready. The good folk of the villages have reinforced much of the weaponry." Acknowledging what Kestron had signed, Gamlon flew off in the direction the arrows were going.

DaVendall surprised Peter by saying, "I hear you have shown great bravery. This will be a hard battle, so please take care and make sure you have enough armoury. Do not hesitate to kill the enemy. They will have no other thought than to kill as many of us as possible."

"Thank you," said Peter. "I will fight any enemy that dares to come near us or our friends. Agreed, Kestron?" Taking in Peter's tone, Kestron replied, "Peter, we'll stand side by side to make sure we get them all." There was no time for anyone to say more, as the voice of Sizan now called his Gorgonians to prepare to attack.

With much activity taking place on the enemy side of the barricade, the roaring voice of Zanus could be heard louder by the moment as he bellowed orders at Sizan and the army of troopers. "Kill! Kill all!" he roared. This was quickly followed by an order for the carts with the armoury to be moved forward. Once the weaponry was placed to his satisfaction, Zanus roared, "Attack, attack!"

On hearing this Deena said, "Well my friends, we'd better be ready." Veber signed, "We'll have to make every arrow and bucket of tar count." With different thoughts going through each of the defenders' minds, Pointer felt an element of apprehension as he watched the enemy draw near to the barricade.

Settled in a position where he could attack any intruder that dared to cross over the barricade, Pointer stood ready. An eerie silence began to filter round the defenders. With Pointer and Moff sensing this, Moff whispered, "There are many brave people ready to defend their land, but I can't help wondering how many of us will come through this battle." It was an anxious time for the defenders as they stood armed and ready. Fearing the oncoming attack, they knew this was the only way to rid Dofstram of these devils. While these thoughts were uppermost in their minds, they continued to observe the enemy.

Using the mist to give them sufficient cover, Zanus and his troopers were able to get closer to the barricade. As they broke through the mist, the defenders were shocked to see what they were up against. Many of the defenders wondered if they had enough strength and weapons to halt the brutes.

Gamlon was still attacking any spy bird that dared to come into his range. Noticing ladders being placed against the barricade and seeing Pointer at the top of the balustrade, he flew over to see if he had noticed them. Pointer was shocked to see the where the ladders had been placed.

"I think I ought to go back and see where DaVendall has got to," said Gamlon. Watching him fly off, Pointer noticed that most of the defenders' attention had been drawn to the carts. Laden with cannons and boulders they rolled over the muddy ground, making the earth tremble under the weight.

Remembering the ladders, Pointer turned his concentration to drawing DaVendall's mind to his. "Something wrong, Pointer?" asked DaVendall in a distant voice. Sensing something was not quite right, Pointer telepathically asked, "Are you OK? Has your injury healed enough for you to be here?"

But DaVendall ignored the question. Realising DaVendall wasn't about to say if he was OK or not, Pointer went on to tell him of the ladders being placed against the more vulnerable parts of the barricade.

"That's just what Gamlon told me," said DaVendall. "I'll see what can be done to support those people. You take care of any unwanted visitors that dare to cross over your part of the barricade." He made his way round the barricade to see what was happening. He came across Soma, the assistant blacksmith

from the village of Hesslewick, and looking at his physique he knew he would be well able to push many of the ladders free of the barricade.
Surprised to see DaVendall beside him, Soma asked, "Is something wrong?"

"Soma, take a look on the other side of this barricade. Try not to be seen," said DaVendall. Without asking why, Soma looked over the barricade and was shocked to see the ladders.

"I never 'eard them coming," Soma told him. Suddenly there was a blast from a unicorn horn. DaVendall thought this was a trick of the Old Crone or Zanus, but then the horn sounded again. This time they knew of only one who would send out two different sounding blasts - Beauty.

Overjoyed at hearing this long-awaited sound, Pointer asked all the telepaths to join with him in reaching out to any incoming telepaths. As each mind connected with another it became a very powerful presence, and one which would get its reward.

A faint voice replied, "Hi, this is Letswick. I can only just hear your thoughts. Binro and I are almost with you. We have to be careful because the sound of the horn will have alerted Zanus to more arrivals."

Concerned that Imelda had picked up the telepathic minds, Moff added, "I don't think we should use telepathy for too long, we don't want it to be picked up."

They knew they would not be the only ones who heard the sound, for Zanus would have been alerted to the arrival of more helpers. Although the conversation had been short, DaVendall, like the other defenders, was relieved that Beauty would be with them soon.

Gamlon asked, "What shall we do about this enemy below? It won't be long before Zanus and Sizan will be upon us."

"I've had a thought about that," said DaVendall. Soma, I'm going to remove the instant threat of this enemy. If any should try to climb these ladders, please make sure they don't succeed."
Looking out at the approaching enemy forces, and aware of DaVendall's powers, Soma smiled to himself. "I'll be delighted, just let 'em come and try," he said.

Covering himself and Gamlon with his cloak, DaVendall

disappeared from sight. Soma, keeping his attention on the ladders, constantly checked there were no enemy about to climb up. So deep was he in his task he didn't hear the arrival of Blacky.

"What's taken your attention, Soma?" Blacky, who was even bigger than Soma, asked as quietly as his deep voice allowed.

"Well boss, it's like this," said Soma. "There's enemy troops down there with ladders. DaVendall is going to do something to them, I don't know what he has in mind, but I have to push any ladders from the barricade."

"I think you might need a 'and," said Blacky. The men stood watching and waiting, with some apprehension, as they prepared to carry out their task.

Settling himself down behind the enemy, DaVendall was about to speak when Gamlon whispered, "There's more here than I thought. What are you going to do?"

"This will need something a little larger than I had in mind," DaVendall whispered. "When I give the word, I want you to cause a little diversion. I think the best way would be for you to give these men a taste of your blade. This will make them think they are attacked by their comrades. We want to make sure their minds are distracted from our friends. While you're doing that, I'll be taking care of the enemy out in front."

"Take care, DaVendall you don't know if the Old Crone is amongst them," warned Gamlon. Giving Gamlon a light covering of invisibility, DaVendall said, "You take care too, my friend. Make these troopers fear for their lives."

Waiting until Gamlon had flown from within the cane, DaVendall set about with his own form of treatment.

Gamlon flew at speed to the enemy. Seeking out which one to attack first, he noticed that some of the ladders were already up and being climbed. About to start with them, he spotted Blacky and Soma push the ladders free from the barricade. Hearing the screams from the falling enemy, Gamlon left them to their role and set about attacking other troopers.

"Did yer see that?" called out a Zanuthian. "They was 'uge!" shouted another. "They weren't like the little people," called a third. Now it was time for Gamlon to do his bit. Before attacking the ones at the bottom of the ladders, he first weaved his way through them, creating a gust of wind as he did so. Passing each trooper, he gave him a teasing jab with the point of his blade. Hearing them cursing the nearest trooper for not keeping their weapons away, Gamlon repeated the exercise. He made each attack count. As the blood ran from the troopers' wounds, the curses got louder and more violent.

"What's attacking me? I can't see nuffin'," shouted one trooper. "Look, I'm bleeding!" howled another. "Just let me get me 'ands on whatever it is."

"I fink we should get out of 'ere," shouted another. For just a moment the troopers went silent, then one of them called out, "An' what do we tell our boss? 'E'll give us the whip, that's fer sure if we don't stay and attack."

Satisfied he'd achieved what DaVendall wanted, Gamlon realised there was one more thing he could do. Catching sight of a few troopers still trying to climb the ladders, with whirlwind speed he sent enemy and ladders crashing to the ground. Swiping the air with their swords, and cursing at not being able to see what they were aiming at, it wasn't long before the enemy gave up. Frustrated and bleeding, they retreated to join the other troopers, fearful Zanus or Sizan might have seen them retreat.

Having heard the troopers shouting and cursing, Blacky and Soma guessed this had to have something to do with DaVendall or Gamlon. There was a moment of delight when the defenders observed the enemy attacking each other, just as DaVendall had said they would. Blacky and Soma weren't the only ones observing the peculiar behaviour of the enemy below. Many of the Ziphers and Jaspers were watching, delighted in what was happening. They all thought it had to be DaVendall's intervention.

"They don't dare go back to their leaders," said Blacky. "They know they will only get worse punishment." Delighted the enemy had retreated, Gamlon flew to join Soma and Blacky. As his cover had faded, he placed himself where he could see what was happening, while waiting for the return of DaVendall.

* * * *

While the attack had been taking place, Sam and Bertram had joined forces with Moff, Kestron and Drewan to assist the Jaspers and Ziphers who were busy battling with the enemy on other parts of the weakened barricade. Themis flew across to let Sam and the rest of the people know what DaVendall had done to thwart the enemy. Hearing this, Sam said, "That's great, Themis, but we have to stop those wretched Gorgonians from breaking through here." Offering to stay and help, Themis drew her sword just in time to prevent being attacked.

Covered by his cloak, DaVendall considered what he should do first. Deciding to check and see if Imelda was among the troopers, he quickly circled the enemy. Satisfied she wasn't there, he removed his cloak and covered himself with a veil of invisibility. Ready to halt this vast army of troopers, his first thoughts were the troopers at the front and the weapon carts.

Hurling fireballs amongst the enemy, he concentrated on the creatures pulling the carts. Recognising this wasn't going to achieve what he wanted, he wasted no time in calling on his friend Gorka. As he waited for his arrival, he continued with the fireballs and added a fierce wind to drive them round the enemy ranks. Screaming and shouting as the fireballs found their targets, the creatures pulling the carts roared in pain. Seeing the chaos, Zanus looked to see what caused it. As he did so, he observed the fireballs hurtling towards the carts. Before he could shout a warning a swirling wind sent the fireballs amongst the troopers.

Zanus was furious. Turning his attention to the troopers he shouted, "Idiots, move those carts!" Fearing at first that the fire was something to do with Imelda, the troopers struggled to avoid the oncoming fireballs. But the fireballs seemed to be driven in their direction. The troopers soon realised they were fighting a losing battle.

Chapter Twenty Five

The Fight for Dofstram

DaVendall now became aware of the arrival of Gorka and his dragon friends. Informing them of what was happening, Grado, the lead dragon, and his companions came to DaVendall's aid. They threw fire from their nostrils, magnifying the flames by breathing out gusts of air from their mouths. Moving amongst the enemy, they surprised many of the troopers as their swishing tails knocked them off their beasts.

Alarmed by what he was seeing, Zanus wasn't sure how to deal with the dragons. As he sat considering the best move, he just missed being hit by a fireball. His horse reared in fright, almost unseating him. Cursing the animal, he roared at his men to kill the flying dragons. When they could not do so, he ordered them to return.

Flying up to reach Grado, DaVendall asked if he and his friends would continue to halt the enemy from moving forward. Assured they would be able to fly for some time, DaVendall added, "I will leave the rest to you and your companions."

"We will gladly stay a while, DaVendall. Anything to rid your land of these unwanted devils," Grado replied, sending out another surge of fire. "Take good care my friends, and thank you for your help."

DaVendall flew down close beside Zanus' horse, then flew into the air and attacked it from the rear. He was soon rewarded when the horse managed to unseat its rider. Red-faced with anger, Zanus was about to take it out on his horse when DaVendall drew the whip from his hand and threw it into the swirling wind.

"Now I know yer 'ere!" yelled Zanus. "Interfering is somefing yer shouldn't do, DaVendall. Or maybe it's that dratted stone." Spinning round, he tried to see which of his enemy it was. "Where are yer? Let me get me 'ands on yer, or are yer too scared?" he shouted.

Frustrated at not being able to see the cause of his anger, he hoped his taunts would be enough to make it reveal itself. Angry that his taunts hadn't worked he yelled, "Yer'll all suffer. The stupid Outlanders'll be begging fer their lives! This is the day I'll grab what I owns."

Not about to give himself away, DaVendall was nevertheless disturbed at Zanus' threats. Flying back to join Soma, he could see him and Blacky busy pushing ladders from the barricade. Landing beside Soma he was pleased to see Gamlon waiting for his return.

Gamlon was equally pleased to see DaVendall return safe. "I see our friends the dragons are doing a good job," he said. "I wonder how long they can stay."

Smiling at Gamlon, DaVendall replied, "They are going to stay a while. I think they are quite enjoying what they are doing." Then, seeing the results of Gamlon attacks, he wryly added, "I see you did a bit of damage yourself, my friend. I noticed you left the results for me to see."

"Not just me. Soma and Blacky have done what you asked and kept the enemy from entering the barricade," Gamlon whispered. Checking to see if his dragon friends were still there, DaVendall noticed the wagging tail of Grado. Realising the dragons had taken shelter above a group of clouds; DaVendall flew up to join them. Greeting Gamlon and DaVendall, Grado explained that they had succeeded in their task and were going to depart. The enemy were in disarray and would need some time to sort themselves out.

Thanking Grado and his companions for their assistance, DaVendall and Gamlon bid them farewell. As their friends disappeared from view, Gamlon whispered, "I hope the Old Crone wasn't alerted to their presence. Like the unicorns, she would relish having a dragon in her hands."

"Grado would have made sure they were covered against

Imelda sensing their presence" said DaVendall. "That's the reason they can't stay any longer." He flew back to join the defenders.

As he arrived, King Alfreston approached with a wry smile on his face. "I see much activity has taken place amongst the enemy," he said.

"We needed a little help," replied DaVendall. "I'm concerned how he will retaliate. Zanus has seen many of his troopers and birds fall, but at least he's stopped his advance. That really worries me."

"Did you get to see how big his army was?" asked the King

"He and Sizan have a vast army between them. That's not counting those cannons. We will just have to hope our friends arrive soon."

"So do I. I wonder why Zanus has chosen this time to try and take over this land. Neither he nor his father could claim any right to these lands. They have always belonged to the Outlanders."

"It could be he wants power over Imelda, and the only way he can get that is if he captures the right people."

Gamlon added, "Or it could be David discovering our friend. And with what the informer must have told him about Lottie, it gave Zanus the idea that this was the right time to destroy the Outlanders and claim their land."

"There is one good thing, he won't be aware of who sent the fireballs," said King Alfreston. As they watched what was taking place further away, they became aware of a rumbling noise. Straining to see what was causing it, they were alarmed to see an army of troopers approaching. Not too far behind the troopers were the few remaining carts, still being drawn by Sizan's malformed beasts. There were hundreds of them.

* * * *

Wishing Beauty would arrive, Pointer suddenly heard DaVendall calling out to her telepathically. DaVendall heard the long-awaited voice answer his call. He moved away from his friends, wanting to make sure it was Beauty and not some trick of

Imelda's. It only took a few moments for him to be certain.

"I wondered if you heard me. I kept my thoughts low and channelled, I didn't want a certain person to hear me," Beauty explained. "We're outside the gate, hidden in a ditch."

"You don't know how pleased I am to hear you," said DaVendall.

"We heard the attacks and felt the trembling ground," replied Beauty. "But after spotting the spy birds we remained hidden. I think this would be the right time for us to enter the courtyard. Please have someone open the gates. I will give these people cover enough to see them safely cross the open ground."

"Take care. I suggest we leave talking until we are together," DaVendall said. Gamlon remarked "It's a relief to know they are here."

Beauty quickly relayed her conversation to her group, then went on to explain why she would be giving them some protective covering. "Although there is only a short distance between us and the barricade, it will be a dangerous part to cross. We will be exposed for a time on leaving this shelter. We'll need to keep silent, as the cover will not hide our voices. When it is clear for us to move, we'll have to keep watch for trofalogues. They won't be able to see us, but they will be able to detect our scent."

Excited at the thought of being with their friends again, the Jaspers and Ziphers struggled to hide their feelings. In a tired voice, Jayne said, "I will be glad to get inside those gates and see all the friends I have missed."

While Beauty concentrated on making sure her group was surrounded by a protective covering, Lema and Vigo were talking about how this had happened on another occasion. Still fearful of the magic that took place, they surprised Eva by clasping hold of her hands. Sensing their fears, she smiled warmly and gave a gentle squeeze of their hands.

Glancing round at his group of friends, Letswick couldn't help thinking luck must have been with them when they had finally left the dungeons and the darkened passages. He recalled how everyone had done their part to gain their freedom. But he had not gone far into his thoughts when he was brought back to where they were, as the warring shouts from Zanus and Sizan got louder and more demanding. Beauty wasted no time in reaching DaVendall's mind and asking for the gates to be opened. Aware Imelda was close to where they were hidden; Beauty closed her mind to DaVendall and asked Lottie to continue.

"It's Lottie. Please ask the men to open the gates and to leave them open until we are all through. Oh, you'd best tell them we are now under a protective covering, so don't be surprised if we appear ghostly."

Anxious to see his friends, DaVendall wasted no time in making his way to the gates. Annoyed it was taking a little longer than usual to walk, due to the wound he received earlier, he grasped hold of Gamlon and whispered, "Hold tight, going to take a quick flight." Flinging his cloak round his body he made his way to the gate, surprising the guards as he removed the cloak. He stepped through the partially-opened gates to see if there were any trofalogues in sight. Relieved not to see any, he turned his attention to the approaching friends.

He glimpsed a lightly-veiled Zipher enter, and soon saw many more were following her. He was eager to discover where Lottie was. Sending out his thoughts to Beauty, he watched as the last of the people entered.

"DaVendall, I believe you are looking for me?" he heard a voice say.

"How good to know you are here and safe, you have brought a good many people, which is a great relief" DaVendall told her. Noticing Lottie and Letswick approaching, he asked the gatekeepers to close and bar the gates as quickly as they could. By this time everyone had emerged from their cover.

Noticing David and Jayne at the back of the group, DaVendall made his way to greet them. "How good to see you both," said DaVendall as he took hold of David and Jayne's hands. Jayne and David returned the greeting warmly but wearily. David saw the concern on DaVendall's face at Jayne's weakened appearance.

"Being held in that dungeon with all the beatings has taken its toll on Jayne," said David. "Once she is rested she will be fine." DaVendall was not sure this was the only reason. Turning to the newly-arrived folk gathered nearby, he added, "I think you could do with some food, drink and rest." He couldn't help noticing the state some of them people were in.

At that moment Moff appeared beside them, "Greetings to you, Moff," Letswick said in a warm and welcoming tone. Moff shook David's hand and gave Jayne a gentle hug. "I'm so delighted to see you. No one was sure if you had really got away from Zanus."

Weary and in need of rest, David warmly replied, "It's so good to see so many wonderful friends. It wasn't a pleasant stay in Zanus' dungeon."

"May I suggest we get these animals into hiding and give them some food and water, then we can discuss strategies?" said Moff.

"The enemy are regrouping, so I think we should start placing the people where they are needed," said Gamlon.

Penny made her way to Lottie and gave her a hug. It wasn't long before a voice asked, "Would you mind if I take a breather? I feel a bit crowded in here." Beauty then asked Penny, "Would you mind helping Yemil and Malla with the wounded? After I have spoken to Alfreston, I will be along to see if I can help."

Delighted to be able to help, Penny and Malla clasped hands and stood beside Yemil, "We're ready to follow, lead on." Smiling at the newly arrived friends, Yemil asked them to follow her to where the food was.

"Ready," said a smiling Yemil. "See you later, Lottie," Yemil and Penny said almost together.

"Do you notice how careful everyone is still being? I hope they don't forget and give you away," Lottie whispered to Beauty.

"These are our friends, they will remember," said Beauty. "The only ones we don't really know are Lema and Vigo. Saying that, where are they, Lottie? Can you see them?"

Looking round the barricade, Lottie was shocked to see the damage. Blood was still running freely on the muddy ground. She turned her attention to the shattered dwellings. She caught sight of Lema and Vigo making their way along the balustrade towards David and Kestron. Moving her lapel to one side, Lottie told her brooch where to look. Wondering when her father had gone to the balustrade, she saw deep concentration on his face.

* * * *

David had realised that Zanus and his army of troopers were preparing to attack in force. Sensing someone by his side, he looked down to see Vigo and Lema looking up at him with fearful expressions. "Take courage," he told them. "Remember what they'll do if any of us are captured. Try and take as many of the enemy down as you can."

Lema stated cautiously, "We'll do jus' that." Then Vigo added, "We won't let yer down." Noticing Kestron observing the two lads, David explained who they were and the help they had given, to which Kestron remarked, "Well young uns, it sounds as if you are sturdier than you look." Peering over the balustrade, Vigo stated, "We're to 'elp fight. We know 'ow cruel they is."

"Do you have any weapons to fight with?" Kestron asked.

"We ain't got nuffing, we lost ours runnin' from the tower," said Lema. "We need to get some." After discussions with Beauty and Letswick, DaVendall made his way back to the balustrade. Vigo and Lema shrank away when he turned his attention to them, intimidated by his height. Bending down closer to the two lads, he spoke in a low voice which only they could hear. Then he turned to Kestron and asked, "Perhaps you wouldn't mind taking our young fighters here and arming them with some weapons."

"Will do," he replied. Then Lottie appeared close by. Giving his daughter a gentle hug, David whispered to Beauty, "Jayne is resting, so I'm going with Kestron to get weapons for our new fighters." Pulling himself away, he noticed the wink from Beauty, and accepted that it was her way of replying.

DaVendall turned to Lottie and gave her a warm smile. "Hello, Lottie. I hope everyone is resting. It seems we have a bit of a battle on our hands. Not quite like the scary ones you and Penny endured." Sensing Beauty had some concerns, he faced her and said, "I feel you have a little concern with regard to our new fighters, am I right my friend?"

"I did, until they proved their worth in helping us to get free of the tower," said Beauty. "They were quite shocked when I introduced myself to them as a friend. They have been witness to a couple of incidents, but they are not sure what or who was doing it. Perhaps it should stay that way," Beauty told him.

"I agree, unless it becomes important for them to know," said DaVendall.

"You're right. But, until that time, we will continue as before," Beauty replied.

Lottie had been watching the enemy move closer to the barricade. She tugged on DaVendall's arm and drew Beauty's attention to what she was looking at. Staring at the vast enemy army approaching, DaVendall knew Zanus was coming to try and claim what he thought was his right, the freedom to rule Dofstram.

King Alfreston, returning from visiting the new arrivals and the wounded, was just in time to prevent an Outlander from receiving a blow from an enemy weapon. Pointer, observing what had just happened, turned his attention to the other side of the barricade. Moving closer to the King he glanced over the balustrade, and didn't like what he saw. He drew the King's attention to what was happening. Alfreston ordered everyone to prepare for an attack. Keeping an eye on the movement of the troopers, he could see Zanus and Sizan at the front.

Hearing these words, the defenders knew the situation they'd been dreading was upon them. With many eyes staring at the enemy, they muttered between themselves about the oncoming battle. Seeing clouds of dust in the distance, their attention was drawn to a weapon they'd never seen before. It was larger than a cannon and many beasts were needed to drag it along. "He's brought his tower," said someone.

"I fear this is going to be a very bloody battle," said Bertram.

"I was just thinking that, Bertram," said Sam. "But you can bet our defenders will do their best to keep the enemy at bay."

Suddenly it went silent. Not another word was spoken by the defenders as they rallied together, armed with whatever weapon they could get hold of.

DaVendall raised his cane to eye level and asked Gamlon, "Do you think the unicorns are near enough to come and help?"

"I would think so," Gamlon replied. "Their greatest fear will be the presence of Imelda. They know how desperate she is to get her hands on them." With similar thoughts, DaVendall sought Beauty's mind and informed her of his plan to send Pointer to bring the unicorns.

Slightly alarmed at hearing this, Beauty replied, "Warn Pointer to take extra care, DaVendall. We still don't know where Imelda is."

DaVendall made his way to Pointer. "We need assistance from the unicorns," he said. "I can't break through to Cedar, so please run and fetch all the unicorns. Gamlon and I will go and seek help from another quarter."

Without asking what DaVendall meant, Pointer set off at great speed to bring back the unicorns. Approaching the cave with caution, he listened for the sound of the unicorns.

Deep inside the cave, the unicorns were beginning to feel uneasy. Sensing someone had entered the cave, Gazer whispered, "I think someone's coming."

"Me too, I heard the sound of footsteps," said Gazer.

"Let's hope it's a friend."

Standing very still and quiet, Gazer called on the other animals to join him and Kerez. He took the precaution of giving his friends a light covering of invisibility, and they stood shoulder to shoulder waiting to see who or what would appear.

Pointer crawled along the ground as quietly as he could, stopping from time to time to listen for any familiar sound. Not hearing the animals, he wondered if he should call out.

"Kerez, Gazer, are you in here?" he called. "It's Pointer. I've come at the request of DaVendall." Remaining still, he heard a low snort come from further on in the cave. Kerez called out, "Come on in, Pointer. We thought it would be wise to go as deep into this cave as possible just in case our scent was picked up by Imelda or one of her beastly creatures."

"What can we do for you?" asked Gazer

"We could do with a bit of your special magic," Pointer explained.

"Come along friends, our help is needed," said Kerez. As soon as the words left his mouth, the other animals came and stood around him. Not wanting to be left out, Pinto asked, "Can we horses help with anything?"

"You could help Yemil with the wounded," said Pointer. "If you come with me to the courtyard, I will take you to her. You all know Penny, she comes to help from time to time." Gathering the animals together, Kerez urged, "Come on lads, let's get going."

"Take care those devil birds don't see you, or any other of Imelda's creations," warned Pointer. Suspecting that he wasn't telling them everything, Doran asked, "What other creatures?"

"Her trofalogues for a start, and there's other grotesque beasts. I can't describe them except to say they are very large and brutal. Sizan is riding one in place of his horse," replied Pointer.

"Then I suggest we get moving," said Gazer.

They agreed that the unicorns should make their own way to the barricade, while Pointer led the horses. As they approached the mouth of the cave, they wished each other good luck. Making sure the other unicorns were with him, Gazer said, "Right here we go, see you later friends." With a final word to take care, the unicorns took to the sky.

Pointer checked that the horses were ready to go, urging them to keep a wary eye out for anything unusual. They all set off.

Although they were not far from the battleground, it was a very dangerous route. Aware of the dangers they could face, Pinto moved closer to Pointer and asked, "What are these creatures like? The ones you warned the unicorns to look out for?"

Pointer thought for a moment, and pictured them in his thoughts. "Imagine a large grotesque animal with a very thick hide. Like the trofalogues, they drool at the thought of killing. They run along in a kind of lopsided way, which makes the earth tremble like an earthquake. I'm not sure how they can be killed but I'm sure a way will be found."

They travelled on in silence. Thinking they were making good progress, Pointer was surprised when one of the more senior horses asked, “Are you all right, Pointer? You seem a little weak in the back leg?”

“I’m all right thank you. Just weary, like a good many others. Let’s hope we get rid of these tyrants for good this time.” Accepting what Pointer had said, the horses walked close behind him. It seemed to Pointer it was taking a long time to make the return journey. He realised this must be the result of his injuries. He tried to go faster but found his injured legs would not allow it.

Knowing Zanus and Sizan were preparing to attack en masse, he also knew their sole aim would be to finish off the folk and take the King captive. His attention was suddenly drawn to Zanus’ spy birds, which had gathered together and were now darkening the sky over the barricade. Urging the horses to try and go a little faster, Pinto asked Pointer if he would like a ride on his back. Pointer refused the offer. “It will slow us down, Pinto, and we need to get back quickly,” he said.

As they approached their destination, the animals were dismayed to see the spy birds dive down in flocks. Aware that the Ziphers and Jaspers would have difficulty fighting off this attack, Pointer reached out telepathically to Moff. It wasn’t long before he heard the welcome voice of Moff. “Why hello old chap, what can we do for you?”

Explaining where he was, Pointer asked Moff to open the gates. “I have brought the horses along,” he added. Moff wondered why.

Almost as soon as Moff reached the gates, he could see they were being slowly opened. “That was quick. How did you know I was going to ask you to open the gate?” Moff asked.

“We’re Ziphers, and we heard what Pointer asked you to do so we did it,” signed the taller of the two Ziphers. Grinning, Moff congratulated them on being alert.

It wasn’t long before all the animals were inside the courtyard. With the gates now closed Pointer thanked them for being so quick. Turning to Moff he said, “I bet you wonder why I brought the horses?”

“I did,” said Moff. “I thought they could help with the wounded,” said Pointer.

"Good thinking," said Moff. Yemil had now joined them.

"I'm going to leave you and Yemil, Pointer, so take care and watch out for any stray enemy," said Moff. "Some have managed to get through on the far side of the barricade." With that he gave a wave of the hand and disappeared from the courtyard.

"I am delighted to have your help," said Yemil to the horses. "If you follow me, you will see why." Pointer went to speak to Bemar, one of the Jaspers, and friends by the well. Noticing he was limping, Bemar said, "I think you had better let Yemil look at your injuries." Pointer quickly assured her he was all right.

At that moment, another flock of spy birds dived down into the courtyard and began to attack the smaller folk. Jumping up and clawing at the birds, Pointer paid no attention to his sore limbs.

With the arrival of the unicorns, King Alfreston wasted no time in asking them to attack from the rear of the enemy. They soared into the sky and headed for the rear of the enemy ranks. Heartened by the arrival of the unicorns, the defenders lashed out with their staffs, swords and other weapons.

Zanus was desperate to get his hands on the two things he knew Imelda also wanted. Not prepared to wait any longer, he roared, "Follow the trofalogues." The defenders watched in horror as the beastly creatures clawed ferociously at the barricade.

Then bolts of lightning and fireballs fell upon the attackers from the sky. Unaware they were being sent by the unicorns, the trofalogues wailed loudly when one hit its target. The defenders battled on with their weapons. It was indeed a sight to behold, thought Drewan; Jaspers, Ziphers, Outlanders and Rancouins standing with the humans, prepared to fight a bitter battle to the end.

Many of the defenders had faced the trofalogues before and knew they would spare no one. Their fangs bared and slime dripping from their mouths, they raced closer to the barricade. Behind them, huge creatures ran lopsidedly behind them, shaking the ground as they did.

"Gorgonians!" shouted Moff.

Sizan was leading a large group of troopers, some of whom

were riding the malformed creatures. Stomping the ground with their black-studded boots, more troopers followed close behind. Feeling the ground tremble under the weight of the army, King Alfreston called for the archers to release their bows. No sooner had these words left his mouth than a volley of arrows flew over the barricade, directed at the oncoming enemy. It wasn't long before the enemy retaliated and sent their own arrows soaring back, claiming many folk. Screams filled the air. Although many enemy and defenders alike had fallen, this had no effect on the trofalogues.

When they heard the screeching voice of Imelda urging the trofalogues on, the folk on the balustrade looked in vain to see where she was. Their attention was turned back to keeping the trofalogues at bay.

Racing towards the weakened part of the barricade, the trofalogues clawed into it, tearing off shreds of material. Once they had opened up a gap, many more trofalogues began to squeeze through and spring out at the defenders. Not realising their stench had given them away, the trofalogues were surprised to see they were face to face with defenders.

Their cruel eyes looked around, prepared to pounce at any opportunity. Staring at their prey and dripping green mess over the courtyard, they slowly and deliberately began inching along the ground. Determined not to let the trofalogues destroy any more of the barricade, the defenders attacked in force, heedless of the injuries they would sustain. It took all their strength to avoid being overpowered. But suddenly they stopped, as if in a trance. Pointer wondered why his friends had stopped fighting and were standing staring at the trofalogues. He realised that somehow they were being hypnotised by the creatures' staring eyes. Realising this could only have been done with one of Imelda's potions, he tried licking the cheek of the nearby Zipher. Having no success, he tried pawing her foot, still without success. After a few more attempts, he gave up and decided to go for help.

Delighted to see Peter, Pointer raced over to him and quickly explained what had happened. Eager to help Pointer break through the trance, Peter listened while Pointer told him what to do.

"Do not look at the creatures' eyes," he said. "Keep your eyes on me. Can you make a loud noise, something to draw the trofalogues' attention away from our friends?"

At first Peter wasn't sure what kind of noise Pointer meant. Guessing it didn't matter too much, he opted to make the sound of warring Indians, as he had once done when he and his friends played cowboys and Indians. The yell that came out stunned both the trofalogues and Pointer. Thinking the sound might be a new creation of Imelda's, the trofalogues raced headlong towards the defenders with claws splayed and fangs bared.

Peter's noise had alerted Letswick. As terrified screams filled the air he ran around the fallen and injured, while telepathically summoning the Ziphers and Jaspers to come and help.

Then from nowhere, Gorka and his phantom reptiles came slithering across the ground like a shadowy mirage. In no time they had reached the barricade and were slithering across the courtyard towards the enemy. The serpents were determined to help rid Beauty's friends of these creatures. Sinking their poisoned fangs deep within the creatures, they began disposing of any trofalogue in their path. Encouraged by what they were seeing, the defenders suddenly found extra energy as they laid into the enemy.

With the hand-to-hand combat becoming more intense, and seeing many of his friends succumb to the enemy, Letswick glanced to see where Peter was, and was relieved to see that he was managing to hold his own. Letswick turned just in time to prevent a sword coming down on him. Soon, with many of their comrades lying dead or injured, the enemy troops wanted only to get away from the courtyard.

The Ziphers and Jaspers lashed out at the enemy with loud shouts of triumph as they began to flee the courtyard.

"Where did those reptiles come from?" Peter asked Letswick. Keeping an eye on the retreating enemy, Letswick half turned towards Peter and explained, "Beauty asked her friends the phantom reptiles to help." Pointing in the direction of one of the larger reptiles, Pointer told him, "The larger one over there is Gorka, their leader. Beauty and DaVendall saved them from falling into the hands of Imelda and Zanus. In return, they have always answered a plea for help whenever requested."

Assured the enemy was defeated, Gorka quickly moved across to Lottie and drew himself up to face Beauty. Beauty gently explained to Lottie these were her friends and not to be feared.

"Thank you for coming so quickly, Gorka," she said. "Once again you have answered my call for help without question. With your help we have been able to gain some control back. I guess you would like to return to your homeland now?"

"Any time, you know we will always come if you need help. Is this the little lady who has protected you, my friend?" Gorka asked, looking at Lottie.

"How do you know that?" asked Lottie. Turning to face Lottie directly, Gorka sent out a hissing noise before he replied, "We all know what was happening in your land, and the bravery you and your friends have shown to our friends."

Blushing and feeling a little embarrassed by what Gorka had said, Lottie was delighted when Beauty took over the conversation. "They have indeed been good friends to us, Gorka. Now, may I suggest you take your friends and return to your home? If we need any further help, I will call on you." No sooner had Beauty finished speaking than Lottie noticed Gorka and the reptiles had vanished.

Peter was making his way back to the balustrade deep in thought when he suddenly heard someone call out, "Trofalogues coming!" At the same time, Lottie saw Pointer coming in their direction. Beauty was about to ask him about further action from the enemy camp, but after hearing that alarm she asked Lottie to move into a more favourable position where she could see the enemy. Standing alongside Lottie and Beauty, Peter and Pointer were only a short way away from DaVendall.

DaVendall's attention was on the group approaching. Staring ahead, he was convinced there was something different about them. Unable to see who it was, he looked to see how far Sizan and his troopers had got.

Lottie felt Beauty draw her attention to the approaching riders. Not sure what she was looking at, she heard Beauty whisper, "I do believe Crocanthus is bringing the informer to us. We will have to be careful this isn't some kind of a trick."

Remembering some of the torment she'd undergone in her own land, Lottie nervously asked, "That bully won't be able to get to me or my friends, will he?"

"Take heart, Lottie, he will have to get past a great many people before he can get to you or your friends," Beauty whispered. Watching Crocanthus riding towards, it seemed his pace had become slower.

Until now Crocanthus had remained hidden by the troopers, but now he decided to get rid of the informer. Taking hold of Norman's arm, he hoisted him up in front of him and threw him across the neck of his horse. Shouting and screaming, Norman realised Crocanthus was taking him to the barricade. He knew David would be there. On reaching the barricade, Crocanthus dragged Norman off the horse and pushed him to the ground.

"What are you going to do with me?" whined Norman.

"Shut up and crawl round here," ordered Crocanthus. Fearing he was going to receive another beating, Norman went down on hands and knees and crawled in front of Crocanthus. He hadn't gone far when he felt something barring his way.

By this time, DaVendall had linked his mind to Beauty, Moff and Letswick. "I guess we'd best keep our thoughts to ourselves," Letswick told the others. "Let's see what Crocanthus is planning." A sudden stillness fell over enemy and defenders alike.

"This I think is a job for Gamlon and me," said DaVendall. "Please be alert to any trickery. Keep Lottie safe, we don't want him getting near her. Ready, Gamlon? When we get to him, remove your blade from the cane and prepare for anything that might happen."

Drawing his cloak round himself, DaVendall made his way to where Crocanthus had halted. When he removed his cloak, Norman was surprised to see who it was. Hearing the gasp that came from Norman, Crocanthus raised his sword in readiness to kill DaVendall. But he was prevented from striking him by an attack from Gamlon. Knocking the sword from Crocanthus' hand, Gamlon said, "Be warned, Crocanthus, leave the sword where it is."

Staring at Gamlon, Norman was shocked to see a knife, apparently with no one holding it, attack Crocanthus' sword, then to hear a voice coming from it. "How did you do that? I never knew a dagger could fly or talk," he said. In response, Crocanthus punched him hard, sending him to the ground.

What DaVendall said next took Norman and Crocanthus completely by surprise.

"Well - well. Who have you brought this time, Crocanthus? Who could this person possibly be? I wonder... could this be the informer? Why have you brought him here? With all the harm he has done to my friends, surely you don't think we want him?"

It took Crocanthus a while to recover from the surprise of DaVendall knowing who Norman was. Before he could respond, DaVendall surprised them once more by saying, "I believe this man is Norman Mansfield." Gamlon, ready to take action if Crocanthus attempted anything else, stayed outside the cane. "You look stupid on your hands and knees, informer, I suggest you stand up," said Gamlon in a disdainful voice. "Be aware, every movement will be watched."

Crocanthus yanked Norman up onto his feet. Glaring at DaVendall, he swiped Norman across the face. "Shut up or I'll kill you right now!" he hissed. Aware Crocanthus wouldn't hesitate to carry out his threat, DaVendall taunted, "That's no way to treat a friend, Crocanthus." Then in a demanding tone he asked, "Why have you brought him here? We have no place for a man like that in this land." Sensing something evil, but unable to discover where it was coming from, Gamlon said, "Careful, DaVendall, I sense another enemy approaching." Not hearing what Gamlon had said and unaware they were being observed by Imelda, Crocanthus dropped Norman to the ground.

Imelda was intent on letting them all know that the stone and Lottie belonged to her. She had disguised herself as a vulture-like bird, known to the people of Dofstram as a creature of the damned. She now flew down to land behind Norman. Only wanting to use him as hostage, she immediately sensed his fear. Feeling uplifted by this, she was determined this human will never leave this land alive.

Fearing these were to be his last few moments of life, Norman stammered, "What is this thing?" He jumped to hear an ear-splitting squawk close to his ear. Then the creature seized him in its long talons and drew him close. Shivering with fear, Norman struggled to get free, only to feel himself pulled closer to the creature. He looked up at its evil face to see something in its eyes which seemed familiar. They were the eyes of the Old Crone.

Imelda slowly removed her disguise and stood transformed back into her true self. Glaring at Crocanthus, she decided she would deal with him later. Feeling the revulsion in Norman and his eagerness to get away from her, she dug her talons further into his arm and snarled, "Yer mine." Norman screamed at the pain. Blood was now running down his arm.

Annoyed with himself for not anticipating the arrival of Imelda, Crocanthus was even more annoyed that she had hold of his prisoner. Quickly moving towards her he demanded, "Why are you here?" At this moment, Norman's terror was like nothing he'd ever felt before. Staring into Crocanthus' eyes, he felt as if he was looking into a black abyss.

"I tried to warn you she was here," Gamlon whispered to DaVendall.

Crocanthus now turned his attention to DaVendall and demanded, "Where is she? Where's that woman Lottie? I know she has the stone. She had it all the time and didn't tell me. She will suffer for that."

With an eye on Imelda, DaVendall warned Gamlon, "Watch for any trickery Crocanthus might use." Staring straight at Crocanthus, DaVendall made no attempt to hide his revulsion at the person in front of him. "You had best be careful, Crocanthus, there are more powers here than you or Imelda can face alone," he warned.

Angered at hearing this, Imelda set out to prove him wrong. With a loud hiss, she lunged towards DaVendall. He side-stepped just in time. This enraged Imelda further, but before she could try again, DaVendall threw his cloak over her. Imelda screamed and struggled to free herself, only to discover DaVendall was drawing her closer to him.

"You will never have Lottie or any of our friends. Be warned, Imelda," DaVendall warned her. Imelda wriggled free and stumbled to the ground hissing and cursing.

"For your part in betraying your friends, informer, I think we should leave your punishment to David," said Gamlon.

Taking advantage of the two men being occupied with Norman, Imelda crawled behind him, eager for revenge. Rising up from the ground, she was about to release a spit of venom on them all when she felt a hand on her arm which prevented her from doing so. Zanus, furious at what was happening, had set off to discover what had gone wrong with his plans. Making his way to join Crocanthus, Zanus saw what Imelda was about to do. "No yer don't, we need to use 'im," he warned her.

Wrestling her arm free from Zanus' grasp, Imelda glared at him and warned, "Don't never do that again."

Still fearful of losing his life, Norman cowered beside her as Zanus demanded. "What yer doin' with this informer? I need 'im fer an 'ostage. 'E's to be offered fer the stone and the brat."

Waving a long bony finger at Zanus, she screeched, "'Oo says yer gonna get what yer want?"

Standing between them and listening to their arguing, Norman thought this might be his moment to escape. But Crocanthus had moved towards him. "Where do you think you're going? We have uses for you. I think we should give them in there the pleasure of dealing with you. Of course that would only happen if they send out Lottie and the stone," Crocanthus warned, in his cruel and taunting voice.

"They's mine, they belong to me!" screeched Imelda. Seeing DaVendall moving closer to her, she screamed, "I'll be back to get that woman an' I'll get me stone too." She disappeared into a green mist, her voice fading as she added, "Be warned."

Crocanthus turned his attention back to Norman and sneered, "If I remember, they don't want you either. I wonder what we should do with you." Aware that the troopers were gathered ready to attack the barricade, Crocanthus turned to Zanus and suggested, "Send this human to ride in front of the troopers. They won't fire, they are cowards. They'll be scared of hitting him." Trembling, Norman begged them not to send him to fight. "I haven't ever been in a fight before," he squeaked. "'Ark at 'im, 'e ain't never bin in a fight!" laughed one of the troopers.

Wondering if there was some other way of using the informer, Zanus decided to go along with Crocanthus for now. Commanding his troopers to follow him, he headed off to where Sizan and his army were engaged in battle. Despite what had taken place, and with Zanus moving off with his troopers, Norman knew this had to be his final moment.

Staring down and glowering at the pathetic man in front of them, DaVendall turned to leave. Crocanthus was angry that DaVendall had not accepted his offer, and he was enraged when he saw that he was making his way back to join the defenders. With the sound of the battle ringing in their ears, Crocanthus was intent on seeking revenge. Glaring at Norman, he ranted at him for being no use to anyone. Then, thinking the defenders wouldn't fight if he was in front of the troopers, he took hold of a nearby horse's reins and prepared to place Norman in the saddle. As he did this, a sudden thought came to mind which made him release the reins.

It was at that moment that Norman became aware of what Crocanthus intended to do. His pleas for mercy were ignored. Suddenly Crocanthus drew a knife from his boot and plunged it into Norman's stomach. Staring into Norman's eyes, he could see the shock and disbelief looking back at him. He held the blade in place and gleefully twisted it, wanting to cause as much pain as he could.

Satisfied he'd done the deed, Crocanthus slowly withdrew the knife and displayed the bloodied blade to the troopers. Their yells of delight alerted DaVendall, who turned to see Norman lying dead on the ground.

He was not surprised by what Crocanthus had done. DaVendall and Gamlon looked at each other and continued on their way.

Checking Norman was truly dead, Crocanthus kicked his lifeless body over onto its back. Then he jumped on his horse, and with the blooded knife still in his hand he rode straight at DaVendall. Busy congratulating himself on getting rid of one human, he thought he could now get rid of another.

With his arm raised ready to plunge the knife into DaVendall's back, Crocanthus was unaware that Gamlon had seen him approaching.

Chapter Twenty Six

Crocanthus Meets his Match

Quickly raising himself free of the cane, Gamlon flew straight at Crocanthus, aiming for his heart. But at the last moment Crocanthus dodged and the little blade struck Crocanthus' shoulder.

Gamlon withdrew and dropped to the ground. Screaming and shouting at the pain from the attack, Crocanthus warned he would get even. He jumped off his horse, with the intention of whipping the animal into moving. It seemed as if his horse knew what to expect, because to everyone's surprise it ran off, leaving a ranting Crocanthus where he stood. Red-faced and shouting in anger at everything and everyone, it was some time before Crocanthus realised he was unable to move his legs.

While this was going on, DaVendall retrieved his friend and whispered, "Thank you, Gamlon. That was a very brave thing to do. Are you all right?"

"I'm all right, but this man is unspeakably evil. We must make sure he never harms another of our friends," Gamlon replied, not taking his eyes off Crocanthus. DaVendall took a moment to think, then with an idea in mind he sent out a telepathic message calling for assistance.

With pain searing through his shoulder, Crocanthus turned his black, cruel eyes in the direction of DaVendall and snarled through clenched teeth, "Your friends will suffer for this!" Standing his ground, DaVendall replied, "It's time to make sure you can never harm anyone again."

DaVendall took off his cloak and threw it into the air. As it began to drop back to earth, it suddenly turned into a cage. It fell squarely on top of Crocanthus, trapping him. He began to scream furious abuse.

Ignoring Crocanthus' screams, DaVendall was relieved to hear the voice of his friend, Gorka. Greeting him and his serpents, DaVendall made his request known.

"Remove Crocanthus to a place he can never return from. Make sure it is a secure place, and be careful of any trickery. I have made sure he is unable to transform himself into another being, but he will try and gain sympathy from any soft-hearted soul. Take great care, Gorka, I can't stress enough how deadly he can be."

Gorka recalled the cruel deaths and torture many of his friends had suffered at the hands of Zanus and Crocanthus.

"We will make sure he never gets free," he replied. "After what he and Zanus did to us, it will be a pleasure to keep him locked up. I know just the place." Noticing a body lying close by on the ground, Gorka asked, "What about this one?"

"That one, Gorka, is Norman Mansfield, the informer from Lottie's land. Crocanthus has disposed of him in his usual cruel way. This is a person who would never have survived in Dofstram once it was known who he was and what he'd done."

Gorka encircled Crocanthus with his long tail. Then DaVendall changed the cage back into a cloak. Crocanthus soon realised his struggling had no affect on Gorka. "I'll find a way back. Be warned, DaVendall I will kill you one day!" hissed Crocanthus. Giving his prisoner a warning squeeze, Gorka signalled to his fellow reptiles, who quickly surrounded Gorka and his prisoner. With a last farewell, the serpents vanished from sight.

Heaving a sigh of relief, Gamlon commented, "Do you think Crocanthus will come back? I dread to think what harm he would do if ever he did."

"Gorka will prevent him from ever getting free, my friend. Remember, it wasn't so long ago Zanus tried to destroy all the serpents."

Mindful that the enemy were still attacking the defenders, DaVendall found his thoughts turning to the eventful day when he and Beauty had successfully managed to rescue so many serpents.

"I think we had better return to our other friends and see what is happening," said DaVendall.

The defenders were still involved in fierce fighting. Lottie was in shock at what had happened to Norman and felt the whole thing was all a bad dream. With her sword seeming to act on its own, thanks to Beauty, she wondered how she hadn't been killed.

"Are you all right, Lottie?" asked Beauty. About to respond, Lottie felt her sword raise itself and attack an approaching enemy. Gathering herself together, she asked, "Why did Crocanthus have to do that?"

"The informer was of no more use to him," said Beauty. "Remember, that's what he did to Ms Beckett. That's Crocanthus' answer to everyone who is of no further use to him."

At that moment, Lottie's thoughts were interrupted by the thunder of approaching enemy boots. Looking down at her sword and wondering if it would react on its own, she heard Beauty whisper, "The sword is in your control, Lottie. Are you ready? This will be a very fierce battle now Crocanthus has been removed. Zanus will be determined to make sure none of us survive."

Lottie wondered what Beauty meant about the sword being in her control. Staring over the balustrade, she was shocked to see how close the enemy were. She murmured a prayer for her friends.

* * * *

Back at the battlefront, Peter was horrified to see a trooper with a large spiked club approaching ready to attack. He aimed for the trooper's arm, hoping to make him drop the weapon. Concentrating all his strength on defending himself, he was surprised to see that his enemy was being attacked by another, Veber. Noticing Peter's predicament, she ran over to help him.

Not taking his eyes off the attacker, Peter lifted the sword over his head and brought it down on his wrist. The trooper roared with anger, his blood dripping onto the balustrade. Swinging the spiked club round his head, he brought it down onto Peter's arm. Peter gasped as the sword was wrenched from his arm. As he fell to the ground, Veber rushed up and plunged her sword in the trooper's stomach. He fell backwards over the balustrade and crashed to the ground.

Moving across to where Peter lay on the floor, Veber saw his injured arm. Opening his eyes and seeing Veber looking at him, Peter struggled to get up. Seeing the blood run from his arm, he drew his arm across his chest to try and staunch the flow.

"I thought you could do with a little help," signed Veber. "I think you must have been caught by the one of the spikes."

"Thank you, Veber. Your help came just in time, I think," said Peter.

"I think you should get that arm seen to." Veber signed.

"I'm not leaving my post, Veber. Tear a bit off my shirt and wrap it round to stop the bleeding. We have enemy to dispose of," Peter told her. He watched as Veber tore off the end of his shirt and wrapped it round the wound, then sat a while longer before gathering himself together to stand up.

"Perhaps you will stay with me?" he murmured. Smiling at him, Veber signed, "I will. Then we'll get that arm fixed."

"Thanks, Veber. Now, I think we had better get rid of some of these ladders," Peter stated.

Ready to dislodge an enemy-laden ladder, they were surprised to hear Moff's friendly voice whisper, "Thought you might need a hand. I saw what was happening, but Veber got rid of the brute before I could get to you. With three pairs of hands, it won't take long to get rid of these ladders."

As they pushed away the ladders, it seemed to them that the more enemy troops they killed the more appeared to take their place. With continuing orders bellowed out from Zanus and Sizan, the battle was building up again. Pointer had lost count of the number of enemy he'd attacked, but wished he could get rid of their foul taste as easily.

Zanus, eager to seek revenge for the loss of Crocanthus, was determined the King wouldn't survive the next time. "Time to die, Alfreston," he grunted. "Along with all yer menials."

Weary and bleeding from their wounds, Pointer and a band of other defenders prepared to face the enemy again. Then they heard the dreaded words yelled across the battleground: "Attack, I want 'em all dead! Leave Alfreston, 'e's mine." Leading the charge, Zanus ordered his troopers to break the barricade down and ordered Sizan to take the other side.

Not content to leave the threats to Zanus, Imelda now sent out her own warnings. "Give me the stone an' the woman or yer'll all suffer!" she screeched. But the defenders were unable to hear her threats over the noise of stomping enemy boots.

Pointer suddenly felt a presence in his thoughts. Recognising David's voice, he asked, "Is something troubling you?"

"Did you hear that old witch?" said David. "I wonder what her plan is. We know Zanus is eager to kill Alfreston."

Before Pointer could respond they were suddenly bombarded with huge boulders hurled over the barricade. Trying to avoid them, the defenders were shocked to see a large weapon being drawn close to the barricade. Flaming arrows shot over the barricade, taking everyone by surprise.

By now many of the dwellings were on fire. Seeing the devastation, Bertram called for any to join him, leaving other defenders to keep the enemy back. Racing to the wells and raising the buckets, they were too busy to see how many dwellings had collapsed before the fires could be stopped.

King Alfreston, concerned for the welfare and safety of the people, could see they were trying to quench the fires with buckets of water. With arrows fired from both sides and swords clashing in hand to hand combat, the shrill squawk of Imelda echoed through the sound of battle. Her vulture monsters were soon attacking en masse. Near misses from the defenders' arrows did nothing to stop Imelda and her creatures dive-bombing the people below.

Drawing Lottie's mind to hers, Beauty explained what she needed to do. Then she closed her mind to everything and everyone around her. As she sent her thoughts far away, it wasn't too long before she heard her friends' response.

She explained the predicament they were in, and the sabre-tooth tigers and locusts promised to set out right away. True to their word, the sky was soon full of flying creatures, friend and enemy alike. Confused at who to aim for, the archers feared all these creatures were something to do with Imelda.

"Don't shoot the tigers or the locusts, they are our friends," called Lottie.

Ready to defend Beauty and her friends, their newly-arrived allies began attacking the enemy with great force. Leaving the tigers to deal with the trofalogues, the locusts flew off to deal with the birds. Delighted to see the enemy falling so rapidly, the defenders fought with renewed fervour. Imelda was shocked to see locusts swarming round her birds and tigers attack the troopers and trofalogues. Staring in disbelief at these creatures, her thoughts turned to the time she and Zanus had tried to eliminate these creatures. Convinced DaVendall or the stone was responsible for their survival, she flew down to join Zanus.

"What yer doin' 'ere? Yer should be attacking from the air!" he yelled.

"Be careful, Zanus. I might not give yer me potions. I might just drop them over the other side. Look at what's happening. I thought yer told me this lot were got rid of years ago."

Zanus was about to vent fresh anger at her for not getting rid of these attacking creatures when he noticed her holding a large phial in her hand. Offering it to him, she said, "In this 'ere is poison. Mix it in water, dip the arrows in it and that'll do away with yer enemy." He snatched the phial.

"I won't warn yer again, Zanus yer don't rule Dofstram, yet," said Imelda. Then she disappeared into the sky. Spurring his horse on, Zanus grumbled, "Warn me would she? Just wait an' see, I'll soon teach 'er a lesson."

There was a small well nearby. Zanus poured the liquid from the phial into it, then ordered one of his troopers to tell all the others to dip their arrowheads in the well. Too frightened to question why, the trooper set off to do as Zanus ordered.

The troopers had soon covered their arrowheads in the liquid. With enough poison to fill a few more wells, Zanus made his way to find other suitable places until the phial was empty.

While Zanus was busy distributing the poison, Sizan and the rest of the army struggled to fend off the tigers and the locusts.

Wondering why the spy birds weren't assisting, he was shocked to see so many of them dead on the ground. When Zanus saw what had happened to his spy birds, he gave an almighty roar. Determined to avenge his birds, he ordered the troopers to fire their poisoned arrows at the tigers.

* * * *

DaVendall, meanwhile, was dismayed at the number of his friends who had been injured or killed and had set his sights on Imelda, aware that like Zanus she wanted to rule over Dofstram with powers stolen from Beauty and Lottie. Thankful Crocanthus had been taken care of, he relayed his plan to Gamlon. Gamlon agreed to what DaVendall planned, and was elated at the thought of ridding Dofstram of its enemies.

"I'm ready when you are," he said. "Just let me know when."

"First we need to see where she is," said DaVendall. "I know she's leading those terrible birds, but I want to see how many she has created." Searching the sky for her, it took a while before he saw where she was. Securing Gamlon back in the cane he spread his cloak round, then soared into the sky and flew as close to Imelda as he could. Sensing his presence, Imelda stopped and looked around. "So DaVendall, yer've come to kill me 'ave yer?"

"You have caused great suffering to my friends," he replied. "The time has come for you and your creatures to move away or die." Gamlon had been watching her every move. Something alarmed him. Carefully and quietly he drew himself free of the cane, prepared to attack.

Then it happened. Before he could warn DaVendall, Gamlon saw a dagger appear in Imelda's hand. A split second later it was flying towards them. Gamlon responded by heading straight for the dagger's twisted blade. Clashing blade on blade, Gamlon saw that the dagger handle had been created in her image. The dagger dropped to the ground. Dismissing it, Imelda lunged at DaVendall, again demanding he give her the stone and the woman. Fending her off, DaVendall hadn't realised one of her fingernails had cut into his arm until he heard her hiss, "The next cut will be to yer 'eart."

Realising DaVendall had been injured, Gamlon rose above Imelda and circled around her, stabbing her at every opportunity. Although Imelda was bleeding from some of the attacks, Gamlon failed to hear her order the dagger to attack DaVendall again. It raised itself from the ground and flew straight at DaVendall.

Turning his cloak into a shield, DaVendall aimed it at the dagger. As it struck the blade it broke it into several pieces, then dropped to the ground.

The cut on DaVendall's arm was now starting to burn. He was beginning to feel the effect of whatever Imelda had put in the wound and his thoughts started drifting away. But Gamlon knew Imelda hadn't finished with him yet. Taking control of DaVendall's cloak, Gamlon turned it into a lightning bolt and sent waves of energy at Imelda.

She reeled backwards, but recovered enough to send a bolt of energy back at him. Urging DaVendall to break free of what was happening to his mind, he continued sending energy waves towards Imelda. At last, placing the cloak over DaVendall, he was relieved to see that DaVendall was coming out of his confused state.

Watching from the balustrade, Beauty sent a message to Manga asking him to assist DaVendall. Lottie grabbed Penny's arm.

"Did you see that?" she said. "I think that old woman has killed DaVendall." Manga soared close to the Old Crone and began clawing at her. He was soon joined by some of his tiger friends.

Imelda was unable to stop them from attacking her. She was soon overcome by the force of the animals. She left the dagger on the ground, hurled one last lightning bolt in the direction of DaVendall, then vanished in a whirlwind of green mist.

Wrestling with his thoughts, DaVendall wondered what had happened. "Whatever she put in the cut seems to have confused my thoughts," he told Gamlon. "I fear what she has planned for her next move. She is desperate to get her hands on Lottie and our friend."

Standing beside DaVendall, Manga turned to Gamlon and asked, "Where did she go? We would have liked to have finished her off."

"We don't know where she goes to when she disappears like that," said Gamlon.

"I think this might be a good time for you and your friends to find Beauty and warn her," said Gamlon. "Remember to take care. If the arrows are poisoned she will attempt to get at least one of you."

Leaving DaVendall in conversation with Gamlon, Manga and the sabre-tooth tigers flew off to see if Beauty needed any more assistance. Landing close to Lottie, Manga quickly told Beauty that they suspected the enemy arrows had been poisoned.

"I will give everyone here something that will fend off the poison," said Beauty. Then she asked if Manga and his friends could assist the defenders at the barricade. They soared off to do battle with the enemy again.

Beauty began telling the telepaths about the poisoned arrows. "I can only give light protection against them," she said. "I don't know what poison she will have used."

* * * *

Having distributed his poison, Zanus was annoyed that his troopers had managed to fire only a few poisoned arrows. He soon realised that Septin and his locusts were persecuting them so fiercely that it was all they could do to defend themselves. Then, as if Imelda knew what they up against, she set off with another flock of her vulture-like birds to get rid of the locusts.

Observing Imelda, Zanus watched to see if the vulture-birds were successful. He was delighted to see many fallen locusts being trampled by the trofalogues. Not wanting any more of their friends to die like this, the locusts turned on the trofalogues in force. Joined by the tigers, who had seen what had happened, it didn't take long for them to turn the tables.

Not prepared to assist the trofalogues, Sizan continued with his battle against the defenders. With the tigers and locusts attacking the troopers and trofalogues below, the defenders had been kept busy with the enemy attacking the barricade. Then they realised that the enemy appeared to be retreating. Peter, fearing this meant they might be getting ready for a fresh attack, asked Letswick, "Where are they going?"

Finishing off the trooper he'd been fighting, Letswick watched as the enemy fell to the ground. "We'll soon find out," he said.

Having gained control of the sky, and with DaVendall back at the barricade, Manga flew across to bid farewell to Beauty and friends. Landing close to Lottie, she alerted Beauty to his presence. Pleased to see her tigers were safe, with just a few minor injuries, Beauty greeted the tigers warmly.

Manga assured Beauty they would return any time she was in need of their support. DaVendall, hearing the end of their conversation warned, "Take care, friends. This has been a hard and bloody battle." With a wave from the other sabre-tooth tigers, they flew up to the sky and away.

Bidding farewell to the tigers, the locusts were also ready to take their leave. Gathering round their leader Septin, they quietly voiced their sorrow at losing so many of their own. They said farewell to Beauty and friends below and flew off into the distance.

With the enemy retreated and their friends on their way home, Beauty suggested to Lottie they should make their way to the injured.

"Do you think Penny and Peter will have regretted getting involved with my problem?" asked Lottie, thinking of the danger she'd put her friends through.

"I think you should ask them," said Beauty. "If you look over there, Peter is doing a great job attacking and killing off many of the enemy. And don't forget, Penny was eager to help Yemil and Malla."

Making her way slowly through the people, Lottie was looking to see where Penny was. Noticing she was bandaging someone's arm, Lottie whispered, "Is it all right if I go to, Penny?"

Approaching Yemil, Beauty asked, "Please pass me over to Yemil for a little while. I want to go with her to prepare some tonic for these people." Seeing the look of surprise on Lottie's face, Yemil said, "Don't worry, I will take care of your friend." Placing the brooch in Yemil's hand, somewhat reluctantly, Lottie made her way to Penny.

Admiring Penny for the way she had helped Yemil, Lottie whispered, "Could you spare me a minute?"

"What's wrong, Lottie?" asked Penny

"It's something I have been concerned about for a while. I will just have to ask outright and please give me a true answer."

"Come on, Lottie, what is bothering you?"

"Right, here goes. Do you or Peter have any regrets at becoming involved with my problem? I never realised it would come to this and I don't want you or Peter to be harmed."

"Lottie Montmerencie, how can you ask such a question?" said Penny. "I wouldn't have missed any of this for the world, whatever world that is. Think of all the wonderful friends we have made. The answer is a definite no. Neither of us has ever regretted a thing. Now, you have things to do out there and I have things to do in here." Giving Lottie a gentle shove, she said, "Take care."

"You too," said Lottie, with a relieved smile.

After collecting her brooch, Lottie told Beauty Penny's response. Smiling up at Lottie, Beauty felt this didn't need any words from her.

* * * *

Assured by Yemil that the wounded were all taken care of, Penny and Peter ran to join Lottie and Beauty as they made their way to the balustrade. Just then a loud scream filled the air, making the three friends stare at each other in alarm. Feeling a hand pulling on his arm, Peter was shocked to see what Froy was pointing at. Turning to face her, he whispered, "Whatever is that green mist? Look, it's closing in on the King."

"I saw a mist just like this one and it turned out to be that Old Crone's doing," said Lottie. Penny let out a gasp. Quickly reaching Lottie's mind, Beauty said, "This might not be safe, Lottie. Make your way to the courtyard, and take Penny and Peter with you."

Gamlon and DaVendall saw the mist too, and knew who would emerge from it. DaVendall made his way to the King. He placed his hand on Gamlon and whispered, "Be ready, my friend."

Alarmed to see how close Lottie and her friends were to Alfreston, DaVendall's first thought was to keep them safe. He was relieved to see them making their way down to the courtyard.

Gamlon wondered if the three young people would they be able to show further bravery in the face of Imelda and her tricks.

Imelda, leaving the green mist to distract their attention, now went in search of the stone. Changing her appearance to that of a warning bird, she flew close to where Vigo and Lema were fighting the enemy. Feeling the discomfort of these two lads when they saw her in her bird form gave Imelda another idea. Pleased with her thought, she took on the appearance of a stable-hand of their own kind. Disguise complete, she tapped Vigo on the arm.

"'Ello, what's yer name?" Vigo asked. Lema and Vigo were surprised when the lad asked, "Where's the 'uman lady?" Not sure which lady he was asking about, Vigo asked warily," Why?"

"I just wanna 'elp 'er get away from 'ere," said Imelda.

Looking the new stable-hand over, and thinking it might have been one of the prisoners who'd been freed, Lema replied, "By the well." He pointed. Imelda hastily moved towards the group without saying another word.

"What yer do that fer? We don't know 'oo he is," said Vigo.

"I didn't fink. It looked like one of us," replied Lema. Vigo, concerned about what his friend had done, went and sought Eram. Finally reaching him, he pulled on his arm and told what had happened.

Suspicious at seeing the mist had gone, Eram ran to find help. Coming across Kestron, he whispered loudly, "We need help. It's possible the Old Crone is in here and has been told where Lottie is."

Kestron ignored the King's warning not to use telepathy and began searching for the minds of DaVendall and Moff. At first there was no response, but when they realised who was trying to contact them they were disturbed by the urgency in Kestron's voice. Kestron quickly explained what Eram had told him. DaVendall advised Moff and Kestron to close their minds and join him at the bottom of the steps.

Still in her new disguise and unaware of what had taken place, Imelda was now imitating the stable-hands' walk. Slouching across to the well, she remained alert to anyone who might suspect who she really was. Taking a glance round, she saw a much weakened Jayne with the defenders. Thinking this could be an opportunity to get rid of her, she slowly approached the group at the well.

Congratulating herself on reaching them unnoticed, she was surprised when Jayne said, "Hello. I'm afraid I don't know your name. Were you a prisoner?" Laughing inside, Imelda replied, "Yeah, it was 'orrible, beatin's an' all." But as she spoke, Lottie realised that something was troubling Beauty. Moving away from the group, Lottie looked into her jacket and was startled to see Beauty with her head down.

"What's wrong?" said Lottie.

"Lottie, that's not a prisoner! Remember the mist on the balustrade? That was Imelda," said Beauty. "I wondered why she didn't emerge. We thought she had come to harm the King, but instead she left the mist to control our friends on the balustrade, and now she is looking for you and me."

Shocked, Lottie turned to take a closer look at the scruffy lad standing beside her mother. At that moment she caught sight of DaVendall, Moff and Kestron making their way over.

"Hello, Lottie. Just thought we would come and check you are all safe. May I suggest you go and see if Yemil needs help?" asked DaVendall. Quick to pick up what he was asking, Lottie asked her mother, Penny and Peter to come with them. They set off towards where Yemil was tending the injured.

At first Penny wondered what was happening, but rather than make a fuss she went along with what was taking place. She couldn't help wondering why they were being told to join Yemil, who she'd only just left. Glancing at Peter, she felt certain she could see the same thought was in his mind.

Just then the shrill voice of Imelda reached their ears. "Me stone, you 'ave me stone! That 'uman 'as it, give it to me!"

Lottie placed a protective hand over her brooch, but Beauty decided this was the moment for her to act.

"Remove your hand please, Lottie. This is something I have

to deal with once and for all. Take me back to where DaVendall is standing, but be careful. Imelda has at last emerged as herself." Lottie reluctantly removed her hand and indicated for her friends and mother to follow her.

Slowly making her way back to join DaVendall, Lottie stared at the bedraggled, evil-looking woman beside him. Loathsome and disgusting were the first two words that came to mind.

Then she noticed Imelda's cunning red eyes staring in her direction. Lottie felt all eyes were upon her. She looked at DaVendall as if to say, "What do I do now?" DaVendall mouthed, "All in good time, Lottie."

"At last, me stone 'as returned," croaked Imelda. "Me stone is back. Come to me little one, come and join the rest of yer stone. Give me the stone, an' that woman. I wants the stone, an' 'er, or all yer friends will die."

Lottie covered her brooch with a hand, as she had done many times before. Imelda was angered that something was blocking her vision. "What's 'iding it?" she shrieked, glaring round at everyone. Angry at what was taking place, and deciding her friends had suffered enough, Beauty stated firmly, "You will never take me again, or any of my friends." She then asked Lottie to remove her hand so she could see Imelda clearly.

Nervous, but certain Beauty knew what she was doing, Lottie removed her hand, revealing the beautiful orange sea-horse brooch. Imelda wagged a spindly finger directly at her.

"So you're the interfering 'uman woman Crocanthus was gonna 'and over to me!" she screeched. "You was to be me reward fer all the potions 'e ad." Without turning away from Lottie she continued, "So me precious stone, yer've come to give yerself to me?" Then to the shock of everyone present, Imelda lunged forward to grab the brooch.

Unaware that Beauty had released herself from her lapel, Lottie was stunned to see her brooch hovering over the Old Crone. She and Penny stood open mouthed as Imelda screeched, "Yer mine, yer belong to me! I 'ave enough of yer powers to draw me close to wherever yer are."

"My powers will never obey you. You only want power for evil, my powers are for good," Beauty told her sternly. Then she flicked her tail at Imelda. Just in time, Imelda soared up out of range. Descending beside Lottie, she placed her scrawny arm round her shoulders.

"Yer might 'ave some of me stone's powers but I'll soon 'ave 'em all!" cackled Imelda. She peered round at the watching people as if daring them to intervene. Feeling their fear, she added, "That's why Crocanthus couldn't find yer. Yer changed ter this." Letting out a chilling laugh she continued, "Be warned, me an' me beauties ain't finished with yer yet. When yer me prisoners I will let me beauties tear yer limb from limb, after I take what I wants."

DaVendall had heard enough. He drew Gamlon from his cane and looked across at Kestron and Moff. Minds joined, they sent a surge of power from their minds to Imelda's, sending her falling to the ground. Taken by surprise, she sent out an ear-splitting screech.

Gamlon didn't need DaVendall to tell him what to do. Raising himself from the cane, he knew he would only have one chance of finishing her off. Flying through the air he flew straight at Imelda. But she had seen him coming and was ready for an attack. As he swooped down, he found himself enveloped in the familiar green mist.

"Another time, Gamlon, not today," she called out. Cackling, she disappeared into the ground.

Staring nervously at the fading remains of the mist, Jayne edged closer to Lottie and placed an arm round her shoulders. Terrified at what had taken place, she just wanted to reassure herself that Lottie and her friend were all right. Lottie, however, was thinking of the times she had spent with the man she knew as Jeremy Thackett, and had struggled to come to terms with the fact that he had turned out to be a cruel killer called Crocanthus. She wondered how she could have been so easily deceived.

Sam placed an arm round Penny's shoulders and whispered, "Just keep the enemy at bay. Don't forget we have many friends who can be called on to help." Not understanding what Sam meant, Penny decided she would have to ask, not yet but later.

Witnessing what had taken place had shaken Pointer more

than he had expected. Hearing King Alfreston urge everyone to beat the enemy back, he made his way to the bottom of the balustrade. The King had taken himself closer to the archers, and called out, "Attack, enemy approaching." The archers raised their bows and sent a shower of arrows towards the enemy. In response many arrows came flying back. Screams came from both sides of the barricade.

Scared, but ready with his sword, Peter looked over the balustrade and saw many more enemy forces trying to climb up newly-placed ladders.

Rushing to help their friends, the people in the courtyard were suddenly confronted by Sizan and an army of troopers. The voice of Zanus could be heard demanding that no one be left alive. As enemy and defender came together, the air was filled with the sound of blade on blade and the screams of the injured. Not being able to help many of the fallen, Sam and Bertram vowed to return later.

Pointer had made his way to join Peter, Veber and Moff in time to hear Peter whisper, "I never thought it would be as bad as this. At one time I thought we were near the end." Sam added, "It's going to get worse, young Peter. Make sure you have enough weapons to defend yourself with."

No sooner had Sam finished speaking than there was a tremendous roar from below the barricade. They were left in do doubt what had caused it when they saw huge boulders being flung against the sides of the barricade. The bellowing voice of Zanus continued calling, "Kill all! Alfreston and DaVendall are mine!" In response to this, the thunderous sound of running Zanuthians and Gorgonians shook the ground like an earthquake.

"More help needed at the far end, the enemy are trying to break through the barrier," shouted Peter, having noticed troopers heading close to where he was. Hearing the call, Bertram and friends raced over to help. Fighting back the enemy, Kestron answered the call and brought more Ziphers and Jaspers to assist. Managing to drive the enemy back, they weren't however able to stop the damage the enemy was doing to the barricade. Bertram suggested they try and repair some of the damage. Turning to Peter to congratulate him on his courage, Bertram was shocked to see he'd been injured. "Peter, what happened to you? Can you still fight?"

Looking down at himself, Peter turned his pale face to Bertram and said, "I'm all right. This is my reward for standing up to the enemy."

"Reward for bravery, more like," said Bertram.

Looking over the balustrade, they wondered if Zanus' forces were preparing to attack again. They appeared to be waiting for something or someone. They didn't have to wait long before they discovered what it was.

Pointer's fear was concern for his fellow defenders, of whom many had received serious injuries. His feelings of concern soon turned to alarm when he heard Sam shout, "Fire!".

"What's happened, Sam?" Pointer asked.

"Look down there," said Sam. Pointer was horrified to see some of the grotesque creatures preparing to ram the barricade. Then a tremendous thud sounded, which they knew must be the impact these creatures were launching at the gates. Glancing at the roughly placed bandage on his arm, Pointer felt a shiver of fear run through him. He feared Peter might not survive.

Then he saw Deena wedged between Sam and Moff. He was alerted to the sound of coarse voices screaming, "No prisoners," as the enemy raced towards the barricade.

Horrified to see many of the enemy enter through another part of the damaged barricade, King Alfreston was alarmed to see them charging through the courtyard, trampling over anything or anyone in their way. Calling out for help, the King made his way down the balustrade steps.

Satisfied that he had prevented a number of the enemy from coming across his part of the balustrade, Pointer decided to check on the injured. As he made his way down the steps into the courtyard, he was shocked at the bloody scene in front of him.

Leaving the trofalogues to their task, Sizan ordered the troopers on foot to stay and kill any defender. Turning his beast round, he ordered the creatures and troopers to follow him. His intention was to enter the courtyard as soon as they fell. Thanks to the creature's enormous weight and strength, it wasn't long before the gates went crashing to the ground. Fearing the worst, the defenders stood shoulder to shoulder, prepared to destroy as many of the enemy as they could.

Trampling over everything in his path, Sizan charged into the courtyard, cutting down defenders on all sides. Alarmed at what was taking place, DaVendall reinforced a protective cover over them. Shocked at the carnage, Pointer raced to DaVendall to warn him of what was happening. DaVendall drew the minds of the telepaths to his and explained what was going on. Soon there were many other Ziphers and Jaspers coming to help the defenders at the place where the gates once stood. Seeing the rapid response from the Ziphers and Jaspers, DaVendall raced to join them. Encircling himself with his cloak, he disappeared off the balustrade. Then he uncloaked and joined in the attack against the trofalogues and troopers. Gamlon meanwhile had raised himself from within the cane.

"Take care, my friend. There are more enemy here than I thought," said DaVendall. Just then he caught sight of Sizan and realised he was riding hard in his direction. It was then he saw how monstrous the creatures were. He was deeply shocked and concerned for his smaller friends, knowing they would have little defence against such monstrosities. They had large bulging eyes and green slime was drooling from their gaping mouths. DaVendall knew instantly this was another of Imelda's creations, and looked around to see if she was nearby.

While all this had been taking place, David had been frantically trying to find Jayne, running round the courtyard and calling her name. It wasn't long before other friends had joined in the search. Suddenly a weak voice called out, "We're over here. We're trapped, over by the fallen barricade."

With so much of the barricade in a state of disrepair, the searchers split up and searched every battered part of the barricade. Finally, Bertram came across Nain and many other defenders. Some were badly injured, while others had succumbed to the weight of the rubble.

With the help of the rescuers, it wasn't long before the uninjured were brought out from under the rubble. That was when they saw who Nain was nursing. Looking up at the rescuers and seeing David, Nain said quietly, "I'm so sorry David."

"No, it can't be!" shouted David. "Not Jayne!"

Taking David by the arm, Sam gently moved him away from the rubble, while Bertram lifted Jayne's limp body from Nain's arms. It was clear that she was beyond hope. Laying her gently on the ground, David bent over her and wept as he'd never wept before. Gently rocking her in his arms, he kept saying her name over and over.

Not wanting to move David, they left him with Jayne and took the injured to Yemil and the bodies of the other defenders to a resting place nearby.

Deciding not to tell Penny or Yemil what had happened just yet, Sam and Bertram left the other defenders to care for the injured and went back to be with David. Slowly they managed to coax him into taking Jayne to where the other non-survivors had been taken. Rejecting offers of help, David carried his wife to the resting place.

How was he going to tell Lottie? This thought brought forth more tears. Bidding farewell to Jayne, he left the room with Sam and Bertram either side of him.

Chapter Twenty Seven

The Last Battle

While this had been taking place, Sizan had left the trofalogues and troopers battling with the defenders and made his way to finish off DaVendall. Noticing more parts of the barricade had fallen, many of the defenders thought this was the end. Sensing their fear, DaVendall was quick to see its cause. More enemy troops were breaking into the courtyard by the minute.

DaVendall quickly called for helpers to assist in the courtyard. As enemy and defender battled for control, DaVendall and Sizan fought each other.

Managing to dodge Sizan's creature as its head was pulled this way and that, DaVendall struck out at the animal's thick neck, only to receive a vicious blow from it. Just managing to stay on his feet, DaVendall was pleasantly surprised to see the unicorns' arrival. He sent a lightning bolt directly at the creature. Stumbling, but managing to stay on its feet, the creature roared in agony as another bolt struck. Cedar, seeing the carnage below, called for the unicorns to send lightning bolts at the enemy.

Ready to attack Sizan, DaVendall caught sight of Moff, Sam and Bertram racing towards them with more helpers. His shout to let the defenders know they were close seemed to stop Sizan from striking out at DaVendall. When Sizan looked back, his enemy had disappeared. Cloaked, DaVendall was still there, but not visible.

Angered at not knowing where DaVendall had gone, Sizan swung his creature round and fled the courtyard. Moff and DaVendall caught sight of their enemy escaping through another part of the barricade. They agreed to leave him for another time and turned back to deal with the enemy still in the courtyard.

The fact that he had got away with only minor injuries did little to calm the rage Sizan felt at not being able to finish DaVendall for good. Making his way to Zanus he was unconcerned as to whether his troopers survived or not.

Fearing the worst was yet to come, something caught Pointer's eye. He looked up to see large creatures flying overhead. He was horrified to see these weren't like Zanus' spy birds, but something completely different.

Having been informed telepathically what had happened to Jayne, Pointer was surprised to see David standing by his side. Seeing the bolts rain down on the trofalogues, David's attention had already been drawn to these other creatures. David asked, "What are they? I've never seen creatures like this before." As the creatures flew closer, David muttered, "They're like bats, but not like ordinary bats. I bet these were created by Imelda."

Zooming down upon the people behind the barricade, the new creatures opened their mouths to reveal bright red mouths with fangs hanging down either side. Fearing the impact these creatures would have, David was desperate to fight them off. Pointer wondered how many of his fellow fighters would come out of this alive. Then he heard the shrill voice of Imelda shout, "Attack! Kill 'em all!"

They were stunned to see Imelda flying in front of another group of bats. As the archers stood prepared to send their arrows across the barricade, they waited anxiously for the command to come from King Alfreston. Within a matter of moments, he commanded them to fire at will.

Hearing a loud squawk from behind, Pointer turned to see one of Zanus' spy birds swooping towards him. The bird spread its talons and reached forward to attack his face. Without hesitation, Pointer raised himself on his hind legs and hit out with his front paws. He was disgusted to see a green and yellow substance ooze out of the wound. Defending himself with as much force as he could, he was pleased to see Cindra had come with others to help. They soon drove off the attacking birds. Pointer thanked Cindra and friends for coming to their rescue and was rewarded with a gentle smile. "Any time, Pointer," signed Cindra.

Observing what had happened, Gazer flew over to join Pointer, and called out, "Thought you might need some assistance." Pointer called back, "Welcome my friend, but I think Farren, Cindra and friends have managed to drive off the birds. But, did you see those bats?"

Joining his friend Gazer, Kerez suggested they fly down and join Pointer on the balustrade. Landing beside Cindra, Farren and Pointer, Kerez told them they had seen the bats, and what happened when they were hit. Pausing for a moment, Kerez continued, "We saw that dreadful Old Crone, but before we could get to her she disappeared."

* * * *

Angered at seeing so many of his birds dead, Zanus yelled out, "Yer'll all suffer, we'll leave none alive!" For many listening to the taunt, it hadn't been so much the voice of Zanus that alarmed them but his jet black horse flaring its nostrils as it stomped the ground, making them appear as one person. Zanus roared for the entire army to attack, demanding they finish off the King and the defenders. But he had failed to consider the unicorns.

"Come on Kerez, we've a battle to fight," said Gazer. Flying off with him, they re-joined the other unicorns, and made ready to attack the enemy and trofalogues. Their lightning bolts disposed of many. Pointer was shocked to see Sizan's grotesque creatures crush everything under foot. Leaving the unicorns to deal with the trofalogues, Pointer and friends attacked any enemy they could reach. It wasn't long before the sound of squawking injured creatures filled the air.

While Imelda demanded her beasts attack and bring the prisoners to her, DaVendall and Beauty were sharing their thoughts.

"We must make sure Zanus and his cronies aren't able to continue attacking these gentle folk," said Beauty.

"I agree. We will need to work together on this."

He asked her to help with what he had planned. Beauty agreed without question. She was eager for this to work. Concentrating her thoughts on creating a circle of dense cloud around the approaching enemy, Beauty joined minds with Lottie and quickly explained what she was going to do. She went on to tell Lottie DaVendall was going to contact the spectres.

Not able to see what was preventing his troopers from riding on, Zanus called on Imelda to come and help. As the cloud continued to hold the enemy back, the Old Crone wasted no time in answering the call.

Satisfied the cloud had restrained the enemy, DaVendall clasped Gamlon in his hand and pulled his cloak around them. Disappearing from sight, they soon arrived where the spectres resided. This was a place secured for them by Beauty and DaVendall many years before as a place of refuge. Removing the cloak, DaVendall and Gamlon were greeted by Lamar, leader of the spectres.

"I think you might possibly want some help, DaVendall," said Lamar. "I wondered how long it would be before you would come to us, especially after I had sent other spectres to help other friends."

"I think it would be better if I told you what has taken place," said DaVendall. Nodding, Lamar invited them to make themselves comfortable first. "Now DaVendall, tell us what's been happening?"

"We are under heavy attack from the same enemies you faced many years ago," said DaVendall. "There is, however, some difference; Imelda has managed to create some zombie-like creatures, real heavyweight. I might add that they have already shown how easy it is for them to crash the barricades."

"This sounds like Imelda's doing," one of the spectres said.

"You're right," replied Gamlon. "These creatures excel all her others. The defenders have fought well, and I know they will continue to do so, but many will not survive. We do have the assistance of the unicorns. But Lottie is under threat of capture, as they know she is able to enhance Beauty's powers."

"I think we should move now," said Lamar. "We are wasting time discussing it here. We will come and see what we can do.

We have our own way of travelling, as you know. We will leave you to travel your way."

The spectres set off. DaVendall and Gamlon travelled back to the balustrade by way of the cloak. Landing close to Alfreston, DaVendall sensed Imelda was about to do more harm. No sooner had he said this than he was aware of a sudden darkness. He knew this was his friends the spectres.

Arriving at the battlefield, the spectres made their way to the unicorns. Just then there was a sudden influx of larger-than-usual birds. Staring at them, Lamar turned to his companions and shouted, "Let's get to them. Don't let any get near our friends below."

Zanus was incensed when he saw the support the defenders had gained. Still enraged by what had happened to his birds, he yelled out, "Yer'll all suffer, we'll leave none alive." For many listening to the taunt, it hadn't been so much the voice of Zanus that alarmed them, it was seeing his jet black horse flare its nostrils as it pawed the ground, making beast and rider appear as one person.

Turning on the troopers, Sizan warned that they would all be severely punished if the task wasn't completed this time. Sizan roared, "Yer'll not 'arm me, Zanus, don't ferget we are needed if yer want to rule Dofstram." Letting out a loud throaty growl, Zanus turned to Imelda and demanded to know why she hadn't given his troopers a potion to get rid of Alfreston and his people. It amused Imelda to see him shudder.

"Be warned, Zanus!" she hissed. "I gave yer troopers poison for the arrows, it's a shame they didn't use it properly." Seeing Zanus go red in the face and about to retaliate, she went on, "Tell 'em to go where the barricade 'as fallen. The trofalogues made good 'eadway into the courtyard. Once they are in, they should finish the job. One thing, Zanus, remember this well, that stone an' that woman are mine. You can 'ave Alfreston."

"We'll see about that," replied Zanus.

Having seen what the enemy were doing, Lamar suggested that some of the spectres should fly down to stop them from getting to the barricade.

As the spectres descended, the troopers roared with fright,

but they laughed it off when they saw it was just a few ghosts. This soon changed when they tried to fight their way past them.

As more of the enemy infiltrated the courtyard the defenders were faced once more with hand-to-hand combat. Terrified of being captured, every able person took up arms to keep the enemy out. This resulted in many being killed and injured on both sides. As blood and earth mixed together it was a terrible sight. Weeping could be heard from within the many collapsed houses. Bertram felt he wanted to go to their aid, but changed his mind when he heard the voice of a weary archer call out, "It looks like those vulture creatures have returned".

Letswick shouted, "Bring more archers, we need to bring those creatures down!"

"I think this is something you should take care of," said Gamlon. "These Outlanders are powerless against her."

"Quite right, Gamlon, I too think this is the moment to show her she's not going to succeed," DaVendall replied. Balancing himself on the top of the cane, Gamlon was prepared for whatever DaVendall had in mind. He didn't have to wait long before DaVendall wrapped them both in his cloak ready to leave.

Gamlon watched as the spectres pursued the enemy mercilessly. As they waved around the enemy and sent them running, he was thankful the spectres were on his side.

Realising Peter was standing close to her, Lottie was relieved to find she had help. They began pushing ladders away from the barricade, feeling a sense of achievement when they heard the screams from the falling enemy.

Beauty whispered, "I see you have been injured, Peter." Feeling a little embarrassed at having allowed himself to get hurt, Peter muttered, "Just a minor scratch, a trofalogue caught me."

Meanwhile, DaVendall and Gamlon were about to deal with Imelda. Before moving off, DaVendall contacted Beauty and told her what he was going to do. Frightened for her friend's safety, Beauty told him she would stay alert and answer any call for help.

Ascending high above the barricade, DaVendall decided not

to confront Imelda immediately; he was keen to see how many other creatures she'd created. As he flew on, he realised there were more than he'd originally thought. He began to dispose of them, but it took a while for Imelda to realise something was happening to her creatures. Not able to see DaVendall, she nevertheless sensed that it was his doing.

"I know what's 'appening to me birds!" she screeched. "I'll make yer friends down there suffer, DaVendall!" Ignoring her warning, DaVendall released Gamlon and left him to fight off the birds. His aim was to get to Imelda before she could carry out her threat. Flying to within a few inches of her face, DaVendall uncloaked and stared straight at her.

"So, yer think yer can kill me, do yer?" Imelda taunted. Flying round her, DaVendall replied, "Your time has come to answer for your evil deeds."

"Is that yer plan? I know yer won't succeed, me powers are stronger now."

Hovering in front of her face, DaVendall drew her eyes into his and in tones of dire warning told her, "Don't think any power you took from the stone will do anything for you. That part of the stone will repel anything you try and make it do."

Angered by what he'd said, but knowing it to be true, Imelda decided to try another approach. She dissolved into a green mist again, the vulture-like birds disappearing from sight with her.

Gamlon delighted in telling DaVendall that he had disposed of many of the bird creatures but was annoyed others had escaped. DaVendall knew these creatures would only stay as long as Imelda was there, but just now he had other thoughts going through his mind.

Wanting to take advantage of what the spectres had achieved, he worked out a plan of action. Descending close to the King, he explained what he planned to do. Together they gathered a number of troops and set off where the gates used to stand. Riding at a fast pace, they were soon fighting side by side with the spectres. They were quickly joined by many other defenders, including Bertram, Sam, Peter, Drewan and Kestron. Beauty was keen to join them but fearful for Lottie's safety.

Aware that many of the defenders had ridden out to attack the enemy, Penny wanted to go along too. Making her way to Lottie, they convinced Beauty they would take care. Accepting their argument, Beauty told them she would give them a protective cover, but warned them to take great care.

Dandy was waiting at the foot of the balustrade steps. He asked them to get on his back so that he would take them to the battle. Wasting no time, they settled themselves with their swords and urged Dandy to go on.

No sooner had they left the barricade than they were faced with troopers heading their way. Raising their swords, and with a little help from Beauty, they soon disposed of them and sped off to the main area of the battle.

DaVendall told Letswick and Drewan where he was headed. Seeing Sizan in the distance, he aimed straight for him. Sizan was taken aback when he saw how close he was to his enemy. Raising his sword, he turned his beast in the direction of DaVendall's horse and charged. DaVendall knocked him from his mount with one blow. Taking up his sword from where it had fallen, Sizan now swore to kill DaVendall at all costs.

Jumping off Cedar, DaVendall sent him back to the stable and turned his attention to the approaching Sizan. They battled sword on sword for some time, fighting over wounded and dead people.

Gamlon considered leaving the cane and helping. However, DaVendall picked up this thought and assured Gamlon all was well. Even as he said this, Sizan came charging at him and was about to plunge his sword into DaVendall's side when Gamlon flew from the cane and stabbed him in the stomach. Clutching his wound, Sizan let out a scream of agony and anger. Before he could say anything, he fell dead to the ground.

"Well my friend, that's another one I owe you," DaVendall said, in a weary voice.

"I think you have been injured, or is that Sizan's blood?" Gamlon asked.

"A bit of both I think, but we don't have time to worry about it now, let's go and help our friends," DaVendall replied. Taking hold of a horse's rein, DaVendall settled himself behind the

Jasper and set off to join the spectres and unicorns as they fought off the birds

"Look! What's 'appening?" screamed one of the troopers.

"Never mind what's 'appening up there, let the Old Crone deal with 'em," roared Zanus. He commanded everyone to attack. Joined by several troopers, the trofalogues clawed away much of the remaining barricade, eager to get to their prey. However, it wasn't as easy as they thought. Flying past, the unicorns saw what was happening below and took action. Soon there was a rapid fusillade of lightning bolts aimed at the enemy, killing many.

While this was taking place, King Alfreston and his group were fighting back the enemy. Pleased to see DaVendall was all right, he noticed Gamlon was fighting alongside the Jaspers and Ziphers as the enemy tried to get through the damaged barricade.

That was when he saw an army of spectres descend from the sky. As soon as they touched the ground, they circled the enemy and engaged in hand-to-hand fighting. Now the unicorns were gaining control of the skies, the King knew there was still much to do about the enemies on the ground before victory was theirs. He now sought assistance from the archers. Wasting no time, he led his group round the side of the enemy. Having seen where King Alfreston was headed, Dandy joined him just as DaVendall called out, "Push them back. Don't let them get near the barricade."

Terrified, but determined to fight on, Penny whispered, "Let's hope we get through this." Lottie nodded. Beauty whispered, "Hang on to Dandy, he will make sure you stay safe."

The defenders heard the King shout, "Go! Attack hard and let's get rid of these bullies once and for all." As the battle went on, it wasn't long before the enemy was surrounded. For just a moment everything went quiet, with exception of the roaring voice of Zanus. Soon even that stopped. Taking a look at all the bodies on the ground, DaVendall saw Letswick, Sam and Bertram moving from person to person looking for survivors. Sad at so many lives lost, they were delighted when they came upon those that had survived.

Making his way over to DaVendall, Sam asked, "Is it possible to get some of the unicorns or horses here to take the injured away?"

"Will do, Sam," DaVendall replied. He called on Cedar to bring animals to help with the injured, and soon Cedar appeared with other horses and unicorns. Moving cautiously around the strewn bodies, they were soon placing the wounded on the animals' backs. Making sure their passengers were secure, the animals took them inside the barricade.

While this was taking place, King Alfreston had learned of Sizan's death and of the loss of many others of his troops. He saw that a number of Gorgonians had made a rapid exit from the battlefield. Where they were going he did not know, and he did not feel inclined to follow them.

Noticing the enemy were scattered over the ground, he asked the defenders to take prisoner the ones that had survived, but to leave the others. Then he turned his attention to Zanus, who lay on the ground covered in blood and grime. He stood over him, and was very tempted to kill him there and then, but decided he would be best taken prisoner, safe in the lowest dungeon at the castle.

Guessing what Alfreston intended to do, Zanus was determined he would never be taken prisoner. Reaching out towards a sword lying nearby, he was about to try to grab it and stab the King in the back when one of the Ziphers spotted him. Just as Zanus' fingers closed on the sword, the Zipher rushed forward and ran his spear deep into Zanus' stomach.

Falling back with a gasp of shock and pain, the tyrant stared at Alfreston with a look of venomous hatred. "One day…" he grunted. But those were his last words. With a final groan of pain and anger, the tyrant slumped back. The onlookers watched as his last breath left him.

"Thank you, my friend," said King Alfreston to the Zipher, seeing the blood dripping from his spear. The Zipher nodded and made his way back to join his fellows. Exhausted and weary, King Alfreston looked round, intending to send troopers wherever they were needed.

It was at that moment that he caught sight of Lottie walking alongside David, her father's arm held protectively round her shoulders. Clearly David was telling his daughter what had happened to her mother.

The King began to congratulate the Outlanders and all the other helpers on their achievements, yet he was still concerned about Imelda's disappearance. Fearing she could come back at any moment, he wondered if now that Zanus and Sizan were dead she would try to collaborate with Crocanthus. It was DaVendall who explained to the King what had happened to Crocanthus. No sooner had Alfreston been told this news than DaVendall said, "Can any of you sense an unusual presence?"

"I'm not picking up the presence of anyone, but I do have a feeling Crocanthus is not dead," said Beauty. "Perhaps he has tried to escape from where he was taken."

"Does this mean we haven't finished with him?" asked Yemil. "Is it possible he might return here?" With voices echoing Yemil's concern, Moff stated, "Gorka and his serpents will make sure he never returns. We can trust Gorka to deal with him."

Sighs of relief followed this statement, but DaVendall added, "His fate would be much worse if he was in the hands of Imelda."

Weary from the battle, the spectres made their way to join DaVendall and their leader, Lamar. Curious as to why Crocanthus wasn't among the enemy, Lamar asked, "Where is Crocanthus? I didn't see him on the battlefield."

DaVendall explained Crocanthus' fate. "Gorka will ensure he will never get free," he said.

Gamlon still had concerns about Crocanthus after hearing his threat as they took him away, but hesitated to say anything. What if he had managed to take some of Imelda's potions with him? Shaking off this thought, he couldn't help wondering if he was the only one who feared this.

With the spectres safely on their way, Beauty said, "I wonder where Imelda went. She won't give up trying to capture Lottie and me that easily."

Checking with his friends that they were all right, Pointer made his way to the balustrade. Slowly climbing up the steps, Pointer forgot about his injuries until Binro signed, "Hi, Pointer, it looks as if you need to get some attention for those cuts."

Sensing something didn't feel right, Beauty whispered, "Can either of you see anything unusual?" Peter looked round to see what Beauty had sensed, then whispered, "Like what?"

"I sense a presence," said Beauty, in a quiet voice

"What sort of presence? I can't see anything," Lottie whispered. Disturbed by what Beauty had said, she looked round, but still couldn't see anything unusual.

Meanwhile Imelda was still determined to get hold of the stone and Lottie. Taking precautions not to be seen, she was about to enter through a part of the barricade that had been destroyed by her trofalogues. Hidden by her invisible covering, she stepped into the courtyard. Now where was that woman and her precious stone?

Unaware of the new danger, the Jaspers took to the air and attacked the remaining enemy from above, while other defenders stood ready to attack any that tried to get away. While Gamlon had been busy with his thoughts regarding Crocanthus, King Alfreston wondered how much longer they could continue. Injured in the hand-to-hand combat, he was determined not to give in. Not having any thoughts at this moment about Imelda, he was unprepared for her reappearance.

"Come to me, I know yer 'ere!" screeched the foul voice. Getting no response, she yelled, "If yer don't give 'em to me, I'll make sure me beauties kill you all!"

DaVendall, having seen Imelda emerge close to where the King stood, cloaked himself. Then he flew over close to the King, and descended just far enough away to prevent her sensing his presence. Watching her peering round about, he knew who she was looking for.

Not able to see where the woman had gone, Imelda let out a terrible wailing sound. Knowing what she wanted, Lottie placed her hands over her mouth to stop herself screaming.

Before anyone could move or say a word, Imelda aimed a long spear straight at King Alfreston. Instantly Drewan leapt through the air and pulled the King to the ground. As the missile landed close to where Drewan and Alfreston lay, it changed into a writhing, venomous snake. Swerving to and fro, it slithered and hissed as it made its way to the King.

Not thinking about the danger he might be in, Bertram tried to grab the snake, intending to throw it over the barricade. He did not realise the snake was Imelda, so he was surprised to see DaVendall standing beside him, calmly asking him Bertram to leave the creature to him.

They watched as the snake turned back into Imelda. "So you still think you can get what you want," said DaVendall. "I think we should make sure you never try to take over these lands again."

Beauty now placed her tail on Imelda and ran it all over her body. Screaming, Imelda tried to wriggle free. This time she was powerless to do so. She lay there like a pathetic old woman.

But she wasn't finished yet. Quickly removing a phial from her person, she drank it down before anyone could stop her. Within a moment, the green mist rose from the ground, and she vanished once more.

Staring down at where the mist had vanished, Lottie asked, "Will she be able to come back and torment these people again?"

"Not any more," replied Beauty, settled once more on Lottie's jacket. "Any power she might have left will have been used up after her disappearance."

A voice from the back called out, "I think we should all return to our families. DaVendall, I believe you have many people to collect from a certain cave. May I suggest some of you go with him and return to your homes, once you have collected your families?"

The Outlanders turned to DaVendall and asked him to lead the way. With beaming faces, and eager to get to their families, they quickly jumped onto nearby carts and any available horse or pony and set off behind DaVendall and Kestron.

* * * *

Quietly gathering together, King Alfreston let the remaining defenders move away from the barricade towards the castle. It was a solemn group of people that made their way there. After the loss of Jayne, Lottie and David felt far from jubilant as they rode along side by side. Lottie had been reunited with her parents for such a short time. She was trying to understand why her father had told her he was going to remain in Dofstram.

Arriving at the castle, they were greeted by cheers. The atmosphere was one of joy and happiness. Glancing round the room, Lottie realised how many friends she had made, and how many she had lost, and how she was going to miss them all. Knowing that Peter and Penny were still going to be with her did little to help her feelings.

With Beauty returned to Queen Matilda, it was a sad and tearful parting for Lottie. Feeling her pain, Beauty closed her mind to others and tunnelled her thoughts to Lottie.

"Lottie, try to remember all the good things we did. Prisoners were freed, the enemy are no longer a threat, and the Outlanders are able to live in peace. Most of all, remember your mother was a very brave person, and will always be cherished by the people of Dofstram."

Tears rolling down her face, Lottie was surprised to see her father standing close by. Wiping the tears from her face, he stood with his arm round her shoulders and whispered words that only she could hear. As they moved a little apart, David added, "We'll see each other again." Looking at her father, she asked, "Are you sure?"

"Let's put it this way, when you see Moff's shop lit up, you will know that's the signal for you to return," he assured her.

* * * *

It was a very quiet group of people who made their way to the Queen's coach, which was waiting at the bottom of the castle steps. Stepping into the coach, they remained quiet, each with their own thoughts. Winston, Penny and Lottie looked across at each other, but it was Winston who broke the silence by saying, "Did it really happen? Did we all come back from a land called Dofstram?"

Arriving at the gateway, Bertram gave his son a gentle push. "Yes Winston, we really did" he said.

Bidding their friends at the gateway farewell, not forgetting the animals, they made their journey to Moff's shop. On the way,

Bertram told them, he and Frances were going to take over Sam and Lucy's shop, and hoped Lottie would become a regular visitor. With a fond farewell from Moff, they left the shop. When they glanced back, they saw it had already been plunged into darkness.

"Would you like to come under my cloak? I'll take you back to Lottie's house," said DaVendall. Within moments, they all found themselves back in Lottie's living room. With a quiet farewell from Gamlon, who felt he had said all he could say on their journey back, it was left to DaVendall to say, "Lottie, you might like to consider rescuing an animal or two." With a wave of his floppy hat, he flung his cloak round himself and disappeared from the house.

They all sat in silence for a few moments, sad to think of the ones they had lost, but happy that Dofstram had been left in good hands.

"I think we'd better see about decorating the Christmas tree," said Lottie at last. "I'll see if there's anything in the cupboard."

"I wonder if we'll ever go back," whispered Bertram to Frances.

"I hope so, but for a different reason perhaps," replied his wife. "Who knows? Now, time for a pot of tea, I think."

* 9 7 8 1 8 6 1 5 1 0 0 6 8 *

ND - #0054 - 270225 - C0 - 203/127/26 - PB - 9781861510068 - Matt Lamination